FRACTURED DREAMS

GK JURRENS

UpLife
Press

Print ISBN: 978-1-952165-01-6
Ebook ISBN: 978-1-952165-03-0
v.200612

GKJurrens.com

DEDICATION

This book is dedicated to all you dreamers,
and to you realists who pay the bills. To one in particular, please do
keep reminding me of the difference between fiction and *all that other
stuff.*

On a more serious note, as I pound this book through its final
editorial paces prior to launch, thousands of you are placing
yourselves in harm's way, *right now,* so the rest of us can cling to some
sense of new-normalcy during this global COVID-19 (Corona Virus)
pandemic.

During these uncertain times, with all humility, I *especially* dedicate
this book to each of you in healthcare, emergency first responders, the
sciences, and all who face scary unknowns *every day* under lousy
circumstances so the rest of our lives can at least creep along. You
provide myriad products, services and transportation. And yes,
political leadership too. A brighter day dawns *today* because of you all.

***Thanks to each of you from the depths of my undeserving but grateful
heart! God bless every single one of us, deserving or not.***

ACKNOWLEDGMENTS

I would like to offer my most profound thanks to:

- **Kay**, my long-suffering partner & most brutal critic,
- **Judy R** for your forgiveness of my casual style, despite your editorial expertise,
- **Tom L** for not only incredible beta read catches, but for your EMF (EMP) idea, and for your TM guidance,
- All you other **beta readers** of my manuscript who were so generous with your time,
- **Joe Y** and **James T**, my flute friends, you jumpstarted ideas for my *Indian Joe* character,
- **Bob W** and your tramper friends, you inspired my Lunatic Fringe characters. You are a model of deliberate and ethical living, and I salute you,
- My helpful friends from **"Writers Helping Writers"** & **"Authors on the Road"** FB groups,
- My mentor, **Judy Howard** of Judy Howard Publishing, for just the right inspiration.
- **Elizabeth Mackey,** you delivered a gorgeous cover design that reflects the story so very well. Thank you.

- And I especially **thank *you*, dear reader**, for purchasing and reading this book.

Subscribe to my email list at GKJurrens.com.
Once you do so, you'll be invited to optionally join my ARC team. I'll then send you my next book two weeks *before* it is published (an Advance Review Copy), absolutely free. You keep the book, and if you are moved to write a short review and post it, maybe find the last few typos, you *stay* on the team for the book after that! Not bad, right?
Do email me at author1@gkjurrens.com with any thoughts you have about the book. Please. Seriously!

INTRODUCTION

Fractured Dreams is the second book in the *Dream Runners* series. If you've read the first book, *Dangerous Dreams*, you will re-intercept several of your favorite characters plus a few more you have not yet met, such as a renegade tribe of quirky desert rats who call themselves the Lunatic Fringe. Each book also stands strong on its own.

For most of us, not only do our dreams often seem fractured in time and perception as we sleep, but we blend our daily experiences with memories of the past and visions for our future after we awaken.

My sincerest and cogent dream—fractured or not—is to hope you enjoy your time spent immersed in the interwoven stories of these provocative characters. Try to appreciate the broad range of eccentricities and ambitions of those whom you are about to meet. As you travel through this story, enjoy becoming acquainted with some old friends from *Dangerous Dreams* too.

I draw inspiration from fascinating people we meet in our travels. Are you also able to relate to one or more of them? That is my second dream. Are you ready to start running this leg of your journey? If so, let's go!

\- GK

HOMECOMING

BLACK ROCK, ARIZONA
2016

A straight line isn't always short.

The next ten seconds changed everything, and changed nothing. Too often in his life Geo Janis measured the distance between joy and terror in precious seconds. He was about to measure that distance at least once more.

Before he picked up Kate's surprise birthday pie at the tiny diner in the eclectic desert town a half-hour away, he read the first of two text messages. His phone's screen lit the car's dark interior with a vague vision of his violent past overtaking him.

Eyes wide and bright, head thrust forward, the chords in his neck bulged and pulsed. He scanned the second text that appeared seconds later. Bile rose in his throat. He tossed his iPhone onto the empty passenger seat, his face a mask of horror. A violent U-turn aimed him back toward the campground, the late-night pie now forgotten.

Geo blasted through the few stop signs and a single traffic light in the village of Quartzsite in Southwest Arizona. He merged onto Interstate-10 East with reckless abandon.

"Get out of the way!"

Left-lane dwellers gorged him with irrational anger. The campground, still fifteen miles ahead, wasn't getting *farther away*, was it? Worse than that dream of wading toward safety in waist-deep molasses while being chased by a monster…

Flashing lights appeared in his mirrors. A glance at the dash of his tiny four-cylinder Toyota surprised him. He wondered how much *this* ticket might cost—ninety in a seventy. Then he realized he didn't care. In fact, an Arizona State Trooper might back him for what could happen next.

Ten minutes later, Geo rocketed onto desolate two-lane US 60 East toward Desert Wells with the trooper still in tow. He struggled to make sense of a jigsaw puzzle of events years in the making as he raced toward danger, maybe even death. Those two single-word texts brought the chaos back into his life he thought he escaped light-years earlier.

Always the adult in the room, Kate warned Geo not long after they assumed their new identities. She predicted their past would overtake them some day. Said she was okay with that. Geo drew from Kate's strength these days.

Their friend, Doctor F Samuel Braxton and *his* friend, the retired senior statesman John W. Stevens, protected them—for services rendered to the United States of America.

Geo feared more for Kate's safety than for his own. He needed to reach her before they did.

Jeez, God, what if…?

He'd made his choice eight years earlier when his country needed him. But he never envisioned life without Kate. Not after fifty years of marriage.

Geo braked hard at the last moment to avoid colliding with the only other vehicle in front of him, a dusty pickup that flashed across his headlight beams as it entered from a ranch road ahead. The truck belched out a black cloud of diesel smoke as the driver accelerated hard to escape collision from the rear.

Speeding up again, Geo's tires protested as he fish-tailed on loose gravel scattered on the asphalt. He passed the panicked kids in the truck, still pacing the Arizona Trooper behind him.

This ticket will cost more. Ninety-five in a fifty-five.

Why did the idea of traffic violations keep annoying him? Maybe because he wasn't used to breaking the law. He sneered in hapless defiance, then in perplexity *as the trooper passed him.* His blue and red rooftop light bar and taillights disappeared in the wind-blown dust over a rise a half-mile ahead.

Eight miles later Geo drifted sideways into the gravel entrance to the obscure Black Rock Campground on his left. He hoped no children played in his path. Not likely. Not at this time of night. Just retired desert dwellers out here anyway.

A piece of him perished as he saw the ocean of flashing red and blue lights surrounding the bus he and Kate called home.

"Oh, God, no!"

A fit-and-trim trooper stood in his way, maybe even the one who passed him, pumping his palms downward in front of him toward Geo. The little red Toyota's front bumper dived to a stop within inches of the trooper's legs. The guy's instincts backed him up an unsteady step or two.

His palms descended to his hips, elbows akimbo. Even though it was dark, with the lights all around, Geo could see his glare. He was livid. And something else.

But that was irrelevant. Their motorhome and attached trailer were still a hundred yards ahead. Didn't this guy understand? He needed to get to his high school sweetheart, to his soul mate, to the woman without whom he was adrift—lost.

Kate trusted her husband because she dared trust no one else. Not neighbors, not cops, only him. And her first text to him was their private 911 signal: *brotherhood.* But it was the second that made him swallow his rising bile: *run!*

Geo realized he was about to say something he'd regret but didn't care, *could not* care. His sweaty palms gripped either side of the padded steering wheel—now sopping wet—pushing, then pulling to the wheel's breaking point.

His jaw hurt. He was gritting his teeth so hard a few had chipped. Realized he'd been doing so since he'd received Kate's two texts twenty-two minutes ago. Nothing since!

He even contemplated running down the trooper to get to her. But no.

Fit-and-Trim marched with purpose toward his window. A general malevolent demeanor hung on him like a shroud, and the heel of his right hand rested on the butt of his sidearm in its holster high on his hip. In a smooth and almost invisible practiced motion, he unsnapped the weapon's retainer loop with his right thumb.

With slitted eyes, he said, "Window."

Tinted red and blue in the ambience of reflected emergency lights, his gold badge glinted at Geo, taunted him.

Aside from an acute case of clear coat peeling off like skin cancer, his eleven-year-old Yaris featured no other options, not even electric windows. He found it impossible to keep eye contact with the menacing trooper while leaning down and forward to reach the window crank with his left hand.

"Freeze! *Do not move!*"

That weapon no longer remained holstered.

Geo complied, although now perplexity layered onto his fear and anger. It was all becoming too much to process. From his hunched-over position, he couldn't see two more troopers running to support their brother-in-arms.

One of them threw open Geo's driver-side door so hard it tried to bounce back. Stopped it with his hip. Pressed down on the back of Geo's head until his back hurt. The other dragged him from the car, head and shoulders and arms first, which made it impossible for Geo to keep his feet and legs under him.

On the ground, he felt rough hands jostling every part of him. He screamed, "I live here! I gotta get to my wife!"

He could taste musty desert dust in his mouth while gasping face down. It tasted gray and gritty. Had he not been near delirious with fear for Kate, his germaphobic nature would compel him to fret over the fungi likely present in that dust. Now in his throat, in his nostrils, in his lungs. In his mind.

"No weapons."

"Turn him over."

He looked up, straight into the blinding beam of a law-enforcement-strength flashlight and maybe the business end of a few gun barrels. He wasn't sure. Of anything. Not any more.

"Pick him up."

On his feet, strong hands gripped each of his arms, then released them. Geo raised his hands high without being told, but clenched his fists against white-knuckle fear, anger, and now rage.

"What the Hell?"

"Sir, state your name and your business here."

He noticed the original trooper held his open wallet.

Geo's voice projected but quavered. "My name is Lee Randle. That motorhome and trailer over there belong to me and my wife Charlotte. Now will someone *please* say something relevant?"

Trooper Fit-and-Trim's voice and demeanor softened as he handed over the wallet. His next words changed Geo's life forever.

"Sir, your wife is dead. Murdered."

Geo took a few moments of squinting to process the words. After torturing himself with this new reality, because he sensed the truth of it, even as his mind ran away from it, his head jutted forward. A feral sneer sculpted his face. Geo spit a guttering scream toward the trooper, his voice gathering volume and a fever pitch as the words tumbled out, each progressively louder and higher than the last.

"No. You're lying! Why would you lie to me like that?"

He fought off the trooper's now gentle hands, determined to get to the only person who understood him, who awakened his deadened passion after… He needed to… He shook, trembled. Melted. Strong hands held him on his uncaring feet.

Then, something even more inconceivable happened. In a smooth motion, Trooper Fit-and-Trim raised his service weapon, aimed it at Geo's right eye less than an inch distant, and fired.

Geo dropped into a welcoming black velvet abyss. Didn't even have time to wonder if Kate had suffered. So why were the trooper's gentle hands still jarring him as he once again lay there in that fungus-ridden dirt? Was this Limbo? Or Purgatory? Or another attempt to finish the job as he descended into Hell's deepest pit of despair?

The shaking continued as he writhed in remembered pain.

Then…

"Sweetheart, it's just one of those dreams again. Wake up, Geo. A bad dream. That's all."

The fear remained. Not *only* in the dream. Kate was a saint.

She put up with this.

But for how long?

PAST SINS

Mesa, Arizona

Nine months earlier, they worried.

But they only worried about weather, equipment, and other mundane elements of life in their motorhome. All of that helped.

The weather hovered just above freezing most winter nights in the Southwestern US. Geo contemplated crawling from under a goose-down comforter so luxurious it curled his toes.

He sensed more than heard the soft whine of their diesel furnace thrumming beneath them in the bus's basement. At last performing flawlessly after a series of costly repairs, he offered a silent thanks to the RV gods. One less worry. For now. The RV—recreation vehicle? Or *reinvestment* vehicle? But the freedom!

Within his semi-conscious state Geo wondered how they would pay off *that* credit card—the one dedicated to coach repairs. Kate worried more than he.

Up to her chin in goose-down, she curled against the shape of his right side in her endearing flannel PJs as she purred, "Brrrr. All the desert offers at night is dark and cold." Kate hugged him, her sleep-heavy slur almost unintelligible. "Nice we have each other, huh, punkin?"

"Babe, why are you awake?"

Reluctant to return too much affection at the moment, he stroked her forehead. They used to do that to the kids at bedtime when they were young. She so needed sleep. He knew by asking her this question for which there was no answer, she'd offer none. Sure enough, ten seconds later, she drifted off again.

He smiled at the silhouette of her profile, vague in the pre-dawn darkness. A few rays of the resort's street lights penetrated their night shades.

At five a.m.—always five a.m.—his mind screamed at him with ideas for the weekly podcast. Writing them down and sharing them helped.

Against his baser instincts, he eased out of Kate's unconscious embrace. When she didn't stir further, he swung his legs to the cold floor with a silent groan.

He slipped both feet into his ragged sheepskin slippers in a single practiced motion. Old friends, those now-ugly wool-lined slippers. They looked ridiculous, but he loved them.

He padded to the bathroom. In the dark, he always sat down to pee as a practical matter.

Geo sought to convince himself his pain and stiffness were nothing more than symptoms of the chilly sixty-three degree thermostat setting. Kate preferred cool temps at night and he was just chilled, that was all. Once more, he tried to believe that perennial lie.

He also tried to forget the real reason for his chronic back and neck pain. And, oh, the headaches. Neither he nor Kate slept well. Worse, another dream still haunted him even though seven years had drifted by, never dissipating the cold fog of its soggy horror.

Never far away, each night brought new terrors; atonement for past sins, Geo was sure. His only defense? To keep sleep and dreams at arm's length.

Most everyone slept. He was different. He'd lay awake. Sometimes he dozed, knowing that to be true only because time passed with gaps, each saturated with fragments of lingering torment. Geo watched the digital clock and would not allow himself to get up until at least five a.m. But neither would he allow himself to lay there one minute past.

Maybe that's why his mind deleted dreams before they awakened him, except for this one, and one or two others. Or maybe because this dream was also a tenacious memory of a monster named Dent Canfield.

Geo remembered a particular night late in October 2008 as if only hours had passed instead of years. There was no forgetting that night in Southwest Florida seven years ago...

A STORM RAGED SEVEN MILES OFFSHORE.

Boca Grande Pass led to the Southeastern Gulf of Mexico. Charlotte Harbor was ten miles across and almost twenty miles long, north to south. Low barrier islands separated this large Southwestern Florida estuary from the gulf.

That the harbor was shallow—less than twenty feet in depth—only meant small craft may fall prey to short, steep, and treacherous waves whipped up in mere minutes by high winds.

THE DREAM WAS ALWAYS THE SAME...

Two men stood less than six feet apart in the sinking boat, facing each other with nothing but the amidships console and naked hatred between them.

Precarious seas rose to five feet. Cresting waves in the shallow waters broke with violent resolve through the pass from the gulf into the expansive harbor. White-caps blew off the waves' peaks in the darkness. That signaled winds from the northwest exceeded thirty knots and approached gale force.

Dent Canfield, a traitorous serial killer and Geo's ex-employee, held a stubby little bat in his right hand. The considerable paunch he carried around his six-foot-three-inch frame did not diminish his deadly intent nor his cat-like movements.

Geo wondered, *Is that bat the nasty instrument of death that killed four of my employees? My friends?*

~

DENT CANFIELD SAW ONLY GRATIFICATION.

At last.

His animalistic madness would no longer to be caged, a two-year erection verged on eruption. There were no adequate words, even if anyone could hear them in the tempest.

His most heinous personal adversary stood right where he needed him—isolated and within swinging distance of his precious thumper. Dent's fulfillment was at hand. It consumed his soul with lust. He took a step closer to fulfilling his wet dream.

Without warning, lumpy clouds delivered a tropical deluge to punctuate the angry wind. The two men became ghosts, shimmering in the wind-whipped brackish water from the harbor that blended with fresh water from the sky. The soggy scene painted a stroboscopic nightmare, barely believable.

~

GEO HAD ALWAYS BEEN A PACIFIST.

He focused on saving or salvaging human life.

Now, though, rage flowed through him like a watery toxin. At first, he felt guilt at this unmitigated fury soon to be unchecked. But then he accepted and reveled in its delicious abhorrence. He spoke out loud, although he knew the storm swallowed his words.

"This is a defining moment. I must find the strength to stop the killing."

~

THE MAELSTROM'S FEROCITY ESCALATED.

Didn't seem possible. Now punctuated with thunder and lightning every second all around them, Dent advanced on Geo. He raised his lethal bat above his head and right shoulder in a two-handed death grip.

A cancerous malice sculpted his face with water dripping from his nose and untrimmed eyelashes. He was within reach of Janis, of fulfilling his dream. He swung.

Geo raised the borrowed pistol within that same moment, aimed at center mass, and pulled the trigger before he dropped to the deck. Dent fell too.

There was nothing left.

Nothing at all.

~

WAS THAT SEVEN YEARS AGO?

Or seven minutes ago?

What's the difference?

What now?

A FAN

Maryland, Eastern Shore

If he were honest with himself, John W. Stevens couldn't wait for his Thursday evening indulgence. He looked forward to the Jack Rhodes podcast for at least two reasons.

First, the guy could spin a compelling yarn that seemed to flirt with fact. And second, he knew Jack's real name—one of Sam Braxton's irregulars. Jack Rhodes—also known as George "Geo" Janis—helped expose the Patriot Brotherhood's meddling in the 2008 national elections when most ignored the evidence.

While he had never met Janis, he recalled Colonel Braxton's accounts of his participation in what they now called the *2008 PB Affair.* That series of epic events was now a piece of American history of which only a select few were aware.

But knowing full well that the PB was still around kept John fearful for his country's future. And that knowledge provided him and his team sterling purpose.

I should connect with this Jack Rhodes to tell him how much I appreciate his stories, and his sacrifice.

He couldn't help but wonder about Jack's sources. And how much some of those tall tales of the future sounded like present-day or even probable near-future non-fictional issues.

John sat at the five-foot table that served as his desk in that small sun-drenched office. During the day, the windows were always swung open to the sea breeze—when they weren't in lock-down, anyway.

The gauzy white curtains blew close enough to tickle the back of his neck. At that, he smiled. He loved this place, especially this room.

Yes, he might give old Jack a call. Just another fan with access to his cover story. He'd clear it with the US Marshal's Service over at the Department of Justice first.

Or would that place Janis at risk?

INTENSITY

GEO JANIS DIDN'T **FEEL** LIKE DAMAGED GOODS.
Before retiring from a successful career as a tech executive, he tenaciously clung to the self-image of a confident leader and a corporate climber. That image permeated everything he did, said, or thought, even as he crossed countless ethical boundaries.

Until so many things changed.

Without end, Geo pondered how his life had evolved. He padded to and from the motorhome's bathroom, as always this time of day, in his ugly ankle-high sheepskin slippers. He sunk into his Stressless recliner in the dim pre-dawn light once more, still wondering.

After his near-lethal encounter with that psychopath seven years earlier, Geo retired at fifty-eight.

Kate had said, "Too soon!"

"No choice, Babe. The job is killing me, even though Dent didn't."

He adopted a demeanor similar to a veteran combat soldier. *It's not so much the age as the mileage,* he thought. The way he walked, talked, and perceived the world around him unfolded in ways surprising to him. It was then his writing began to reflect a certain bedraggled intensity.

Terry, one of his devout listeners asked him in all sincerity, "Love your podcasts, man, but why did you choose the mid-twenty-first century timeline for *The Alley*, Jack?"

Geo sat alone at five a.m. in front of the motorhome's passenger-side desk. The filtered light of the green glass desk lamp lit his iMac's keyboard, and little else. The twenty-seven-inch monitor cast a blue-white mood light. He started typing, not knowing what he would say.

"Terry, first, thanks for being a loyal listener. So why the year 2050 for *Redemption Alley?* I once assumed I chose this timeframe for my podcasts as an arbitrary literary device, something authors do sometimes. You know, to make the show interesting, maybe a little different. Perhaps it's more than that.

"Or I'm peering into someone else's future. It's as if a voice from the far side of some future grave speaks to me, and it is compelling. Most authors might call that inspiration, but it's more than that to me.

"That voice warns me that period of yet-to-be history is a time of revelation, the pinnacle of humanity's indecent exposure, and I must tell that story. Now.

Maybe these stories warn of what today's follies will yield. You know, like fruit of the barren tree? You decide, Terry. And thanks for asking."

His producer who only knew him by his pseudonym expressed dark concern, but there would be no deviation from the script.

Zaya French, his main character, would remain a man of integrity. Zaya possessed two unshakable traits—he would not deviate from his ethical standards, and he would never quit.

He cherished all the attributes that Geo himself abandoned long ago and now sought a measure of redemption by trying to vicariously recapture those attributes through his fiction.

Silly, but it helps.

Geo—as Jack Rhodes—listened to his latest podcast with grim satisfaction. As he pressed play on his iPhone and listened to the opening sound effects that set the scene, he thought, *Could this really be what our future holds?*

If so, how do I know of this? Now?

M ESA, ARIZONA

"Home is where we park it."

That's what Kate and Geo often said.

Geo thought, *Without anonymity, we're dead. But we know what we're doing. At least we think so.*

They parked in an RV resort with over 2,500 doors. Almost two-thirds of those doors opened into mobile homes called park models—small, manufactured, and transportable trailers meant to move once or twice in their lifetime.

More substantial and stationary residences—full-size mobile homes, or larger manufactured homes—numbered in the hundreds. And almost another thousand RVs of all types stayed in this resort from a few days to a few months to enjoy the amenities before hitting the road again.

Kate and Geo treasured the relative anonymity of large cities.

Mesa was such a place, part of the Phoenix metroplex, the largest population center in Arizona.

Before moving into their bus and embarking on a journey of indefinite duration, they lived in New York, L.A., San Francisco, Austin, Detroit, and Fort Myers. City kids. Mesa felt comfortable and casual.

Seven years earlier the couple lived aboard their cherished pilot-house motorsailer *Sojourn.* After thirty years of weekend and vacation sailing, and many months sailing to and anchoring near secluded tropical islands after retiring, and to avoid detection, they almost drove each other crazy in their self-induced isolation. They concluded life at sea was not for them, at least not forever, as idyllic as those memories remained.

Besides, not long after they returned to the mainland, that madman Dent Canfield burned their boat to the waterline, thinking they slept inside.

Now they took their time adjusting to what was supposed to be a serene desert life. As long as it lasted.

Geo looked over his shoulder.

Every waking hour of every day.

And every night in his dreams.

As he pressed *play* on his iPhone to listen to the latest episode of the weekly podcast of his creation called *Redemption Alley,* he looked forward to some self-indulgent time free from those dreams.

Before the show finished, he slept.

But the dreams would not be denied.

MAKING A DIFFERENCE

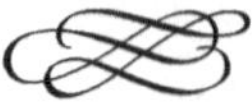

W ASHINGTON, DC
2016

Stewart Atherton—America's first black commander-in-chief—reflected, *I haven't slept five contiguous hours in almost eight years.*

Apnea was not the issue. First, he lived in constant fear for his beloved nation, and second, for his own life. With good reason. He survived more assassination attempts during his tenure than any other US president. Nobody outside a small subset of official Washington knew of this.

President Atherton couldn't wait to leave the job he worked so hard to get. Twice. Now doubt plagued him. He had made a difference, hadn't he?

If Julia were still alive, she'd joke about his hair transitioning from black to white—almost overnight—halfway through his first term. She'd hoist that mischievous grin and say, "Stew, some might say you appear more distinguished. To me you just look old and scared. But you're still the love of my life. And always will be."

God, he missed her, in particular, her romantic sarcasm. Every long day and every longer night.

Now he cut his snowy hair so short he might as well have shaved his head. They advised him against that. Besides, that would not fit his style. That would admit a small defeat, and Stewart Atherton did not possess that character defect. Although a shaved pate *would* streamline his early morning workouts in the White House gym under the watchful eye of his personal security detail.

That the president used the services of a *private* security team agitated Adler Stavers, head of his Secret Service. This broadcast the president didn't trust Stavers or his team. They were right. More fodder for the occasional news cycle.

Conspiracy theorists went nuts over that detail, though nobody was sure how they gained access to such a juicy tidbit.

Washington.

"Mr. President, you have another full day ahead of you starting in thirty minutes with your Chief of Staff and National Security Adviser to prepare for the daily intelligence briefing."

Another gray DC winter day back-lit Atherton's impeccably clad athletic seventy-four-year-old frame behind the Constitution desk in the Oval Office. Armament-resistant window glass jaded one's view.

"Thank you, Janice. Please get me a secure line to John Stevens."

"Of course, Sir."

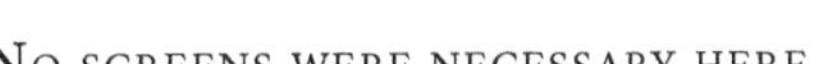

No screens were necessary here.

Thanks to the non-stop sea breeze. John's arrow-straight Roman nose drank in the dank but invigorating salt air through the window thrown open behind him.

He set down the mug of French Press coffee to grab his ever-present satellite phone now sounding its annoying symphony of paranoia. He stabbed the green button.

After the beeps and pops of rolling encryption subsided, he glanced at the screen with surprise. The display appeared dim in the brilliant ambient light of the small sunroom he'd converted to his office. He waved at the Captain to give him the room.

Captain Cheevers, sitting at attention across the desk from him, arose. Disappeared from the room without a sound, sliding together the heavy eight-panel double pocket doors behind him.

In a cheerful tone, but one that bespoke all business, John said, "Mr. President, I imagine you're pressed for time. What may I do for you?"

He forgot about his coffee.

It wasn't often that his friend Stewart Atherton graced him with a call. He closed his eyes and imagined his erstwhile political opponent standing in the office he still missed. Stewart didn't sit unless he had no choice.

"John, you are correct. And I won't ask where you are. This is your almost-lame-duck president asking a knowledgeable insider if I made a difference during my two terms. You must understand this feeling."

John considered his response.

"Stew, you need to hear this. As a friend who has been there, I imagine you are interrogating yourself without just cause. You wonder if it has been worth it. Doubt is tingling your every nerve ending.

"First, you survived. That is a singular achievement since they hatched a plot to do away with you the day you beat me in 2008. By the narrowest of margins, I might remind you, Sir."

Both senior statesmen indulged in a soft chuckle.

"Second, you've set a shining example as the first black president in our proud nation's history. They elected you. That would have been enough. But not for Stewart Atherton."

"John, I wasn't trolling for a love fest here."

"With all due respect, Mr. President, shut up and listen. You took huge risks that paid off. You instituted monumental changes in public policy I could not have imagined during my tenure. And you pulled this nation out of the worst recession since the Great Depression, damn near single-handedly. Oh, I almost forgot—you also took a cabal of traitors off the board.

"I could go on, but to answer your question, yes, you've made a difference. You've screwed up, too. Guess what? If the public were aware of how many times *every single president* has screwed up, well, we can only imagine. Let that go. It's just static. Stew, you should be proud. Now, what else?"

"Thanks, John. I guess I needed to hear that. One more thing. I need you to tell me how you do it. And how I can do it too. Assuming *he's* elected, how do I continue to serve my country after this madman takes office? How can I become another wizard behind the purple curtain?

"I'm scared, John. Not for my personal safety. I've lived with that fear through both terms, but Jeff Redding? Our worst fears for this country may soon come true. Not to put too fine a point on it, John, but he scares the crap out of me. What can *we* do going forward? How can I help?"

"We'll talk further once you emerge from your cocoon next January, farther from your oath of office. You have my number, Stew. Use it once you're a private citizen again, assuming we're still both alive and taking nourishment. Now I suggest you go do your job. Sir."

John hung up on the almost-lame-duck President of the United States. That elicited a small smile.

His coffee was cold.

A GOOD DEFENSE

C ALI, COLUMBIA

She mastered four languages as a child.

Carmelita Dega spoke Spanish, Portuguese, English, and German. Growing up in a multilingual neighborhood, not a day went by she didn't speak at least three of those four languages.

And because she spent every waking moment anywhere but in her abusive home, she studied and practiced every conceivable form of self-defense. To survive. Anywhere she might gain experience or even a free lesson, she also mastered the dingiest streets of Cali, her home-town—the third largest city in Colombia.

At fourteen she became an arranged bride. Later that same year, she gave birth to premature twins. Lita wanted neither marriage nor children. But she learned to love her girls.

So she gave them up before her abusive husband, twenty years her senior, expressed an interest, got his calloused hands on them. It would have been only a matter of time. Little Lita found it impossible to forget what her father had done to her as a child.

Less than six months later she orchestrated a summary divorce administered by Mr. Nine Millimeter—a friend of a friend.

What happens in the barrio stays in the barrio.

The emotional abuse and physical mauling ended overnight. If Lita only knew at fourteen what she knew at the age of fifteen-and-a-half...

Lita learned to be as tough as she was small. Nobody messed with little Dega. By eighteen, everyone recognized her as someone never to anger. One young man learned the hard way.

"What's with the pink mohawk, Chiquita? ¿Está un poco loco?"

This was no compliment.

She seethed. With a quiet menace, she said, "It is *not* pink, es oro rosa—rose gold. I *am* crazy, and it is *not* a mohawk, Puta."

Also no compliment.

Some suggested Lita wore her natural raven hair like that to elicit a reaction so she might have an excuse to respond. Nobody did. Until that young tough who committed the ultimate triple transgression. He sneered, *and* laughed, *and* tried to touch her hair.

What occurred between his next two heartbeats proved consequential. It only took that long for Lita's tormentor to taste the greasy dust of that alley off that side-street in Cali.

She turned and walked away before his nose even hit the dirt. His impertinence earned him two snapped ribs and four fingers broken and dangling at odd angles. He no longer laughed.

She smiled and thought, *At least he lives.* Decided it was time for a change in her hair style anyway.

Lita also changed her fighting style.

Among her ruthless street survival skills, Lita studied Judo, achieving a sixteenth-grade brown belt. She wormed her way into the heart of an expatriated American sensei—her martial arts instructor—who gave her all the lessons she could handle. He liked her.

So obvious, but he is so very nice.

Lita's progress impressed him. This hard-throwing pocket-rocket might have become a serious contender for the top female Judo competitor, or Judoka, in Colombia had she not shied away from formal competition. Its meaning escaped her.

Then a specialized branch of the Army recruited Lita. The Fuerzas Militares de Colombia, Contrainsurgencia, the country's elite counterinsurgency, or COIN unit, recognized her potential.

Such a grizzled twenty-one-year-old displayed stellar career prospects. They viewed her countless near-misses with the law, and her hard-knuckled approach to life, as "experiential assets" to jump-start a promising career.

Do I have Sensei to thank for a recommendation?

After just three months of training and six months as a COIN squad member, Lita distinguished herself by leading several challenging operations. Her squad leader seemed incapable of doing his job which placed the entire squad at risk.

The team respected this little dynamo's take-charge attitude, her fearless demeanor, and recognized her as their de facto leader.

Then, before being appointed the official lead wolf of the pack, based on her mates' enthusiastic recommendations, a series of altercations with her commanding officer detoured her future.

"Carmelita, my little bonita, I could help you if you help me. You are so strong, but so tiny. What do you say? Can we help each other?"

She found ignoring him accomplished nothing but unspoken threats of insubordination.

The CO would regret one fateful incident until he would be tossed into his coffin. He approached Lita from behind in the go-team's locker room late one evening. Caressing her well-muscled left buttock in his left hand, he tried to squeeze her ample right breast after reaching his right arm under hers. The smell of stale cigarette smoke and cheap rum revolted her.

He became disfigured over what he called a misunderstanding.

Lita filed a report. The dishonorable discharge papers arrived, authored and signed by the CO within forty-eight hours of the incident. Criminal charges never materialized.

Her corpulent CO would never forget Carmelita Dega. The stylish patch he'd wear over his hollow left eye socket for the rest of his life would not permit him to do so. During honest introspection, el Jefe admitted to himself he never saw her right thumb coming at him over her left shoulder. Bested by a woman, and one so small, punished him enough.

Lita's friendship with her Judo teacher and neighbor from the barrio had blossomed. She grew to respect this opinionated Americano. They understood each other.

Bitter and disillusioned but determined, Lita sought employment in the private sector.

Sensei provided her an email address.

RHODES' ALLEY

M ESA, ARIZONA

"Is this Jack Rhodes of *Redemption Alley?*"

After a lengthy pause, wondering how this guy got his number…

"That depends. If you like *The Alley* podcast or Jack's novels, I'm your guy. If you hate them, I have no idea who you're talking about."

A breathy chuckle. "Hello, George."

… They found us!

Geo's first impulse urged him to hang up and run. He jumped out of his lawn chair so fast it up-ended, crashing into the trailer's tongue at the rear of the coach. In that instant, his blood pressure shot directly into deep space.

Kate sat next to him in the shade of a dwarf palm. She stiffened, eyes wide. Dropped her open paperback face down onto her lap. She clutched the plastic arms of her chair with bone-white knuckles and feared what might happen next.

As a precaution, he covered the phone as he mouthed and pointed, "Char. Inside. Now."

He never failed to use her cover name outside the coach, and now with a suspicious and unknown voice on the phone—

She complied without question. Walked to the forward end of the bus on the passenger's side and disappeared up the steps and in through the open door.

He partially recovered, looked at the cell hoping it might reveal the caller's identity. Blocked ID.

"Sorry, name's Jack here. You must have the wrong number."

Torn between hanging up and learning who from within Hell had tracked them, he opted for the latter.

"Jack, my apologies for the drama. I can't imagine living under an assumed name for so long. And the stress of living a double life? Believe me, I understand."

So this must be someone from way back. What are the odds I remember this guy? But that voice...

The unidentified caller continued.

"We've never met but we have a dear mutual friend—a doctor and cantankerous old Confederate soldier. Are we as one here, Jack?"

After a moment's consideration, Geo said, "Yes, yes! Who is this?"

"Just an old retired politician. I'm John. And I am a huge fan of your work."

Geo thought hard. Who did he know that was a friend of Sam's named John. With a jolt, he tagged one impressive name to that iconic voice. He'd heard it countless times. Oh. *Shit!*

"Ahhhh, John W?"

"You nailed it, Jack. Colonel B told me you were sharp. I'm covered over here, but suspect your line is open. Appreciate a little craft. Nice."

"Sir! What? How? Why?"

"Okay, so you're a better writer than a speaker." He chuckled.

The former president continued, "Look, Jack, I wanted to reach out, to tell you how much I enjoy your podcasts. I'm a loyal subscriber."

"Wow. Thank you, Sir. That means a lot. Sometimes I wonder if it's worth the effort."

"You compel your listeners and readers to analyze their own values through your fiction, Jack, and that's an invaluable talent. Too many no longer bother with critical thinking. You make it fun if not somewhat, well, dark. And I'd appreciate it if you'd call me John. Calling me 'Sir' makes me feel old."

"Well, um, John, I'll struggle with that, but I'll do my best. If you don't mind my asking, do you have another agenda for calling this humble writer well into his retirement, and yours?"

"Correct again, Jack. You performed an invaluable service to your country toward the end of my last term, and you left everything behind. That could not have been easy. It's as if I know you better than most from that, and from your podcasts. As one of the few who knows your background today, your stories seem insightful. More than I would expect. Can't help but wonder, not that it matters."

"Sir? Uh, John?"

"Be careful, son. You're damn near broadcasting your identity. From there, it would become easier to pinpoint your location. Meantime, I will remain a loyal subscriber. Thank you. Again."

Click.

Geo held the phone to his ear for another thirty seconds, staring at nothing, seeing nothing, hearing nothing. Then he stared at the phone for a long while. Finally, he slipped it into his pocket and turned on his heels with a smile and hollered.

"Hey, Kate! Guess who just called? An *Alley* fan. Another retiree!"

RAW RECRUIT

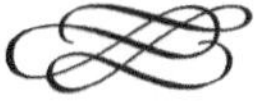

POTOMAC, MARYLAND

THE BROTHERHOOD NEEDED RECRUITS.

Malc Frieburg sat in his plush high-back desk chair behind his opulent desk. Even though the idyllic weather at his Potomac estate beckoned, he drew tight the curtains on the large window in his den. The desk lamp provided the room's only illumination.

Quick to respond to Carmelita Dega's email inquiry, he sensed just enough desperation that might qualify her for his army of covert malcontents. Her inquiry came as no surprise after a revealing chat with his old acquaintance, the sensei from Cali with whom he shared a certain history.

After he looked deep into Dega's background, it was time for an interview with one of his trusted South American operators, a hard case named Yuri. Standard recruiting practice.

"Hey, hombre, I need you to vet somebody for me over in Cali. Her name is Carmelita Dega. Sounds like a real hell hound. Can do, amigo?"

"Sí, Señor Frieburg. Am I looking for anything in particular?"

"Yeah, Yuri. Find out how hungry she is for our kind of action and dig into her history. I need a real desperado who isn't afraid to commit, well, everything to the job. ¿Me entiendes?"

"Claro que sí, Señor."

Twenty-four hours later Yuri assured Malc that Dega looked promising, but Malc still needed proof she was rock-solid under fire. Too many things had gone wrong lately. Besides, he needed some expendable assets for what could well be a one-way mission. Objective: test the defenses of a high value target.

~

CALI, COLUMBIA

SHE NEEDED TO PROVE HERSELF. AGAIN.

During the next two weeks, Carmelita Dega received several encrypted emails in her small but clean apartment in Cali's massive barrio. In response to her increasing interest, and she suspected their continued vetting of her background, each email contained more detail outlining her first probationary mission.

As part of a team of ghost operators, Lita's mission would support a former US president's retirement with extreme prejudice. Time-frame: six weeks. Prep: acclimate to a team by training in rural South Carolina. They'd be looking her over. The pay? Obscene.

Looking out her second-story window onto the same dirt street where she had taught a young man an important lesson many years ago, the magnitude of her first mission told her much about her prospective employer. To trust her participation—an unproven asset —for such a significant mission?

They are shorthanded. And these people are not afraid to take huge risks, both on unproven assets and on bold missions with broad consequences.

These revelations both frightened and excited her.

After one interminable day considering whether she would accept such a bold charter, and whether it fit her code, she replied to a final encrypted text requesting her commitment.

In for a centavo... Besides, I have never been to Los Estados Unidos.

So began the game.

TRICKY BUSINESS

P OTOMAC, MARYLAND

The man was the father he never had.

Enoch Slattery had been Malcolm Frieburg's dearest friend, mentor, boss, and his, well, everything.

Right up until the day he disappeared.

Malc's mood swung to maudlin, sitting in the darkness of his den, curtains drawn tight against the night. The only light came from his desk lamp and his phone's screen. It occurred to him this twenty-four room mini-estate was a waste. He only used this room and maybe four others to eat, sleep, shit, and to store all of his cool stuff.

When Enoch was snatched in October of 2008, thanks to President John W. Stevens and his minions, Malc took over as the Patriot Brotherhood's muscle czar. That was all because of Enoch.

Among his effects, Malc found a recording between a guy named Palmer Xavier and Enoch. The PB's founding father had directed

Enoch to give Xavier a full briefing on their dirty tricks organization before Xavier joined the PB. He was just another client at that point.

Xavier didn't know that Enoch had recorded their conversation—the guy never missed an opportunity for a backstop.

Malc played this recording now and then, for the comforting sound of Enoch's sharp voice. Yeah, Enoch's voice. He had copied this recording to his smartphone years earlier.

Once again, now sitting in darkness, alone, he pressed *Play* for the fifth or sixth time in the last month as he remembered the man he loved and respected more than any human being, alive or dead…

"Meeting in Midtown Manhattan.

"On my way into the Madison Avenue office of Palmer Xavier, Chief Operations Officer of Greater Global Solutions. *The Man* directed me to provide a *complete* briefing to this client, against my better judgment. They got plans for this guy, I guess. I'm not trusting him yet, but orders are orders. HOO-yah.

"Here we go.

"… like I always say, Mr. Xavier, 'push a point, then jump back before getting splattered by whatever doesn't stick.' Sad commentary. Made me rich."

"Mr. S, you have work. Urgent. Pays well. Can do?"

"Name it, Sir."

"I'll email you the details, usual channel. On another topic, I'd like to understand your range of services better."

"Sir, politics is one of our mainstays. Every political campaign uses back-room operators. We do the nasty stuff the big boys can't dirty their own dicks on. Same with big business. And Sir, I can't remember a dirtier political campaign—ever—or one that got this intense, this early.

"When I think I've seen every sort of twisted thinking, the crap gets even slimier and more profitable. The work is tricky, but the pay is obscene. And there's nothing wrong with watching—with a recording device in hand. Sometimes, more is required.

"And I'll tell you something else, Mr. Xavier. One of my secondary services involves information leverage. You can guess what *that* involves."

"Well, you've enlightened me. More dimensions to your work than I had imagined. Scope?"

"Sir, I use more than a hundred operatives worldwide. Most are ex-military, ex-intelligence, or most often both. They contract with my firm. They've checked their ethics at the door, along with what remains of their otherwise-purposeless lives, which is often why they work for me. And I only hire by word-of-mouth.

"We've no fancy name, or motto, or company song. These ghosts just get things done, I pay them well, and they never go home. No point. For most of them, my shop is their last stop. And one lap with one of my guys or gals is all it takes to get done whatever needs doing."

"It all sounds so melodramatic. How do you find these people, Enoch?"

"Sir, you cannot understand how many of these somewhat rusty swords are lying around out there on overgrown battlefields that nobody will ever hear about. I'm the guy who picks up and collects those swords.

"We're a retirement home for active adult spooks. Here, retirement age isn't guys in their sixties or seventies. Most of my operatives are in their forties and fifties. They're at the top of their game and looking to double-dip their pension with side jobs. Or they have no pension and no other options.

"They're hardscrabble as Hell, with tradecraft oozing outta their anal retentive sphincters. Some became disillusioned after losing their sanctions. Because they got their rocks off twisting protected titties, or using the wrong third-world asshole's cat or dog or wife for target practice. Or they screwed the wrong guy's goat.

"Besides my overlooking all that, I pay way better than government service, and I offer a great benefits package. Sometimes they get to burn the stuffed shirts that flamed *them,* and they get to watch it on the six o'clock news. Satisfying work. You get the idea."

"How discreet are your people, Enoch?"

"Let me put it this way, Sir. I'm as discreet as they come, outside of you keeping your own dirty little secrets to yourself. No offense. Everybody has 'em. Everybody. And nobody's secrets are safe forever. Between any dork and his prayers to the Almighty, though, is me with my recorder.

"Until I was referred to you, bet you never heard of me, right? Now we know each other, and are guaranteed mutually assured destruction if either violates our code of silence. That's how it works. So to anyone but my clients, I am a ghost. My discretion is my trade, but that ain't worth jack unless I deliver results.

"I'm one of the better-trained spooks you'll ever meet outside of government—any government—and I get the results. Always.

"Spookville is an exclusive community. My guys might guess others they know are around, but we have no central office, no head-quarters, and no company Christmas parties. These tight-asses prefer privacy and solitude, so all they can do is guess. Most don't even care to try.

"Operationally, there's nothing. Nothing at all. Deep, dark, empty space. Tight compartmentalization makes for tight security.

"Look, Sir, this is more than I've talked in years. Are there other questions you might have for me?"

"Not right now, Enoch. Thank you."

As he exited an elevator to the empty late-night lobby of 555 Madison, Enoch said into his recorder, "End interview. On my way out. Now, I gotta dig up some dirt on a handful of GGS execs per Mr. Xavier. Deadline ASAFP. End file one of two."

～

GOD, MALC MISSED THAT MAN.

Enoch was the father he never had.

Mr. M assumed the mantle of leadership over the Patriot Brotherhood shortly after Enoch disappeared eight years earlier. Malc briefed his new boss on what his team could do for the PB. He used Enoch's briefing to Palmer Xavier—which he had memorized—as his blueprint.

Malc's friend and mentor always told him, "Gotta have a Number Two, somebody you trust who can take over for you at a moment's notice. And in our business, it's not *if* something happens, it's *when*."

When Enoch went missing, Malc activated *Hat Trick* as agreed. He had even bought the small estate in Potomac as homage to Enoch, to commemorate the day he was transformed from a soldier to a general in that town.

Still sitting in his darkened den, and not yet finished reminiscing, Malc could recall every detail of that day, almost nine years earlier— the day he activated *Hat Trick*...

❧

I wasn't frightened, more concerned.

Despite all my attempts to connect with my friend and counselor, no word from Enoch in over forty-eight hours meant trouble. That never happened. Something was wrong.

I recalled an earlier conversation with him.

"Malc, I want you to once again recommit to me."

I remembered thinking, *This conversation? Again?*

"If you don't hear from me for seventy-two hours—ever—something is very wrong. We've discussed this. Execute *Hat Trick*. Promise me. Can you commit to that, one more time? This is vital, Malc."

I said, "Absolutely, Bossman. You can count on me."

It seemed a melodramatic precaution but Enoch was a legend.

Our agreement comprised a sacred oath between two high-level operatives. *Hat Trick* was a high-priority. Ever the operators, we even code-worded this contingency plan.

Only me and a handful of senior operatives in our organization of mercs knew of its existence.

Early the following morning, clouded by dread for my friend and guide, I found myself giddy with guilty anticipation. The security guard opened the front door of the nondescript Wells Fargo Bank on Falls Road in Potomac.

Hat Trick stipulated I assume Enoch's mantle of leadership. Vital information awaited in a safe deposit box. The working assumption? Something or someone had compromised Enoch.

I would receive precise directives to destroy certain documents and files, to change keywords and passwords, to move funds and select personnel. I would establish new double-blind communication channels with specific operators. And Enoch's written instructions would mandate that I move certain digital and hard-copy information to a new location known only to myself.

I'd then craft *Hat Trick 2.0* with a successor of my choice after the prescribed brief wait time. And so the covert chain of succession would prevail.

I wore that safe deposit box key around my neck for almost a year. Should Enoch show up later, he'd resume control with my close cooperation and we'd establish a new set of contingencies. No question. *Hat Trick* would then have just become part of my tradecraft.

The time arrived. After seventy-two hours of deafening silence, I opened the triple-briefcase-size box in the bank's opulent private viewing chamber. Stacked its contents on the small glossy table.

So began my review with some bound paper journals. Then, less than a minute later…

"Oh, my *God!*"

As many briefings as Enoch conducted with me, that cache of info carried me beyond my wildest imagination. I wasn't looking at dynamite. I was fondling an armed weapon of mass destruction.

As I gazed at the materials scattered across the slick surface of the high-top table at which I stood, what I saw paralyzed me. With difficulty, I arrested my reverie and continued to scan a phenomenal body of intel.

I scanned lists and descriptions of operations, financial transactions, small journals describing dirt on major public figures, pay-offs, including long-standing blackmail transactions with the title 'Annuities' going back years.

Now jittery as Hell, I backed off a step and surveyed the treasure trove. I guessed the DVDs and flash drives contained thousands of incendiary images. Enoch had labeled each with provocative and descriptive titles in various colors.

A hard plastic case protecting each DVD featured copious hand-written tables of contents with legends for a simple but comprehensive color coding scheme. They cross-referenced back to various hard-copy journals in the box.

There was more. Much more. I realized Enoch must have collected this material over *decades*.

I glanced over my shoulder to ensure nobody else was in the tiny room with the frosted green-glass door. The fancy gold-tone deadbolt remained in place.

Not seeing any cameras either, I shoved the array of explosive materials into the oversized briefcase I brought with me. The thing now weighed at least thirty pounds. More a medium-size suitcase than a briefcase.

Before departing the private viewing room, I once again donned a mask of neutrality. Difficult but not impossible. The volume of materials forced me to also pack every huge cargo pocket of my olive drab Army field jacket—briefcase overflow.

I shivered. I exited the bank into the sunlight dappling Falls Road through the branches of maple trees with their golden leaves barely clinging to life.

The street appeared much the same as when I entered the bank thirty-three minutes earlier, but I remember thinking, *I've just entered a different world. In this world, I'll play by a very different set of rules visible to perhaps a handful of people.*

Anywhere.

~

ON THAT DAY—EIGHT YEARS AGO NOW—

Malc's incredulity had overwhelmed him.

It was back then—in 2008—the Brotherhood's power and influence began to collapse. Thanks to Stevens and those two operators of his, Braxton and Janis, who exposed so many of the PB's assets.

His opulent den, still dark as ever, pressed in on him. Malc chastised himself. He never got around to implementing *Hat Trick 2.0*, including the choice of his own Number Two.

He found trusting anyone impossible. Betrayal was such a part of his fabric. Enoch never knew that about him. Had he known, would he still have trusted him to take over?

He always supposed he needed to groom his own Number Two, but never did.

Stupid. Greater good, and all that. Maybe I should decide who I distrust least.

But first, he needed to finish some business.

S OUTH CAROLINA

Darla Evans needed no one.

Not emotionally, anyway. Now—naked and bleeding—she cast that premise into a cloud of drug-induced doubt as she stumbled through the cedar forest.

The deep bruises on her arms and legs, and the copious amounts of dried blood on the front and inside of both thighs, painted a gruesome drama. She hated drama.

Dar was a woman of precise action. She decided she would *not* be a casualty. Not today.

Held for two days and tortured—that's how she preferred to think of it, the parts she remembered, anyway—escape and evasion now became her top priorities.

She never failed to achieve her priorities. Survival made the top of her new list, the list of a soldier caught behind enemy lines in the throes of a tactical retreat.

Someone had erased two days. Only the last two hours replayed like a high definition video in an endless loop...

She lay spread-eagled.

Tied atop a smelly old metal bed frame and box spring, it was covered with a thin fabric in tatters that was more stained than not. Upon wearing through her plasticuffs, she discovered an ancient landline in the next room with a rotary dial. *And* a dial tone!

Her shaky but terse message to the 9-1-1 operator, gasping between each semi-delirious word:

"Darla Evans, US Army. Imminent danger. This location. Contact Captain Derek Cheevers, Fort Bragg, North Carolina. Send help. ASAP."

Dar imagined she was still active military. More specifically, that she was still one of the few female members of the First Special Forces Operational Detachment-Delta. Most folks spoke of that elite US Army detachment simply as *Delta Force.* She had retired six years earlier.

She hid the off-hook receiver best she could and stumbled out of the secluded ramshackle cabin. No other combatants in sight.

Dar could not know that her team leader, Captain Derek Cheevers, also US Army Retired, already tracked her. Barefoot, she headed for high ground—SOP, or Standard Operating Procedure.

In her febrile state she collided with Cheevers on the rocky trail. He led another of Dar's teammates, Mick Sandstrom and three South Carolina state troopers.

Dar would not cry. She would only fight. She would always fight. But with no strength left, not even enough to recognize her teammates, she collapsed into somebody's arms.

～

Then... "Derek?"

"I gotcha, little sister. I gotcha." He wrapped his coat around her scratched arms and shoulders, scooped her up. She weighed five-foot-two of nothing. *Maybe* a battered but grizzled buck-ten.

Derek carried her toward safety and medical treatment. Broke his heart to see her in this state, but she was one of the toughest soldiers he'd ever worked with, retired or not.

She's okay. Has to be.

Twenty-four hours later, Derek sat at Dar's bedside in a sixth-floor private room at the busy Roper Hospital in Charleston. Mick paced nearby, pissed at whoever did this to their sister-in-arms. There *would* be payback.

"Hey… guys. I called. You came."

Dar's weak smile peeked out, her tiny voice little more than a dehydrated croak. She was receiving a fast drip.

"Hey, little sister. You look like Hell and back."

"No shit, Cap. Um, Derek, I can explain about the no-clothes thing. Assholes stole 'em. And my sidearm."

"Geez, Dar. *That's* what you're worried about right now? You *are* a piece 'a work. Isn't that right, Mick?"

Mick sauntered into her limited field of vision, brushing his cheeks with the back of one hand. No words.

From within a slow morphine slur Dar said, *"Hey… Big Mac!"*

To Derek, she said, "They're telling me kids are now out of the question for this now-never-baby-m-momma. BFD, huh?"

Two big tough veteran Delta operators both misted over. Again. Dar smiled. Sort of. Or was that a defiant sneer?

One tough operator.

Trying to recover, Mick found his voice. "The three bears, Sistah! Big Mac, Lil Sis, and Jus' Right." He winked at their team leader. His eyes misted more, much to his dismay. Another swift back-of-the-hand brush of his cheeks.

Dar said, "We gotta debrief. These assholes. I think they wanted to know about where I work. I gave 'em nothing."

"You know what, Dar? That can wait. Right now your mission is to get better. We need you sharp. Got that, soldier?"

"Uh, yessir." Her eyes rolled, most of them whites. Lids flitted a few times before clamping down.

The men tried not to stare at her purple sleeves of bruises and shallow lacerations in sharp contrast to the white hospital gown and bandages.

"Good. Now rest and we'll be back in a quick four."

"Uh, yessir..." Dar's eyes remained closed as her voice faded into a lumpy snore.

Derek and Mick would not disturb her for *twenty*-four.

MOST SCARS HEAL.

After five weeks of rehab and mandatory counseling, an astounded Doctor Stacy Delgado cleared Darla Evans for full duty. There was a reason Darla had been one of the few successful female members of Delta Force.

Now retired and working private protection, she'd allow this woman to protect her any day.

But what had this episode cost this soldier?

GHOST HUNTING

P OTOMAC, MARYLAND

He found science fiction his great escape. He happened upon a Jack Rhodes novel, and that was it. He then purchased, read, and analyzed all his published works over the next six weeks hoping for more clues.

Those stories *had* to have been written by the object of his rage—George Janis, the pen name and fictional disclaimers notwithstanding!

He didn't so much enjoy Rhodes' work as it intrigued him, or maybe disturbed him. As much as he hated to admit it, he found himself compelled to listen to every single episode of his *Redemption Alley* podcast every Thursday.

Malc found his subsequent search for intel on Jack Rhodes unsatisfying. Nothing existed beyond the author's website, and links to all the major book and podcast retail sites. This guy was a ghost, and *that* he found revealing.

The tip from his contact in Washington had yet to pay off, but Malc sensed the hunt was afoot.

Let's see what old Jack will expose of himself *this* Thursday.

ESCAPE TO THE BEACH

M ARYLAND'S EASTERN SHORE

Time does not heal *all* wounds.

Especially after today.

John shunned the customary Secret Service protection. He had his reasons.

Two months after the abduction and torture of Darla Evans, former American President John W. Stevens continued to lead a small covert group of dedicated specialists.

Their mission? To thwart the treasonous activities by a group of thugs known as the Patriot Brotherhood. This had been their mission for the last eight years, ever since Stevens left official government service.

He insisted his team—the women and men who followed him—call him John. Most were in the field today, not unlike most days. Today, only his private protection detail remained on site with him.

They operated out of a large two-story home on the east edge of the peninsula known as Maryland's Eastern Shore where they over-looked the Atlantic. The states of Virginia and Delaware also claimed portions of that same large spit of land between the Chesapeake Bay and the Atlantic Ocean.

To call their refuge a beach house would have been a pretentious euphemism, so John discouraged it. They chose this house because it was far enough off the beaten path for security purposes, but with ready access to commuter airports at Ocean City and Salisbury.

THE PRESIDENT WAS IN IMMINENT DANGER.

Someone compromised their rural location—a well-guarded secret—and a team of at least a half-dozen well-armed mercenaries now laid siege to the house. No doubt at all, these were Brotherhood thugs.

Once breeched, their perimeter collapsed to the walls of the house itself. An incoming grenade and a heavy small arms barrage pene-trated windows and walls. Driven back and down, the escape plan mandated they make their way to the basement storm shelter. Its back wall led to a tunnel to the nearby shore.

The team leader shouted over the maelstrom as the four of them stumbled down a dim stairway. Bare incandescent bulbs hanging by ancient electrical cords from the ceiling lit their way. The path to safety led them through the shelter that doubled as a panic room for the ever-paranoid previous owners.

"John, we need to get through the tunnel. Now!" He propelled John by his belt with firm pressure from his knuckles against his charge's back.

Over his shoulder, he said, "Wait, what of the others, Captain?" Even though Derek Cheevers retired from the Army six years earlier, John insisted on referring to him by his former rank.

"We confirmed they're gone, Sir. All respect, *move!*"

A tunnel hewn from the living rock generations earlier connected a honeycomb of caves. This gave them egress to the rocky Atlantic shore which was sheltered by several small barrier islands.

"Dar, rear guard. Buy us ninety seconds, then collapse the passage behind you."

"Copy."

A small but seaworthy boat awaited John and his three surviving team members, all veteran Delta operators. This hardened trio served under President Stevens near the end of his last term while on active duty and were proud to continue protecting him now as private contractors.

They lost five souls today, including new recruits and old friends, to a well-planned and executed attack.

Time for grief and recrimination later.

Derek Cheevers and Mick Sandstrom hustled their leader—their president—to relative safety, they hoped. Their adversaries were a small but determined force.

Whump!

A gray-brown dust cloud spewed from the tunnel's tiny exit at the base of the rocky hillside pock-marked with sand and saw grass. Dar bolted from its epicenter at speed before she tumbled to the ground. One of the opposition on the ridge atop the hill had fired down on her —a single shot pierced the back of her left calf.

Already on a small dock with a smaller boat moored to it, Mick dropped his machine pistol. He hollered over his right shoulder, "Cover!" as he bolted toward Dar.

Onboard, protecting John with his own body and a Kevlar vest, Derek let loose a precise barrage, and Dar's hilltop attacker fifty yards away collapsed. Another prepared to fire only to fall beside the first shooter, also a casualty of Derek's lethal aim.

For good measure, he launched a beer-can-size grenade over the edge of the ridge a few moments later.

Poom!

Whump...

"Payback, assholes!"

It gratified him to witness a small cloud of sand and rock explode skyward atop the ridge.

Mick carried the one-hundred-fifteen pounds of Dar's rock-hard grizzle in a fireman's carry. She craned her neck up and away from Mick's broad back. With her sidearm bouncing to the cadence of his heavy footfalls, she added her rapid semi-auto fire toward the top of the hill.

She hit nothing but sand and rock, but she wasn't about to just have her ass hauled without paying her way. That was Dar. She couldn't see that Mick grinned as he trundled this pocket rocket across his back down the sloped beach to the stony shore.

All aboard the tiny vessel, no sooner had Mick slipped the lines from their cleats than Derek shouted, "Brace!" He jammed the shift lever into its forward gear and the throttle to its maximum.

The powerful twin 250-horsepower outboards launched the light craft from a dead stop to over forty knots in seconds. Massive torque slammed the steering cables twang-tight. In less than a half-minute they were beyond the range of the small arms fire from shore. That was their hope, anyway.

They felt the mild chop of Sinepuxent Bay transition to the deeper and longer swells of the Atlantic Ocean as they rounded the northern tip of Assateague Island.

Off their starboard bow—ahead and to their right—another small boat appeared on a northerly course. This was no pleasure boat—the attackers' Plan B. Their rapid closure rate left no doubt. This boat would catch them, even if they ran.

"Shit! Everybody hit the deck!"

Derek's shout saved them. For the moment. Two seconds later the other boat thrashed theirs with an impressive fusillade from four or five shooters. The quarter-mile distance between the crafts dissipated much of the barrage's ballistic energy and ocean swells further reduced its efficacy. The countless hits did not penetrate their fiberglass hull. Yet.

Then Derek did the unthinkable.

He ordered everyone to cease fire as he yanked back on the

throttle but kept the big twin engines idling in neutral. The attacker's boat continued roaring toward them as their own boat dived and settled into a trough between two swells from the sudden loss of momentum.

He whipped open the hinged door near the bottom of the steering console amidships to grab a quart of two-stroke motor oil. Sliced off its top in one swift stroke with the classic KA-BAR fighting knife he always kept strapped, top and bottom, to the outside of his right thigh. He preferred the USMC version since it was an inch shorter than the Army version. Still almost a foot long, an awkward addition to his tactical gear, it came in handy for times like these.

Derek twisted the protective cap off a marine safety flare and struck the igniter on the cap's top. He thrust the brilliant red magnesium flame deep into the can of oil. Nothing except a vacuum would put out that burning metal incendiary. He dived for the deck again to duck below the smudge cloud and waited with solemn eyes squinted against the noxious smoke.

Greasy plumes billowed skyward, carried on the slight breeze from the south. Incoming gunfire ceased as the bad guys closed in for the kill of what appeared to be a beaten force, out of ammo, in a disabled boat. The smoke blew toward their attackers. While John looked perplexed, Mick and Darla got it.

Derek croaked, "On my signal…"

The moment they heard the engines of the approaching boat throttle down, Derek shouted, "Now!" The three combat vets pulled themselves erect, took aim. Darla braced herself against Mick.

With their B&T APC9Ks on full auto, they began emptying thirty-round clips into center mass of the black craft still closing on them. Burned through their mags in seconds with devastating effect. The oncoming boat drifted to a stop twenty yards off their starboard bow.

John was still prone on the deck with Derek's protective foot on the back of his bullet-resistant vest for insurance. Moments earlier, Derek had popped a high explosive round into his launcher, propped the loaded weapon against his right shoulder. Fired.

Toward the end of the staccato song of their sustained gunfire,

Mick and Dar heard the hollow *poom* of the grenade's launch, felt its hot exhaust. All three dropped where they stood amidst the billowing smudge of burning oil.

They knew what came next.

Whump!

Debris whistled overhead. Burial at sea.

Seconds later, as a blanket of quiet settled over them, they checked each other for wounds. Didn't find any physical damage other than the tiny hole in Dar's leg. It bled, but not much—no tourniquet necessary—a clean exit. Small-caliber, high-velocity hardened round from a long gun, probably a sniper's weapon, thankfully not a hollow-point.

But now they took a moment to experience profound grief for their fallen brothers and sisters. Their friends. Derek's eyes misted as he tossed the still-burning flare overboard. Watched the flame descend into the depths between swells.

Mick's neck muscles convulsed—checked his weapon. Angry at her own display of weakness, Dar sobbed under her breath as she gripped her leg.

"Hurts like a bitch," she muttered. She continued to lean on Mick.

And John, now on hands and knees, humped his back, vomited on the deck. Derek patted his back between the shoulder blades.

"You're okay, Mr. Pres…John. *We're* okay."

Smudge-faced Derek then said to nobody in particular, a voice dripping with bitterness and a post-combat adrenaline rush, "So how did these assholes find us?"

Dar cast her now-slitted eyes downward. As if to inspect her bloody leg. It hadn't been her. Had it? They were going to move, just in case. Now…

"So what now, Mr. President?"

"I need to make a call."

Derek passed him their encrypted satellite phone.

～

"WE NEED OUTSIDE HELP WE CAN TRUST."

If he were to trust anyone outside the trio that just saved his life, John Stevens knew he would remain in imminent peril. But he must go into hiding, even farther off the proverbial grid. No more underestimating their opposition.

Maybe some help from old Colonel Braxton's irregulars is in order.

ALEXANDRIA, VIRGINIA

HE RETIRED, BUT HE HADN'T DIED.

Sam Braxton, physician, Army officer, and intelligence operative, hung up his spurs a decade earlier only to be drawn back into the game before retiring yet again.

He once possessed such purpose. Now ensconced in his favorite latigo-tanned-cowhide arm chair and ottoman, he just worried about his friends, and the opposition: the Patriot Brotherhood.

The encrypted cell laying face down on the table by his right elbow buzzed like a hornet to interrupt his worrying. Or had he dozed off?

John W. Stevens said, "Sam, I need your help."

"Mr. President, you have but to name it."

MARYLAND'S EASTERN SHORE

LITA DEGA CHECKED FOR A PULSE.

She confirmed yet another teammate's death. The ferocity of the opposition's resistance surprised her, although she wasn't sure why. The protection detail of an American president will be well-trained and dedicated. Envy crept over her.

Such high purpose.

With several teammates down around her, she exercised extreme caution. That did not deter her from getting eyes on the objective, now escaping.

Whump!

The ground beneath her feet trembled.

One of her team—Brick—by-passed the now quiet house to recon the grassy ridge ahead of her.

She heard, "They're making for a boat."

As Brick reached the ridge, he established his firing stance, aimed more down than out, and fired his long gun.

Crack!

She approached the ridge at a full run as the guy behind Brick fell. She had forgotten his name.

At the ridge seconds later, Brick collapsed onto the coarse grass and sandy soil six feet in front of her as if someone deflated him. She dropped beside him as a precaution. Felt for a pulse. None.

She commandeered his sniper rifle. Recognized it as an M24 SWS. A Sniper Weapons Systems—accurate, reconfigurable, and it fired 7.62 NATO rounds—ubiquitous worldwide. Impossible to trace. Smart.

Peering over the ridge, she watched as one of the president's detail bolted from the dock back toward shore. Near the base of the hill he retrieved a fallen teammate. Lita judged it was a woman by her slight build.

Brick's tactic: wound one to draw the others away from the prize. Effective. The little woman was on the ground, trying to get up.

After the big man hoisted her over his shoulders, he charged back toward the boat. Though inverted, the woman still fired her weapon up toward the hill. Lita could see her face through Brick's scope, a mask of ferocity.

Lita ensured a round was in the chamber of the M24, centered the tiny woman's back in the scope. Easy, but her priority was the prize. She swung the M24 to her right and up toward the more-distant boat.

These high-velocity armor-piercing long rounds could penetrate most anything, even both the prize and the human shield in front of him. One round would tear through two Kevlar vests and two torsos with ease.

Lita hesitated.

She admired the obvious loyalty within that team. She, however, was nothing more than a hired gun. That wounded woman? A fierce warrior with a real cause. Then, less than a second later…

Whump!

A good thing she lay prone in a dip at the ridge. Had she been standing, the grenade launched from the boat below would have cost Lita her life.

What would she do now?

Malc Frieburg slouched in the back seat.

A dark blue rental SUV a quarter mile up the beach road was parked behind a second identical vehicle parked just ahead. Their rally point. The operation was a disaster.

Yet another.

He glowered at his on-scene guy who stood before him at the SUV's open right rear door. Not a question, Malc said, "He got away."

He noticed blood just outside and below his man's vest, but saw it all on his face before he spoke.

"They took heavy casualties. So did we, Malc. We were up against hardened combat troops. That was obvious."

"Excuses? You're better than that."

"Yeah, you're right, Boss. This guy's a bitch to pin down. We'll start again."

"You okay?"

"I took a round in the side. No big deal. Next move?"

"I'll let you know once we get more intel."

"Hey, your recruit, Dega, she's good. Strong moves. Took fire. Not only did Lita stand her ground, she advanced and fired on the enemy. Survived."

"Good. Appreciate the after-action. Get treatment and stand by."

His vendetta would never bring back Enoch Slattery. His friend and mentor disappeared eight years earlier, wounded, or dead, but gone.

Malc's personal mission list remained short and selective: Braxton, his buddy Janis, and Stevens. They had ordered Enoch's hit. So far he was oh-for-three.

With today's lack of results they would need to back off aggressive operations for a time.

Their time will come. Soon.

Malc's simmering anger escalated. So did his jitters. He needed to let Mr. M know in case of consequences.

Yeah, consequences.

He couldn't wait.

CHEWED OUT

W ASHINGTON, DC

Vice President Norman Sealey seethed.

He scanned the stately den in his home at Number One Observatory Circle in Northwestern Washington on the grounds of the United States Naval Observatory. They built the white nineteenth-century house in 1893, but within the last eight years the old pile gained some hi-tech upgrades.

Neither his office in the West Wing of the White House, nor his offices in the Eisenhower Executive Office Building would suffice tonight. Both suffered from an egregious lack of privacy despite Secret Service protection. Maybe because of it. Here, at least, he achieved some distance.

The vice president drew in the scent of oiled wood as he rounded his ornate desk and approached the most secure safe ever manufactured. Installed in the east wall of his den, concealed behind a secret door in the opulent walnut paneling. He pressed the near-invisible latch and a panel sprung open.

Within that safe rested the most secure satellite phone available. Anywhere. He was told it used a proprietary AES 512-bit end-to-end rolling encryption algorithm. *Whatever that is,* he thought. Sealey retrieved the phone, the only contents of that small safe's top shelf.

The phone's vendor assured him conversations between two of these phones would remain private. Guaranteed. Still, he verified this claim with the top asset protection experts loyal to the Brotherhood. He silently chastised the manufacturer, *This damn thing is heavier than my other cells, and too damn bulky.*

Once again, it was time to risk using *that phone.*

But first, Sealey flipped a switch under his desk to lock down the den which doubled as his panic room. Not that he'd ever panic. He was rewarded with several satisfying *thunks* as well-oiled deadbolts engaged.

Dead-air space between bullet-resistant panes of the only window in the room mitigated the risk of audio surveillance able to detect the tiniest of vibrations made by any audio source. Even through heavy glass.

After pulling down on the antique incandescent desk lamp's chain, he sat and bellied up to the posh executive desk in the subdued light. Crafted of the finest ebony, he reflected on his affinity for naturally dark wood. His back was to the window with the shades drawn. Annoyed by the blotter on his desk crooked by a few millimeters, he gruffly straightened it.

Next, he retrieved a remote from his shallow upper right desk drawer and pressed its red button. A sophisticated anti-surveillance device generated a noise source that masked thousands of cataloged audio waveforms from invisible microphones. He'd heard one of those Secret Service drones bragging about it.

The device created a sound-canceling envelope within the room. At least that was the theory. The damn thing sounded like a slow-turning and hissing fan that varied in speed.

The Secret Service swept these premises daily for intrusive

devices, but he never took chances, not when he needed to use *this phone.*

At last, Sealey dialed the number—no speed dials or numbers saved in memory—and waited for a computer-generated key code.

Once received, he hung up, redialed, and after a series of atonal beeps and whistles, entered the key code from the previous call by rote to complete the two-level authentication.

Someone else then performed the same paranoid ritual.

A guilty dance.

Vice President Sealey heard that voice.

Reminded him of fingernails scratching an old-fashioned chalkboard.

"Yes, Mr. Vice President. How may I serve?"

"You can do your damn job, Martino!"

"Sir, no names, please. I know Old Soldier is a burr under our saddle, and he could sink us..."

"Ah, stop already with your sophomoric mixed metaphors. John Stevens is not only a threat to our brotherhood, he's jeopardizing our chances for success in the upcoming election. And you've not only failed to rid me of Atherton, you can't even handle an old ex-president! I'm thinking you've outlived your...

"Look, we can not afford these incessant failures, Mr. M. And you need to do something about that idiot Frieburg."

Sealey spoke the "Mr. M" using a tone saturated with disdain.

Martino's sat phone case creaked.

He gripped it so hard, he thought it might break. It did not.

Before he assumed leadership of the Brotherhood, Sealey was his sponsor. In return, he expunged several of Sealey's records. Otherwise, some conflagrations could have blemished his record and ruined his chances at the VP slot when the sitting VP fell ill and died in 2009. In private, Norman remained nothing but an arrogant politician who talked too much.

"It would seem we have helped each other out in the past. Now is no time to fail our mutual allegiance."

"Is that a veiled threat, Michael?"

"Not at all, Sir. We'll get Stevens. Though he has put into play unexpected assets, he will not be an issue much longer."

"And Atherton? It's almost too late in his final term for his death to mean anything. The last thing we need is a martyr for the opposition. I suggest you continue to make Stevens your priority, Mr. M. We need him gone. After I leave office, we need to have a different discussion.

"Fair enough, Sir. Consider the Stevens issue resolved."

And then the smug politician hung up on him without another word.

PRODIGAL SON

WASHINGTON, DC

Michael Martino mopped his brow.

Sealey was an ass, but he was right. His organization failed to retire Atherton. They failed to eliminate that pain-in-the-posterior Stevens. For all their resources, these two miserable failures transcended excuses and promises.

The temperature outside soared, but it didn't matter. Ensconced in his favorite Italian leather armchair in front of a fire in the library of his Chain Bridge Road mansion, the oiled wood-paneling glowed from the reflected flames.

The small amount of smoke that escaped the flue tinged the air with the sharp hint of hickory. But the opulent surroundings and pleasant odor comforted him not.

It would seem Enoch Slattery's protege wasn't the man for the job. But he would gain nothing by taking his frustrations out on Frieburg.

He needed dramatic action and blamed himself for taking so long to come to this disastrous conclusion.

Just then, a pocket of air popped as it escaped a crackling log. An omen? No, he took no stock in such nonsense. Still…

Considering his failures, maybe Malc's bloodlust didn't run deep enough. Or perhaps he wasn't a strategic thinker with intuitive tactical roots. Michael's gut told him he must call for reinforcements.

Palmer Xavier once worked for Michael Martino in the corporate world before either of them were recruited by the Brotherhood.

Mr. Z—Abraham Zelokov—was a legend on the geopolitical stage. As the founding father of the Brotherhood six decades earlier, he recognized Xavier possessed the raw materials of greatness.

But Mr. Z thrust Palmer into leadership before he was ready. After things fell apart for him, Mr. Z whisked him away before retiring himself in 2008 and Martino had stepped in hastily to chart the Brotherhood's future.

Since then, Palmer trained and operated within the hardscrabble Eastern European arm of their organization most devoted to Mr. Z. A marriage of convenience. Michael told them to groom Palmer as the next Mr. Z, the next great leader of the Brotherhood.

Palmer had made stellar progress over the last eight years eliminating three considerable chinks in his tarnished armor.

First, a decade ago, he lacked a knack for invisibility. Second, with no practical field experience, he did not command Mr. Z's or Enoch's raw physicality. And third, Palmer possessed no widespread trusted networks. Nobody knew him.

Michael reflected he too lacked field experience, to this day. At his core, he was still just a corporate guy. But he made it work.

Another log popped in the fireplace. Hickory flames danced without knowing why. Michael Martino continued to think about Palmer Xavier.

Dedicated and sustained effort to eliminate Palmer's three shortcomings were the conditions of his survival. Palmer understood. Above all else, he was a survivor.

Countless personal and organizational victories heralded his time in exile as he excelled at completing complex operations across Europe and the Orient.

Michael had diligently monitored his erstwhile mentee's progress abroad. Some very competent operators told him Palmer was now as hard as hammered steel. Also, he emerged as a respected leader within an important international arm of the Brotherhood.

He possessed raw talent in abundance—always ruthless and never afraid to take huge risks; he never wavered from his duty to the Brotherhood, no matter the turbulence.

Once clad with battle-hardened physical and emotional armor, he developed his expertise in the nefarious arts. And he established a profound rapport with Mr. Z's most infamous international cabals as they rebuilt after the 2008 debacle. Seemed he exploited power and influence in the most visceral manner possible. Did it still leave him wanting?

Yes, Palmer was ready to return from Purgatory. Time to bring him home the victor. He would like that. He would take Frieburg's place who would either work for him or perish.

The flames in front of him and to his left reflected anticipation in Martino's eyes. He grinned as he remembered one of Palmer's favorite aphorisms: "Kill 'em all. Let God sort 'em out. And may the strongest carnivore get the prime cuts."

That was Palmer.

And now, with his formidable training and international connections? If he proves himself here, Palmer could yet lead the Brotherhood in his place. That assumed they survived the next six months.

Michael reflected how weary he was. But he knew Palmer was a hungry lion on the hunt, no longer an impetuous cub.

God help those who stood in his way!

BALTIMORE, MARYLAND

THE STENCH OF THE CROWD SEEMED NORMAL.

The International Arrivals Terminal at the Baltimore-Washington Marshall Airport stank old and musty this afternoon. By comparison, a high school locker room smelled sweet. Too many sweaty people hustled with purpose, too long from a shower, somewhere to be.

Whatever.

The temperature outside crept into triple digits. The throng carried its body odor into the building like an overweight bag. Windows dribbled with condensation, and humidity did its best to sneak in every time an automatic door squealed open.

To make matters worse, huge invisible air conditioners failed their only mission on this midsummer day near Charm City. The Chamber of Commerce loved that name.

Yeah, right. More like Mobtown, what with the wife being a proud member of the Mobtown Mommies.

Vinnie Testera held a handwritten sign, waiting, as the dank air wheezed in and out of his frail lungs. Twenty years of triple-pack days.

He wished he were sitting down, but the flight landed and passengers wandered past either to claim their checked luggage or to seek an exit.

Nearby, angry and tired voices expressed frustration. Half of the baggage carousels off to his right featured handwritten out-of-order signs.

Nothing crankier than pissed-off international travelers.

His fare would have no checked bags. Bored, he leaned back against a railing and propped the sign on his generous belly like an artist's display easel. In his most formal style he had scrawled *Stockton* on white cardboard with a fat black marker pen. Vinnie kept a dozen of these twelve-by-twenty-four-inch cards and two Sharpies in his trunk. Tools of the trade.

Almost as if by magic, a lanky character at least seven inches taller than his own slouched five-foot-ten materialized in front of him. Nodded with brief eye contact. Could this be his VIP?

"Mr. Stockton?"

Another tiny nod. No smile. Intense darting eyes. Vinnie found it hard to ignore the granite expression punctuated by several short scars on his fare's face. An involuntary shudder caused Vinnie to blink his widened eyes in rapid succession before recovering his composure. Not what he expected. At all.

"Hey, no offense, Mr. Stockton, but my Maryland hack license requires me to ask for ID. You understand." Not a question.

That was bullshit, but here he faced an unusual dude, and he could be anybody. Or nobody. But the guy produced an opened US passport in his left hand, like he expected the request. Vinnie stared at it for two seconds, and the damn thing disappeared even faster. Slick.

"Thank you, Sir."

He grabbed the guy's ratty tan leather valise as he gave his charge another sideways and upward glance.

Crummy dresser. He sure needs a shave. Tall drink of water, this one, but something about him. I'd better not underestimate this guy.

With deference, he said, "I have a comfortable car waiting just outside, Sir."

He received another nod but still no words. Stockton snatched an old wide-brimmed felt hat crushed into the side-pocket of the valise already tucked under Vinnie's left arm. Crammed it onto his head in one smooth motion with one hand.

This guy doesn't look like any VIP I've ever picked up. He slouches, like he's too tall or something. Even stinks a little. Euro-trash? Looks more like one step up from a bum. No, that's not right at all. Moves like a damn cat. There's something else... Oh well, money's good.

VAN STOCKTON WASN'T SURE HOW HE FELT.

This was no homecoming. In fact, no place felt like home any more. And that was just fine. Gave him perspective.

He looked forward to seeing his old friend, Michael Martino. To anybody else, he was a ghost. What freedom! The last eight years were the finest graduate program he never could have imagined.

The ride to DC took time. He welcomed any period of inactivity to review: weapons, tactics, mental mapping, interrogation strategies, friends and enemies lists, points of influence and leverage… He kept them fresh, like well-oiled tools on his workbench.

A very different world than he knew existed before going into exile. Yes, exile. More like the Z University. He'd always admired Mr. Z in life. Grew to love him in death. He wanted to inspire that kind of cruel loyalty too. And he would. Palmer Xavier was no more.

Good riddance.

WASHINGTON, DC

THEY PULLED INTO THE CIRCLE DRIVE.

The stretch Lincoln rolled to a stop under the elaborate porte cochere in front of the gray granite manse on Chain Bridge Road, northwest of downtown.

The inevitable sense of déjà vu crept over Van. He lived here for a short time an eternity ago in another body with a smaller mind.

Not sure what to expect, it was not his old friend Michael Martino standing on the broad steps of the grand double doors. Two serious middle-aged men in casual attire flanked him.

Michael's once thick black hair, now white and thinner, ruffled in the slight breeze. When Michael was his boss at Greater Global Solutions, Van couldn't remember him ever out-of-doors unless transiting between his limo and his beloved Gulfstream G550 on the tarmac in front of some general aviation terminal. His smile seemed too broad. Something else. Deference?

Van exited the right rear door of the gunmetal gray limo in a graceful arc, not waiting for the driver to open it. He pulled the old valise out behind him. He thwarted the driver's earlier attempt to place it in the trunk. Trust issues.

Michael descended the steps with a subtle limp to greet his old friend and corporate mentee. He had not aged well.

"Mr. Stockton!"

Michael oozed with enthusiasm. Did not allow the driver to observe his generous wink as he reached out to embrace his old friend, Palmer Xavier.

Van pulled back. Two protective palms shot up with bent elbows on their way to locking, and clashed with Martino's attempted embrace. Michael's shocked expression forced Van to re-evaluate. *Bad tactic*, he thought. He adjusted in less than two seconds, and his protective palms converted to open arms. He pulled Michael in with reserved enthusiasm.

Michael laughed at the sudden reversal of his old friend's demeanor. Mouth to ear, Van croaked, "Sorry, Michael. Habit." He realized he hadn't spoken three words in as many hours.

~

THEY SAT AT A DIAGONAL TO EACH OTHER.

Once this was Van's favorite room when he lived here as Palmer Xavier, Mr. X, head of the PB. For three short weeks, he sat in Michael's chair. But an ugly SEC investigation into his personal affairs brought an end to his reign of invisibility which incited his exile.

The Brotherhood could ill-afford the attention. His own damn fault. Lesson learned and cataloged. The only reason he was alive? Mr. Z wished it.

~

THE FIRE RAGED.

As they both half-faced it and each other, that fire now retrieved fractured memories of Mr. Z. For both of them.

"Palmer, I'm amazed at your transformation. You've changed so very much in what, eight years?"

"Yes. You too, Michael. And it's Van. Please."

Van's eyes darted around the room before coming back to gaze into Michael's again. Van's eyes were hard. Suspicious. And the way he sat toward the front of his chair, ready to… what? Pounce?

"I assume you sweep often?"

"Yes. Daily. Remarkable."

"Meaning?"

"I no longer see an ambitious and ruthless but soft executive before me. You *are* an operator. I've heard the reports. I read every single one, Palm… Van. You've become a legend, my old friend."

"Michael, I love you like a brother. But you talk too much. You need to be crystal clear with me. Why am I here? Now? Net net."

Taken aback, but recovering, Michael once again smiled. Like he and Van shared a secret.

"Very well. The Brotherhood is in trouble. You already know that. We never recovered from 2008."

"Yes. And I own partial responsibility for that. I'm prepared to make amends."

"Good. *You* are what we need right now. Malcolm Frieburg replaced Enoch Slattery, but he can't do the job. He's a solid soldier most of the time but he can't think fast, hard, or long-range enough to lead. Prove yourself on this side of the pond. You are a leader, Van, and that's what we need. Here and now.

"Mission: I need an ex-president retired. ASAP. You have the skills and the respect to make that happen. What do you say?"

"I'll need introductions, details, access to resources. Timeline?"

"Yesterday."

"When will you introduce me to Frieburg? Better yet, I will introduce myself."

Michael's jutted chin rested on the tip of his left index finger, his elbow on the arm of his chair closest to the fireplace. His head angled to gaze upon Van Stockton's casual stare at the fire. He could almost hear the hum of his machinery planning next moves, contingencies, implications, consequences, alternatives.

He refused to ask about Palmer's… Van's new scars outlined by skin more pale than the rest. Michael realized he dared not ask. Curious, and yet…

"Remarkable."

For the first time, Van rewarded Michael with the smallest smile, or smirk.

Michael pondered, *Who **is** this guy? He must already know the end game: he is again being groomed to lead the Brotherhood once I retire.*

Yes, this is what we need right now. I can't wait to discover Malc's reaction to Van's introduction.

OBEY OR PERISH

Potomac, Maryland

Malc Frieburg could be hard on himself.

Harder than anyone.

He realized he was in way over his head. Not only had Mr. M lost confidence in him, he had lost confidence in himself.

He realized he was happiest when alone—the incredible shrinking man. In his sprawling semi-rural home near the end of Falls Road, he found himself half-way through another night of fitful sleep. Alone.

A third of the way through this night laced with one cracked nightmare after another, he sensed something out of the ordinary in his secure third-floor bedroom that doubled as a panic room. Not sure what he sensed.

Something.

He opened his eyes to focus on the business end of a Glock. A big-ass forty-one? Holy shit! The next sound introduced him to a new set of visceral emotions.

Clack!

Malc winced, convinced his life had ended. But no finale—just a little disappointed. After peeing a little in his boxers, he mustered sufficient false bravado to dredge up some righteous indignation.

"Who in Hell are you, and what's going on?

The business end of that Glock backed off with a horizontal waggle. Message: sit up. As he arose, he spotted his two-man inside security detail zip-tied and gagged on the floor at the foot of his bed. Were those his socks stuffed in their mouths? Looked like calves hog-tied at a rodeo. Not that he'd ever been to a rodeo.

How did this guy do that? And my three outside guys?

Shick-ack!

The Glock's slide racked in a round.

"Now a live one in the chamber awaits your next words, Mr. Frieburg. Either meet your maker or live. Your choice."

"What?"

Blam!

Gee-ZEUS!

That freakin' forty-five caliber discharging twelve inches from his right ear jangled his bell. He could hear nothing, and his ears would ring for days. This guy knew that, didn't speak for a while until Malc could hear something again. Took his time. When he spoke, he did so at volume.

"What is your decision?"

"Uh, ah, I don't want to die. What will it take?"

"Yes, that's better, Malc. You now work for me. Any deviation from my orders will cause your summary execution. Is that clear?"

He'd play along with this lunatic. For now. He nodded. No words.

Still in a loud voice and close to Malc's right ear, in a flat voice Van said, "Now, get dressed."

More a survival reflex than anything else, Malc said, "Yes, Sir." And he meant it. Was he headed for his execution after all? Naw, this guy would have done that already. What else? No idea, but he'd play ball with this nut job. For now.

With the Glock pressed against the middle of his back, they walked down to the first floor kitchen.

Did he smell coffee? What in *the* Hell?

"Sit."

Malc complied, sinking onto a bar stool at the island in his spacious kitchen. Now more surprised than ever, he watched the tall hardscrabble guy lay the Glock on the island between them. Within reach. He walked over to the coffee pot, filled two mugs, and said, "Black, three Splendas, right Malc?"

"What? Uh, yes. Geez, Mister, who *are* you?"

"First name Van, last name Stockton. Like I said in that ridiculous bedroom of yours, I'm your new boss. You've screwed up too many times, Malc. Lucky for you that first trigger-pull banged the pin against an empty chamber. The Brotherhood doesn't tolerate failure. And more than one? Mr. M must like you or you'd already be dead. I suppose because Enoch liked you. I liked Enoch. So did my old comrade, Mr. Z.

"I see your eyes, Malc. If you are to reach for that pistol, now is the time. Otherwise, you and I can do some business. You get a reprieve, I make you a hero. Here's your coffee."

He slid it across the black granite island right past the pistol—still within easy reach.

"Time for your next decision."

"Holy shit! You knew Enoch?"

Heard his voice creep up an octave. But this Stockton's voice? As hard, flat, and cold as the granite under the heels of his hands. The guy strolled around the island, stood over him, looking down with those flinty eyes under a hooded brow. Malc stared at the four small pale scars that broke both his eyebrows in two places each. Like short claw marks. Nice.

"Look, Malc, I've just said more in the last two minutes than in the last two months. Do not make me repeat myself. Now, or ever."

"Yes, yes! Look, Mr…"

"Stockton. I'm repeating again."

"Sorry, sorry! Mr. Stockton, I'm your man. Truth is, I'm in over my head. I love the Brotherhood, and I loved Enoch like a father, but I think he overestimated my leadership skills. I'm a decent trooper, but I'm no general. Geez, you knew Mr. Z! How?"

"Alright, Malc." He laid a paternal hand on Malc's right shoulder with his left hand as he scooped up his pistol with his right.

"First go cut your men loose and tell them there's a new sheriff in town. You'll find the outside guys collected near the front door. Your gate is unattended at present. Fix that and meet me in your den. We need to talk."

"Yes, Sir!"

The relief in his voice at being given an order he could execute with confidence broadcast his willingness to work with this take-charge man of mystery.

~

MALC ENTERED HIS DEN—VAN'S DEN NOW.

Mr. Stockton sat behind the desk. Malc dropped into the middle of three guest chairs opposite. With a pecking order now established, Malc said nothing, oozing with respect, but still exhibiting some hesitation. He waited while Mr. Stockton finished on the phone.

"Someone wants to speak with you. Go ahead. He's here."

"Malc, this is Mr. M. You've met Mr. Stockton. Are you onboard?"

"Geez. You guys don't fool around. Yes!"

"Good. Don't screw this up, Frieburg."

Click.

"Look, Malc, I know what it's like when someone else comes in to take charge. So I will work with you. But I will abide no hesitation or holding back. Your life now belongs to me. Can you live with that?"

He emphasized the word *live*.

"Yes, Sir."

"Okay, and just make it Van. Think of me as Enoch two-point-oh. Now, do you have a key for me?"

"Oh, you know about *Hat Trick*." Not a question.

"I know everything. Let's have it."

"Yes, Sir… Van."

He nodded, noting that Malc took the key from around his neck not only without hesitation, but with haste. As if he were delighted to get rid of the damn thing.

"Wells Fargo down the road, correct?"

"Yes, Sir!"

"Tone it down, Malc. While I appreciate your enthusiasm, let's keep our working relationship immediate but casual."

"Sure. Would you like me to go with you?"

"Yes. You'll drive. We'll need two men."

"Okay, Van."

MALC WAITED BEHIND THE WHEEL.

The huge armor-plated white Suburban idled silently. One man from his personal security team stayed in the front seat with him. He kept a loaded Mac Ten at the ready across his lap.

The other, also armed, waited in the bank's lobby while Van retrieved the box's contents. He stood, he did not sit, per Mr. Stockton's orders, with one eye on the door, the other on the bank's staff and customers.

Van was one paranoid cat, but then Malc remembered how he disabled his entire security detail in absolute silence. And held a gun to his near-naked ass in his own bed in the middle of last night. He was a capable man to fear and respect. Reminded him of Enoch. Only taller.

Once more, Malc recalled every word of the conversation that got him here and what he experienced at this bank almost a decade earlier for this same purpose.

Fifteen minutes later, Malc watched Van exit the bank flanked by his man who carried the suitcase they brought with them. He supposed it now contained the entire contents of Enoch's box.

Malc had kept that stuff where Enoch left it—and where he found it—back in the day, because that was easiest. Even bought a house just down the road from this bank.

They spoke no words during the short drive back to the house. Malc dared not speak.

Upon their arrival, Van directed him to gather his entire five-person security detail at the property's front gate fifty yards down the gentle S-curved pea-gravel drive. Then he asked Malc to verify through binoculars from the den's window they were all accounted for down there.

That tempted Malc to ask if these extreme precautions were necessary, but kept his mouth shut. Instead, he tried to learn.

Now they both stood in the den shoulder-to-shoulder behind Malc's desk with their backs to the window, curtains drawn, warm incandescent lights glowing, in the middle of the day.

Van opened the suitcase to their right on the desk, with Malc's Apple iMac three feet to its left. An old-fashioned desk blotter partially obscured the glass-covered space between.

The blotter featured leather trim on both sides for tucking loose notes, and a large blank paper pad in the center for doodling. The only writing on the pad were a few of Malc's scribblings. A small piece of note paper peeking out from underneath the leather trim on the right side appeared to be a short grocery list with a curled corner, long ignored.

Malc said, "What now, Bossman?" That's what he used to call Enoch. Seemed fitting now, no disrespect to his old mentor. There was a new sheriff in town.

"At first glance, and with what I already know or suspect, I estimate *at least* forty percent of this material is now worthless as of our massive 2008 exposure. Worse, we might now trust those who are no longer trustworthy. Have you culled materials related to compromised assets from this material?"

He spread his hands over the open suitcase.

"Uh, no, not really."

"Malc, we need to be ruthlessly honest with each other from this moment on if this is to work. 'Not really' or 'not at all?'"

"Sorry, Van. Not at all."

"Then that's our first order of business. As long as it takes. We need to be certain whatever remains in this tome is one hundred percent valid, current, and trustworthy to mitigate the risk of further exposure. Let's get to work. I'll pull media, you man the computer."

"Got it. What say we tackle the paper first, together—the notebooks, journals, reports, and we edit as we go. Then we plow through the hard media like CDs, DVDs, and flash drives. We use the computer and editing software as needed to upload and revise files. But we review everything. That'll get you up to speed faster too, and I can answer questions real-time."

He held up his right index finger to preclude interruption and continued on his enthusiastic roll. A second finger shot up.

"Then, as a second phase, if you agree, we digitize all the paper stuff either by scanning or transcribing—you read, I type. If you want to add notes, you dictate to me. I can type, like, fifty words-a-minute, Van. And we merge it all into a single encrypted database that we can better conceal and access—from anywhere. Okay, Bossman?"

Malc smiled. He knew that was the best way to proceed. He didn't add that's what he intended to do himself, but never got around to it.

Van rewarded him with an appreciative grin and a pat on his right shoulder. "Very good, Malc. Very good indeed."

"Yeah, well, once you pointed out my lack of data maintenance after all those folks got busted, I figured I owed you a few ideas."

"The past, Malc. Let's create a new future. Together."

Geez this guy is a hard read. Twelve hours ago he held a gun to my head and pulled the trigger. Twice. Now I'm ready to follow his ass to the grave. Yeah, this guy is something special.

"Radio your lead guy. Inform him we'll be in here for as long this takes. Could be hours, even days. Every six hours, they are to send someone for food and drink. You'll radio them when we're ready for ours. You'll fetch those provisions from the front door. They will return to the gatehouse. They are to remain on high alert, standing shifts as necessary. Clear?"

"Yes, Sir… Van."

"Do you have a hard-wired alarm from the front gate to this room?"

"Yes. A buzzer will sound in here when they push a button in the gatehouse. It's our panic signal."

"Good. Any prearranged patterns?"

"No. If the buzzer sounds, we hunker down. We wired the place to blow too, if necessary."

"New orders. Direct your man to signal one buzz when food is incoming. Two buzzes if he needs to talk for any other reason, but only for urgent matters. Three or more buzzes means our perimeter is about to be breeched. While we're in here, Malc, we power off all radios and cells. Disable your computer's Internet access. Clear?"

Five minutes later, Malc finished turning off his radio, phone, and wi-fi without question.

For the next thirty-four hours they slaved over their trove, culling wheat from chaff. Malc made an occasional phone call for an external inquiry, verification, or confirmation. Via encrypted sat-phone only. They crafted dozens of initial test missions to re-vet their highest level operatives.

Malc brought in a coffee pot and supplies—including several one-gallon jugs of water and lots of Splenda—from the kitchen down the hall. Infusions of caffeine were their life's blood for the next two long days and a short night in-between. They did not leave the den the entire time other than for restroom breaks. One or the other would power nap on the plush red leather sofa for twenty minutes. Then back to it.

The volume and diversity of intel spanned personal, political, criminal, law enforcement, and religious boundaries. It impressed Van, although he avoided showing that. The magnitude of compromise, however, surprised them both.

This was the first precise analysis of arrests, convictions, disappearances, and other types of impact to their assets during and after 2008, spanning both domestic and international scope.

Malc seemed more embarrassed as time wore on. He could provide few decent answers to Van's countless tough questions.

Re-validate *trusted* assets? Never occurred to him.

Test known-reliable communication channels for potential blowback? *Geez.*

❧

UNBELIEVABLE.

Van could neither understand nor condone such a fundamental neglect of intelligence asset management, not after that devastating sweep of so many critical assets by the authorities *eight years ago*.

He needed to inform and maybe even chastise Michael. He was looking at negligence of the highest order. As he reminded Malc, that was the past.

Now things must change. And they would.

Or heads would roll.

FRAGILE REDEMPTION

W ASHINGTON, DC

The ever-present fire crackled.

As he waited in the Chain Bridge mansion's library, Van Stockton thought, *Michael must burn a tremendous volume of wood.*

The passionate tradition of an eternal fire paid homage to the legendary Mr. Z, founder of the Patriot Brotherhood. Mr. Z used to say, "This fire is a symbol of our burning passion, of a hot-blooded commitment to our cause, and to our organization." Michael would not break that tradition.

This was going to be bad.

When Michael Martino, Mr. M—the current patriarch of the PB—entered the room, Van's dead-serious demeanor worried him. He held Van's gaze awaiting the assessment for which he and Malcolm

Frieburg sequestered themselves for two days. Michael saw fatigue and iron resolve in Van's face.

Suspecting a paucity of good news, or worse, Michael called to his chief of security who appeared in five seconds from the hall next to the library.

"Thomas, please clear the house. Secure all comms. No exceptions. Await instructions from the porte cochere with your team, if you please."

"Yes, Sir. Allow me sixty seconds."

Thomas performed an almost military about-face, exiting the room at a brisk pace.

HERE WE GO…

As Van and Michael waited in silence, both staring at the fire, Van considered Michael's words, "Secure all comms." Realized that would include recording in this room. Michael offered a slight apologetic shrug and conciliatory smile. Van offered a slight nod. He recalled their previous meeting and what was said.

So Michael possesses some craft. Good.

After a minute, he offered an upturned palm toward Van as if to say, "All clear." He needed no words

"Michael, I am sorry to report your organization is in a precipitous state. Almost half of your assets are compromised or no longer accessible, much less mission-ready. The other fifty-five percent you cannot trust without aggressive confirmation of their loyalty. We must assume all assets are compromised until we re-verify their commitment to the organization's charter."

MICHAEL'S JAW DROPPED AND STAYED THERE.

He swung his gaze toward the fire in slow motion. Smoldering shock consumed him. He remembered the veiled threats he and the

VP exchanged less than a week ago. Van had stopped speaking to let the import of his words soak into Michael's consciousness.

After two full minutes, Michael spoke in a whisper. "I hope you're overreacting, Van."

"Well, it's your conviction and arrest at stake, or worse, but my analysis is unimpeachable, Michael. We must regroup. Every asset needs revisiting. This in-depth re-vetting process will require extensive resources, but I assume that will not be an issue.

"Test missions will exercise every asset's commitment. Until then, you can trust me, and you must tell me if we can trust Malc. My sense after spending a few days with him is that we can. For now.

"Your boy let you down, Michael. He may be salvageable. If not, I will slit his throat myself. Malc appears to be a motivated soldier with some initiative, but a screw-up as a leader."

"Fuck!"

"*Now* you're where you need to be. Sir."

Not one to wallow in regret, Martino remained a man of action. With resolve he said, "So how do we proceed?"

"If you need anything executed with urgency, the three of us are it. In parallel, I'll start with Malc's most trusted assets, test them with rigorous medium-risk jobs, and watch for any backlash. Once they're proven solid, I'll recruit them to do the same with *their* most trusted assets.

"This process must continue until we can once again trust the entire organization, to the extent that's ever possible. Those who cannot will become examples for others. But this could take months. Agreed?"

"Yes. I've placed too much trust in Malc. I assumed since Enoch placed him…"

"Okay, bad assumption. We'll get this back, but we must invest the time and energy. For now, we start with your personal security. Now my question for you Michael. Do you trust me?"

Michael did not hesitate. "Without equivocation. You hold my absolute trust, Van, though you also frighten me too."

"Good. Then first orders of business, we re-vet your personal protection detail, your cybersecurity, your physical systems such as alarms, and all contracted facilities across your estate for negative intrusion. We start at the top. Any contacts you have, we test, no matter who. Everyone except you is expendable, including Malc and me.

"Our first principle—we protect you. Then we work our way down with brutal rigor. I've already chosen a job for Malc that will challenge his loyalty and his ability. He will rectify his failures. If he can't, he's gone. Then we go down from there. Still with me?"

Michael wrung his hands as if washing them. His lips tightened, his brow furrowed as he gazed into the fire.

"What?"

"Oh. Yes. Agreed. One hundred percent. There is at least one asset with whom we may have a problem. This will be tricky."

Redding didn't worry him, but Vice President Sealey did. Based on the major surgery Van was proposing, his loyalties needed validation too, but how? He shared this concern with Van.

"Would you like me to handle that for you? Mr. M?"

The flat casual tone behind those words chilled Michael's every fiber. And Van was back to 'Mr. M' after a deliberate and formal pause.

My God. Such a casual offer to murder the Vice President of the United States for me.

After the chilling thrill passed, he could but revel in who and what his once ruthless but feckless mentee had become. Who was the mentor now?

"Not yet, Van."

POTOMAC, MARYLAND

Would he survive this new boss?

While it relieved Malc to work for a strong leader again, he dared not screw this up. Or he was dead. He was okay with that. He would deserve it.

Van spoke of their failed attack on Stevens' beach house. His indictment was clear. "You failed and lost several loyal operators."

The man spoke in plain words. "Finish finding Stevens. Or I will finish you."

So Stevens still topped the list. Van said outright this was a test. Do it alone. Trust nobody. Yet. And that was fine too. He didn't want to get anybody else killed. For a while, anyway.

Van said, "Think like a cop. Look at known associates, no matter how obscure. You have access to data: public records, search engines... Use them. But no footprint. Stevens trades on his brand equity for appearances to stir up anti-PB sentiment, and though he's gone to ground, he will possess few if any alternative identities. Use that too."

Van manned the sat phone in Malc's den to work Mr. M's network top-down. Meanwhile, Malc camped out in his small library at a giant antique roll-top desk with his encrypted cell and a pad on which to take notes and doodle.

Malc recalled his time with Enoch who told him of an operation then-President Stevens ran in Russia with his administration's intelligence teams. Their sources at the time had surfaced Doctor Sam Braxton's name. From a trusted White House contact they discovered a meet-and-greet with the president in the official 2008 visitor's log.

Three other names were logged for that meeting. Per the confidential transcript, Stevens congratulated a young officer named Derek Cheevers. He was to pass on the president's special thanks to two of his team: a Mick Sandstrom and a Darla Evans.

Malc had assigned a four-man team to locate, detain, and interrogate this Evans in South Carolina several months ago. They assumed that as a female, she'd be easiest to break. That's how they'd discovered President Stevens' beach house location, even though the task proved far more difficult than they could have imagined.

Even though that attack failed, with Stevens escaping, Malc still gained some actionable intel. The president's up-close security detail and most trusted confidantes did not bother with false identities. Interesting. Van was right.

Malc trusted one of his newer operators. He figured he could count on Lita Dega since she was a recent recruit—long after all that 2008 nonsense.

Dega described the three characters that escaped the beach house with Stevens in a boat. Malc matched the descriptions and photos from the files for Cheevers, Evans, and Sandstrom he bought from a source at Veteran's Affairs—personnel files of inactive vets. Good to know. That took some doing, but he had to trust a *few* folks to make progress.

So counter to Van's orders, he talked to a sprinkling of other contacts for identity and cell records searches for Stevens, Evans, Sandstrom, and Cheevers. And because of his personal vendetta, he included Braxton and Janis in the hunt.

He wasn't too concerned about violating Van's choking restraint to distrust *all* of his contacts since this was low risk.

Malc's research paid off. Nothing on phone records for Stevens or Cheevers or Evans. But he got a hit on Sandstrom. Maybe the retired Delta operator was getting soft. Called a lady in Scottsdale.

One more tidbit. Braxton, the old spook, holed up in a rest home in Alexandria.

Soon, you meddling old menace! And who is this guy, Lee Randle, you called in Mesa? Might that be your old friend Janis, under another name? You have so few friends, Braxton, and we know from back in the day Janis was your BFF. Enoch told me so during his last op before he disappeared. Can't hide in plain site without agency cover, old man.

Bingo! All trails lead to Arizona.

CO-CONSPIRATORS

W ASHINGTON, DC

Some business he only attended to here in this sanctum sanctorum in the residence at One Observatory Circle. He locked it down and activated those elaborate counter-surveillance measures.

Immediately after extracting his secret phone from the wall safe behind the hidden panel, he initiated its two-level encryption process. God, how he hated using technology, but loved what it could do for him. They built this absolute privacy stuff for just this game.

"Hello, Norman. I always enjoy this symphony of secrecy. A little foreplay eases tensions when contemplating risky behavior, does it not?"

"Jeff, I'm not in the mood."

Jefferson Davis Redding, the Brotherhood's front-running candidate for president chuckled as the VP played into his little joke without meaning to do so.

"To business, then. Today's topic?"

~

Sealey said, "I'm worried…

"about the election. I've done all I can for the Brotherhood from within this administration over the last eight years without exposing myself. We have yet to bounce back after that 2008 disaster and we did not remove Atherton, and I am not at all happy. I suggest you worry too with Stevens still out there stirring up the opposition.

Redding said, "Norman, you worry too much. The most important commodity we must leverage is our matchless war chest.

"Our pro-business lobby and international investors continue to court us, now more than ever. And the technology they're buying for us? Voters won't know what hit them.

"We get them to swim in a sea of insecurity during the run-up. And we drown them in it before we threaten to rescue them—on our terms. In other words, we buy the presidency."

"Well, Jeff, you played that same tune during your run-ups to '08 and '12. What's different this time? You know this will be your last hurrah. In any future elections you'll just be another spoiler candidate to the majors if you do not win this one."

~

This ruffled Redding's sensibilities.

Nobody attacked his potency as a candidate. Not even this popinjay.

"I will remind you, Mr. Vice President, our strategy was sound in '08. The trolls did their job, we ensured the right stars aligned, but at the eleventh hour some piece-of-shit accountant *within our ranks* betrayed us.

"Do try to keep Mr. M from allowing this to happen yet again, won't you? And 2012? Well, we just weren't well-funded. Now, if we succeed with our current strategy, our odds remain favorable."

Redding hated naysayers.

"It's still a roll of the cosmic dice, but let's make sure we continue to load the dice. Okay, Norman? Our administration will complete the transition started seventy years ago."

"You just do your job, I'll do mine."

Pop, click.

IRREGULAR AFFAIR

U NDISCLOSED LOCATION

Former President Stevens loved action.

Since he left the Oval Office almost eight years earlier, he continued to serve his country as a concerned private citizen. He led a small but dedicated group of patriots who fought on behalf of an oblivious nation.

Most of his activities remained disguised as innocent but opinionated public appearances or political endorsements. In some situations and with certain individuals, however, they pushed harder.

The Brotherhood's influence once reached deep into government, law enforcement, and big business. Maybe still did. This prevented him from operating in a more overt manner in certain matters, and that was just fine with him.

If he were honest with himself, he relished the intrigue after his eight-year tenure as the most powerful *public* figure on Planet Earth. His love of the country and of the American people did not diminish when voted out of office—by a narrow margin, he'd always remind himself.

Stew Atherton was a good man, and John vowed to support his successor by any means possible. So far, he was only somewhat effective in doing so.

Now Stew was ill. Frustration consumed him.

Is the Brotherhood responsible? But what is the game plan? The worst-case scenario? Vice President Sealey would step in as president. And he is solid... or is he?

Sealey was a hard read. Intelligence sources declared him a patriot and a good civil servant. But now this on the heels of so many assassination attempts over the last eight years?

The vice president was the one person within Stew's administration who gained the most should the president become incapable of executing his duties. And what better stage from which to throw his own hat into the ring for the next election?

Prior to the 2008 campaign, intelligence sources reported no ties between Sealey and the PB. They found no shadows of doubt when Stew sought a new candidate for veep even as he engineered the demise of Sealey's traitorous predecessor. And no misgivings had surfaced relative to VP Sealey since then.

Sealey's earlier record as governor of Maryland appeared stellar. Still, John wondered. Would he cast suspicion on himself with such an obvious ploy if he were dirty? John knew he'd have to dig deeper than ever. It's the least he could do for his long-time now-ailing friend from across the aisle.

He would reach out to a trusted old acquaintance outside of official Washington. He recalled the *Nosy Cherry* operation from eight years earlier, a major op against the Brotherhood's collaborators before he left the White House. The core of his current detail came from that mission.

John had kept in touch with the old Army physician and NSA war dog, Colonel F Samuel Braxton, more so after Sam's wife Mary died two years ago.

Sam reminded him of a frail Mr. Spock from Corpus Christi. Now well past ninety, he had landed in an assisted living facility in Fairfax County.

ALEXANDRIA, VIRGINIA

JOHN WASN'T USED TO TRAVELING INCOGNITO.

Rather than risk compromised communications, he ditched his security detail for the morning. He trusted them but took no chances with the visibility of an entourage.

So he visited Sam Braxton in person and alone as invisible as possible for an ex-president. Wearing casual clothes, ball cap, and shades, he arrived in a taxi and signed in with an alias. The works.

John knocked and entered when invited. He found Sam hunched over an old computer in his sun-drenched suite. The too-high round table next to a small balcony's sliding glass door, the too-low padded arm chair, and the too-large laptop all looked gigantic compared to this incredible little man. Once a giant, a legend in the intelligence community, he now appeared desiccated, but with an internal furnace that still burned white-hot.

As John stood at the open door, Sam's surprised reaction delighted him, but felt his standing and saluting too much. He observed the onerous effort required to do so. Old soldiers, old habits, but always brand new respect.

"Mr. President? I am honored and perplexed, Sir!"

His speech still belied Sam's Deep South heritage, as the last word oozed out as "Suh!"

"Hello, Sam. Please, sit. Been awhile, my old compatriot. You look well."

Sam chuckled as if this were a joke.

"No offense, Mr. President, while you are ever the penultimate diplomat, you are an atrocious liar, Sir, if you don't mind my being blunt. The curse of an honest man. A pleasure and an honor, but a monumental shock to receive a visit from you.

"Sir, several things stand out."

"All right, let's have it." The president didn't even try to suppress an affectionate smile. Ever the analytical old spook, Sam delivered his from-the-hip assessment.

"First, you appear to be here without your entourage. Second, our last official intersect point was the *Nosy Cherry* operation near the end of your second term. Third, I've enjoyed every one of your Christmas cards, but July 4th is next week. And fourth, your attire appears casual to the point of a contrivance.

"So I'm left guessing you're off the books and need help or advice from this old codger. The Brotherhood, perhaps?"

Sam continued without awaiting a response.

"Now unless you want to cause another major coronary event, to which I am no stranger, please tell me what is on your mind, Mr. President. Before I expire from an acute case of suspense. Respectfully. Sir."

Sam knew he was spot on and issued a dry chuckle at his own small joke.

Then it was the president's turn to chuckle.

"As perceptive as ever, Sam. And let's cut the 'Mr. President' crap, okay? My name is John."

"Yes, ah, John."

"Good. My concerns may be unwarranted, but I prefer to be proactive. I fear for the safety of my old friend, President Atherton. The reports say he's taken ill, and cannot perform his duties."

"You are recalling the 'illness' of his traitorous first VP engineered by President Atherton's team six months into his first term."

"Yes I am, Sam. Your memory and your instincts still serve you well. That event removed a high level operative of the Brotherhood from the White House without devastating his new administration. That may have been a foreshadow of what I now suspect is a similar event engineered by that same traitorous group of… thugs.

"Sam, I fear for my friend's life, and I need some discreet help. Discretion was always your strong suit."

"Oh, dear. Well, my network at the agency has grown stale. I fear my help must be at a lower level. I still know a few trustworthy soldiers, but they're helpless in the political arena. Do you still trust and maintain contact with Admiral Mannheim?"

"Hell, Sam, I'm not sure why I'm even here. I just need a dependable non-political ear to bend. Perhaps a brainstorming partner. Even though Greg is no longer NSA's director, he might help. He's a good man. I'll keep him in mind. But I trust you more than him."

John continued.

"For now, let's assume Stew is a potential victim of an attempted palace coup. I still have some White House access, but no ideas for finesse, let alone a rescue plan should that become necessary."

After a thoughtful pause, the president pressed on.

"Good grief. This may be my paranoia blossoming. What do you think, Sam? Am I letting my imagination get the best of me?"

"Sir, you dare not ignore your gut,

"but we do not yet have enough information. Reconnaissance must be our priority. Can you seek a private audience with President Atherton?"

"I'm sure his handlers will throw up road blocks. Mine would. But former presidents retain a few perks. I might bully my way in to see him for a few minutes. Under the guise of worry for a sick friend—not as one president to another. Even if I'm unable to see him alone, that would be better than total ignorance."

"Good. So let's assume you can make that happen. Do you know his physician's name?"

"I should, but no. I can find out. Why?"

"I still have a decent network at both Walter Reed and Johns Hopkins. Retired chief surgeons retain some modicum of respect, not unlike former presidents, I imagine. Odds are fair that President Atherton's physician is an active member of the military, and I can probe his or her proclivities."

"What would that tell us?"

Sam smiled and thought, *Us? Me and this great man? A unique honor.*

He said, "Well, since neither of us likely know him, we dare not approach him directly. But we are embarking on a reconnaissance mission and we may learn something of value for our use later. Perhaps as leverage. Only *after* we gather information, do we analyze it."

"Careful, Sam, your spy is showing. Okay. Then what?"

After a few moments of careful consideration, Sam spoke with somber deliberation as if what he was about to suggest entailed great risk.

"Okay, John, here's what you will do, Sir. You must get in to see the president, even if it's at his bedside. Tomorrow. This is imperative. If he's conscious and still possesses his faculties, whisper Dilleford's name in his ear. That will remind your friend he may be a victim, unwitting or otherwise.

"If you are not alone, ask him to blink twice if he believes he is in mortal danger. Watch his reaction.

"However he responds, this next action is critical to our abbreviated timeline. You will advise the president to demand a second opinion from an old acquaintance, Doctor Elijah Rudstone. Immediately.

"Elijah was one of my most trusted and competent interns at Hopkins over a decade ago, and he has some agency background. He's now a respected department head, so he is a natural choice for an outside opinion.

"Even if they hear your advice to your friend, they will be hard-pressed to decline this request. I'll brief Elijah to expect a call. He will ask the right questions. And he will share his prognosis with us.

"Meantime, I'll collect intel on his current physician. But Sir, this plan is risky. If your suspicions bear out, we may even accelerate the president's demise if they perceive a heightened risk."

~

ONLY A COLD MOMENT LATER, JOHN SPOKE.

"I understand, Sam, but if Stew is merely a victim of my boundless paranoia, no harm, no foul. If my suspicions are correct, however, he could be dead either way. Correct?"

His own last declaration took the wind out of his sails. But he had made hundreds of tougher calls during his eight years in the White House.

"Yes, John, that is possible."

"You talk with Dr. Rudstone today so I can bully my way in to see the president tomorrow. Agreed, Sam?"

"Of course, Sir."

"AND SAM, THERE IS ANOTHER ISSUE.

I would appreciate your counsel. There is no doubt my life is in imminent danger."

Sam reeled from this revelation. "Excuse me, Sir?"

"A hardened team of mercenaries attacked my team and me two weeks ago. Several of my detail did not... survive."

It was as if Sam could *see* the lump rising in John's throat as well as hear it in his voice. A sheen of sweat arose above his granite brow, glistening in the sunlight that drenched the small living room. The man suffered.

Losing even a single member of his team tortured his sensibilities. But several? His micro-expressions told the rest of the story. Sam respected this great man for his courage *and* his heart.

"The only reason I escaped was thanks to your old *Nosy Cherry* acquaintance, Captain Cheevers and two of his team. This disguise serves a broader purpose than a discreet visit to ask for an old friend's help.

"Sam, I am on the run, and not at all sure who I can trust outside Captain Cheevers and his team. So I am trusting *no one* inside official Washington, including the Secret Service. Any advice for this old fugitive?"

While the aged spy didn't freeze because of panic—he operated far above that sort of static—he froze in deep analysis of this news, of his important friend's question.

John was smart enough to let him think. Now entangled in not one, but two simultaneous operations of import? He could see Sam still loved the game. After almost a full minute of silence and chin scratching, eyes half open as if in a dream-like state, Sam spoke.

"John, after you visit the White House, you need distance. Posthaste. How do you feel about the desert?"

<h1 style="text-align:center">RESCUED</h1>

B ALTIMORE, MARYLAND

The phone rang seven times.

Finally, his old mentee answered. A gruff voice demanded who dared call.

Sam said, "Elijah! It *has* been a long time, my old friend. Still pissing on interns and residents?"

The voice softened in an instant.

"Sam? Sam! How long has it *been*? So you *are* still alive. I'd heard rumors."

"Still kicking. Well, limping, anyway. Sorry for not calling. Got me in one of those assisted living facilities. At least I can come and go. I'm even still driving. I need to ask. Are you still open to freelance consults?"

"Right to the point, eh, old man? I keep mighty busy over here at Hopkins now, Sam."

Not comfortable discussing this over the phone, they agreed to a brief meeting in two hours at one of their favorite old haunts. Twisted Teahouse, in the Hampden neighborhood of North Baltimore, was near the medical center.

Sam did not begrudge the long drive up from Alexandria, an essential precaution. So was the stop at the Montpelier exit off I-95 to relieve his petrified bladder.

After a ginger backslapping fest, Sam and Doctor Rudstone settled at a tiny window table near the bakery counter. Its curved-glass cover remained half-fogged over by the steam from buttery-warm ganache-stuffed pastries and still-steaming bagels inside.

Elijah leaned forward. He looked Sam in the eye, and said, "Now what's with all the mystery, Doc?"

"How about offering a second opinion for a sitting US president? At his request?"

For a moment, Elijah wasn't sure he understood his old friend and mentor. Sitting back, open palms face-down at the end of extended forearms and locked elbows, he dropped his chin to his chest and stared at Sam over his spectacles. He braced against the table as if he feared Sam would shove it against his slender waist. Then his eyes widened as comprehension dawned.

"Whoa! Well, Atherton's illness is all over the news. What do you know, you old spook? Give it up. Did you recommend me?"

Sam explained the entire situation to his trusted colleague forty-four years his junior. He was taking a risk, but one that he and John agreed was unavoidable.

Without further hesitation, Elijah said, "Sure. Once they let me in, I'll do a full work-up. Eyes only?"

"Please. We suspect foul play at the highest level, so do exercise caution, Elijah. Might be a slow poison. I suggest you first arrange an introductory call to Doctor Joshua Sampson, the current White House MD, a Walter Reed guy, as soon as John and I get the green light. Might ruffle fewer feathers that way.

"Sampson follows the playbook with a solid rep. Most of the time. If they ask you for your findings, tell them that's between your patient and you. They'll think you evasive. That's okay. Once again, it is unclear who we trust."

"Sam, this isn't my first cold consult under dubious circumstances. It'll be fine. And it's *John?* Holy Heather, man, you're a high flyer these days. Don't get too close to the sun, my friend. I'd hate to see your wings melt. I must get back."

"Thank you, Major."

"A genuine pleasure, Colonel. I'll await the call."

WASHINGTON, DC

PRESIDENT ATHERTON WAS BEDRIDDEN.

They told John his old friend convalesced in the large bedroom in the presidential residence recovering from a severe case of influenza.

Recovering? The flu? Good grief.

Stew almost disappeared in the huge bed among clouds of pillows and comforters. After entering, John walked a full twenty paces to his bedside, the right side. Doctor Sampson, Vice President Sealey, and the president's steward gathered ten paces from the foot of the monstrous canopied bed. They each appeared inconsolable—to a fault.

John ignored them beyond a cursory nod.

"Stewart, my old ally. You've looked better."

Without being prompted, the president signaled John to come close with a weak hand resting outside the bedding tucked perfectly around him in precise symmetry. Instead of using his feeble voice, he waggled two fingers to signal his wish.

John hovered his sympathetic hand on the president's shoulder as he leaned in close and whispered, "Like Dilleford? Blink twice for yes."

Blink. Blink.

"Demand a second opinion from your old friend, Dr. Elijah Rudstone from Hopkins, Stewart. That's Elijah Rudstone."

Blink. Blink.

So everyone in the room could hear, John said, "I'll let you rest, my friend. So good to see you. Get well, Mr. President."

The entire interaction took less than thirty seconds.

~

TOO MANY OPINIONS!

Doctor Josh Sampson, the White House MD, appeared offended at having his expertise challenged, but the time to seem conciliatory had arrived. And the time had long passed when he should have called in a second opinion himself. But that pup Rudstone? From *Hopkins?*

Adler Stavers, Atherton's alienated Secret Service Director, realized the same, and frustration hung upon him like a wet wool overcoat.

~

THERESE DIDN'T LIKE IT.

This other doctor sniffing around the president's illness spelled danger. Discovery would mean disaster—treason, attempted murder, the works. She would not submit to that, but a direct attack on this new MD was not practical either.

If her orders weren't to make Atherton's death appear as natural as possible, more white powder folded into the president's morning oatmeal would make short work of him. She warned them of this risk, but they gave her no choice.

"Is the president's breakfast ready yet, Therese?"

She said, "Almost. I need his oatmeal to be just the way he likes it—al dente."

"Good. His guy will be here in two minutes to deliver it to Anthony. Finish, please."

"Yes, Sir."

Therese spent her life perfecting her profession. Now, however, it seemed the precise time to abandon this two-month assignment—

plus six months of vetting before that—in favor of a survivable exit strategy.

How had she let this happen? She finished the president's breakfast tray, stirring in a lethal dose of the white powder retrieved from within her hollow medical alert bracelet, and after a quick stir, slipped away from the White House kitchens. Forever.

Was *she* now a loose end?

∾

THE TWO OF THEM SAT QUIETLY.

The spacious bedroom felt cold and desolate to both the infirm president and his faithful steward.

Anthony propped up his charge with an additional pillow after stalling with a few lame jokes he heard in the dining room earlier. Breakfast had arrived late.

He helped the president eat his oatmeal these days as he was too weak to do so by himself. As he opened his mouth to accept the morning's first spoonful, Doctor Rudstone stormed into the bedroom and issued a polite but loud command.

"Stop. Please."

Ever loyal to his president, Anthony sensed something awry and froze with a sharp intake of breath.

"Has he eaten anything yet this morning?"

"No, Sir. What is happening?"

"I need his stomach empty for a blood test." Anthony accepted the ruse without question. Whatever was best for *his president.*

Stew Atherton's drooping eyes widened at the intrusive exchange. A large plastic bag appeared in this new doctor's right hand. With hastily donned plastic gloves, he swooped up the oatmeal—bowl and its contents—into the bio-hazard container, and sealed it carefully.

∾

Just as Sam and John feared...

Doctor Elijah Rudstone discovered a low-grade poison in President Atherton's bloodstream. He guessed someone introduced tiny doses of arsenic trioxide into his food daily for *weeks*.

An assassin's favorite, arsenic was difficult to detect in very low doses. He might have missed it until too late if Sam hadn't suggested what to look for. But the analysis of the bowl of oatmeal he snatched that morning revealed it would have killed President Atherton that same day, no doubt a lethal dose in reaction to soliciting a second medical opinion.

Once he found arsenic, President Atherton's symptoms made perfect sense: gastric distress, esophageal pain, vomiting, and diarrhea with blood.

By this time, he confronted Josh Sampson with his findings who seemed surprised. The inquiries would reveal the facts. At least now he seemed ready to go to any lengths to help.

*He's an incompetent fool or an accessory to attempted murder. The freaking **flu**? But if you're not **looking** for foul play...*

Doctor Rudstone rushed the president to Walter Reed in an ambulance. A four-vehicle escort led by two Metro PD motorcycle officers with emergency lights blazing and sirens blaring made short work of the eight-mile drive to the military medical center in Bethesda. Adler Stavers expedited the entire move with a full complement of Secret Service agents and vehicles.

While the president would suffer significant side effects for years, he would recover. He remained at risk for certain cancers because of his prolonged exposure. But one fact was indisputable. Elijah Rudstone, consulting physician, saved the president's life that day.

As an added precaution, John directed his own team to the hospital alongside Stew's team and Stavers' agents. John installed Mick Sandstrom undercover inside the hospital, just in case. Their president would not die on their watch.

Rudstone continued to oversee Atherton's treatment at Reed. He made the time—at President Atherton's request. This raised eyebrows, but they were taking no chances.

The White House was in chaos searching for the traitor, or traitors.

NO FEAR

M ESA, ARIZONA

The dream would not die...

Time tore past like fast-ripping paper in an otherwise quiet room —abrupt and noisy and jagged. Subliminal emotions startled him while awake *or* while sleeping.

When they awakened him, Geo could think of nothing else, long after, even though his dreams only offered vague notions of fear and horror.

When awake, a distant gaze was often interrupted by a sudden jerk of his head or a hand's involuntary twitch.

Was he going crazy?

He wasn't sure which punished him more. Was it the paralyzing memory of being struck down and left for dead years earlier on the deck of a sinking boat in a storm at sea? Or was it the burden of having taken a human life? Either way, he'd awaken devastated. Most nights.

At least he could walk now, with almost no limp, although running was no longer an affordable luxury. He hated running anyway. What *was* the point?

A short eight years earlier, every aspect of Geo's life had changed. He and a few friends stumbled onto a nasty organization called the Patriot Brotherhood. The PB rivaled the proportions of a first-world shadow government.

A brilliant young man named Dent Canfield worked for Geo back then. Dent's job at Greater Global Solutions was a cover for his real mission as a technical operative for the PB.

Geo fired Dent from GGS for egregious sexual harassment, and Dent returned the favor by trying to kill Geo. After later discovering the truth of Dent's involvement with the PB, Geo became instrumental in Dent's demise.

This act exposed a significant portion of the PB's operations with help from a retired US intelligence operative and now dear friend, Doctor Sam Braxton. Sam had turned Dent.

The 2008 genesis of Geo's predominant nightmare would also have been his own demise if not for a timely rogue wave. He would be dead along with four of his employees, his friends. A memory of survival. Little else. Yet another lie. Yet another day.

Before that, Geo survived three decades as a technology executive at one of the world's largest multinational corporations.

Since all of that, he had made every attempt to abandon his past, and failed.

During these post-retirement years, writing became his life, his greatest joy. He loved watching words flow onto the page, as if by magic. He cherished every reader. And every listener.

～

HIS WEEKLY PODCAST DEADLINE APPROACHED.

Just forty hours away from showtime, Geo left Kate snoring like an adolescent puppy at 5 a.m. After sliding the bedroom's heavy maple pocket door closed behind him, he made his way forward to his office in the main living area.

The subtle glow of red and green equipment lights scattered around the bus's dark interior sent a small thrill through him each morning.

My twenty-three-ton home features eight wheels, an 8.9 liter diesel engine, and lots of other cool gadgets. How many can say that?

Geo promised himself he'd take his anti-cramp tablets, anti-allergy supplements and anti-inflammatory meds later. He stumbled to the keyboard and stabbed the *Fn* key to wake up his iMac—his anti-depressant device.

While the computer shook off its own stupor, he switched on a desk lamp. Twenty-six inches away sat the valiant Mister Coffee. He always loaded MC before going to bed. Four cups of triple-filtered water dripped at a ponderous rate through three heaping scoops of Starbuck's French Roast espresso-ground beans.

Geo loved how Starbuck's over-roasted—some say burned—their beans. Robust. With a bite. Not subtle. Like him. When he was writing, anyway.

He reached behind and to his right while half-reclined in front of his computer. Punched MC's *Brew Now* and *Brew Strong* buttons in a quick practiced sequence.

His clean and empty mug waited atop MC, already primed with his favorite powdered Vanilla-Caramel creamer, including its vile mix of sugar-free preservatives and flavor beads. The mug would be toasty by the time Geo poured his morning's magic source of inspiration. Yet another lie he chose to believe.

Scrivener, his author software was more awake than he. It was time to further punish his fictional characters, much to the delight of his hundreds of thousands of devoted readers and listeners.

While he sometimes agonized over placing his beloved characters in precarious scenarios born of conflict, that's what comprised great drama. If he were honest with himself, at times he found a perverse and vicarious delight in ruining the lives of others. With no consequence—other than to increase his readership. So did that make him shameless, or worse?

This bothered him, a lot. Without hesitation, he'd complicate, maim, and murder. He tasted the bittersweet irony. Beyond his fiction, his life was a testament to peace, love, and the search for tranquility. So what sort of person was he?

Geo's six-foot writing desk—forward of the kitchen, aft of the cockpit's passenger seat on the starboard side—dominated the bus's interior. As a lifelong sailor, nautical terms made more sense to him than 'in front of,' or 'behind,' or 'the right side.'

His huge desktop dominated the living space, and often motivated Kate's gentle bitching because of its eternal surface clutter. The twenty-seven-inch Big Mac always had lots of company.

Various colored *Post-It* Notes clung to every vertical surface, some with curled corners. Five rings of keys—all within easy reach—peeked from under the brim of a cowboy hat covered with national park and motorcycle rally pins. Three Native American flutes piled atop Geo's TV and DVR remotes.

The mellow incandescent sheen of a green glass desk lamp with its tubular bulb and tarnished telescoping brass base bathed his desk with guarded optimism in the pre-dawn hours.

His command center.

A wireless keyboard and track pad, both in need of a compressed air blow job, awaited in anticipation for his attention. His closest friends. They perched atop a cheap padded lap desk beneath his hands. The Mac's brilliant screen sat at a forty-five degree angle to his chair, but that didn't matter. It was the dream that mattered. Geo was living on the road, writing, publishing, and casting.

With his feet on an ottoman, the king of his realm labored in near darkness. He slaved on his blog, on the next novel, on podcast scripts, email marketing, or on social media posts in support of his *brand*, until Kate arose between eight and nine. She stayed up later at night than Geo.

This morning, in solitary silence, Geo banged away at his frustrations, aspirations, pain, and happiness, transferring them onto the e-pages of his weekly near-future sci-fi script.

His exploding audience emailed him with probing questions about what was coming. They'd chime in on a social issue addressed the previous week that wasn't really fictional. Or they'd ask why certain characters behaved the way they did. Or why the story took a certain turn. It seemed they couldn't wait for the next podcast. He teased them, and they waited.

They loved him for it, even his inscrutability. Some listeners also provided story ideas. Geo encouraged this. He was fond of saying, "We're all in this together." And he meant it.

His readership continued to grow almost to the point of a cult-like social phenomenon. This both delighted and scared Geo and Kate.

He muttered to himself, *Yeah, I'm blessed. But day-dreaming without producing a two-thousand-word script won't get the next episode written, edited, recorded, and posted on schedule.*

So the process began anew. A new day, a new episode, and new adventures for people who don't exist. But their issues do. If they only knew.

TUCSON, ARIZONA

THEY SETTLED INTO A RHYTHM. AGAIN.

After checking in with the Marshal's Service, they had moved the rig out of the valley near Phoenix to a higher elevation east of Tucson, farther southeast, almost three months earlier. A smaller town, a new town, a little cooler. And more flute aficionados.

Their lawn chairs faced each other at a diagonal. Geo watched Kate rock. She was a rocker. He was not.

Between them, a small white steel table with an inset blue and white mosaic top held her protein shake. Geo's giant coffee mug sat next to it, empty as usual. He kept trying for another sip, a few more drops, even though he'd emptied the mug thirty minutes earlier. He limited himself to one mug per day. His protein shake remained ignored on the table.

They sat in the sparse shade of the only nearby tree—a tall palm with a trimmed top. A gentle breeze from behind drifted between the bus and its disconnected trailer. The soft rustling of fronds overhead hinted of a relaxing scene, but belied the tight mood between them.

Geo's hair, now long on the sides and back but balding on top under his ever-present pin-festooned cowboy hat, blew across his eyes. He didn't bother brushing it aside. Reminded him he could still *grow* hair, *and* of his brief tenure in nineteen-sixty-nine San Francisco where he was but another rebel without a clue. A damn hippy, as his sainted father in Minnesota used to say. And the stupid hat protected him from a merciless desert sun.

Geo long-suspected the old man had taken a fall from grace decades earlier before he found Jesus, but he wasn't sure.

Rest in peace, Daddy. Your hippy served his country for four long years. Sorry you had to die before seeing that.

Kate stayed with Geo through three decades of alcoholism. Together, they faced a murderous ex-employee who tried to kill them both eight years earlier. Despite all that, the couple drew upon a multitude of incredible memories they crafted... together. Their retirement years were the best, as long as Geo stayed busy.

But now this.

He needed to say something, even though she remained silent. He tried for one last micro-sip of coffee from the empty mug. Again. Stalling. Then...

"I didn't intend my fiction to echo our life, Babe. But they say that a good author's work will carry a certain autobiographical authenticity."

She remained silent for a strong thirty seconds before speaking. Then, with gravitas...

"Aw, Geo, I know how much you love writing, but can't you try to understand *why* you write? It's obvious it's now taking us somewhere we don't want to go. Now it may put others at risk. Maybe if you wrote something else for your podcasts?"

Geo could not help himself. It seemed events of the past were once again catching up with him. With them. This caught him off-guard, and he hoped they would survive. Again.

As the author of a weekly podcast and several novels, he recognized one sign of success was listener and readership engagement—fan mail. This included email, comments from blog subscribers and followers, and social media group interaction: shares, shout-outs, tweets, retweets…

Sometimes a few of his followers took a dark turn down *The Alley.*

Nobody likes everything any author publishes, he thought. *At least not work that stands for something.*

He'd seen a serious up-tick of threatening mail, even hate mail, in recent weeks. Comments appeared on multiple social media platforms as well as reader comments on his own site—anonymous entries. Even some malicious texts.

Curious, and unsettling. This… *dark mail,* as he called it, seemed to originate from just one or a few determined and anonymous sources. No coincidence, he was sure. Or was his a hopeful dream only *imagining* it was just a sprinkling of malcontents? These ravings sounded personal.

"Babe, this nasty stuff is *not* why I became an author, but it was inevitable. Believe it or not, this is a symptom of success."

"Oh, Geo, you big jerk, you're still rationalizing. Haven't we worked past that by now?"

"You're right, Babe. I'll work with Bluehost and WitSec to make sure we're doing all we can to mask our location and our identities. Just in case. But I'm not too worried. Let the marshals worry for us."

All published authors envision their work being adored by thousands, perhaps millions. But belittled and discouraged by threats, some of violence, shocked him. These threats, though veiled, bode ill and were unmistakable. Oh well. *Was* this the inevitable price of success?

～

ANOTHER DAY HAD PASSED.

The desert sun capitulated to the western horizon, but the small city's lights in the medium distance diluted the stars' intensity. Since the sandy soil did not hold heat like grassy or wooded landscapes, temperatures plummeted as quickly as entering a walk-in fridge. That was always the cue to either start a fire or retire to the warmth of the bus's interior.

Geo dreaded what was sure to happen soon, but he needed sleep. He could put it off for a while longer.

Their quiet conversation continued for another hour before they retired.

"Babe, let's try to get some sleep. I love you."

"Okay, Geo. I love you too, but I do not want to live in fear—ever again."

"You know what? Maybe it's time to move again. Just as a precaution. What do you think of Quartzsite? Maybe some boondocking? Lots of flute players down there too."

Now too tired for discussion, Kate said she wasn't sure about drycamping—without hook-ups for electricity, water, and sewer—and they'd talk in the morning.

As Geo snapped off the last remaining light above their bed's headboard near the rear of the bus, his thoughts echoed her previous admonition.

No fear. Got it.

He knew that was already no longer possible, but had said no more.

INVISIBLE POISON

T UCSON, ARIZONA

HE COULD'T HELP HIMSELF.

Geo broke a dozen Witness Security rules he had sworn not to violate, including the one prohibiting contact with old friends and family. He didn't care. Roots were important despite the risks.

He sprawled in his favorite ratty old lawn chair by the side door of his trailer near the rear of the bus. He used every opportunity to keep that damn cell phone away from his brain, but would grudgingly acknowledge it was a useful tool.

Like a chainsaw, respect but fear the tool. So he kept it away from his head by streaming audio to his Bluetooth hearing aids. Made it harder for folks to listen in, too. He'd just risk the Bluetooth.

"Hey, dude. What's happening with you, man? Olivia and I can't keep track of you guys. And you're evasive when you do call about where you're parked. You're supposed to be out there enjoying your retirement, right?"

The tone of Tommy Reese's voice broadcast unmistakable concern for his old service buddy of four decades earlier. If Geo were honest with himself, the events of eight years ago still clung to him like stinky bayou mud on his boots. A lingering case of post-traumatic stress?

Whatever.

"Look, Tommy, you mean well, but I'm still wrestling with some stuff. Hey, my state-of-the-art security system in the bus might amuse you. Complete. When this baby touches off, they'll hear it coast-to-coast!"

"You still agonizing over that episode with your old ex-employee serial killer traitor? Yeah, you told me about that back then. Hey, that could be the title of a grunge-goth horror flick. Geez, Geo, let that garbage go! It'll nibble away at you and Kate. I know, easier said than done."

"Yeah, Tommy. No worries. Say, thanks for emailing that article on toxic EMP a few months ago. Something I worry about. I appreciate that, old friend."

"Hey, you saved my life back in the day. Now I worry about you, brother. Sustained and escalating electromagnetic pollution, or should I say *poisoning,* is not something our physiology can tolerate, nor can our psychology as a society comprehend. We don't even yet understand what it's *already* doing to us, and the entire ecosystem.

"And this whole argument that non-ionizing radiation from radio waves is okay? Bullshit. Gonna get a lot worse in the future, the direction we're going."

Tommy was Geo's lead petty officer for a short while during their tenure in the US Coast Guard Search and Rescue Teams. A rogue wave caused Tommy's head to hit a steel bulkhead—hard. Knocked him unconscious and threw him overboard during a SAR mission in a raging storm. Geo had thrown himself in after Tommy and pulled him to safety. Tommy never forgot.

And Geo never forgot that *another* rogue wave *saved* his life not so long ago.

"Yeah, I've lined the trailer I tow behind the motorhome—my studio—with about five hundred bucks worth of fine copper screening. Just a precaution. I spend a lot of time in that trailer writing, painting, and recording, so I protect the ole brain pan from getting microwaved. Plus, it gives the trailer's interior an interesting steam-punk vibe."

"You *what*, Geo? Aw man, I was just advocating a grass roots push for some decent legislation to leash those greedy telecoms from polluting and saturating the planet with microwave radiation. But kudos for taking action, I guess. Geez, Geo. *Nothing's* half-assed with you, is it? So now your trailer is a gen-you-wine Faraday Cage? Dude, you kill me! What's Kate think of that? I can guess."

Tommy chuckled. He knew Kate well. He and Olivia had been dear friends even spanning years of separation. They'd been on several Transcendental Meditation retreats together over the years. In the old days, that is, before the madness.

"Well, I explained that it was part of my amateur radio station's set-up. A wonderful counterpoise for the ole HF/shortwave radio transmissions I don't send or receive any more. But I might! It's a decent cover. She does not need this worry. I do enough of that for both of us. Her biggest bitch was the cost. Once an accountant…"

"Aw, Geo. After almost fifty years of marriage, you're still keeping secrets from her? And I forgot how much of a nerd you were—are."

"Very few secrets, Tommy. I appreciate the heads-up, though. These higher frequencies are bad enough, but now this short-range line-of-sight shit? Gonna require towers and repeaters *everywhere. And* higher power transmissions. Soon with clouds of satellites in the mix? You and a lot of others convinced me the science is irrefutable. Just another goddamn example how big business's profit motive comes at the expense of our general well-being."

"Whatever, man. Hey, I gotta scoot. It's always great catching up with you. Remember, all things in their time."

"Hi to Liv. Love ya, brother."

"You too, Geo. Keep your powder dry. Here's hoping you need not use it, my old friend. Namaste."

The click on Geo's cell, or rather, the sudden cessation of back-ground noise, possessed a certain finality. Was he over-reacting to *any* potential threat? They say hyper-vigilance is a symptom of post-traumatic stress. He'd been to several VA clinics for various reasons over the years, but never for *that*.

His current dilemma remained more pressing. How could he convince Kate to let him line their motorhome with copper screening too? And maybe the car?

INDIAN JOE

I NDIAN JOE *WHO?*

Nobody ever seemed to recall Joe's last name. But Geo knew it was Blackfeather. He also told Geo in confidence that Ernesto was his first name, with a middle name of Joseph.

Indian Joe performed at the Ritz Carlton on Dove Mountain north of Tucson two nights a week when he was in town to supplement his income as an entrepreneur. He designed software for the construction industry part-time.

With his commanding presence, Joe seemed much taller than five-foot-six. He took pride in his mixed Native American and Hispanic heritage, reflecting that pride in how he dressed.

Ever-present faded blue jeans and a frayed jean jacket framed a turquoise choker that hung outside a faded t-shirt conspicuous by its lack of logos or slogans.

And there was the ever-present bandana worn high across a tanned and creased forehead. That blue and white bandana held back his thick brown-black medium-length hair. Some would say he wore his hair long. But no hat. Joe never wore a hat.

A three-inch vertical scar on his left cheek, and a separate one that slashed through his left eyebrow enhanced an angular and handsome face. The stitch marks on both scars appeared self-inflicted. Amateur first-aid? Battlefield triage?

Geo stared sideways at Joe as they sat at a diagonal to each other in two of Joe's beat-up old lawn chairs in front of his ancient bumper-pull travel-trailer. Plastic tumblers of sweet tea sat on a low white table between them sweating circular puddles.

The late morning sun would toast them if it weren't for Joe's blue-and-white striped awning over their heads. Reminded Geo of circus canvas. Several rips and more than a little sun-rotted fabric would not keep them dry in a heavy rain, but they needed the shade during the day—Geo more than Joe. With no wind, that awning stayed put 24/7.

"Besides, rain is rare," Joe would say.

Geo couldn't recall ever seeing Joe not wearing that jacket, choker, and bandana. He wore another bandana high around his throat, under that choker, tied at the side with the slightest flare. Like the old cowboy, Roy Rogers. He always wore that entire "uniform," even in triple digits. About that Geo wondered. Between sips of too-sweet tea, he said, "Hey, 'Joe-Two-Kerchiefs,' why do you always keep your neck covered with that red-and-white hanky?"

"Not cool, man. Private, okay? Another day."

"Sorry, Joe. Just making conversation."

The way he sometimes squinted suggested impaired vision, but Joe wore no glasses. Desert eyes. It struck Geo that he always smelled clean, and his creased jeans stayed that way. He could tell because constant ironing makes jeans a lighter blue at the crease. He seemed a twenty-first century anachronism.

Joe's jeans always looked clean, even though a little frayed at the rear of his cuffs. And another thing—his cowboy boots were always polished, *never* dusty. What *was* it about Joe? Something else. Then Geo realized Joe seemed like a vigilant but patient warrior between skirmishes. Maybe a soldier without a war.

He wondered too about that smell—subtle but noticeable. A perpetual hint of cardamom and sage floated around him, and good humor. Yeah, that was it.

Joe self-published a modest e-book on the art of crafting Native

American flutes from desert plants such as yucca and agave. Sold a few dozen copies, or a few hundred, maybe more. He couldn't say. Didn't much care. It was about sharing his craft.

Geo met Joe at a flute circle in Tucson, and they became instant fast friends. The irascible flutie taught Geo how to make a yucca flute *and* the finer points of performing with it. He even showed Geo how to harvest his first yucca stalk most suitable for making a flute with minimal tools. "Much like the Old Ones," Joe would say.

Joe and Geo sat in threadbare lawn chairs facing a small fire. Pungent mesquite smoke rose in the cool night air as they rubbed their hands over the fire. Their plastic cups of strong sweet tea, ice melted, sat forgotten on the table between them.

Tonight, Joe was more talkative than usual. Over the years, performing on the casino circuit taught him how to handle abusive drunks and insensitive tourists.

In his quiet sing-song voice he said, "Yeah, the tourists love to hear me perform on my anasazis. Some call rim-blown flutes *pueblo* flutes instead of *anasazi* flutes. Tribal politics, I guess. Speakin' of politics, they don't much care I let folks call me *Indian Joe*. Name just stuck. I don't pay much attention.

"Out-East Gringos come to see how red the redskin looks compared to what they see in the movies. Or compared to the color of their own necks. Most are nice folks from somewhere else with different ideas. It's all good. At least I try to keep it that way.

"I got kinda pissed at this one ignorant cedar chopper from North Carolina, though. He asked real loud what happened to my feathers, and would I do a rain dance for him. He was tryin' to be funny for his friends. They were as drunk or as high as him.

"I smiled, put my arm right tight 'round his shoulder, and from my lips to his left ear I explained, real patient-like.

"'Pardner, I'm sure you don't mean nothin' by that. S'just that what you said just now brings me close to whippin' out my rain stick and slappin' you with it n'order to educate you. Don't be sayin' shit like that, 'kay?

"Now you want me to play a tune on one 'a my flutes from my

proud and honorable heritage as a Native American? I'd be glad to oblige your European immigrant ass, 'kay pardner? Here's a coupon for a free spin at the roulette wheel over yonder. No hard feelin's. I'm Joe.' Offered him my hand.

"The dude's eyes grew to the size 'a Sunday dinner plates lookin' for a suitable smart-ass comeback. Instead, he busted out in a foolish grin, took my hand in both 'a his. Said, 'Aw, shit, pardner, I get it—now. Sorry, man. And thanks…Joe.'"

That was Indian Joe.

~

GEO AND JOE HEADED EAST ON I-10.

The next morning, they hunted yucca in Geo's little red *toad*—as in the vehicle they sometimes *towed* behind their motorhome. They did so when venturing where the length of the bus towing the trailer with the car inside would be a burden, or would cause an over-length ticket —in California and Coastal Oregon, for example.

The toad was a no-frills Toyota Yaris. Didn't even have electric windows or cruise, but got the job done, *and* fit into the trailer, along with two motorcycles and a bunch of overflow from the bus.

The duo now headed south on US 83, one of the more scenic routes to Tombstone where they'd end up if they traveled too far.

"C'mon, pardner, let's hike. My spirit guide tells me we go this way." Geo had driven them for an hour from their RV resort east of Tucson before they parked in the Santa Rita mountains and started walking.

"Spirit guide?"

"Ah, yeah, a little spice in my recipe for the tourists who expect, well, something mystical from every native. Just making conversation, white man."

Other than his changing-the-topic expression, Geo couldn't tell if Joe was serious. Didn't seem like he was joking. They had left the little car parked at a roadside turnout four miles shy of the intersection to

Sonoita and Patagonia. Joe said he knew there were "righteous yuccas just over the next rise."

Right. *Just over the next rise* in Joe-speak translated into the better part of a sandy mile over rolling dunes in serious high-desert scrub country. They kicked up copious amounts of dust en route. Geo worried about contracting Valley Fever from dormant fungus in that dust, but they were in the mountains, so no worries, right?

"Only a few chollas up here. That's a good thing." Joe explained, "Here's one, pardner. The cholla is a nasty cactus. Pronounced CHO-ya. They're called jumping chollas, or teddy bears. Look all fuzzy, don't they? Lots more of 'em down in the valley."

"Yeah, a cool light green. I can see why they might call them teddy bears."

Geo sometimes hiked in the desert near their resort and saw chollas from a distance. He reached out a curious hand.

"Stop!"

Joe's shout from behind and to his right startled him. He jumped back and dropped his left hand to his side before he froze.

"Hey, man. You spot a rattler or something?"

"Nope. Just trying to keep you from making a painful mistake."

Joe explained in his patient sing-song voice, like he was a bored minimum-wage tour guide who expected zip for tips.

"The cholla is one of Old Apache's best friends, but not yours. All that fuzz is thousands of near-invisible and almost weightless barbed spines. The slightest breeze unhooks 'em when they're dry. Once airborne, if they land on, or *jump* to an ignorant hiker—no offense— those tiny barbed spines will grow under the skin if not removed fast.

"And then there's the pain. Starts out itchy, then gets infected and swells up all puffy and, well… not pretty.

"In the old days, Apaches threw them at invading cavalry to infect them, or they loaded their sticky arrows with those barbs. In real bad cases, if you don't get them barbs out fast, and if enough of 'em grow in ya for a spell, they can paralyze or even kill ya. Steer clear, man. Nasty. But they make great rain sticks."

Geo loved this hike. Great story material. And danger gets the blood pumping, right? His heart rate wasn't yet back to normal.

"Rain sticks?"

"Yeah. Makes the sound of falling rain. I've owned a monster rain stick for twenty years. Five feet long and four inches across. I'll show you next time you're over to the trailer.

"Old dried cholla stalks have hundreds of seeds inside. You push the woodier spines into the stalk. But real slow, long after the fuzz is dead 'n gone. Tipping the stick end-for-end causes the dried seeds to tumble against all them spines for a good while. Like the sound of falling rain. A rain stick."

"News to this city boy."

"Do yourself a favor, pardner. Buy one instead of making your own. Hey, lots of yuccas up ahead. Got your handsaw and gloves ready?"

"More desert plant defense mechanisms I need to know about?"

"Well, matter 'a fact, the stalks you want grow up the center of the big spiny yucca bush. You'll see they're a spiky ball a few feet across and a few feet tall. The razor-sharp points on the ends of those long stiff leaves will go right through your jeans and stab ya if they get the chance.

"Not poisonous, but hurt like hell. They'll even go through those leather work gloves you got. And do *not* rub even your gloved hands *downward* on the dried stalks themselves. They'll sliver ya. Even their cute little dried leaves. No big deal but you should be aware. Clean 'em up later with your heavy gloves and sixty-grit sandpaper."

"Geez. No wonder these plants survive out here! I'm glad you're here to keep me from doing something stupid."

Joe's quiet sing-song voice soothed while scaring Geo yet again. His next words did not match his tone of voice.

"Yeah. Oops. Too late. Freeze, Lee. I mean right fuckin' now…"

After stepping over a desiccated scrub trunk of a fallen eucalyptus tree, Geo heard the crescendo of an unusual rustling sound, still thinking, *Rain stick.* No, that wasn't right. From three feet to his right, Joe reached out in a smooth but quick motion to grasp his right arm with his left hand in a firm vice-like grip. Drew him back ever so slowly. Geo let it happen.

Joe reached to his right and picked up a crusty fallen branch four feet long. He brought it around and poked it two feet in front of Geo's feet. The stick discouraged a four-foot rattler from thinking about striking. Once the snake headed for safety from these callous invaders, Joe let out an exasperated sigh as if to say, *Damn city folk.*

Then Joe moved on as he continued to talk with an unsettling sense of sing-song calm. "Rattlers can't strike unless they're coiled—that young fella wasn't there yet. Don't mean he wasn't about to.

"Yuccas up ahead on the ridge. See those six- or seven-foot stalks with droopy seed pods up top? Good and dry. Get your sawin' arm ready, white boy."

Glistening with sweat that also now soaked his t-shirt, Geo whispered, "Son of a bitch!"

T UCSON, ARIZONA

CHET BRAVERMAN STOOD IN THE DARKNESS.

Standing outside his ancient motorhome, he conversed in low tones on his encrypted satellite phone. Dogs barked in the background. The night chilled the back of his bare arms, but not uncomfortably so, though he wished he'd worn long sleeves.

Had there been more light, several new bruises and more than a little blood might have shocked a passerby.

He cradled the phone between his hunched-up shoulder and head cocked to the right as he massaged his right forearm.

"But are they okay, Chet?"

"Yeah, Doc, both Char, and Lee are fine. Before he got home from his Thursday night flute circle—don't ask—I chased this guy away from their rig next door. But he showed me some moves, Doc. This was no hillbilly burglar or lost camper.

"The dude moved like a panther. And he put *me* down *twice* before

I spanked his ass and he ran off. Whoever he was, someone trained him. One mean SOB."

"Objective?"

"Dunno, Doc. Might've just been a recon since he was alone. Char was inside the coach reading, and she hadn't locked the door. He headed in that direction, but he did not get there before we mixed it up.

"After, I knocked and talked with Char. Stood outside in he dark. Asked her for a paper coffee filter I didn't need. Reminded her to lock her door until Lee got home. I'll talk with Lee too.

"Dumb not to lock the damn door. Even out here. They're getting lax. Lucky I was on a perimeter check. What're we lookin' at, Doc?"

"I doubt you need to worry about a major incursion, Chet. Just the same, I suggest you remain vigilant, but keep our talk between us for now. Thanks, old son."

SAM BRAXTON DISCONNECTED.

He needed to think. He worried more than ever about his old friend George, and his lovely bride. The last two days brought imminent danger into sharp focus. He and his old partner needed to talk.

Soon.

BLOOD IS THICKER

*D*ING.

Chet needed a break. Out of the corner of his eye he realized he just might have one coming his way.

His old iPhone, already swabbed with alcohol, informed him: *'Notification: New Podcast, Redemption Alley, Episode 6-23, by Jack Rhodes.'*

He smiled, realizing Thursday had snuck up on him. Well, not the entire day, but this part. The fun part: Lee Randle's weekly installment of semi-dark escapism.

Bob and Weave barked outside, but there was no help for that. Chet shuddered at how much noise those two Newfoundlands generated when upset—four to five days each week.

That'll piss off the neighbors, again.

He'd try to explain later. He already did so with Lee and his wife Char next door.

Weave and Bob sensed what was going on, but didn't understand. Couldn't. But dogs smell stress and potential danger.

"Hey, Jess, after we're done, how 'bout we listen to this week's podcast from Lee?"

Her voice quavered, just enough to further shake his confidence. "Sure."

Unspoken: "If you don't kill me first."

Chet dreaded every session in the back of their old 2002 Newmar Dutch Star motorhome, but anticipated its results. Sterility was a huge issue in their forty-foot bus with two giant slobbering and shedding dogs while parked in a dusty RV site.

With fondness, he remembered jamming with Lee next door in the trailer he towed behind his bus the night before last. Chet could only dream of having that much space in his own rig. He remembered that early March evening that meant so much…

"Hey Chet, you're a talented performer.

"You make my old guitar sound good, man."

"Thanks. I have an acoustic-electric too. Stowed under the bed of the old Dutchie but no time to play it, or even to un-bury it from the cases of fluid. Like, since we left Oregon six months ago."

"Must be rough. Four, five hours *every other day?*"

"Yeah, but Jess is a new person after each session. It's fine. Just a pain in the ass to get 'er done in the bus. Turns our tiny bedroom into a little shop of horrors. But we make it work. An extended road trip is her dream."

"And you're making it happen."

"It's a nightmare in Paradise both for me and for Jess."

Lee picked up on that right away.

"And?"

Chet stalled, then answered with all candor—not his nature. At all. Since they hit the road, Lee was the first person with whom he shared a good deal in common. Lee seemed genuinely concerned—about *him*.

Strange since they just became neighbors. Already Chet was pouring his guts out, and they were playing music together. Chet on Lee's guitar, and Lee on one of his flutes. They jacked into his small travel amp with a little reverb and a touch of echo fed by two microphones. The evening unfolded with more ease than he remembered feeling for months.

Lee even hinted they might even try to record a track or two onto his iPad with its GarageBand software through his little ten-channel mixing board. Just for grins.

Chet thought, *Amazing. Darn near a mini-recording studio in this trailer.*

He said, "But every treatment day I worry about screwing up the session. Not trained as a medical professional, I... I fear failing Jess. In-between days, I have trouble sleeping, or thinking about much else. But I see how different a person she is after each session. I mean, in every way! I just didn't realize what a commitment I was making. And now..."

"Now, you're wondering how you'll continue doing this forever between the fear and the joy."

"Yeah."

"Did you train for this?"

Chet was nervous talking about his lack of certification. He thought, *If anything significant goes wrong...*

"Her specialist and the medical equipment supplier required a six-week course, including a formal certification, but we had to cram it into three weeks because we had committed to hit the road. Weather and stuff. So no certificate *and* increased liability. If I could go back...

"Anyway, it was a crash course, and we got distracted with visions of exploring scenic byways together. Now I wonder all the time what did I miss? What *didn't* I learn?"

Lee guided his thick white mustache off his upper lip with the pinched-together thumb and forefinger of his left hand, drawing them apart. He rested the palm of his right hand across the top of the big-leaf maple flute he'd made that was laying across his lap.

His gestures and his gaze were Chet's touchstones. Somehow, Chet calmed down a little. Lee's eyes never left Chet's as he cocked his head to his left, inviting him to continue.

"The machine weighs a lot, and the thirty cartons of dialysis fluid under the bed and in the bus's basement weigh over a thousand pounds. I place most of it over the drive axle. So the bus is overloaded and running on old rubber I can't afford to replace. A blow-out always costs a lot more than new tires, but…"

Lee was a good listener, but then he jumped in. He explained he was an author who wrote fiction and published as Jack Rhodes, always eager to collect stories.

That explained the black t-shirt with white letters and poor grammar that said, 'I make stuff up.' He even said, "Be careful what you say, because you might end up in my next novel or in one of my podcast's story lines."

Chet had met no one like him before.

The more time they spent together, the more guilt Chet felt about keeping secret his relationship with Doc Braxton to watch over him and Kate—Char.

But Doc said to stay quiet about all that.

Without pressing too hard, Lee probed Chet for personal details he didn't mind sharing, even if it ended up in a book.

That might be a good thing.

Chet continued to open up. "Well, first, they taught us that sterilizing everything is a matter of life and death."

Lee said, "And that's damn near 'Mission Impossible,' right? Parked in the desert with constant winds kicking up God knows what?"

"Well, yeah. And her dogs shed copious amounts of hair and whatever else. Before each session, they get put out, and I dust and vacuum the entire bus—ceiling to floor. Jess and I both shower with that pre-surgical antibacterial stuff that stinks.

"Then without a stitch on either of us to contaminate what feels like a crime scene in the making, I swab everything in sight with isopropyl alcohol from a sterile bottle and a freshly laundered rag I keep in a zip-loc until we need it."

"Geez, man."

"Yeah. It's a scene out of a horror movie building up to something bizarre. Still weirds me out. And freakin' nerve-wracking, not to mention exhausting. Reasons I never became a medical professional.

"The procedure itself is always scary. I was hoping to get used to it. That day ain't here yet. With gloved hands I have to swab her port sites, again. And I take the sterile caps off two different tubes, attach a needle to each of those tubes, and then insert one needle into her vein port, and another into her artery port. Then there's the machine end of each tube. That's how her blood gets filtered and returned. And me with just two hands.

"And, oh, man… One of the first times I tapped an artery without the needle snapped all the way into its tube, blood sprayed *everywhere*. A lot. Unbelievable pressure! Looked like 'Helter Skelter.' And we both freaked.

"Lee, I'll never forget what I saw in Jessie's eyes at that moment. Now I lay awake at night wondering if I'll screw up the procedure and kill her *tomorrow*. Four or five days every week. Forever. She doesn't have diabetes, but an inoperable tumor on her kidney screws up the kidney's function, along with some other stuff."

Chet knew Lee would wonder about that, but he always seemed upbeat—at least when he was with him—looking for the sweet spot. Didn't ask if Jesse's condition was terminal.

He said, "But you do it because you love her, and the miraculous improvement in her demeanor. Are you aware what a hero that makes you? Damn, man! Cool."

"Aw…"

"Let's make some music!"

That was then.

OLD BROTHER-IN-ARMS

Y UMA, ARIZONA

Another park welcomed them.

After moving almost four hours west toward Mexicali, Geo and Kate settled into a small park outside Yuma. They wanted to visit a couple with whom they crossed paths all over the country. Kate loved their dog, Zeus, a gargantuan German Shepherd. Geo thought she wanted to visit Zeus as much as his owners.

Not long after they settled in at the Shangri-La RV Resort, they received an unexpected but welcomed call. Geo shouted into his cell, "Sam, you old so-and-so! What a delight. It's been almost a year! How are you faring at that old folks' home?"

"Old son, a pure pleasure to hear your voice, Sir!"

Geo grinned as Sam's Old South enunciation came out *'ta hay-ah yaw vawce, Suh!'*

"And I will remind you I do *not* live in an *old folks' home,* my young friend. I have retired to an *active seniors residence,* thank you very much. My only hardship is a three-to-one ratio of aging cougars to me and my weary geriatric brothers."

Geo smiled both at Sam's description of his accommodations and myriad memories they had made together. Sam saved his life more than once, and together, they foiled a plot to stab Lady Liberty in her heart. At least they slowed that plot to a treacherous crawl. Together.

"So, in what shenanigans are you embroiling yourself these days, old son?" A rhetorical question, the answer to which Geo suspected Sam already knew.

"Sam, I am now exercising my true calling. Compared to you I'm still a pup, but at sixty-nine, I'm having the time of my life as Jack Rhodes, itinerant vagabond, author, and podcaster."

"Well deserved, m'boy."

"Sam, due respect, you old spy, you do nothing without at least two reasons. I'm glad you called, but I can't help but wonder why. I mean, the other reason."

"I'm talking with many old friends. There is a storm brewing. I wanted to give you a heads-up. Do you follow politics?"

"Well, your tone of voice just transformed into agency-speak, so now I'm spooked—uh, no pun intended. Reminds me of the first time we met aboard *Sojourn* in Baltimore and I asked if you worked for the NSA. If looks could slice 'n dice!

"But to answer your question, my old friend, I somewhat follow politics. You were close to President Atherton's predecessor, President Stevens. And I see this new guy trying to sneak into the Oval Office on the shoulders of his pro-business platform while preaching a sour ration of white nationalism. Beyond that, I try to preserve my sanity by remaining agnostic. Why?"

"Well, *Lee*, y'all will not want to learn of this. I am quite sure the 'new guy' is a PB lackey."

Sam was right. He didn't like Jefferson Redding's platform, but this confirmation horrified him. Old storm clouds once again swirled through Geo's consciousness. His stomach took a monumental acid dump, and he fell ill within that very instant. "Oh, shit!"

"Precisely. I'm hearing the agency and others are abuzz preparing for the worst. Lee, this country's climate is approaching explosive proportions. It will get worse. Much worse. You need to know."

"Sam, I can't go back. That whole episode of our shared past damn near killed me. And I mean more than almost turning me into a corpse. I still get sick headaches waking up from the nightmares. Why are we having this discussion now?"

Geo's tone had grown unintentionally strident.

"*We*, Lee? Well, *we* lean on our friends. You go on enjoying your retirement, but with a more watchful eye.

"On a different topic, you may be amused to learn I'm one of Jack Rhodes' most avid readers and listeners. Imagine that. This desiccated quasi-corpse reads fiction and listens to podcasts! For someone who claims to be a political agnostic, however, your podcasts articulate some mighty opinionated sentiments, old son."

"Sam, it's fiction, and science-fiction at that. Nothing more."

But just then, Geo asked himself, *Is my **writing** now lying to me in my own voice?*

Sam continued. "Well, I advise caution. Like it or not, you are a public figure, your false identity hiding behind a thin pseudonym notwithstanding. Your readership and listeners have made you a celebrity of sorts. And celebrities are not immune to hate crimes that some might classify domestic terrorism. Or conspiracies. Evidence? Your growing collection of 'dark mail.'"

"Sam, how do you…"

"M'boy, you *are* adorable! Remember with whom you are speaking. I live in an old folks' home, but I keep in touch with old friends, *and* some new ones—I still have something to offer. They still call me. And I watch out for *all* of my friends, Lee."

Geo could only bask in wonder! Ever the spymaster. His gut continued to churn like butter in an old-fashioned beater.

Without warning, Sam embarked on a fit of coughing. He covered the phone, and a nerve-wracking half-minute elapsed before he returned to the phone.

"Sorry. My lungs have a mind of their own these days. Nothing serious."

"Sam…"

"I must go soon. You and Charlotte travel a great deal. I suggest you avoid isolated rural areas in the Deep South. If you are able, favor urban or suburban areas in the Southwest, or anywhere in the Midwest. And do exercise an additional modicum of caution when articulating your, ah, opinions, with anyone face-to-face, or while not under the cover of your alter-egos."

Sam did not elaborate—*I must go soon?* Did he mean ending the call soon? Or was his health at his advanced age worse than he was sharing?

"Oh, Sam, I hope you're all right. We're fine, although you're frightening me here."

"Good. No need to over-react. I just ask that you remain vigilant and consider tempering your rhetoric in your podcasts, even just a little; however, I know that's a big ask. You are a man of unshakable integrity. *And* you are one hell of a writer, old son! Who *is* your producer? Outstanding product! I can't wait for next week's episode. My most fond affection to dear Ka… Charlotte. Until later, Lee."

Click.

Did you know you can hear a wry smile over the phone? If you just listen?

Armed with his now-more-vigilant point of view, Geo considered having published his latest book in a new light. Under the pen name of Jack Rhodes, he had published an anthology of what the book's tagline called, *'an adventurous collection of provocative poetry as a colorful social art form.'* Also to become an audiobook.

He had indeed come off the political sidelines and offered bold opinions in his poetry and essays. Against his better judgment. But it felt good. Until now.

Not sure who might read such a book, his concern wasn't quantifiable. Although this diversionary effort into published verse in addition to prose garnered more attention than he had dared hope, likely launched by his podcast audience.

This brewed more expectations. Of yet another book. Not to mention more visibility to his burgeoning political proclivities. And to his critics. Armed with Sam's warning, he now expected more 'dark mail,' or maybe worse.

There was no doubt in his mind. His retirement had just taken an ominous turn. But he always walked the talk with the cliché, 'Plan for the worst, hope for the best.'

Geo suspected but could not know the worst had already become someone else's plan for him.

But for now, he had work to do.

TUCSON, ARIZONA

CHET BRAVERMAN HAD A BAD FEELING...

He had entered their ancient motorhome ten minutes earlier from his hourly perimeter check. He began reading one of Lee's latest books—of poetry. Like his *Redemption Alley* podcasts and novels, he published it under the pseudonym of Jack Rhodes.

Poetry was not what Chet enjoyed reading most. But because Lee was his neighbor, though they were currently visiting friends down in Yuma, he enjoyed learning more of his buddy through his published works. Even his poetry. He discovered the book to be thought-provoking and entertaining.

Still tied out, the dogs began chuffing. One barked once before both fell silent—*at the same time.* Now Chet's six senses screamed *danger!*

He laid down the book and creeped to the bedroom in the bus's rear where Jessie read a new release from her favorite romance-mystery author.

"Honey, get behind the bed and stay there."

"What's going on. Does this have something to do with that call from Sam?"

The skepticism in her voice was unmistakable as she gently closed her book.

"I heard you talking to him outside last night. That was him, right? You didn't mention it to me, but I could see it rattled you. And do you want to tell me about those new bruises, hon?"

"Now is not the time. *Please.* We have visitors. Not friendlies. Catch my drift?"

He saw the sudden advent of terror instantly etched into her now-distorted features. Couldn't blame her. She was an intelligence analyst at the agency before retiring, not a field agent like him. He blew her a kiss and flashed a confident smile. Then he went to work.

Chet stayed low as he crept forward through their motorhome's living room, back toward the front door on the passenger's side. He cursed himself for having lowered the opaque windshield and cockpit window shades. That afforded them privacy, but he now needed to know what was going on outside.

He recalled Sam's warning to stay vigilant. Now he condemned himself for putting the love of his life in danger. Neither he nor the good doctor thought it would come to this. At least not so soon.

Chet saw movement outside. Spotted the shielded rays of at least one flashlight near a driver's side window—the blind side. He most feared an explosive device tossed under the coach. He realized he needed to carry the fight outside and away. Chose not to turn off the lights inside. That would signal he knew they were out there. So with some speed, he might be able to effect some surprise, a tactical lever.

Standing in his sandals on threadbare beige carpeting, the unlocked door to the overhead gun safe swung wide to reveal its contents. Chet clutched the compact nine millimeter Beretta APX by its short barrel. He flipped it in mid-air to shift his grasp to its handle heavy with an internal thirteen-round clip.

With his other hand he switched off the weapon's safety. Slid the slide back just enough to ensure a round was in the chamber. He grabbed a handful of t-shirt at his waist, lowered his head, and mopped his brow with it. Salty sweat in his eyes for the next fifteen seconds would not be acceptable. He knew his time was here. Now.

Speed and agility must be his best allies. After kicking off his flip-flops, he threw the entrance door open. It banged hard against its hinges and latched open. He skipped the steps, jumping down almost four feet to the pebbled RV site. Pain shot through his calloused feet but only intensified his resolve. Started a tuck-and-roll, and that's when it hit him.

He splayed forward before being pivoted by the impact's momentum. A pile driver had pummeled his back left of center, up high. Chet landed face up. Through the instant fog of his paralysis he watched as two men crept up the old Dutchie's steps.

They passed through the door he had thrown wide. Had he lost time? He saw tendrils of... fog? Then flames. He spurred himself to action, but remained frozen in his nightmare, despite his resolve.

Two men in masks dragged him through the swirling fog—or was it smoke?—up into the coach. Curious. The faint odor of propane gas. He knew propane was odorless, but they infused it with skunk juice so lethal leaks became obvious to the nearest nose.

Both small flames *and* the smell of skunk juice made no logical sense. But the creeping blackness left him not caring. At all. Why was that? He knew. Moments before, he was so motivated to... what?

Had Jessie suffered?

DODGED BULLET

Y UMA, ARIZONA

K ATE SHRIEKED IN THE BUS'S LIVING ROOM.

He heard her scream as he finished brushing his teeth in the bathroom farther aft.

Even though they were in Yuma visiting friends, their satellite TV still picked up the local Tucson news stations.

"Geo, come here and listen to this story out of Tucson. An RV fire and explosion. They, uh, they think it's us! Oh, no. Are they really talking about Chet and Jessie?"

Geo could just hear the TV mounted above the windshield from the bathroom, came rushing out.

"Oh, shit. Rewind. I want to hear the story for myself. Remember? Their reservation expired. And they wanted to stay another week at Voyager, so they'd still be there."

"Did this happen because they moved their motorhome into *our* site in front of *our* trailer? That must be why they identified the bodies as ours! *Oh, poor Jess and Chet...*"

Now sobbing without restraint as the news took root, Kate side-handed the remote onto the couch next to her as if it burned her hand. She stared at the accidentally paused DVR image of a burned-out fiberglass bus carcass crouched in front of their own trailer. They saw its familiar nose cap discolored from the now-extinguished fire.

Geo and Kate had not told the resort's management of their arrangement with Chet and Jessie, so the mistake made sense. Their site, their trailer, two incinerated bodies, and to the uninitiated eye, a similar motorhome—burned out to its aluminum skeleton and chassis. He could even see the tires melted into dark gray-green puddles.

The two large black dogs the camera crew caught loitering at the site must be Bob and Weave.

"Babe, that fire was meant for us."

Then Geo's anger surged beyond his grief at the loss of two friends. This was no accident.

How might this relate to Sam's recent call? If so, why now? Should he call Sam? Were cell calls secure? Then guilt pummeled him like a boxer who takes an intentional beating in the ring. If someone were looking to harm them, but now assumed they were dead, was that a good thing? But instant remorse pinned him to the ropes.

The horrifying memories from eight years earlier flooded Geo's mind. Once again, they threatened to beat him senseless in yet another all-consuming round of bitterness, grief, and anger.

Not again!

DIRE NEWS

TUCSON, ARIZONA

THE TV NEWSCASTER DRONED ON.

April Somebody-or-other on the ABC affiliate KGUN 9 sounded like the story bored her, but she tried to sound shocked. Too much inflection in her voice seemed contrived and her expression displayed more-than-appropriate sorrow speaking of victims she didn't know or care about.

None of her melodramatic performance reached her apathetic eyes. They remained frozen in too much make-up and Botox-induced facial paralysis.

"The tragic motorhome fire at the Voyager RV Resort east of Tucson left two dead—a retired couple, Mr. and Mrs. Lee Reynolds Randle.

"According to the Pima County Fire Chief, Joseph Santiago, a propane gas leak appeared to cause the fire and subsequent explosion. They use propane gas in recreational vehicles for heating and cooking.

"Mrs. Randle passed away in her sleep. They discovered her remains in the rear bedroom of the motorhome. They found Mr. Randle in the kitchen area. Chief Santiago speculates that Mr. Randle may have realized something was wrong and went to the kitchen to investigate where smoke inhalation apparently overcame him before the devastating explosion."

WASHINGTON, DC

AN ALERT SOUNDED.

Since the US Marshal's office keyed off any news stories containing the names of protectees, the story caught Marshal Cassandra Nobles' attention. The Randles were her team's protectees.

She was in Washington on other business, and contacted her supervisor to start the inevitable investigation. They must consider the possibility of foul play. The Randles' high profile sponsors—a senior NSA officer and a former US president—would demand it. Unbelievable. But first, the hardest part.

ALEXANDRIA, VIRGINIA

WILL IT EVER END?

Doctor F Samuel Braxton, veteran intelligence operative and hardened spook long retired, was one of the toughest nuts anywhere. Right now he just felt old and vulnerable.

He stooped more than stood, but only for short periods before he'd lose his balance, or his will.

These days he could only endure sitting in his room reading intelligence briefs on his laptop for an hour or two at a time. But he looked forward to Wednesday mornings. The old farts that played Bocce sometimes even made him smile.

Sam left his ninetieth birthday behind more than a half-decade ago, but he could still roll a damn fine ball down an astroturf lane. Or whatever they called that green crap now.

God, he still missed Mary, gone now just too damn long. As he limped toward the Bocce courts his cell vibrated.

Seconds later, Marshal Nobles' call forced him to drop onto a nearby bench at the edge of the Bocce courts. Otherwise, he might have collapsed where he stood.

"Colonel Braxton? Sir?

"This is US Marshall Cassie Nobles."

"Oh, please no. Are they gone?"

"Yes, Sir. I'm afraid so."

"*Goddammit*, what *happened*?"

She shuddered at the feral seething she could hear in this intelligence legend's voice, and her own body language reflected, what, fear?

"Sir, we've just begun investigating, but…"

Colonel Braxton's next words were soft, but definitive.

"Marshal Nobles, there is a leak. And it cost two wonderful people their lives. Find the leak, or I'll have your job. And then things will get nasty. Copy?"

"Affirmative, Colonel. I'll keep you posted."

"You do that, young lady."

Was his voice breaking? Shit!

In a daze, Sam stumbled home.

He dropped into his recliner and stared at a treasured photo. Geo,

Kate, and a younger version of himself relaxed on the foredeck of *Sojourn*. They met when he sold that stout little sailing ship to them in Baltimore, November 1995, after which they became fast friends.

That boat—later exploded and burned in 2008 by a vindictive Patriot Brotherhood operative—remained an indelible memory. And now this delightful couple dying in an explosion and a fire eight years later by a different killer? The irony ate at him like corrosive emotional acid.

How long did he sit there? How many questions did this erstwhile chief worldwide interrogator of the National Security Agency ask himself, not finding any answers? Geo and Kate gone? How did those bastards find them? Why now? He tortured himself for hours.

His cell vibrated. It rang. He did not answer. This happened three more times. After he wearied of the vague disruptions to his pity party of self-loathing, he dug the phone out of his sweater vest's pocket in slow motion. Call ID blocked. Answered anyway.

"This is Sam." The next two seconds put this hardened veteran into a tail spin. He recognized the voice in an instant, and his heart swelled.

"*Sojourn Portable*. Shanghai-La, Yuma. In 48. Out."

Click.

COLD GRIEF

Y UMA, ARIZONA

Were Chet and Jessie's deaths an accident? I want to believe so, but they told us to assume the worst.

Sam engaged the US Marshals Service back in 2008—almost nine years ago—on their behalf. So Kate and Geo relocated under new identities. Sold everything, at least on paper. They began a life on the road in their motorhome. They were ghosts in the wind. Had it been cavalier or even arrogant to assume they had succeeded?

GEO TOOK REFUGE IN HIS WRITING.

That did not quell the grief, but it helped. He sat at his desk and dived in.

He thought, *Some levity? Yes, a distraction.*

Kate saw him working. "You're still producing *The Alley*? After all that's happened?"

"Why wouldn't I? C'mon, I'm a writer. Do we stop living because someone else died?"

She had been walking away. When she heard that, however, she turned. After an icy pause, she said, "Oh, Geo, *that* is so very cold."

"Is it? Did it occur to you that maybe someone is *trying* to get me to stop?"

"Under threat of death?" Her question was rhetorical and an indictment of his lame excuse. "And that's your motivation to keep publishing?"

"Well, Kate, it's what I do. And I find it therapeutic as hell."

"Okay. Whatever."

His words had not mollified her, but with nowhere to stomp off to in her anger and frustration, she plopped down into her recliner next to him. Her body language screamed she considered him a callous ass.

We all deal with grief in different ways. Maybe a few thousand words will... Whatever.

He tapped the right-pointing arrow on his iPhone to listen while he began on the script for another episode.

WELL MET

CURIOUS...

Geo's friend, Indian Joe, showed up at the same RV park not long after their arrival in Yuma. Kate dismissed it as another path-crossing so common with full-time RVers.

She was just glad Geo had a friend. Otherwise, she worried he seemed happiest when he was by himself these days. As they migrated to increasingly remote locations, they felt both safer *and* more isolated, including from each other.

Even though Kate loved dogs, she didn't own one. After her boxer Banger died thirteen years earlier, she decided not to repeat that heartache. Instead, she lavished affection on other people's pets.

Today the lucky recipient was a new friend's French bulldog named Jax. Geo called him Tank because he was built stout and heavy even though he was only fourteen inches at the shoulder. Jax loved Kate too, especially when he walked with her. Still, he tried to get as far ahead of her on their walks as his extendable leash allowed.

As Kate passed Joe's vintage bumper-pull trailer, she spotted the younger man sitting in the shade of his awning playing a lovely flute, soft and serene. Even though Joe and Geo looked so very different, they were much alike.

The music stopped. "Hey, Char, who's your friend?" She'd *never* get used to being called Char.

"Hey, Joe, meet Jax. He's even more ill-behaved than my dear hubby."

"Jax, dude, how you doin' little man?"

The gray-black Frenchy looked up at Joe with his squished-face, his too-long tongue dangling to the left over his serious under-bite. He just snorted in defiance as if to say, "She's mine, you fool!"

Joe amused Kate. He seemed to understand what the dog was saying. She realized he was so much more perceptive than most anyone she had ever met.

"No offense, little dude." When he spotted Kate's quizzical gaze, he said, "He looks jealous."

Kate laughed. She wasn't doing much of that these days. Then she got serious.

～

"Joe, can I ask you about Lee?

"Does his behavior strike you as unusual?"

He'd need to exercise care here. "Um, define unusual."

"He's having lots of awful dreams. And this whole copper screen thing, for example. Do you know about that?"

"Well, yeah. He told me he took a nasty beating a good while ago and has suffered from it off-and-on ever since. Not sure if he meant body, mind, or both. I assumed the latter after he told me the story. Not unlike returning from combat."

Comprehension peeked out from the desperate denial in Kate's eyes. Joe backed off to a more conventional approach.

"Look, Char, each person deals with grief and stress in their own way. This is how Lee copes. This is how my ancestors dealt with theirs. They reach for a base of clarity amid confusion. It's okay, Char."

"I didn't think of it that way. He's lined his entire trailer with wire mesh. Says it's for his ham radio stuff that just collects dust in boxes. I'm worried."

"Yeah. He's been researching electromagnetic poisoning—EMP. The science behind that is solid. It's a real thing. More a matter of degree. I'm not sure. Lee says it's gonna get worse, and he's preparing for that. Saner people are out there prepping for the zombie apocalypse. I'm not there yet, but I'm just an ignorant injun."

"Yeah, sure you are." She debated whether she should mention another reason for Geo's—for their—emotional distress. She proceeded with care.

"Joe, we also lost two other friends a few weeks ago."

"Jessie and Chet?"

"Uh, yeah. How *d'you* know about that?"

"Well, Lee must have mentioned them. A motorhome fire, right?"

Kate's antennae wriggled, but she resisted broadcasting her doubt.

"Yeah. Over in Tucson. Although they didn't know each other long, Geo bonded with Chet. I liked Jessie. And then they were just gone. What should I do, Joe?"

"Hey kiddo, besides processing your own grief, you're doing it. Just listen. And pay attention. Lee's a complicated guy. I don't think he's any crazier than me, but *that* might worry you. I've introduced him to some of my friends, and that is nothing but positive therapy.

"If a TBI jarred his wiring back in the day, along with the recent loss of friends, the best we can do is support him. And you. So sayeth your resident red man."

Realizing this was her longest conversation with Joe to date, she appeared embarrassed.

"Thanks, Joe. I love that wingnut so much, I worry, even when I don't have to. It's the mom in me."

"Yeah, Char, Lee told me that. He worries about you too. That's why you guys are still together. And Char?"

"Yeah?" She sensed what was coming.

"I've seen combat. So has Lee, but as a civilian. That's much scarier than as a trained dogface. And closer to home. Makes it different, but the same. The Coast Guard trained him for search and rescue, not for combat. Send his ass to the VA to talk to a professional."

"Thanks, Joe. Hey, when we move, again, we always do, Geo's going to miss you."

"Same here, Char, but you never know. Remember, I'm footloose too. Our paths will cross again. And things have a habit of working out more often than not for good people, kiddo."

But Kate could see or hear that Indian Joe had a bad feeling.

~

SAM SNAGGED A THRILL ESCAPING...

That's what he thought each time he got out of that residence he called *God's Waiting Room*, even if only for a few days.

Out in the field again, he felt ecstatic at the great news about his dear friends. Some days were better than others. Much better.

They embraced as if resurrected from the grave. Kate and Geo *had* been—resurrected.

Sam found the motorhome's five steps daunting and was not shy accepting help from his friends climbing them. Nobody wanted to stay exposed outside.

Sam said, "George, old son! Or should I say, '*Sojourn Portable?*' You remembered your tradecraft! I'm so proud. And yes, I miss that old boat too."

~

GEO SMILED.

Kate saw more than pride in Sam's face.

He is so much older.

They hadn't met face-to-face in almost eight years.

Geo said, "Sam, you old coot. I'm surprised you're still alive. God, man, you got so *old!*"

The smiles could not have been brighter or wider.

"Hey, you pup of a sea dog, you used the word 'old' twice. Must be true. When you're threatening to kiss a hundred years of age yourself, I'll listen to your derogatories. I am still vertical and taking nourishment, albeit less perpendicular to the ground as time passes, and I'm 'eating' more liquid than solid these days."

Sam turned to Kate. Without saying a word, he embraced her. She found her next breath more of a throttled gasp. He released her, gripped her by the shoulders, stared up into her fierce blue eyes without uttering a word.

Watching his lower lip quiver, she said, "Sam, I swear. You not only grew older, you're shorter too."

Standing in the motorhome's living room now cramped with three standing adults, these old friends laughed hard—too hard. Six eyes watered. This cathartic release of nervous tension offered them a temporary blanket of mutual warmth.

After they all sat, Sam with some difficulty, Geo explained their escape from death. Their collective mood darkened.

"Old son, I am so sorry about the loss of your friends." A long introspective silence.

"But to the business at hand, we must assume you were the intended targets and the likelihood of imminent danger should anyone discover you have not passed. We must assume this error will out. And soon.

"So let us discuss how we will leverage this temporary cloak of invisibility for which your friends paid so dear a price."

Kate's uneasiness at this sudden transition to leverage their loss was obvious.

"Sam..."

"Kate, a monumental tragedy, the loss of..."

"Jessie and Chet. Braverman."

"Yes. Jessie and Chet. Now we need to think about *your* safety. As I used my tradecraft to get here undetected, Geo was right to send me a cryptic message. Someone close or inside leaked your identity and location. We need to discover who, leaving you in your shallow graves for as long as possible. Does that make sense, my dear?"

Kate couldn't help but offer a weak smile as she heard, *'mah deah.'*

Sam always coaxed a smile, even amidst grief and fear. What an amazing little man. They would *so* miss him some day soon.

Then, another pregnant pause. Sam's momentary silence spoke volumes.

"You okay, Sam?" Something else weighed on his mind. Geo shut up and listened.

"George, since your home features wheels you can move quickly, correct?"

"Yes. But we're booked for another month over at Voyager in Tucson. The trailer is still there. This trip to Yuma was just a diversion. But now…"

"Old son, you are no longer safe, neither in Tucson nor here. Retrieve your trailer with minimum fuss if you must—I can clear an unofficial path—and move to a more remote location. Can you do that?"

Kate looked at Geo. She didn't need to say the words. He knew she was thinking, *You promised no more fear.* But she was strong and offered the slightest nod.

Geo finally said, "Uh, yes. We visited a small remote campground two years ago outside an almost-ghost-town. They're never busy, and people out there mind their own business more than most. Hotter than the heart of Hell this time of year, but cozy and off the beaten path."

"Perfect. I suggest you make preparations. Now if you would, please hail me a taxi, I must attend to other urgent business."

Both Kate and Geo offered to help Sam up from his low perch on their sofa, but he declined with a too-sharp sideways shake of his already-hatted head. He took some time rocking back and forward to gather momentum before shifting the bulk of his hundred-pound weight onto the four-footed cane he gripped with both hands between his knees. An awkward but practiced routine to watch. They respected his wishes. A proud little man.

While he was getting up, Geo said, "So soon? Hey Sam, didn't we get you retired?"

"No longer, old son. No longer. Time is now of the essence."

~

Joe just showed up knocking.

Without calling him over to meet Sam, he just appeared at their motorhome's door as they prepared to usher Sam out. Geo found Joe's impeccable timing unnerving.

How he appeared after every move also perplexed Geo, but that was not uncommon. They saw the same folks in different places wherever they went. Paths crossed. Lives intersected.

"Come in, ole buddy. Perfect timing."

In addition to his eclectic appearance, Joe's heavy footfalls up the stairs and relaxed shoulders announced his casual demeanor. His eyes darted upward and around as he ascended each step, conscious of all overhead obstacles. This hinted that a low ceiling and cramped spaces required such diligent habits in his own trailer.

"Sam, I'm delighted to introduce you to another dear friend. This scrawny outlaw is Indian Joe. That's a pretentious alias—not one of his own choosing, he tells me. Joe is a stand-up guy whatever we call him.

"Joe, this ancient codger is our dear old friend, Sam. I love you both and I'm pleased you could meet.

Sam said, "A pleasure, Sir!"

Setting aside his walking stick, quick to remind everyone it was *not* a cane, Sam pumped Joe's hand with both of his own. Meeting his gaze, he judged his character as he spoke. Nothing escaped Sam, ever the interrogator.

"Likewise, Sam. Heard a lot about you, Sir."

"All lies, Joe. At least as far as you know." Smirk.

Sam continued to observe Joe's body language, inflections in his voice, and his micro-expressions. He liked what he saw, but for reasons he couldn't explain, he would hazard no guesses. Not yet.

~

Joe said, "Thank you...

"… for watching the boy's back, Colonel." He knew Lee found this amusing since he was at least thirty years Joe's senior.

"We take care of each other. And Lee, you talk too much. Joe, these are dark times. I'd appreciate discretion in your relationship with this young man and your knowledge of me."

Sam chuckled for a moment at Joe's double-take in Geo's direction.

"Yes, I consider anyone younger than my ninety-six years, and that includes Lee here, to be a 'young man.'"

But that was not the reason for Joe's double-take. He wondered what the old man knew about himself that he wasn't telling? Most wouldn't have noticed, but the way old Sam looked him over unsettled him, and he was impossible to read, but Joe did not allow that to show.

Joe recovered and said, "Sir, I am discreet. Lee can tell you. Are we in danger from some big city folks out here, Sam? No matter. We stand ready."

"So you read people too, Joe. You possess admirable powers of perception and observation. I would just say that your current situation calls for vigilance. I've shared as much with Lee."

Geo—Lee—said, "Yeah, old news that refuses to fade. We'll be careful."

"Now I must depart. Lee, if you please, that taxi?"

ISOLATED CONCEPTS

B LACK ROCK, ARIZONA

But this summer was eery, and anything *but* quiet.

Sam had suggested they move to a place more quaint—more rural —a month ago. So they took a day soon after that to move and set up at this remote campground in the middle of oblivion.

En route, the trip to Tucson to retrieve their trailer was a quick in and out. All evidence of the fire had been cleaned up, except for the discoloration and some buckling of their trailer's aluminum-skinned nose.

Kate thought, *Here, Geo hangs around strange folks who fill his head with stranger notions. They call themselves the Lunatic Fringe? Really? Like a club of geriatrics who gravitate toward high drama? Or a gang? Whatever. Friends of Joe's, so...*

She believed their trips to the Fringer's camp out in the desert harmless enough. Geo visited now and then with Joe in his ATV. She'd squint her eyes and admonish them with a look of concern, but would dimple her cheeks and shout, "Play nice, boys."

Geo seemed happy here and happier out there. That was good enough. But Kate worried the heat might compound other worries about his state of mind.

And she pondered Joe following them from Tucson to Yuma, and now to Black Rock. But wanderers wander. Not uncommon. Joe explained this was where he grew up. Had lots of friends 'round these parts.' Serendipity?

He had moved his old bumper-pull trailer three sites north of them. Closer to the fence that separated this small park from thousands of acres of low desert that stretched east and south all the way to the border.

When not chasing around in Joe's ATV, the boys spend a lot of time sitting out in the shade of our trailer most evenings, or over by Joe's.

She smiled.

Especially once the sun sets and the temp drops into the nineties, I always know where to find them.

She really was glad Geo had a friend to hang with, even though Joe was, well, even more eccentric than her hubby. She liked him, and if Geo trusted him, that was good enough for her.

Sometimes she heard them playing their flutes. Geo said Joe was an awesome flutie, not that she cared much for that music. She was a Moody Blues fan.

When it was quiet, she'd take a short walk for some exercise. She also wanted to see what the boys were up to. If they weren't chatting, she knew closed eyes and slack jaws meant they were meditating.

Kate tolerated Geo's evolving eccentricities. When he presented her with his latest bolt of inspiration, though, she said, "Isn't this kind of radical, Geo?"

In response, Geo spoke so fast Kate struggled to understand him. She reeled at his energy, even in this oppressive heat, low humidity notwithstanding.

And it seemed he'd moved on after losing Chet and Jessie. Should that please her or trouble her? Was he now over-compensating? Were

Joe and his deep-desert friends exerting too much influence on him? But this latest inspiration didn't seem to come from them.

"No, no, this is not all that radical, Babe. Most people just haven't researched this. The science is solid. Dangerous proliferation is imminent.

"With new generations of wireless technologies deploying soon, increasingly unhealthy electromagnetic waves will bombard us not only from our phones and tablets as they communicate with thousands of towers and other devices all around us, but also from clouds of satellites in space.

"Like climate change, most will deny the correlation between EMP, or ElectroMagnetic Poisoning, and its symptoms. But before long, it'll be too late for an entire generation growing up inside a planetary microwave.

"Look, I know this sounds crazy, but…"

"Yes, Geo, it does! So that ham radio explanation for all that chicken wire in your trailer. That was bullshit, wasn't it?"

～

"So let's talk about insurance…

"Remember all our discussions about God and religion?"

"Geo, you had better not ask me to just have faith. I *will* hurt you."

She was joking, but serious at the same time. The anxiety in her voice was unmistakable.

His words continued to tumble out, fizzing with exuberance. His eyes seemed on fire. He was out of breath since he wasn't taking enough time to breathe. She couldn't recall ever seeing him so animated, and her heart swelled while her mind fretted.

"No, Babe. Let me explain. You can read the sixteen or seventeen papers I've studied if you like, all by credentialed academicians. And that just scratches the surface. Never mind all that now. Remember *Pascal's Wager?*"

"Uh, yeah. Pascal's Bet. Blaise Pascal, French philosopher, eighteenth-century, right?"

"Yeah. Seventeenth-century mathematician. Anyway, Pascal posited that we bet with our lives that God either exists, or He or She doesn't. Pascal even calculated the mathematical probability of God's existence.

"But here is one take on this. Whether you believe in God or you don't, why not hedge your bet? Believe, and if the whole God-thing is nothing more than a societal or moral control mechanism, you've lost less in life than a potential eternity in Hell.

"Same with EMP. A few bucks for some copper screening, we call it our homage to steampunk decor or something, and enjoy a little extra cheap insurance that *may* never be necessary.

"Logical, forward-thinking, not irrational. Besides, what a wonderful way to inspire conversation with visitors? The Fringers would *love* that!"

He was a little boy asking a petulant parent if he could keep the puppy he just found. All expectant and eager and not even considering a disappointing answer.

"Oh, geez, Geo, go get your stupid screen. But we're gonna get a decorator to help us install it so it looks better than that mess you stapled all over the inside of your man cave. Agreed?"

"Sure, sure! Great. I'll order it right away!" He pecked her cheek with gratitude. Rushed off to order materials at the small hardware store fifteen miles away in the village of Quartzsite. His local friends encouraged him to patronize local businesses instead of mail order. *We gain more positive energy,* they said. Or something.

Kate's brow took on a permanent furrow of worry.

OPERATION FAMILY VALUES

LEXANDRIA, VIRGINIA

Sam's rooms were pleasant enough.

He collected two government pensions. The first came from the US Army, and a second from the NSA. Together, they established his financial independence. Add the annual stipend from Walter Reed as their retired Chief of Surgery, and he easily afforded his well-appointed but small apartment in the Hermitage Assisted Living Community.

Sam's curved middle-floor balcony featured a plate glass railing so as not to impede the view, such as it was.

He knew he was blessed, and appreciated the marvelous staff who cleaned and delivered his half-dozen newspapers each morning.

Sam always enjoyed a young person with whom to chat. He made a point of opening his door to the hallway at the precise moment a staffer arrived with his papers and mail. *Just* before they knocked. Never failed to startle them. Simple pleasures.

A wonderful dining room served bland food about which everyone complained. Since Mary passed, his diet had suffered, until this place. He shouldn't have a care in the world. So why did he worry so? And why did he feel so useless in this gorgeous gilded cage?

The slight and fragile Colonel Doctor F Samuel Braxton remained a friend to presidents, to politicians, and was still an intelligence community legend. At ninety-six, Sam considered the possibility he didn't know himself at all. Even after almost a century of practice.

He mused, *I've been in the business of reading people, understanding and exposing their deepest secrets, and protecting my nation for eight decades. Yet I still fear my own confused mental meanderings above all others.*

Weeks passed since an RV fire killed two of his agency friends. Why hadn't he told George or Kate that Chet and Jessica Braverman were old comrades—two of his agency irregulars after they and he retired? And why didn't he tell them that as a favor to him, Chet's vigil over them likely already saved their lives at least once? Before it cost them both of theirs?

He must tell them, hadn't he?

Sam had resisted cracking his near-perfect mask of indifference at the death of his friends when he talked with Kate and George about their murders. They suspected nothing.

In his grief, George told him of Jessie's dialysis sessions, and how taxing they were on both her and Chet. That surprised Sam. In retrospect, he realized Chet had dropped clues of Jessica's infirmity, but that didn't suit his narrative, did it?

*Lord, what have I become? Despite hardships, they acquiesced to my plea for help, to watch over another couple in potential jeopardy. **And why am I keeping this to myself?** Would this devastate George? Whose feelings am I trying to spare here? God, I miss Mary!*

Sam envisioned his beloved wife every time he saw how George looked at Kate. He now felt every day of his ninety-six years pressing down on him. A profound weariness engulfed him, but he had work to do.

At that he almost smiled.

The phone in his hand seemed heavy as he dialed his friend and waited for the encryption algorithm to finish its task. After completing the connection and he heard the voice of perhaps his closest friend, Sam got to the point posthaste.

"George, I'm going to ask that you plan for your long-lost uncle and his family to visit you for a while."

"Wait, what?"

"Old son, there's been another attempt to assassinate President Atherton *from within the White House*. They meant his death to appear a natural illness. Such a sophisticated attack could only happen with a collaboration at the highest levels of our government. Sound familiar?"

BLACK ROCK, ARIZONA

GEO'S STOMACH FLIPPED.

He stared at the back of the motorhome's passenger seat as he sat sideways near his desk, tugging on his right eyebrow in need of a trim. His left hand held the phone. It became slippery with sweat. *The Brotherhood?*

"Oh, God, Sam, not again."

"George, not again. *Still*. Although they've identified no perpetrators yet, suspicions run rampant. No one is trusting anyone outside a select few. Again.

"Further, a recent attack on President Stevens has compounded matters. John tells me neither he nor Atherton trust his Secret Service Director. For the first time in history, both a sitting president and his predecessor employ *private* protection. Also, Atherton just fired his, still recovering from his bout with arsenic poisoning. That's how bad it is."

Sam paused. Nobody spoke. George's rapid and shallow breathing dominated the call. Then...

"George, President Stevens appealed to me for desperate help in disappearing outside of *any* government orbit. *And* if we orchestrate this with care, we might just jump onto the offensive. For the first time, we have high-level intel from *inside* the Brotherhood. We may have them on the ropes, George. With your help we could finish this. Interested?"

After the shortest of introspective pauses and an effort to overcome the nausea that threatened to overwhelm him, amidst his noisy shallow breaths Geo said, "Sam, you already know I am. Whatever it takes. If we can end this madness, I'm all in."

"Well, for now, old son, you and Kate will play gracious hosts. You are an operator again, my friend!"

Geo scratched his head and rubbed the back of his neck. His chest tightened like a raw egg in a vice as Sam explained his outlandish strategy.

But what if this works?

~

SAM FELT SOME COMPUNCTION USING GEORGE.

He and his orbit would be bait, but for the greater good and all that. Would he do this to his friends? And to use an ex-president as a shiny lure to catch some big fish? A bold plan. He took solace in his confidence and in the people executing the plan.

This could work.

~

SAM TOLD A PRESIDENT JUST WHERE TO GO.

He directed John W. Stevens and his security team to drive—not fly—to Arizona in two mid-size SUVs rented by the least-known member of his team. From some large rental agency in a large nearby city.

John asked Mick Sandstrom to handle this. Mick rented two Ford Edges in his own name at the BWI Airport outside Baltimore. None on the team possessed false IDs with backstories, but nobody knew Mick, did they?

~

Sam then directed Geo what he must do.

He was to rent two small mobile homes, the kind popular with vacationers and snowbirds. One was for John, and the other was for his three-person detail led by Sam's old acquaintance, Derek Cheevers.

Sam had never met Darla Evans nor Mick Sandstrom, but Derek said they helped save John's life from certain death in Maryland recently.

~

Next, Sam would recruit Cassie Nobles.

She was the US Marshal and supervisory agent responsible for Geo's and Kate's placement and maintenance within Witness Protection, also called Witness Security, or WitSec.

Since his friends were still alive after years of Marshal Noble's protection, despite the one incident involving the Bravermans, Sam would trust her, but only her.

He asked her to visit him in Alexandria. She resisted the notion until he mentioned this was a request from her protectees' *other sponsor*. As she was in Washington on other business, she drove to Alexandria that same day.

After Sam briefed her, she made a call of her own to one of her assets. To Sam, she seemed the consummate professional, but he observed her darting eyes, and the sheen of sweat that beaded on her brow as they talked.

One hand clutched and flexed the other as if in a white-knuckled prayer. She told Sam his plan was way above her pay grade, and she struggled when he told her in no uncertain terms they *must not* get her chain of command involved. But that *so* broke protocol.

Sam warned her, "We *are* wandering outside protocol, Marshal, but protocol could get our president killed if we trust the wrong person. John and I need you to contain this within your team. We'll straighten all this out once we know who we can trust. Alright?"

"Doctor Braxton, I'm not sure…"

"Marshal Nobles—Cassie—this is imperative. Any other approach could cause the death of innocent people, decent people. You'd jeopardize your protectees, President Stevens, and his security detail. Not to mention collateral damage. *Do you understand?*"

After a few moments of reflection, Sam noticed a different set to her jaw, her left eye squinting more than her right, and a definite pucker in her left cheek. Her eyes ceased their darting about. Her posture leaned into any residual doubt, and an abrupt nod of finality completed her transformation.

The brevity of her uncertainty impressed the old spook. With her career on the line, she would execute what she now knew to be the next right series of moves. On her own.

Bravo!

"Yes, Sir. I guess I don't have to like it. My job is to protect and to exercise initiative. Yes, I get it."

"I will ensure Presidents Stevens and Atherton coordinate with Director Banfield at Homeland. We keep this circle *tight.*"

"Wow."

"Well said, Marshal."

TRIP PLANNING

P OTOMAC, MARYLAND

JUST TWO PEOPLE TALKING…

The brief call from an operative to her handler entailed risk but conveyed important intel.

She said, "They're desperate to control the next election. They see Stevens as a significant loose end. Sounds as if they are now less interested in Atherton. They're just trying to get past all that poisoning business."

"Good news, that. What else have you discovered?"

"Some other major operation. Not much chatter. I overheard mention of World Horizons."

"The phone company?"

"This op has everybody nervous and excited. All I have on that."

"What else?"

"They are *very* shorthanded. They trust new recruits more than they should and do not trust old-timers. I get the sense they trust all operations to only a handful of operatives. For now. Seems they are still reeling from whatever happened back in 2008. Now more than ever."

"Why now? So many years later?"

"They attribute several failed operations to compromised assets. I think they are re-vetting the entire organization. Operations include less sophisticated plans and more brute force. A new guy has everyone spooked. He is driving all operations now."

"Name?"

"Van Stockton. A very serious player. He has taken over muscle, at least domestically, from Malcolm Frieburg who remains in play as Stockton's second."

"What else?"

"Stockton is at or near the top, Señor."

Boom!

BLACK ROCK, ARIZONA

"Hi... Sandra?" Geo read her name tag.

"Beautiful morning. I'm Lee Randle in site sixty-nine. You rent park models. Any available?"

Sam had called Geo again that morning. After traveling an indirect route to ensure discretion, and to handle some orthogonal business, President Stevens and his detail would arrive soon. He said something cryptic like, "The stars are aligned. It's time." Ever the spy, old Sam.

The buxom seventy-something work-camper behind the chest-high counter in the Black Rock Campground offered a most ostentatious display of flaming fire-engine-red hair. Stacked high atop her chubby pink face it looked like ratted straw. No doubt its asymmetry came from sleeping on one side more than the other.

Several strands of bright ceramic beads hand-painted every primary color adorned her ample neck.

He detected the not-so-faint odor of gin that either oozed from her pores or emanated from her breath. Or both.

For a moment, Geo considered criticizing her choice of attire by informing her every major fashion center in the world now banned the Hawaiian muumuu. Symbolically, in most first-world countries, anyway. But he reconsidered.

Besides, she seemed a free spirit who long ago graduated from such petty considerations as what others might think of her appearance.

"Yup. Sure are, Sweetie. Take your pick. Slow 'round these parts. Most folks like to be closer to cities or have headed north to escape the heat. Now if y'all wanted to find a rental up near Phoenix or Tucson-way at the last minute, still slim pickin's and mighty spendy."

"Wonderful. We have relatives coming to visit. Can I rent two next to each other?"

"Can do, Sweetness. You're sixty-nine." The cheerful old gal shot a lascivious wink Geo's way, but he declined nibbling at the bait for that tired sexual innuendo.

He responded, "Yes, that's correct. We need them furnished for a short-term rental, and two of your newer units if possible."

"Well, you *are* in luck. We have two brand-new furnished units we rent for the owners, but they'll cost you more than some others. You could put your family in Numbers 6 and 7 in the B row back next to the fence. Nice and private, but still only a hop, skip, and a jump from your rig.

"They're gettin' two hundred a week for each, but real nice units. That's dollars, not pesos." She appeared grateful for her hilarious self-endowed sense of humor.

When Geo didn't laugh at her clever levity, she appeared disappointed and continued in a less-than-magnanimous tone.

"Room to park one vehicle by each. Even have covered porches and car ports. For how long?"

"Perfect. I'd like to book those for two weeks starting today. Visa okay?"

"Better than cash, honey. Book them under your name, Mr. Randle?"

~

"Hey, Kate! Guess who's arriving today."

~

"It's good to have a plan A, B, and C."

That was Kate's motto. What-if planning relaxed her, no more than when her consumption of anxiety meds outpaced their prescription. More so these days.

And now, expecting a game of danger and intrigue? She admitted to both high anxiety and cautious anticipation. If they could finally rid themselves of the need to run every time a new rumor surfaced?

Or if they never again placed any of their friends in jeopardy? Might they even be able to shed their false identities if Sam's crazy plan works as designed?

Well, she'd just up her dosage for now and help.

Scared to apoplexy, she still managed a smile. They had a plan to finish this.

DEAD WHISTLEBLOWER

Washington, DC

Eternal embers crackled and smoldered.

The library's fireplace in the Chain Bridge Road mansion was never dark or cold. The remnants of tinder-dry oak logs performed a comforting and familiar dance today.

Like his fire, Mr. M, the third patriarch in the Patriot Brotherhood's eighty-year history, smoldered.

Michael Martino's short past tenure as Chief Executive Officer of the $100 billion multinational corporation, Greater Global Solutions, proved inadequate training for his current position.

He now commanded the oldest and most powerful, yet least known organization on Planet Earth. At least he still imagined so, despite myriad setbacks.

The PB commanded formidable resources. When his Chief Operating Officer at GGS preceded him in this post of unspeakable influence, he was happy for his mentee. But Palmer Xavier lost his cloak of invisibility and paid a bargain price—exile instead of death. Mr. M had been next in line.

"Malc, what in Hell is going on? Can you tell me that?"

"Mr. M, a whistle-blower at World Horizons is making noises. I'm on it."

His voice rasped in low tones, dripping with molten malice.

"Look, I've done favors for these people. Do you understand? *Favors.* I want this static to dissipate before it turns into a worldwide tidal wave."

~

MR. M'S INNER CIRCLE KNEW HIM FOR HIS CLUNKY METAPHORS.

"Yessir."

Malc had a recruit in mind for this minor annoyance. A dress rehearsal for the main event.

He called one of his favorite Central American contacts moments after Mr. M hung up.

"Yuri, change of plans. Call Dega."

~

"DEGA, ARE YOU PREPARED TO GO TO WORK?"

"Sí, Señor. I am bored."

"World Horizons. Cyril Dunstone. Extreme prejudice. Can do?"

"Seguro, Señor Yuri. ¿Cuando?"

"ASAP, Señorita."

"No hay problema. Gracias."

FREMONT, CALIFORNIA

CYRIL DUNSTONE SQUIRMED.

He sat stewing in his condo across the bay from Palo Alto. The sun bathed his face on the tiny balcony as he overlooked the water. A delightful seventy-eight degrees belied the clammy dread in his gut.

Doubts about World Horizons' latest product launch strategy ate away at him like battery acid on rusty steel.

As the senior project manager for the massive launch, their new telecom mission didn't bother him despite a concern over device emissions. New devices replaced older ones at a lightning pace these days and their R&D team leader assured him all their new devices included better shielding, making health dangers marginal.

But there was something far more worrisome happening. He'd heard the word *surveillance* several times. Why would that topic apply to a telephone company's new products? Even if Internet and TV were part of the package?

While he had his suspicions based on hall whispers around the lab and at the HQ offices, every time someone muttered anything related to this topic, the discussions just stopped. By edict.

And when he caught wind of more extensive dangers with later generations of this same technology, not only to humans but to the entire planetary food chain, he became concerned about *personal legal liability* in addition to his already anemic ethical standards.

This had all become very real to him.

But real right-now panic set in at the mention of *targeting*. Cyril felt compelled to take definitive action. But what?

His supervisor, a real ass-kisser, saw no cause for concern and said so. In no uncertain terms.

Cyril needed to tell someone, but who? He could trust nobody within the company. Calling the media might help, but that might also paint a target on his back. These were serious high-level executives running this campaign.

Who knows what they might do? Trusting anyone inside World Horizons makes no sense. So someone within the government? The FBI maybe? Yes! The FBI.

Should he just search for the phone number of the local FBI office? Was it that simple?

He Googled *FBI Fremont CA* and the Palo Alto field office on

Bayshore popped at the top of his search results. He jotted down their number from his laptop's screen onto a piece of scrap paper. Considered dialing.

God, what am I doing? This is crazy.

And that's when something cold and hard gently and then more firmly pressed against the back of his neck.

Terrified, he said nothing, did nothing, other than to turn a pallid white.

He heard, "You move, Señor, you die." A husky voice.

Time slowed to a ponderous crawl. He trembled, felt faint, but not before his bladder got a mind of its own. Just a small spot.

"You have two options only, Señor. Uno, you disobey one word, I create a small but effective hole in the back of your skull con mí pistola. The tiny bullet, she scrambles your brain like soft eggs.

Or dos, you dial that number on that piece of paper, and we wait together for your friends from the FBI. That is who you were to call anyway, no? Then we stage un poco teatro. You pretend to die, and they carry you to safety in a body bag. So, uno or dos, Señor?"

T UCSON, ARIZONA

Geo drove to Tucson.

Both he and his car shared an intimate relationship with this road. Indian Joe referred him to the perfect place on East University Boulevard near the perimeter of the U of A campus. Not far from where he told Kate he was meeting an author friend for coffee on campus.

A compulsion for anonymity driven by paranoia mandated his actions. He paid cash for two hours use of a private soundproof computer booth in the exclusive WayFair Internet Boutique. They were accustomed to being paid in cash, but also accepted credit, debit, or bitcoin. No checks.

He locked the heavy half-glass door to the five-foot-by-four-foot cubicle. Double-pane glass walls reached to a high unadorned ceiling above desktop-level on three walls.

The computer desk occupied the entire five-foot dimension of the fourth sheet-rocked wall decorated with expensive prints of futuristic scenes.

He drew the vertical wall blinds and horizontal door blinds closed, turned on the overhead lights and the tasteful desk lamp.

Once settled into the comfortable high-back desk chair in front of a respectable personal computer connected to lightning-fast Internet, Geo powered off his iPhone and iPad. Even with their location services disabled, he wasn't taking any chances.

Next, he pulled a pair of headphones with an integrated noise-canceling boom microphone from his shoulder bag and jacked into one of the PC's USB ports. Popped the phones onto his head and prepared to join the massive online teleconference based on intel from Sam's agency friends.

He entered his falsified press credentials, also courtesy of Sam, and his location: *New York, NY.* He masked his actual location with re-direct software loaded onto the PC from a high-density CD he carried with him. That was Sam's one hard and fast rule before he'd allow Geo to do this, even though he knew Geo would find a way to do this anyway.

Game on.

Within a few minutes he heard, "Welcome to World Horizons, soon to be the global leader in communications, television, and Internet services..."

Blah, blah, blah...

World Horizons' secondary aim was to court public opinion. Their primary objective, however, was to apply a liberal dose of political lubricant. Only Geo and a few others deduced that so far, or even cared.

The moderator of the massive *live* online audio press conference announced their newest technology, billing it as a quantum leap forward and of huge benefit to, well, everyone. This teleconference of unprecedented scale was but one example of their new offering's capabilities.

They announced they would also soon become the world's premier Internet and satellite TV service provider. Their revolutionary line of deluxe new smartphones, tablets and wearables would all be game changers.

As the first devices to take full advantage of their global 5G telecommunications technology, they set the stage for far greater capabilities.

Geo thought, *If the public only knew...*

He had found credible research published on several obscure websites that postulated WH's motivation to offer their own line of smart multifunctional 5G devices went much farther than their published objectives. But the most credible and most imminent danger documented the likelihood of widespread health risks associated with this powerful new 5G technology.

With the quantum leap forward in capability, electromagnetic radiation presented a significant danger to the public. But so few people were talking about that. Not surprising.

So WH devices offered additional shielding necessary to protect mobile and home users. They presumed other device manufacturers would follow suit, and that those precautions would suffice.

They were wrong.

On a broader scale, they would soon blast 5G *at strength*. These high-powered high-frequency signals would emanate from a dense network of satellites onto an unsuspecting planet.

Towers numbering in the hundreds of thousands and millions of smaller repeaters would re-broadcast these potentially lethal signals, more concentrated in densely populated areas. But they guaranteed ubiquitous coverage around the globe. These towers and toaster-size repeaters would then re-broadcast 5G *everywhere*.

A few—Geo among them—worried this saturation bombing of the planet placed every body and mind at risk. Moderate at first, more serious later, he could smell the stench: a profitable vortex of slow-rotting death in a target-rich environment.

And not so much as a hint of any environmental impact statements. Why? Buried under a mountain of lobbyist money?

His inescapable vision? The smell of human and non-human soft tissue cooking and dying.

Scattered among the crackpot conspiracy theories littering the back alleys of the Internet, Geo located more and more substantive articles on prolific EMP—ElectroMagnetic Poisoning. This was the only territory not censored by *Big Telecom*.

Respected physiologists suggested the danger was real to anyone who might listen. And with each successive generation of this same technology, the problem would inevitably grow to epidemic proportions, better device shielding or not. The danger would be *atmospheric*. Unless someone did something...

One article received almost no attention, except from Geo, a few thousand other concerned critical thinkers, and a throng of conspiracy theorists. This article suggested a strong telecom lobby in Washington pushed legislation for "enhanced *device* shielding standards despite the costs as this new technology proliferates."

Political opponents, however, pushed counter-legislation for "additional precautions to mitigate the broader *atmospheric* risks of EMP as an essential public safety measure."

The powerful telecom lobby ensnared this counter-legislation in bureaucratic sub-committees and partisan filibusters describing it as "the baseless meanderings of ultra-left alarmists contriving rhetoric that is fueled by little more than a handful of conspiracy nuts."

This same well-funded lobby gained *public* funding for a comprehensive network of 5G telecom satellites numbering in the tens of thousands—the initial round. As an enticement, they offered free bandwidth to military and government intelligence users.

The promises included vast improvements in communication and surveillance capabilities—*offered only to US government agencies as an act of patriotism.*

Some, however, suggested *World* Horizons made the same offer under the table to other wealthy foreign constituents; however, Geo found little in the way of hard evidence to support that supposition.

They offered this massive online launch event simulcasted to the public to make it more dynamic, and accessible later via re-broadcast on syndicated outlets.

Advance press on the topic captured the public's imagination with promises for a quantum leap forward in personal communications and entertainment.

And the recorded event posted later online would target millions more not at the huge live event. They expected a media splash with simultaneous email, TV, radio, and podcast campaigns.

SUCCESS HUNG ON A THREE-SECOND DELAY.

This built-in safety net guarded against crackpot journalists or nay-sayers from broadcasting live. The producer monitored the live feed.

His fist hovered, ready to pound the big red button. This *hook* would censor incoming commentary and truncate it before broadcasting. He would then delete the offending remarks from the conference feed before it was rebroadcast or posted later.

GEO ONCE WAS A BROADCAST ENGINEER.

Before he joined corporate America in 1977, one of his college jobs at a large FM station provided him valuable experience. He knew how it worked.

So using his nom de plume, he posted his name in the queue and awaited his turn. Twenty minutes into the Q&As, that turn arrived.

"JACK RHODES, FREELANCE TELECOM NEWS.

"This announcement offers *amazing* opportunities for consumers and broadcasters. Congratulations! I *am* curious—how will you address the inevitable global electromagnetic poisoning risk posed by 5G and later generations of that same tech?"

This reporter's opening congratulatory remarks seduced Steve Forbes, the producer. Exhaustion from lack of sleep slowed his reflexes. He was a second too slow on the big red button to censor the live feed. The guy's last words broadcast live to millions of listeners were *global electromagnetic poisoning risk.*

"Son-of-a-bitch! Who *is* this guy?" Steve knew his job at *World Whore-Icings,* as in cold promiscuous bitch—how he thought of World Horizons—was now at risk. A difficult company to work for, but the pay was ridiculous. Now another crackpot who could stir up a universe of conspiracy theories!

He warned the fat-cats broadcasting live carried a huge risk despite the potential reward of a dynamic listener experience, or some such shit. He'd be able to say, "I told you so," but that wouldn't save his job. At least they could edit this asshole out before posting the re-broadcast online.

Then the phone rang. Against his better judgment, he answered it.

"What the Hell was that, Forbes?"

He knew that voice—his executive director.

"Sir, we're still live. With all due respect, we'll talk later."

And Forbes hung up on his boss. Shit!

LOST?

R ANSOM VALLEY
NEAR QUARTZSITE,
ARIZONA

That was a real thing. Jennifer Daley belonged to that social media group, as did Geo.

Authors who maintained a mobile lifestyle adapted to life on the road by commiserating with other authors via the Internet.

She and Geo knew each other online but had never met IRL—In Real Life. She came to the area for the Tucson Festival of Books as a keynote speaker in April and stayed in the area for some extended desert research.

They met at Jennifer's small but deluxe van-style Class B motorhome on nearby government land. Geo drove out to her site on the far side of Nowhere Bluff. Her location revealed her love of dry-camping in seclusion.

Jennifer seemed nice, and legitimate, but he tried to follow at least some of the Marshal Service's rules. He was only known to Jennifer and 'the Warriors' by his pen name, Jack Rhodes.

"So how did you get on the list, not just once, but *seven times*, without losing your sanity, Jennifer?"

The two of them sat facing each other in tiny tripod lawn chairs under a scrub mesquite tree. Between the tree, two low dunes, and the low angle of the sun, they enjoyed a seductive hint of shade and a few degrees of relief.

Jennifer achieved what some authors view as a pinnacle, or a launch pad—that of New York Times Best-Selling Author—a coveted form of recognition. There were other lists, but this was *The List.*

Geo spoke in staccato phrases, as if getting them out were a matter of some urgency. After ten minutes of banal chatter, he was getting to what was foremost on his mind.

"Um, in practical terms, does the line between your real world and your fictional world ever blur? For example, *I can smell her hair, I know what she's thinking, what she wants, because it's what I want. Like I'm a God. At that point guilt overcomes me because I'm married IRL. So I punish myself by punishing her. She hates me for it.*"

Geo dropped his head in, what? Shame?

Jennifer said, "Punishing characters and getting inside their heads is a basic part of writing good fiction, Jack. You need drama, and conflict creates the tension which drives dramatic events. Besides, creating compelling characters *demands* we get close to them. What happens then?"

She'd been there so often. Second nature to her. Maybe first.

"Well, *we make up*. Then I write her into yet another catastrophic situation. She responds, without… honor. Geez, what the Hell am I saying? *We make up?* See what I mean?"

Her eyes cast an understanding glow in his direction. She said, "The good thing? She's no longer perfect. Makes her a deeper character and provides you some useful distance."

"I guess. But she and others pop up in my most intimate dreams and even invade my memories, alongside other things that happen in my real life.

"Sometimes it's hard to distinguish where I've intruded into that gray zone, in an in-between scene. Happens with all my characters during a serious work in progress, but it's my relationship with *her* I feel must end.

"Do I kill her off? Write her out? Or transform her into some kind of unlovable monster? Will I find the courage to let her go? Easy, right? But it's not fair to her. Oh God. Am I falling into some Hemingway-esque abyss here?"

"Jack, there is a fine line between good authors and their characters. First, a well-crafted character reflects your own character, good and bad, at least to some extent. They aren't you, but they are a reflection, like looking into a deep pond that's smooth, then rippled.

"You aren't the pond, but sometimes you go for a swim. As long as you get back out and dry off you'll be fine."

"Yeah, maybe. But worst of all? My villains frighten me. I create them as I dredge up my own worst memories and amplify them. Now I have elevated and committed those memories to words in scenes that live forever. They too invade my dreams, over and over again. Not sure *real life* still means what it once did. I take precautions, but…

"Is this just the darker side of my imagination, Jennifer? They say inspiration from life experience is a good thing in good fiction—not always true, is it?"

"This profession extracts a price, Jack, one that would surprise most people, even less-dedicated authors. Like any profession. You need to ask yourself if you're willing to pay that price, or not. Either way, it is a decision. *Your* decision."

"Is it like a progressive disease?"

"Oh, Jack. That's why I'm learning to adore you. The perennial drama hovers ever near the surface. Remember, you're writing good fiction. You're keeping the craft close to your heart. And your mind must be the traffic cop between the drama in your scripts and experience in your life. Enjoy the ride! What's the problem?"

"Well… scattered among the few non-writing days in my life, I'm telling stories, sharing memories, some of which never happened outside the pages of my novels. It's automatic. Knee-jerk.

"Does that matter as long as it produces good scripts? I know it does, but what does it mean when my characters become my friends? My family? My memories? Or vice versa? Is this the anatomy of a good author? Or a pathological liar? Or both? Or worse?"

Geo realized his emotions were... escalating. He took a deep cleansing breath.

In a patient voice Jennifer said, "Look, Jack, what we do is important if we embrace our craft. Our readers know that; however, our friends and family may *never* understand. *We* may not always understand. But I believe in a principle critical to the serious author."

Jennifer Daley's next words would burn into Geo's mind forever.

She said, "The weave of society's fabric is guided by the direction of its threads. Those threads are the stories we tell. Both fact and fiction uncover fundamental truths. We should never take those truths and our role in articulating them for granted. If an author's passion is real, that is not fiction.

"Jack, storytellers play an important role in determining the direction toward which society drifts. Is it any wonder why we sometimes blur the boundary between our stories and our lives? You just need to find your own balance point, your fulcrum. And then keep coming back to that."

Jennifer didn't say so, but concern sculpted her brow as she gazed into his darting eyes.

The sun dipped below the western horizon. They both already felt chilled as the desert temps dropped with the sun.

Was he willing to accept the cost of recognition, real or imagined? He wondered if time would reveal his personal truth—real or imagined.

As he departed, she said, "Remember, Jack, find your fulcrum."

Finding his way back to the road in the approaching twilight proved challenging, but the time had come to seek his fulcrum.

DEAD AND ALIVE

F REDERICKSBURG, VIRGINIA

He would not be needing his own wheels.

So Sam left his old car in the underground garage back at his *active seniors residence* in Alexandria.

After he got off the bus in Fredericksburg, he caught a cab. Damn cane made entering the taxi an awkward maneuver. No matter.

The beige twenty-five-year-old suede coat hung on him like draperies on a skeleton. Been a while since the last cleaning which explained the shiny cuffs and stained collar. Even his wrinkled khaki slacks bunched in all the wrong places as he hunched in the back seat of the smelly taxi now hurtling him toward his destiny.

He adjusted the angle of his treasured long-barrel pre-Civil War Colt Dragoon nestled in a large custom inner pocket at his left breast. Like his favorite jacket, these old slacks, and himself, the large-caliber revolver was yet another historical artifact.

Nobody paid attention to an invisible old man stooped forward, and lumpy in the wrong places. Sam reflected that as he aged, his belt line crept farther north, closer to the ear and nose hair that sprouted faster than his short ill-trimmed white-on-white goatee.

He thought, *This good old Colt isn't as comfortable as it once was. Seems longer. And heavier.* Its barrel and front sight jabbed his thigh through the jacket's silky liner. So he sat up straighter.

Could he have missed his dearest Mary any more? Yet each day, he did. He smiled.

That was now a short-term problem.

A trusted agency compatriot handed Sam his personal Holy Grail —Malcolm Frieburg's location. PB's number one henchman was in Fredericksburg. Or so he thought.

SAM'S FRIEND COULDN'T HAVE KNOWN.

Nobody at the NSA could trust such critical intel to just one old retired spook. But he offered his old boss a thirty-minute lead on the posse. Out of gratitude.

This favor sacrificed every oath taken to God and country. But the currents of their friendship ran that deep. Sam said he just wanted eyes on the prize. He owed Sam that much—and so much more—even if questions surrounded this piece of intel.

MOTIVE, MEANS, AND OPPORTUNITY... CHECK.

MOTIVE: Unknown to his friend, Sam assumed the role of anonymous assassin in the unexpected crowd. *This mongrel must be put down.*

The posse had beat him to Ground Zero. He did not know what Frieburg looked like, but that mattered little.

MEANS: If all went well, a forty-four caliber round just twenty inches above the handcuffs, center mass, would offer him a fulfilling retirement gift. *I'm sure there is one trigger-pull left in me.*

The FBI Hostage Rescue Team had breeched a gentrified second-floor loft. The Fredericksburg PD secured the perimeter. One officer thought nothing of granting access across the tape to a distinguished elderly gentleman who flashed his impressive credentials with panache. Like he belonged there with all the other Feds.

The officer raised the tape just a few inches to allow the old agent underneath. He was that short and stooped.

Sam barked with authority to nobody in particular over his shoulder, "Too many spectators here. Move 'em back!"

He surveyed the scene, chose his tactical location, now wearing his falsified credentials outside his blousy jacket, and waited.

He heard, "Get this arrogant prick out of here."

OPPORTUNITY: Target acquired, Sam waited. He wasn't expecting Malcolm Frieburg to be black. Closer… Closer… He reached across his desiccated chest and into the jacket with his bony right hand. *The long revolver feels so very heavy. But not too heavy.*

Its tall forward sight snagged, then came free. Kept it just out of sight until… *Wait...*

Someone hollered "Gun!"

Wham!

The fusillade of bullets that came Sam's way in the next instant closed the lacy curtain on a life well-lived. He might have spotted Mary's shadow in the crowd as he crumpled. Absence of regrets made the fall shorter and easier and almost pain-free.

His body now spent, he was sure a smile of fulfillment etched his wrinkled features as he took flight from that decrepit husk. Sam took his mind with him.

Maybe Geo and Kate were safe now.

That was enough.

THE CHAOS SUBSIDED.

FBI Supervisory Special-Agent-in-Charge Granville Franks, the on-scene commander, looked down at the minuscule corpse, his torso riddled with holes. The little old man still gripped an ancient revolver.

"Now who the Hell is *this* guy?"

By the time they identified the body from his credentials and after a few calls from the scene, the mystery only deepened.

"Why would a distinguished long-retired Army doctor want to assassinate a minor-league player in a local kidnapping ring? Or did this Jesruda Nevison have enemies in high places? And how could that make *any* sense?"

This old soldier's mission guaranteed suicide. But why? Must be personal.

Agent Franks could smell another cold case in the making unless this gentleman left other clues behind. Worth a look.

BLACK ROCK, ARIZONA

KATE ADORED EDUCATIONAL TV PROGRAMS.

One of her favorite shows on the Discovery Channel describing the unique flora and fauna of the Galapagos Islands didn't interest Geo. Kate kept the volume low. They respected each other's limited space in the motorhome.

Every morning Geo scanned three different national news feeds on his iPhone. He realized this was out of character since prior to a few years ago, he *never* listened to or read the news.

Diffused sunlight filtered through translucent window shades from the large window on the driver's side. The exterior awning over that window allowed in more light with less heat. His coffee mug, empty for hours, sat to the left of his keyboard. A glorious morning dawned until he read an article posted by Fox.

Unknown to Kate, a blazing electric shock stiffened and paralyzed Geo. Stomach acid gorged half-way up his throat. He found part of his voice.

"Sam's gone." Geo squeaked out those awful words.

Kate muted the TV. Not sure what he said, much less what he meant, she said, "*What* did you say? Sam? Gone? As in *dead?*"

Geo's next strangled words came out so slow as if some nasty little demon who crouched inside his throat prevented their easy passage.

"They shot him after he assassinated a kidnapper during an FBI bust in Virginia… *Aaaaghhh!*"

That guttural scream and soul-chilling news turned Kate's face ashen. Her chin trembled with both lips quivering as if she were trying to say something that refused to escape *her* constricted throat.

She stared through her mid-air disbelief before swiveling a blank gaze toward Geo's tortured expression, afraid of what she might see.

He had become stone, animate life suspended, still on his feet, as if Medusa had transformed him into a cold uncaring pillar. Minutes passed with no sound except her labored breathing and sniffles.

At last, with a creeping belief that Sam could be dead but not under such absurd circumstances, she dared say, "*What?* That's *crazy!*"

But she felt the scenario just too outrageous for fiction.

Almost to herself, she mumbled, "Sam was old, but I can't imagine he's just… gone. Like *that.*"

The stone pillar disintegrated. Geo collapsed into his recliner and wept, his face in his hands, hunched into his grief. He didn't trust the article, but his heart believed. Somehow, he felt the truth of the story. Even though the circumstances seemed too, what? Contrived? Staged?

Geo's mind surged off in myriad directions. His mentor and protector since November of 1995—just gone. They shared the field of battle. The little man saved his life. More than once. A dear, dear friend. *Another* friend. Gone.

"God*damm*it!"

Profound grief and vague belief transformed into irrational anger. His empty mug became a missile, missing Kate by inches, bouncing off the steering wheel of the bus, shattering the glass of the speedometer on the dash. Too stubborn to break, the stout mug came to a spinning rest on the cockpit carpeting.

~

KATE SAID NOTHING.

She didn't seem to notice the near-miss, or care, amidst her soft sobbing. But out of the corner of one misty eye, she saw the chords in Geo's neck pulsing dangerously. They seemed on the verge of exploding. That frightened her from within her own grief.

Geo stormed out, slamming the heavy door. The window did not shatter. He needed to be alone. Didn't it occur to him she suffered too? She feared his self-pity might turn into something far more perilous. And reckless. He and Chet and Sam. Now, just him.

He slumped on the hard folding chair.

His trailer, his man-cave. Where he and Chet made music. Gone. Now Sam. So alone. The only noise penetrating the trailer's painted interior plywood walls and closed door? The *humma-humma* from trucks punching in their jake brakes.

That distinctive sound punctuated the constant buzz of cars doing sixty on two-lane US Highway 60 a hundred yards to the south. Trucks decelerated into Brenda, on that sunny fucking highway, but nothing could drown out the cacophony of Geo's agony.

Then he realized he was not only crying, he was *screaming*. His temples throbbed a primal jungle beat, lent his white-hot headache a satisfying rhythm.

A subtle sound—a voice—piggybacked on his despair, and then grew louder.

"Are we not enjoying ourselves, George? Pity parties aren't much fun, are they?"

In mid-sob-and-sniffle, still clutching his temples with white knuckles, Geo snapped his head up so fast he heard something pop in his neck. He ignored the thin mucus and tears running into his mustache and beard.

With sudden desperation and bloodshot eyes more white than not, and very round, he sought the source of the sound. He searched the confines of the trailer's crowded interior with manic resolve, realizing his grief now deluded him.

Geo shook his head before he returned to remembering poor old Sam.

"Poor old Sam, my ass! Pull out of your nose dive, George. This is not the time. We have work."

"What the…" Sam's diction, that unmistakable Georgian drawl. Or was it Texan? He realized he wasn't sure, never knew, never cared. But how…?

"Yes, I'm here, George. It seems I have unfinished business. Some-one's looking to end you and Kate. He tried to end me too. I tried to beat them to it by taking out some trash. Too bad it was the wrong trash."

"Sam?"

"Guilty as charged, old son. You fit to talk?"

"I don't understand. You're… *dead!*"

"We old soldiers don't allow a trivial thing like death to stand in the way of our duty. I guess I am not yet ready to leave the field of battle."

Am I insane, or is this a part of a reality I've never been able to accept —until now?

Geo rocked and rattled his head, trying to clear it. Just made it ache more.

"Sam, what is going on? Am I crazy?"

"No, not yet, not now. No time. With all due respect, George, shut up and listen. We weakened the PB when we exposed their underbelly in 2008 and 2009. Diminished, not disappeared.

"You and I remained high-value targets to someone within what remains of that organization. I tried to sever the head of the snake, but don't imagine I did. Bad intel."

"Is that why the FBI and Virginia State Police shot you?"

"I took a chance. I did not hit the jackpot. But they hit me."

"Sam…"

"That's all I got, old son. I must depart. For now."

"But Sam. Sam? Shit. Wait. That guy who tried to shoot us at the marina in Florida back in '08, but your guys got him first. I wonder… one of his friends?"

"Believe it, George."

"Oh, my God! That's it!"

Silence, except for the faint hum and buzz of highway traffic. Sam was gone, but the headache was not.

Energized, Geo bolted from the trailer. He knew he dared not share this with Kate.

He was on a mission. Again. He had found… clarity, such as it was.

SPIRIT VOICE

THE GRAY CANVAS LOOKED BLACK.

Lounging in those tattered lawn chairs alongside Geo's trailer in the dark, they sipped cold sweet tea Joe brought over from his trailer.

Geo remembered red plastic cups like these, white inside—the kind from the high school keggers he always tried to avoid. They too looked black in the dark.

Joe's tea tasted spicy-weird, but he made no comment, thankful for the distraction.

Joe said, "Fair warning, pardner. This ain't none of that decaffeinated shit. This here's high octane."

Almost midnight. Kate slept in the motorhome not ten feet away behind a closed window and directly under a soft-humming rooftop air conditioner. She remained oblivious, consumed by her sorrow for Sam's passing. Geo's eyes remained swollen and his nose congested, but Sam's voice…

He now needed to cling to what was left of his sanity.

The imminent conversation was likely to be bizarre, and they would need privacy. Dark and almost quiet, the susurrus of the RV park whispered to them like a country cemetery, which felt appropriate.

"Appreciate you coming over, Joe. Didn't want to be too far from Kate. I have a problem."

With a straight face, Joe said, "You called the right guy. I *am* a solver of problems. Well, other people's problems. Besides, couldn't sleep. And finished my work at least an hour ago. Not my best work. So I have a little time."

Geo smiled. That wit.

"Joe, you said something on our hike that day in the Santa Ritas above Tucson. I thought you were joking. Now I'm not so sure. I need an honest answer."

"Geez, Geo, get *to* it already."

"You said something about your, ah, spirit guide, that he showed you the way to a good patch of yucca."

"Yeah? So?"

"I'm hearing the voice of a dear friend who just died."

"No shit."

Then, a single beat later, Joe said, "It's a gift, isn't it? Loud or soft?"

"So you were serious." Not a question.

"You weren't ready to accept that yet."

Geo thought, *Much **has** changed since that day.*

"Well, I think I am now. *Or* I'm out of my mind."

"Can't tell you about that, brother. Crazy people hear voices too."

"How can I tell the difference? What the Hell is going on?"

"Well, some people call this stuff intuition. Some, a power outside themselves. Those are coping mechanisms for lesser mortals with minds snapped shut more than not.

"My ancestors believed the difference between life and death was a continuum, not a boundary. If you know the voice, and comes from someone you trusted with your life *in* life, odds are you're not crazy. No guarantees."

"So what do I do?"

"Come on, Geo, you're a smart guy. You listen. You act. Assuming those actions don't violate your personal code. And if the voice is your friend instead of your insanity, things work out. After that, there are always pills.

"At first, I thought I was nuts too. That's when my old friend helped me out. As he did in life. Been with me ever since."

"Did you ever tell anyone?"

"You nuts? Oh, sorry." That smirk, further evidence of Joe's weird wit.

"The short answer is no. Not unless I joke about it. Like with *las touristas*. Like I did with you. Then for more serious discussions, only with people I trust and I know to have an open mind. Gotta be careful, man. Most folks wouldn't get it.

"Hard to tell whether you've got a guide or whether you're delusional. Or both. Hell, maybe we're both bat-shit crazy. Just flow, man. Just flow. Like water. See what happens. Sometimes our senses evolve through a mist of emotional pain."

Geo looked sideways toward Joe and said, "That's profound shit, Joe."

"Yeah, well, I'm a profound guy. Some say I'm *full* of profound shit."

Joe talked as if these phenomena were so natural. But why keep all this a secret? He knew why. Joe had said it.

As if a patient teacher with an impetuous child, Joe said, "Sometimes Ed whispers so soft I question his presence. Sometimes the son-of-a-bitch screams at me. Remember when you were about to touch that nasty cholla cactus on our little yucca quest? I wasn't even watching you, but Ed hollered. So I hollered. Faith.

"I've learned to trust his instincts—like when Ed and I were cellmates. So it was Ed who saved your punk ass from that cholla that day, through me."

Joe fell into a silent reverie, remembering something. No telling what.

"You were in prison?"

"Another day, compadre. For now, give your newfound sense a test run. See what happens. Just remember as soon as you disbelieve—

assuming you're not bat-shit crazy—your spirit guide's vibe to this life might snap. Up to you, amigo.

"I dunno. Next-level shit, Joe. I'm a tech guy. How can I rationalize this?"

"You can't. Don't try. That *will* drive you crazy. You forget I'm a tech guy too? Part-time, anyway. Time away from all that allows this gift to make sense, no pun intended. They call that meditation. *And* isolation from the other *noise*."

He emphasized his last word with a gentle index finger to his right temple.

"Joe, Sam tells me Kate and I are in danger, that we're on some hit list somewhere. And he has an idea who it might be. My… intuition… also tells me this is plausible. Our past…"

Joe surprised Geo by his lack of shock at such an outlandish hypothesis.

"Hey, you had *better* listen, man. And if he's wrong? Well…

"But if he's right…"

PURPLE FRINGE

THE TIME HAD COME, APPARENTLY.

Indian Joe hoisted his lanky frame out of the sagging lawn chair. Turned to Geo, offered him a hand, pulled him out of the other one that sagged worse than the one he just escaped. It was now well past midnight, time to enlighten his friend.

"Dude, follow me. You're ready to meet someone. Don't worry about that. You're protected. Let's go."

Geo had turned to close and lock his trailer's small side door. He feared someone walking off with his flute collection, mixing board, microphones, guitar, and all the other stuff lying around in there. It all seemed important until...

But he stopped at Joe's words and followed him. Act of faith, he guessed.

Protected? Huh.

They talked as they walked. At first.

"I don't want you to freak out, amigo, but you need to meet a fellow flute player. Randy is a helluva guy. But he's different... in a good way."

"Should I have brought a few flutes?"

"Naw, we're just gonna talk. He's interesting, and I know how much you love meeting interesting people. Randy is part of a group of unusual folks. We dig deeper than most are able or willing."

"We?"

"Yeah. I are one too, kimosabe."

"Well, okay, but I'm not into cults or any shit like that."

"Geez, man, don't worry so much. Just flow, baby!"

Geo's furrowed brow reflected his perplexity, but he trusted Joe who seemed aware of his bewilderment. Worse, he enjoyed it.

Joe fell silent. Both kept walking. Each retreated to his own reverie.

They continued at a brisk pace.

Turned three corners in as many minutes. This small RV park was bigger than Geo imagined. Spread out. He hadn't explored it until now. Tucked into a distant corner of the park, they approached the longest and most elegant triple-axle Airstream bumper-pull trailer Geo ever saw. An expensive rig. At least thirty-four feet long and very shiny.

But its less-than-conventional tow vehicle captured his greater interest—a raised and rusted one-ton pickup almost as old as its caked-on prehistoric dirt. Steps descended from the cab doors to make climbing up into this relic easier.

The monster truck featured a flat-black brush guard in front of the grill and coarse black screen protected all six headlights—two above the front bumper, and four more on a roof-mounted light bar. The thick layer of dirt disguised the truck's color.

The contrast between the gleaming aluminum trailer with only the slightest dust sheen, and this customized but crappy tow vehicle could not have been more striking.

Before Joe announced their presence, and before he touched the closed door of the trailer with his knuckles, the curved door swung open—fast.

Geo jumped back. Joe smiled. A delicate hand held it against the evening breeze.

"Welcome! Enter at your own risk!"

The voice projected vitality far more robust than the gaunt but cheerful face that greeted them. A pale hand belonging to an old gentleman's papery white arm appeared first. That translucent arm draped with purplish veins disappeared into the bulky sleeve of a loose-fitting purple robe tied at the waist with a deeper purple waist sash that kissed the floor.

He appeared not much more substantial than a skeleton adorned with loose pallid flesh and that outrageous floor-length robe. Geo guessed he was eighty or eighty-five, depending on his off-road mileage.

This little guy drives that huge truck outside?

His gnarled feet peeked out as he stood twenty-eight inches higher up inside the trailer. They were bare on the floor's plush but dated shag carpet, also purple. That carpet looked new. Everything in that trailer looked new, except him.

Geo wasn't sure why those misshapen hooves fascinated him. Looked to be at least twice as old as the rest of this duffer's body, and more damaged. That this old guy could even get around on those gnarled stumps Geo found surprising. Intriguing. He found it hard not to stare.

This animated cadaver extended his pale right hand, veins and all. Full arm extension. Geo accepted it, and that arm drew him up into the trailer with unexpected strength. They didn't have far to walk.

With a musical voice that came from a much younger man, he said, "Hi, I'm Randy. And you would be Lee."

"Guilty as charged. So you guys have talked about me?"

Joe said, "Randy knows you've started talking with your dead friend."

Geo grumbled. "But when? We just…"

"Oh, lighten up, man. Randy is one of us!"

That caught his attention. Us?

*I'm already part of an **us**?*

He did need help figuring out all this weirdness somehow.

"Well, any port in a storm, I guess."

Randy chirped, "That's the spirit! Pun intended." Ancient wrinkled smirk. Not unlike Joe's.

The old boy got them seated around a table in a cozy booth. He had covered that table in an intricate linen damask embroidered in varying shades of purple.

Joe and Geo slid in on one side, Randy on the other. Tight quarters compared to Geo's larger bus.

Randy smoothed the tablecloth with his bony palms and crooked fingers. Geo recognized chronic rheumatoid arthritis, a disease which attacks the body by weakening its immune system. His fingers all pointed in the same but wrong direction. *That's* what he felt when Randy's hand held his a minute ago.

Geo offered a nod toward Randy's hands as they brushed the damask.

"RA?"

"Yup. You know someone, don't you?"

Geo said, "Yup. Hurt?"

"I have days. Some are good. On those days, I play."

Joe said, "Randy plays an awesome pueblo flute. Depends on a friend to build 'em with custom finger holes. This man right here is our resident rim-blown flute guru, among other trivial shit. Right, Rand?"

"You nailed it, red man, despite your colorful vernacular."

Swiveling his gaze toward Geo, Randy said, "I manage the worst symptoms with holistic healing instead of traditional medications. Who's to say whether I'd have been better off with pills than with poultices and proper ruffage? I harbor no regrets given the hands life has dealt me—pun very much intended. Again."

Walls inside the trailer curved upward and inward toward the ceiling. This made the interior appear smaller than what he had imagined standing outside. Interior cubic footage shrank even further with the violet drapes covering almost every square inch of the walls and ceiling. Geo wondered whether those drapes concealed any copper screen.

"Yes, they do."

"What?"

"You were wondering whether I'm a *bird*, as some would say. Yes, these drapes hide my cage, my copper shield. I hate to scare the straights. I'm sure you understand, better than most."

"Wait. You can read minds, Randy?"

He chuckled. "Deduction. I read people. Joe told me you're redecorating your rig. Saw you staring. Prudent wager, I'd say."

Randy reminded Geo of an aging vampire—realizing that was an oxymoron—and his trailer the inside of a posh coffin, even though it's exterior looked like the fuselage of a 1940s airliner.

Serious vitamin B deficiency at least, Geo guessed. Not the outdoors type. At least not during the day. Geo understood. His own Dutch and German heritage caused him to burn in the shade on a cloudy day.

Randy's intense gunmetal gray eyes bored into Geo's baby blues.

Geo thought, *They are kind eyes, but he enjoys some private joke—head cocked left, opposite brow raised, one dimpled cheek? Yeah, he's chuckling inside, but at what?*

"I try to know folks who wish to become better acquainted with our eclectic little enclave. I'd like to know you, Geo. But as Joe may have hinted, we possess fragile sensibilities. *You* also need to learn what *we're* about so you can make up your own mind.

"Most of us don't mesh well with mainstream society's intellect. We're not isolationists, mind you, at least not all of us. Joe, for example, meshes better with others and lives a more conventional lifestyle.

"For others, though, the noise is too great. Or the melody is disturbing: atonal, disjoint, even horrific. So some of us live out in the desert, or in the woods, or in the mountains, as a matter of survival. That will seem lunacy to some. That's okay. Each of us finds peace and freedom down a different path.

"You've acquired a voice. How's that going for you so far, my new friend?"

Geo squirmed on the plush padding of the settee's bench. He noticed the cushion under him was also purple. Or violet. Like the carpeting, the draped walls, Randy's robe, and most every significant surface in the trailer. Some velvet, some satin, maybe? Even a purple formica countertop! Felt like the inside of a gypsy tent.

So why did this seem like he was cheating on Kate? Crazy. She had been asleep for hours already, and she would understand none of this.

"To be blunt, Randy, this is all so different. My first inclination? I've suffered a psychotic break."

"Well, could be you have. Any inclination to hurt others?"

"Only those who threaten me and mine. But I've always feared taking another life, human or otherwise. My hypocrisy also troubles me. To eat flesh someone else has killed is not an issue for me. I am no vegan. Not yet, anyway. I lack the discipline. And I am not at all sure why that troubles me *or* why I just shared that with you."

"Outside of combat or law enforcement, have you ever taken a human life?"

"I intended to do so eight years ago. Shot him in the chest. I was convinced I had killed him, but he survived. He was very sick—a monster. He, um, murdered, um, four of my friends."

Geo's throat constricted as he dredged that memory from the bottom of a painful psychological trash heap yet again. Tried and failed to swallow.

"I had to stop the killing. Worst day of my life, even after I learned he survived my attack, and I his. I most feared my *intent* to kill another person, even a monster."

Still clinging to that odd expression, Randy said, "Okay, so let's try to rule out a few things. First, you don't seem psychotic, so I'd rule that out, at least for now. Second, you have a good heart. A courageous heart. And third, we *are* talking. *Right now.*

"You're sitting in a lunatic's trailer opening up with all candor to someone you just met. You present yourself with a refreshing openness. From these observations I can see you have an open and trusting mind with a sense of moral integrity."

"You a psychologist or something, Randy?"

"Well, I play flutes and I'm a fair judge of character. But yes, I was also a psychologist in one of my many past lives. Outside the group. Some out there still call me Doc. Here, I'm just another weirdo doing what he can to contribute and to thrive."

"Ah. Well, Doc,"

"Randy."

"Okay, Randy, so what's going on with this voice I heard? In here?" To stress the point, Geo jabbed his left temple with an index finger—not a soft jab, nor just one.

"Lee, be gentle with yourself. Many mysteries keep life interesting more than maddening. We can't explain everything, nor should we try. We need to be okay with that. You heard the voice of a dear friend who shed his mortal coil. That's not too surprising."

"But it was so real. Like an invisible man sitting next to me in my trailer conversing with me."

"Some of us accept reality as relative, tenuous, ephemeral—in its current form, at least. Take dreams, for example. Are dreams real? Some would say they aren't. Dreams are as real as breathing, but different. We *know* that.

Randy continued. "Is death real? We know that too. We say death is real, but it is not an ending. Instead, it's just a transition.

"Evidence? Physicists tell us that nature never destroys matter. Rather, She converts matter to another form. And we all matter. Empirical evidence.

"I and others believe death is only a transition to another form of living. To what, though, none of us can *know*, and that's where our feelings, our emotions, serve us better than our five finite senses. Are feelings and emotions any less real than the external physiological data and stimuli fed to us by our five senses? You decide."

"Geez, I have a headache."

"Overload, Lee. A lot to absorb. Just flow with it for now."

"That's what Joe says."

"Joe's a sharp guy."

Joe offered a nod to Randy for the compliment, followed by a self-deprecating shrug and smirk for Geo. He shifted his forehead bandana to satisfy a sweaty itch. Joe never sweat.

Randy grinned like he'd just found a charmed Morgan 1886 silver dollar in the dirt outside his trailer.

"For what it might be worth to you, Lee, I believe you would make a fine addition to our merry little band of lunatics. At the risk of seeming too conventional, I've authored an informal pamphlet.

"In there you'll find I've captured the few key mandates most of us feel best defines our group's conscience. A little light bedtime reading. Take this back to your rig. Let Joe and me know what you think. Okay, my new friend?"

He stretched his gnarled hand across the table to Geo who grasped its awkward shape once more, all angular and bony. Now, though, it felt softer.

GEO'S MIND SWAM IN THE DEEP END.

During the walk back, Joe told Geo that Randy would move on soon.

"Big city melodies interfere with his own. But even this small park can only be a stop-over for a few days. Long drives are difficult for him. We keep in touch. He knew I was here.

"Randy is one of those wonderful spirits whose body has already started its transition. You'll better understand once you've read that cheesy little flyer he's so proud of. Pay attention to number ten."

"Where's he headed?"

"To a better place, he says. In conventional thinking, that means the deeper desert down at the base of the Harquahala Mountains for now. Some holy places out yonder. Then?"

Another smirky shrug. *Huh.*

Geo crawled into bed at 1:13 a.m. That's the thing about digital clocks. Not "about ten after one," but 1:13. Both he and Kate *needed* that clock with its big green numerals. The damn thing doubled as a nightlight.

MANIFESTO

KATE ACKNOWLEDGED GEO.

She rolled over to deliver a concerned kiss and a grunt upon his arrival in bed. Left him to his worrying. So obvious.

She had slept for two fitful hours before his absence awakened her. Reading settled her turbulent mind. Geo looked at her back. A JD Robb novel absorbed her. She kept contrasting his authorial efforts to Robb's.

She thought, *Robb is able to crank out a new book every forty-five days. Why does it take him a year or more? Maybe if he'd lose that damn podcast. Maybe if we weren't always moving...*

Once he came to bed she tried to recapture slumber. She closed the book, set it aside, doused her reading light.

Kate feared Geo was taking Sam's death too hard. They had been so close.

~

"LIGHT READING," RANDY HAD SAID.

After Kate's peck on the cheek, Geo hunkered under their goose-down comforter and between Kate's favorite Egyptian cotton sheets to read Randy's pamphlet.

Joe was right. This 'manifesto' was nothing fancy. Just a single sheet of cheap white printer paper folded in half along its shorter dimension, like a child's homemade greeting card.

An unusual all-upper-case font was printed on Randy's ink-jet, no doubt.

With the paper's now-long dimension vertical and its crisp fold to the left, it featured a simple but provocative title in the center of the page:

LUNATIC FRINGE

Beneath that, he saw a crude hand-drawn smiley-face emoji with small hollow circles for eyes... all three of them in a triangle, one over two.

He flipped to the next page. Nothing to the left of the fold, all printing appeared to the right. He continued reading a unique and precise font and style he did not recognize.

It looked almost gothic, but he'd bet anything Randy just sought a unique, maybe mystical appearance, and just a little hard to read... Intentional? You had to want to read this:

COMMON PRINCIPLES
(37TH INCARNATION)

WE GATHER AS AN ACTIVE HUMAN RIGHTS GROUP,
A LOOSE FEDERATION OF LIKE-MINDED FREE
THINKERS. NOT MUCH STRUCTURE.
A SPONSOR AND INVITATION NEEDED. WE MAY ASK
YOU TO DISASSOCIATE LATER IF A MAJORITY
FEELS YOUR THINKING HAS EVOLVED AWAY
FROM THE GROUP'S COLLECTIVE CONSCIENCE.
NO OFFENSE, AND NO HARD FEELINGS. IT IS A

*NATURAL EVOLUTION. IT IS OKAY. WE COME,
WE GO.*

*WITH ORGANIC INTENSITY, WE BELIEVE IN A
COLLECTIVE AND INDIVIDUAL ENTITLEMENT
AS MEMBERS OF OUR WONDROUS AND
MYSTERIOUS SPECIES, AND OF THIS GROUP, TO:*

*1. LIFE INDEPENDENT OF OPPRESSORS OF ALL
KINDS,*
*2. FREEDOM OF EXPRESSION, AS LONG AS WE CAUSE
NO HARM TO ANY BODY OR MIND,*
*3. DEFEND OUR PERSONAL AND COLLECTIVE
ENERGY,*
*4. PURSUE STATES OF HIGHER CONSCIOUSNESS
UNFETTERED BY CONVENTION,*
*5. SHARE KNOWLEDGE AND WISDOM WHICH
OTHERS MIGHT ACCEPT, OR NOT,*
6. A CLEAN PLANET ON WHICH TO NEST,
*7. RESPONSIBLE PHYSICAL, EMOTIONAL, PSYCHIC,
AND SEXUAL FREEDOMS,*
*8. SUPPRESS OPPRESSORS AS DEFINED BY OUR
GROUP CONSCIENCE,*
*9. SUPPORT OTHERS' FREEDOMS AND OUR OWN BY
APPLYING FORCE SUFFICIENT TO THE TASK,
ONLY AS A LAST RESORT,*
*10. CHOOSE THE TIME, PLACE, AND
CIRCUMSTANCES OF OUR OWN PHYSICAL DEATH
EVENT.*

*THE FRINGE IS SELF-SUPPORTING. MEMBERS
MIGHT POSSESS SUBSTANTIAL MEANS, AND
THAT'S OKAY. IF WE SHARE OUR BOUNTY WITHIN
THE GROUP OR BEYOND, WONDERFUL. IF NOT,
THAT'S OKAY TOO. THE ONLY PRINCIPLE
OFFERED IS THAT A MEMBER'S MEANS SHALL*

*NOT CONTRIBUTE TO SOMEONE ELSE'S
PHYSICAL, EMOTIONAL, PSYCHIC, OR SEXUAL
DETRIMENT.*

~

THAT WAS IT.

No contact info, no location or names either. And a weird choice of words, as if this was written and revised endlessly by a committee... or a community.

This was one provocative little manifesto!

Then he recalled Joe's words, "Randy is one of those wonderful spirits whose body has already started its transition. You'll better understand once you've read that cheesy little flyer he's so proud of. Pay attention to number ten."

10. CHOOSE THE TIME, PLACE, AND
    CIRCUMSTANCES OF OUR OWN PHYSICAL
    DEATH EVENT.

Geo thought, *Damn!* Then the voice whispered. "You said a mouthful, old son." He glanced over at Kate. She slept.

Double-damn!

B LACK ROCK, ARIZONA

No, please. God!

The sweaty ghoul pressed his knife against Kate's throat.

In the dim light, Geo saw its razor edge gleam as its tip penetrated her pale skin millimeters from her jugular. Dark rivulets dribbled down her neck onto her familiar flannel pajama top.

Geo screamed his plea to kill him instead of her. His hopelessness transformed into despair-fueled rage.

"She's done nothing to you!"

"No, but you have, asshole. And if slitting this little throat causes you anguish, that's reason enough. But I promise your pain will be short-lived."

"I'll do anything! What do you want?"

"Not much. Watch, and then die. No more talk."

With little effort, that knife cut through the flesh and muscle of Kate's neck. Instead of a breathy scream, she only whistled through her severed trachea now flayed open and gurgling as it filled with blood, choking her.

Kate's assailant clutched her from behind. Even though bound to a steel and wood chair bolted to the floor, this monster embraced her as she faded. Geo looked into her eyes in the dim light six short feet away. She gazed back at him.

First those lovely blue eyes sprung wide in shock before they relaxed in resignation to her fate. She fell quiet as she slipped from her body. Then he heard a familiar husky voice. Hers?

Geo struggled against his bindings to no avail. Screamed until nothing remained. Only a soft sobbing wheeze.

The assailant's wild-eyed sneer now just inches away filled Geo's entire field of vision. That's when the first penetration occurred, avoiding his vital organs to prolong the torment. The knife pushed in with a slow and deliberate thrust near the left side of his torso.

Geo's only response to the searing burn was a long slow exhale. Didn't care. Not anymore. Next, his attacker withdrew and re-plunged the five-inch blade through the tender muscle mass just below Geo's collar bone, pushing against resistance with both hands. To the hilt. Twisted the serrated blade, enjoying Geo's exquisite but silent contortions as he devolved into a baser animal.

The monster moved to the next calculated insertion site. Through the shock of it all, Geo felt more than heard that hot breath. With a subtle smoker's whistle from diseased lungs, his voice warbled against Geo's left ear. The madman methodically continued his work.

He stunk of stale cigar smoke and hate.

Toward the end, Geo's brain demanded an inhale after a constant series of silent screams from empty lungs. Somehow he drew in a breath despite the malevolent barrage of assaults while in the embrace of this sweaty killer.

Geo screamed as loud as he could. Not loud at all. One last plea. Little air remained to be expelled from the anguished lung that still functioned.

"Finish it, you evil bastard!"

~

HIS HANDS BROKE FREE.

He struck his attacker.

"Geo! Geo! Please!"

Too late.

"Geo! Wake up, for God's sake!"

"What? Where?…"

Kate defended herself from his trembling blows. Then he reeled from the sight of those wild eyes of innocent fear. Tried to process…

"Kate? Oh! God. I'm sorry, I'm *so sorry!* Are you okay? Fuck!"

"I'm fine, Geo, but we have to talk."

She pulled away from him on the bed, rubbing her left forearm, nursing her… *defensive wounds?*

Still sullied by the nightmare's pain and the fog of sleep, he remembered little. But he would *never* forget the terror in his beloved bride's eyes just before he stopped his clenched fist from striking the monster's—*her*—face with all his strength.

Minutes later, they sat side-by-side, both still in their pajamas, in the motorhome's living room. A floor lamp they brought with them from their last home bathed them in an amber glow, a peaceful glow.

Now this.

Kate looked hurt, the pain much deeper than the bruises about to blossom on her arm. She sat to his left with deliberate space between them. She stared straight ahead, not at him. After several minutes of debilitating silence, she spoke after drawing in a deep breath.

"Do you remember what I told you when we started dating as teenagers?"

He remembered, even though they hadn't been teenagers for a half-century. She came from an abusive home. Was she now living in yet another?

He dredged up his next words slowly, in an embarrassed voice.

"Babe, I remember. You said, 'If you ever hit me, we're done.'" He choked them out, head down, tears rolling down onto his chest, onto the stupid long-sleeved Abercrombie and Fitch Water Polo sleep shirt given to him. Someone's discard? Like him?

"Do you remember what your response was to that ultimatum, Geo?"

He remembered.

~

"I said, 'Why on earth would I *hit* you?'"

"Geo, I knew right then you and I might have a future together. You asked that question with such innocent confusion on your face, I saw someone whose entire childhood did not crawl and claw through violent nights.

Before that, I thought physical and emotional abuse was normal, not to mention the other stuff. I know what just happened wasn't you, baby. But we need to find out who that was, and *why* that happened. Or we *are* done, no matter how much we love each other. Do you read me, Geo?"

"Yes, yes. I was dreaming, but can't remember much."

With more breath than sound, she whispered, "*What is going on with you?*" He seemed to get smaller. She didn't mean for her words to take such an accusative tone, but they had.

The lump already in his throat, still growing, and the tears on his face convinced her this man had seen too much, and cared too much about, well, everything.

It was no surprise to her that he was more fragile than she. Her childhood had been a brutal boot camp that trained her to withstand emotional blows, among *all the other stuff*. But his scale had tipped. Now hers was close. Again.

Geo grew up in a nurturing and loving family. He would never appreciate the profound difference in their backgrounds. She had shared hers all with him, but words could never tell the complete story.

She'd had the dreams too. She forgot *none* of hers.

Similar to one sober drunk confiding in another, Geo would believe her next words without equivocation. Her voice softened.

"Honey, you need to talk with someone, just like I did after you rescued me from my step-father. Make it happen. Make it happen."

She needed say no more.

He got on his knees between hers. They embraced, his head on her chest. He could not see the residual fear in Kate's eyes as she stroked his blonde-turning-gray hair.

TUCSON, ARIZONA

THE WORDS ALWAYS REMAINED THE SAME.

Each time Geo called Veteran's Affairs, anywhere in the country, they offered the same recorded message that never failed to strike a dissonant chord somewhere deep inside. The only variation was the location:

> "Welcome to the Southern Arizona VA Health Care System. If you are
> having a medical or mental health emergency, hang up and dial 9-1-1.
> If you are having thoughts of suicide, press seven now to be connected
> to the veteran's crisis line."

He made an ASAP appointment. Drove over to Tucson six days and five sleepless nights later.

As he waited in a small reception area that tried not to appear antiseptic, the normal waiting room detritus caught his attention.

Almost too tired to read from lack of sleep and the four-hour drive from Black Rock, he expected to see at least one copy of *Psychology Today* or *Better Mental Health*. But he only spotted a three-month-old copy of *Wired* magazine—appropriate—and a cover tease for an article on Battlefield Yoga. *Battlefield Yoga?*

What caught his attention more than anything on a nearby table was a clear plexiglass cube a foot on each side and open on the top. It contained twenty-two heat-sealed plastic bags within—he counted them—each containing something red and silver with a handwritten note on a white piece of paper inside each baggie. Like each was packaged by a volunteer.

The sign taped on two opposite sides of the cube explained: *Free gun locks. Courtesy: Vet's Crisis Line.*

He caught the receptionist monitoring him pawing through the bags. He looked like a Marine drill sergeant. The guy spoke with a seismic rumble.

"Go ahead, man. Take one. They're free. For safety."

Before he could respond, peripheral movement to his right caught his sudden attention. A slender woman who he guessed might be in her early forties appeared through a doorway and called his name without raising her voice.

Her smooth movements amplified her feline physique. But there was also a touch of controlled masculinity in her step, in her stance. Like a cop. Hard to explain.

She opened the woodgrain door to his right, gestured with her right hand, and in an authoritative voice said, "Come in, Mr. Randle. Please." Not a request. More a command.

She remained silent as they completed their short walk. Nor did she speak for what seemed like a long time as they got settled in her office.

Was she giving him time, or assessing him? She had guided him to a guest chair facing the door through which they just passed—good— and a view of the only window to his left in the smallish but pleasant room.

Once seated, they faced each other almost knee-to-knee. She crossed her legs, smoothed her loose-fitting black slacks with both hands before recovering a yellow legal pad from the small table to her right.

"So your primary care physician referred you, Mr. Randle. Says you're dealing with some issues. Care to talk about what's on your mind? And remember, what we discuss is confidential, so please don't hold back."

"Sure. I've lost some folks close to me, and I'm having some scary nightmares."

"That it? "

"Well, sometimes my anxiety level, um, escalates."

"Look, Lee, let me be blunt. What aren't you telling me?"

Walls crumbled, as if by magic. Geo appreciated how this worked. He learned from Alcoholics Anonymous that by keeping things inside they grow septic.

Just occurred to him he and Kate hadn't been to a meeting in months. So much—too much. Just excuses.

He kept rubbing his now-sweaty palms on his upper thighs. Up and down and up. Lift. Up and down and up. Lift. He did that a lot. Kate needed to spray the front of his jeans legs with stain remover every time she did the laundry. She asked him about that—he couldn't explain. Didn't even realize he did that until Kate mentioned it. That thought occurred to him now.

He saw Kate's eyes in his mind again, and the fear in them. Realized she was too selfless to fear for herself. She feared for him. Well, maybe for both of them.

"Doc, for the first time in fifty years of marriage, I struck my wife."

He'd sob if he had any tears left. His dull gray eyes, all cried out, stared out the window. Just a hoarse exhale longer than each shallow inhale of his breath. Like he was trying to empty his worthless self.

"I was coming out of one of my nasty nightmares. I didn't mean to hit her, but I did."

"What emotion came to the surface?"

"When I realized what I'd done? Shame. Naked shame."

"What was the dream about?"

"Not sure. Involved shooting and chasing. No, wait. In this one, someone was cutting our throats. We were tied to chairs. I dunno."

He fell silent, gazed at the corner of a sunny rock and cactus garden outside the now-too-tiny window as he attempted to dredge up something he long tried to forget. His eyes darted over to the therapist's.

A nondescript double-wide trailer housed her office, the kind they use for temporary office space. The government was ever utilitarian. At least when it came to veterans.

Geo continued. "Even after two years of dating and fifty years of marriage, we still hold hands. We argue, but we also take every opportunity to touch each other, to hug, to kiss, like newlyweds. And I fucking *hit her?* What in Hell is wrong with me, Doc? No, wait. I know. This is where you tell me I'm stressed, right?"

Now he was snapping at this nice lady who was only here to help him.

"Lee, too soon. You said you've suffered losses. Who have you lost?"

He realized he was getting agitated and needed to settle down. He felt the center of his stomach quivering and pulsing like a tiny battering ram inside that hammered his gut without *anyone's* permission. Like his heart was trying to squirt up and out through his throat.

The therapist—he couldn't remember her name—looked concerned. Her voice calmed him, for the moment, but underneath, he knew she was anything but calm.

Geo bet there was a panic button in her pocket if things, well, *escalated*. MPs outside, maybe? Did they have MPs at the VA? No, here they hired ex-MPs to be VA Police.

Or she'd buzz that skyscraper of a receptionist just on the other side of that feeble plastic door?

He and the managers who worked for him at GGS always used a panic button when dealing with agitated corporate employees. Most often they were firing them for no good reason other than budget cuts. Orders. They used to joke about passing the *hot button* around to the manager with someone in the hot seat *du jour. Geez.*

This was not going well.

Geo choked it out. "A dear friend of mine passed several weeks ago." He decided not to mention Chet and Jessie.

"How?"

"He was old. And they shot him."

She stopped, surprised, waited, stared at him with calm concern. That frustrated him. Head cocked toward her left shoulder, brow just a little wrinkled, she still left her serene hands folded on top of the yellow pad with only a few words scrawled on it. His name and today's date?

Geo blurted out, "Sam was ninety-six and tried to assassinate someone. The FBI and local police killed him in Virginia."

She said nothing. Neither did her expression. Jotted something down on her pad. Then she hooked the pen onto the right side of her pad four inches down, and folded her serene hands on top again. She leaned forward.

He pondered every nuance of her body language. Why did he do that? Ever the analyst, the observant author, he guessed. Yeah, that worked for him.

"I don't know the whole story, but I'm sure he was trying to protect my wife and me. He was trying to eliminate an ongoing threat."

Geo realized she likely considered this a fabrication or a delusion, but he didn't care. Felt good to say it out loud.

She said, "Look, Lee, I consult with folks who deal with classified information, who solve big problems, folks who manage unbelievable levels of responsibility and stress. I also talk with combat veterans who struggle just to manage their own lives.

"I don't probe, I don't judge, I listen. Maybe I offer a little guidance. And it goes no further. So what else? Any other traumatic events that might trouble you?"

Geo surprised himself. He did not hesitate.

"Yeah. Eight years ago, a serial killer hunted my wife and me for months. One of my many disgruntled ex-employees. He killed four of my friends. Almost killed Ka… Char and me.

"Blew up my boat—our home at the time. He assumed we were in it. We loved that boat. Her name was *Sojourn*. He beat me with a bat. I shot him. We both survived. Later, he was assassinated. Now sometimes I have headaches. Sometimes I limp. Geez, sounds like a load of crap, doesn't it?"

Now the words were tumbling out. Talking about things with which he'd suffered in silence for years became a cathartic event.

She said nothing. Head still cocked, serene hands still folded, still leaned forward, just a little more. But she wasn't writing anything down!

"Char and I were drinking a lot. We've been sober for almost six years now. Better, but not the dreams. Now they're worse again. Now there's something else going on I can't talk about, but we're scared. Again."

"Did you ever talk with anyone about this old business, Lee?"

"Well, yeah, after it all happened. The friend I lost recently, a physician, set us up with a counselor back then, and that was good. Lasted about six months. Then we started moving. A lot. And that was that."

"Lee, do you have trouble sleeping? Is your anxiety ongoing or cyclical? Beyond your recent altercation, does your demeanor trouble your wife? Do you harbor any thoughts of harming yourself or others? Anything like that?"

"Uh, well… Shit. Sorry. Yeah. To all of that. Off and on. Mostly on. I fall asleep okay, but I'm up very early. Nowadays, I guess since Sam passed, I'm up at two or three in the morning.

"Other times, I just don't wanna get out of bed. On bad days. I'm not suicidal, I don't think, but with me hitting Char, I'm worried, Doc."

"Okay, it's good that you're worried, Lee. One more time. What else?"

"I feel like we're in constant danger."

She grabbed her pen, jotted a few cryptic phrases on that yellow pad. Otherwise, what useful purpose did it serve just laying there on her masculine lap?

And why should he care what she wrote or didn't write?

Geez!

Then she spoke again after two full minutes of thinking, then writing, then clipping her pen in the same damn precise place on the right side of her stupid pad.

"Lee, you display many of the symptoms of post-traumatic stress, or PTS. We often see this in soldiers returning from combat. Sometimes years downrange. Has anyone ever diagnosed you with PTS before, Lee?"

"Well, the person I talked with in 2008 and 2009 suggested I reacted as expected, but I guess I handled it pretty well. Even better after putting the plug in the jug.

"I held an executive position at a large international firm at the time and stress from that job pushed my buttons, I guess. Another reason I retired at fifty-eight. Besides that almost-getting-killed thing. That was almost nine years ago. But *now*, I hit Char?"

A long one-minute pause gave both time to think and to settle down. Again. She started taking deep breaths. He followed suit.

"Okay. That happens. PTS can worsen over time, often exacerbated by the lack of ongoing treatment combined with additional stressors like the loss of your friend recently.

"And under violent circumstances? This is more likely to dredge up hostile emotions you've already processed, maybe only partially, but can compound them nevertheless.

"I'm prescribing something for you to take the edge off, a minimum dosage to treat your anxiety. It's called Citalopram."

Geo didn't like the sound of this. He worried.

She read his expression and said, "Don't worry about addiction. It's not that kind of medication. Take it the same time each day. And Lee, it is important you keep taking it even when you feel better. That means it's working. Okay?"

"Okay, Doc. Geez, I hate this, but I know I need something."

"Can we talk for an hour each week for a while, Lee? That might help."

"Sure. That'd be fine. What's your name again?"

"Doctor Cassandra Nobles. Just call me Cassie."

GEO CONTINUED TO SEE CASSIE FOR WEEKS.

She always asked him about the meds. After he hinted at hearing

Sam's voice, she seemed to accept that, but upped his Citalopram dosage 'merely as a precaution.'

She didn't believe he suffered from schizophrenia, but suggested he should at least know of the symptoms. Schizophrenia was a scary word, but if he remained vigilant, she thought it unlikely he'd strike his wife again.

The more he dwelled on it, the more PTS made sense. *It's hard to see the shit when you're swimming in it.*

Cassie was right. His symptoms were classic.

UNBROKEN CIRCLE

C ANYON HARQUAHALA GRANDE, ARIZONA DESERT

He could see them beside a fire atop a small breezy plateau in this valley. Indian Joe had told him this was sacred ground.

As he hiked with the padded quiver of flutes slung over his right shoulder toward the perimeter of the stone circle, twilight silhouettes of distant mountains in every direction with no other lights in sight signaled this holy place was untrammeled. Randy and Joe had invited him, an honor with this group in this place.

A dozen dedicated flute aficionados, some of whom were also makers, sat cross-legged or leaned up against large rocks. Or they sat in low sand chairs around the tight circle ten feet in diameter.

They were here to play and to listen and to celebrate life—a pleasant mix of First Nation citizens and North American descendants of European invaders.

The sparkling tinkle of a small steel triangle struck at intervals hinted of magic here—real or imagined. Two buffalo-skin drums softly pounded out a campfire beat for anyone who wanted to offer a traditional or improvised tune to the rest of the expectant group.

Two accomplished performers blew life into a rhythmic Cherokee melody at the circle's edge. They chose to stand. One bass, a fat low A-minor flute three feet long, found its harmony with a skinny high A-minor pocket flute only a foot long. The duet worked the thumping rhythm as if it were a giant heart pacing them in synchrony.

Bright paints and leather lashings anchoring a few feathers and colored beads embellished a pair of inverted rain sticks. All that enhanced their appearance. Gravity enabled their performance. Held at a gentle angle, the hollow sticks created the soothing sound of a gentle summer rain. Seeds inside meandered over the sticks' myriad inward-facing thorns.

Everyone listened along with their floating inner muse.

Between songs, all sat in quiet contemplation. The desert offered its own dry susurrus of soft anticipation as they awaited the healing power of this valley. In the middle distance, a coyote bayed at the quarter moon.

Distant blue-white heat lightning ripped near-horizontal bolts across the sky beyond the mountains with no thunder at all. A few deep sighs made their way around the circle as they listened. And watched.

And waited.

A bundle of sage and white cedar smoldered in an Abalone shell at the circle's geometric center to dissipate negative energies.

Magic. Nature. Therapy.

This group embraced these poultices as their lifestyle, more than just the heart of a spiritual evening.

Less than ten yards away a medium-size fire of dried mesquite warded off the cool night temps from within its small stone-ringed pit. Even the drifting smoke and the crackle of burning wood contributed a sense of spirituality to the circle's atmosphere.

Little more than a reflex for these experienced desert dwellers, all maintained a casual one-eyed watch. A rattler or the occasional scorpion might seek heat from the nearby fire, or warmth under someone's lap blanket. Anyway, most lay dormant after dark.

The desert's quiet song descended unending, freeing mortal minds to seek immortal truths. Geo remembered that the philosopher Nietzsche once said, *"When you look long into an abyss, the abyss looks into you."*

Did he now find himself in the twilight of early wisdom as he opened his mind to new possibilities? Would he find hazards through his now-more-open spirit as he sought counsel from beyond the grave? As he undermined his existing norms and values by creating new ones, did he risk losing himself? Or finding himself?

And if Nietzsche's abyss was what deep truth looked like, might Geo discover some startling surprises? He thought, *Oh, what did Nietzsche know, anyway? This feels so right. Besides, I am not compelled to seek all truth—only that which fulfills and keeps Kate and me out of our own graves a while longer. And me out of an asylum.*

After almost twenty minutes of listening to the desert's subtle song, first one rain stick picked up again, then another. They had responded to the haunting melody from one of Randy's rim-blown pueblo flutes. A low E-minor? The drummers knew to stay silent as Randy's rhythm traveled a haunting journey.

Now and then, two or three tiny thumb symbols accented the low meanderings of the slender yard-long Anasazi flute over the almost inaudible chitter of handcrafted rain. Together, they softly celebrated thousands of years of human tradition in sync with Her elements, their earth mother.

Later, Joe, Randy, and Geo took turns performing more cheerful extemporaneous tunes to a small but grateful audience. But Randy was *the* rim-blown guy. These flutes were the hardest and most traditional flute of all to play well. Randy said he was channeling Coyote Old Man, whatever that meant. Also a master of Anasazi music and rim-blowns, Joe could play anything. Geo felt more at ease here than anywhere in recent memory.

Indian Joe said Bearfoot—Ed, his spirit guide liked that name—must sleep this night. Old Randy just smiled. Geo waited in vain for Sam to speak to him again. After Sam's death, that first time he heard his voice almost tipped him into Nietzsche's abyss. He wondered, *Has Sam met Bearfoot? Oh, boy!*

NEW PATH

I NTERSTATE-10 EAST, ARIZONA

THE TIME HAD ARRIVED FOR THE NEXT LEVEL.

Despite the lack of cruise control, the weekly four-hour drive to Tucson in his little red Toyota smoothed Geo's rough edges as much or maybe more than the meds.

He collected his apprehensions and sorted through them. Then he pondered over what questions were worth contemplating. And who might offer answers if he asked the right person, or... guide.

This meant he contemplated which questions he could trust asking Cassie, and which he'd reserve for the Fringers. Sometimes he discussed what was on his mind with both to contrast and compare scientific and spiritual perspectives. As a researcher he found this comparative analysis gratifying.

Cassie, Geo's VA therapist and now confidante, grasped the scientific bones of his concerns, but she wanted to keep increasing his meds. He did not find that satisfying.

Several of the Fringers reinforced the wisdom of his EMP precautions, but many felt real danger from ElectroMagnetic Poisoning was still decades away. He'd fall back onto the wisdom of Pascal's Wager—his own adaptation—against which there was no substantive argument: believing and acting hold less risk than dismissing or ignoring.

So Geo cranked up his authorial rhetoric to protect humanity from itself, as futile as that windmill might be to tilt. As a result, through the voice of fiction and the contents of his weekly *Redemption Alley* podcast, he increased his personal danger by at least an order of magnitude. This according to Joe, Randy, and an occasional kick in his ethereal hindquarters from Sam. These warnings he ignored. After all, he trudged a righteous path.

NEW LIFE

H OUSTON, TEXAS

Ernesto Joseph Blackfeather…

Deputy US Marshal Blackfeather, aka Indian Joe, died one night, and has been alive ever since.

White collar crime ran rampant in the 1990s with all the dot-com blunders and infantile Internet security. Joe pioneered security software during those wild days. He found his skills in high demand, but his amateur investment adventures wandered everywhere except the market's sweet spot.

Joe won and lost more than one fortune before being accepted into the US Marshal Service's Felony Apprehension Unit, a rare honor and his dream job.

Details remain sketchy, but Joe's software acumen, combined with his physicality, served him well. Those skills also provided him high-value credentials for serving in Witness Protection after a successful two-year assignment with Felony Apprehension.

After years of denial and quiet shame, Joe rediscovered his heritage and wished to shame that heritage no more. He was a new man. Becoming a Deputy US Marshal completed his personal transformation. But his past left him with emotional and physical scars.

Joe made many friends in FA. He also made countless enemies.

One evening while retrieving a fugitive from his home back at the turn of the twenty-first century, Joe and his partner became targets in the tiny backyard of a rundown rambler in the Houston suburbs. He couldn't even remember being mauled.

But his attacker—a vindictive neo-Nazi with a grudge, posed as an anonymous tipster informing on a neighbor, allegedly the high-value felon. He struck Joe from behind before slashing his throat. This was after he shot Joe's partner, Ed Insner, at point blank range.

Left for dead, two teammates found them seconds later, Joe with copious blood loss, and no pulse from either. One teammate trained as a first responder brought Joe back to life—chest compressions, mouth-to-mouth, the works. He directed *his* partner to sustain pressure on Joe's deep neck wound with a bunched-up nylon windbreaker. The large-caliber hole in the center of Ed's forehead spoke for itself.

The bad guy escaped.

An ambulance arrived within six minutes; a hospital was just four minutes away. Against all reasonable odds, Joe recovered after emergency surgery and months of rehab.

At least he recovered from his *physical* injuries.

During his rehab Joe started hearing voices. Well, one voice, with many moods. His deceased partner, Ed, gave him a non-stop stream of unsolicited advice like *Get your head out of your ass and get back out there.*

Later, the voice recalled their jail time together. During a rare undercover assignment in a county detention cell, they squeezed a confession out of a reactionary scumbag who murdered three Department of Justice employees. Ed said, *Yeah, that gig was a nice diversion from the street shit, eh, partner?*

One day during his rehabilitation, instead of trying to pretend he heard no voice, Joe started talking back. In private. Ed explained in his best pseudo-sardonic tone—that was Ed—he was now someone Joe's ancestors called a spirit guide.

Ed would say, *Whatever. Just know I'm still here for you, buddy. Hey, that butt-ugly scar on your neck healed to a nice shade of magenta, huh? Magenta! Musta learned that fancy word since I croaked. Ha!*

Sometimes, in response to comments like these, Joe gave his spirit guide the mental finger.

Joe's supervisors remained concerned over his adoption of a kinder, gentler demeanor—the polar opposite of what they needed in Felony Apprehension. Not long after returning to duty, the USMS reassigned Deputy Marshal Blackfeather to WitSec in the Tucson Field Office. Joe had requested Arizona, his childhood home. Doctor Marshal Cassie Nobles was his boss within the Arizona Federal Judicial District, although he learned Cassie moved around. She was a recent transfer in. Lofty career goals, no doubt, but she seemed honorable.

Joe survived with lifelong mementos of that betrayal in Houston—a magnificent scar high under his chin, and an intolerance for intolerance. Few had heard this story. So far, his new buddy Geo Janis was not one of them. Some day he'd have to tell Geo about his day job, but not yet.

VENDETTA

U NDISCLOSED LOCATION

Malc Frieburg's day job kept him busy.

But two names burned his frayed nerve endings: Sam Braxton and George Janis.

Braxton died from law enforcement lead poisoning. What sweet irony. Janis, however, had yet to pay. One of Malc's operatives intercepted an archived report that had collected dust for years. His blood boiled, and he *would* be appeased.

Enoch Slattery had been Malc's only father figure. His own asshole father died claiming any sperm that took root was no offspring of his. Rot in Hell, *Dad*. But he idolized Enoch.

Until eight years ago Enoch was his mentor, his confidante, and his only friend. That ended when Braxton and Janis ordered him whisked away to some black site to suffer and maybe die from unspeakable torture. Now the time was long overdue for his last real enemy to die.

The old report of Enoch's capture galvanized Malc and his team into action. He had deployed a hundred operatives for any chatter of Enoch's captivity, even though it's what the cops call a cold case. He would never forget his friend. But every channel went full black after the report of his capture. Enoch was gone.

Not only did these two toadies deprive him of his father figure and friend, they forced his beloved Mr. Z to ghost himself. Mr. M was okay, but nobody could ever replace the venerable Mr. Z. The old Russian had influenced world events for sixty years.

But when those shit rockets closed in on him, the Great Man, a god among men, ate a bullet from his cherished Makarov. What choice did he have?

Yeah, the last of this pair of assholes would pay.

REVEALING NEWS

B LACK ROCK, ARIZONA

Another beautiful evening twilight...

They sat with their backs to Geo's trailer in tattered lawn chairs, side-by-side, facing west. The tiny trenches in the pea gravel beneath those chairs showed they spent many hours sliding those chairs to practice the rigor of tracking sunsets.

Geo furrowed his brow. Indian Joe tried not to notice, enjoying the remnants of another dramatic desert sky glowering in defeat. They had jammed earlier for two hours on their flutes in the trailer, sometimes with Geo on his guitar, the three-chord wonder that he was.

They jacked into what Joe called an electric canyon—Geo's small amplifier with just a touch of echoing reverb, like the acoustics of a real canyon.

Then they just reveled in silent and comfortable companionship by the light of a small fire for another half-hour.

"Joe, we've been spending a lot of time together."

"Well, don't get all mushy on me. This ain't no bromance or anything, right?"

"Aw, c'mon, you hard-ass. I'm trying to tell you something here. One friend to another."

"Sorry. Old habits. I spend a lot of time alone. Good for me. But you… Dunno. Been real interesting. And you got a natural talent for telling a story with your flutes. Not a bad maker, either. Plus, you got balls for a city pussy. No offense."

"Damn it, Joe. I'm worried. I have something I need to tell you. I don't want to put you in danger."

That caught his attention. He leaned farther toward their dying campfire, and into the discussion, but still couldn't resist making another remark."

"Huh. What? Something from your little desk job back in the dark days? 'Fraid I'll catch a contagious paper cut? You don't need to worry about your buddy, Joe. I can take care 'a myself. Even have, on occasion."

"Damn it, Joe, this is serious. Will you just shut up for a minute and let me tell you what's on my mind?"

"Okay, pardner. Sorry. Shoot."

"Eight years ago, I held an executive position at a big international company. That afforded me a comfortable lifestyle. But the stress and a running battle with my ethical standards tore me apart.

"Then I discovered my boss was leading a double life. He was a covert operative for another huge organization—of bad guys. Freaking traitors. I exposed some of them, retired early, changed my name, and started running."

"You shittin' me, man? You punkin' me?"

"No, Joe. Honest injun."

"Kiss my red ass, gringo. Sorry, go on."

"Well, me and my friend and mentor, a retired intelligence officer —you met Sam in Yuma—helped bring hundreds of traitors to justice. Some folks died. Kate and I almost got killed too.

"I'm in hiding because I think these assholes may still view me as a loose end even though we're years downrange. Based on some stuff happening now, it isn't over. Not yet."

"Well, damn, son. That's quite a tale. And old Sam is a spook? Huh. Well, let's assume it's all gospel. Why are you tellin' ole Joe about it?"

Joe was younger than Geo, but he persisted in portraying himself as older. A cultural thing, perhaps?

"Well, I fear those around me could become collateral damage. Not that it matters, but my real name isn't Lee. Same for Charlotte."

After only a brief beat, which surprised Geo, Joe said, "Hell, son. What's in a name anyway, but I find this all interesting. Look, Lee, or whatever you answer to, none of this makes any difference. That's true at least as concerns our friendship, which I value and find enriching.

"Or regarding potential threats to my personal safety, even though we've only known each other for a few months, do not worry about that for a single moment. I'm in. Hell, the scenario to which you've just alluded is far more interesting than writing code or making flutes. Or than cow-towing to flatulent tourists. Or than dealing with obsequious casino managers. What's next, gringo?"

Geo's eyes widened with incredulity. His friend's command of language transformed during the last few *minutes*. And his drawl became far less-pronounced. This seemingly ill-educated desert rat now possessed the demeanor of a sophisticated college graduate. Maybe even from a prestigious Northeastern University. Holy shit!

"Joe,"

"Yeah, the tourists like to think of a guy who looks like me in a particular way. That's fine with me. In fact, I encourage that. To a certain extent. I so enjoy being forever under-estimated. A tactical advantage.

"But you, my friend, have shown the utmost respect for me and my heritage, all that notwithstanding. I love you for that, man. And when you whipped off your mask, I am now compelled to do the same. Even?"

After a stunned silence, Geo got them rolling on some barrel laughs he sensed were healthy for both of them. Geo stood. Joe did the same. In the post-twilight darkness by the dim yellow light from their dwindling fire, Geo embraced Joe in a hug of appreciation and a round of back-slapping. Joe did not object, but also did not engage with the same enthusiasm.

They continued laughing and then chuckling between contented sighs after they descended once more into those cheap lawn chairs around that pitiful fire. They weren't sure why it all just felt good.

Good enough, Geo thought. *Two chameleons in a pod. Do chameleons have pods? Or is that only whales? Or peas?*

TRUST AND GUTS

W ASHINGTON, DC

He could wait no longer. Had to be now.

It took several days to get onto the president's calendar.

Adler Stavers, longstanding director of the United States Secret Service, now sat across the famous constitution desk from President Stewart Atherton in the Oval Office.

Yet another gray day broadcast its presence through the armament-resistant window behind his president. An ill omen?

Director Stavers cut right to the chase. Events developed too fast for idle banter. Besides, this belligerent president might lose patience with him before he delivered his message.

"Mr. President, thank you for taking my meeting. You are in danger. Again."

He saw naked disgust on the aging face of his president who still suffered from the most recent attack on his life. Could he blame him?

After several moments of silent consideration and what seemed to be a blank stare with malevolent undertones, the president spoke in a low voice.

"Well, Mr. Stavers, that's been true throughout my entire administration, has it not?"

"Sir, it's no secret we share little or no trust. You made that clear when you brought in your own personal detail on day one eight years ago. I understand why, even though at first I viewed it as a personal affront."

"Mr. Stavers, we need not do this."

"With all due respect, Sir, yes, we do. Now more than ever after that recent attempt to poison you. I should have caught that."

Stavers felt the president's bristling diffidence toward him on both a personal and professional level. Resolute in his mission, Stavers pressed on.

"I've given my life to this service. If for no reason other than respect for my office, Mr. President, allow me to offer you an olive branch. Lacking your trust, I've long cast myself in the role of a silent protector behind the scenes.

"Sir, your fine team has foiled some designs on your life because of your trust in them, even though like me, they failed you recently. Your adversaries are getting too close. You may not know that my team and I also prevented several attacks on you that otherwise would have proven fatal.

"Now I am duty-bound to share a dossier of several such events as proof. I only offer this to you now because your direct involvement is critical. I can only help by emerging from the shadows of your doubt. How can I earn your trust before it is too late, Sir?"

"Mr. Stavers, I will deny nothing you've articulated of our tempestuous relationship. My actions provide the prima facie evidence. But I've made it clear I love my country above all else. And I appreciate your candor. If what you say is true, what would you ask of me?"

The president's voice emanated profound eagerness for this useless meeting to come to a quick end.

"Sir, grant me a test to prove my fealty to our great democracy, and to your administration, despite your longstanding skepticism.

"You know of the Patriot Brotherhood. You and your predecessor dispensed justice in 2008 and 2009 to a list of known traitors and collaborators. Since then, my agents and I kept our heads down, seeking less traditional ways to serve.

"Even now this cabal of traitors reasserts itself with renewed efforts to dominate the American political landscape. I hold proof vital to the survival of President Stevens and to his efforts to derail this gang of thugs.

"More to my point *today*, Sir, I must now also surface proof of treasonous complicity *from within your administration*. This will also be prima facie evidence of my loyalty to you, and of my attempt to fulfill my oath to defend and protect you and our great nation.

"To build a bridge between my best intentions and your distrust, I suggest you read the encrypted dossier I sent to your *personal* email account. Ask your team to verify its provenance, and its veracity. But Sir, time is short as events unfold even as we speak. What say you, Mr. President?"

Prolonged silence met Stavers' question. Thirty seconds passed. Adler wasn't sure President Atherton remained engaged, but said nothing.

"Give me four hours, Mr. Stavers. Thank you. Dismissed."

STEW ATHERTON WOULD LOOK INTO IT.

As the almost-lame-duck president endured his final days in office with both anticipation and dread, he still swung a big stick.

Specific to today's task, he issued several terse commands to a cadre of trusted officials in the US Intelligence Agencies. But his most trusted inner circle included his director of the NSA, Admiral Jake "Gunner" Mahoney.

Five hours after his ten-minute meeting with Adler Stavers, he received a call from Admiral Mahoney.

"Jake, give me your best gut on this Stavers dossier."

"Sir, better than that, Stavers' claims appear factual. Ninety percent confidence, anyway. While we still have more work to polish this assessment, my best analyst believes you're looking at the real deal.

"It appears Stavers pulled your presidential ass out of hot grease more times than we could have imagined. What you might find most surprising, Sir, is that you are still alive thanks to Adler Stavers and his team even more than due to your own private team's efforts. And he contained this within his department until now, for reasons of his own. Sir."

Stew loved Jake's colorful vernacular, and even more so because he felt comfortable using it with his Commander-in-Chief. This shocking news was hard for him to accept. But since he trusted Jake Mahoney with his life, maybe it was time to set aside longstanding grievances for the sake of the nation.

"Thank you, Admiral."

"Sir."

TRUST AND TRAITORS

THE TIDE TURNED.

This time, President Atherton summoned his Secret Service director to the Oval Office. His own private security team leader, Stan Farley, attended this meeting with them.

The president had directed Stan to sweep for bugs that afternoon, just prior to this meeting, even though that daily event would take place again early the next morning.

Director Stavers arrived. He registered concern at Farley's presence. An unspoken uneasiness existed between them, but it was clear his attendance was not optional. The two security chiefs sat next to each other in guest chairs across the desk from their boss.

President Atherton spoke first. "The room is clean, cameras are off, and Stan is up to speed."

Farley nodded to Stavers, a tacit acknowledgement of the value Stavers and his team brought to Atherton's well-being over the past eight years.

Farley had told the president that to the extent the dossier's contents reflected reality, they all owed Stavers and his team an unpaid debt of gratitude. But both remained somewhat skeptical.

"Adler, let's say we further verify the impressive contents of your dossier. I would first offer you and your team my thanks. Second, if we continue down this path of building mutual trust, tell me something else I don't yet know. You made a brash claim earlier. Please explain."

Stavers' reluctance stemmed around this *civilian* in the room, but the president was driving, and he wanted Farley present.

"Mr. President, your VP is a traitor."

Adler waited a moment, not for the inevitable disbelief to dissipate, but to ensure he had their full attention. Two granite faces stared at him. Then he forged ahead.

"Long suspecting his motives, I placed his Observatory Circle residence under surveillance some time ago. My unilateral authority. A recent conversation over which Vice President Sealey could only believe was private became available to me."

"You expect me to…"

"No, Sir, I do not. Nor you, Stan. This will help."

Stavers produced a digital playback device from his inside breast pocket and placed it on the president's desk. He touched *Play…*

∾

"Yes, Mr. Vice President.

"How may I serve?"

"You can do your damn job, Martino!"

"Sir, no names, please. I know Old Soldier is a burr under our saddle, and he could sink us…"

"Stop already with your sophomoric mixed metaphors. John Stevens is not only a threat to our brotherhood, he's jeopardizing our chances for success in the upcoming election.

"Now you've not only failed to rid me of Atherton, you can't even handle an old ex-president! I'm thinking you've outlived your…

"Look, we cannot afford these incessant failures, Michael. And you need to do something about that idiot Frieburg."

∾

ADLER STAVERS TOUCHED *STOP.*

He remained silent, embarrassed at his unsanctioned surveillance of the vice president of the United States, present circumstances notwithstanding.

The president also remained silent for several minutes. Then he asked Stavers to play the recording again. More awkward silence.

The two subordinates were smart enough to remain silent, awaiting the president's pleasure at the grenade just lobbed onto his desk.

"First, I'd recognize Norman's voice anywhere. I've had my suspicions. But this, this is… high treason. Stan and I owe you a heartfelt apology, Adler. Due diligence demands I have that recording analyzed."

Without hesitation, Adler pushed the recording device sideways to his right on the desk toward Stan. Without saying a word and before picking up the device, Stan offered his hand to Adler with a small apologetic smile to back it up.

Adler accepted the only apology he suspected he'd ever get from Stan Farley. Nodded in return. It was enough.

Adler said, "Yes, Sir. I would expect nothing less. And I can provide intel on the other two names mentioned on the tape. I suggest I meet with Stan and your analysts to deliver my deposition. These treasonous acts must not stand. Sir."

The president said, "I will expedite our next move. How can I further test the veracity of your claims, Adler?"

"Sir, I suggest you meet with Vice President Sealey. I further suggest you take a call with President Stevens, ostensibly to learn what he has discovered of chatter you're hearing. Tell Sealey you and he need to circle your administration's wagons.

"He should be eager to take part, and will see this as an opportunity for Patriot Brotherhood operatives to trace the call and to locate President Stevens.

"My most trusted team member sweeps Sealey's residence daily, and by my directive, always leaves one discreet listening device in place that cannot be defeated. I suggest one of your team accompanies my guy on the next sweep to retrieve the latest recording together.

"If we can verify that he is collaborating with the PB, you will have your confirmation. Meanwhile, we can plan next steps and react to real-time events should something else shake loose. Is that acceptable to you, Sir?"

The president didn't take long.

"Let's do it, gentlemen. And men, we're on our way to burying a big hatchet. Let's make sure we bury it in the right treasonous heart."

FAMILY REUNION

B

ALTIMORE, MARYLAND

Other than anonymity, the Sleep Inn and Suites featured one advantage: its proximity to the Baltimore-Washington International Airport. Only two-star accommodations, but they could ill afford to have anyone recognize former President Stevens.

Mick Sandstrom on Captain Cheevers' team booked the room under his name as he was the least-known member of their party. Mick was proud of his minimal digital footprint.

Their suite was clean, featured two queen beds, a sofa bed, and a single bathroom, but little else. That was just fine for their party of four. After two days, however, with no housekeeping, the room grew gamey. The president's friend, Sam Braxton, called with final arrangements made for them with Geo Janis in rural Arizona—*way* off the grid.

"Mr. President, are you sure?" Uncertainty circled Captain Cheevers like a ravenous jackal.

"Provide me with another alternative, Captain. Who do we dare trust?"

"But a trailer park? Sir, with all due respect, that is not a hardened facility."

"Captain, we hardened the beach house, took every precaution, and look where that got us. No, given our dubious circumstances, stealth is our best option, however unconventional. And I'm told it's a small RV resort that also has *hardened* permanent trailers."

John risked a smile with his small serving of humor.

"Please help us make this happen, Derek. And if we are to hope for any chance of success, you must call me John. Or maybe even Uncle John. We're to be a family."

"Sir. Uncle John? You know, it just occurred to me you are enjoying the prospect of going undercover."

Spit-and-polish Captain Derek Cheevers dared risk a smirk in the general direction of the man who used to run the free world.

BLACK ROCK, ARIZONA

KATE STRUGGLED WITH THE IDEA.

"Geo, is the president really hiding out with us? This can't be happening." She had been cleaning the motorhome non-stop ever since they received the call.

The oversized reddish sun descended through the tops of the tall palms lining Apache Way. That broad gravel drive separated the row of pull-through bus-style motorhome sites from a row of small 'park model' mobile homes on the far side.

With no grass anywhere in sight, small translucent watering tubes emerged from their subterranean home inside a hand-molded crater of muddy sand around each thirty-foot palm. A gentle hiss signaled the watering system cycled and offered the tree next to their site a long crater-filling drink.

Geo's attempt to slow Kate's cleaning frenzy yielded results at last. They weren't relaxing, but they sat in lawn chairs on a grass mat anchored with tent stakes at its corners. Insurance against evening breezes sweeping their pea gravel site with grit. Those tiny round rocks allowed almost no desert dust to ascend from beneath. But beyond the park, the occasional dust storm challenged all fastidious housekeepers' efforts. *And* painted the sun blood-red.

He set the tone by speaking softly.

"Babe, they'll just be our park neighbors. I don't know how long they're staying, but he'll have his protection detail with him.

"The president's lead, a guy named Cheevers, told me we must keep up appearances. They're to be just four family members coming to visit for a week or so."

"Oh, God. I can't do this. *Family?* I'll lose it, Geo. He used to be *president!* Everyone will *know* him.

"Cheevers said John will be in disguise. He said they do this all the time."

"*John?* Geez, Geo, you're on a first-name basis with President Stevens?"

Geo smiled. "Kinda cool, huh? But we do need to low-ball this. And *please* keep your voice down, babe."

"Yeah? Really? Okay, I'll stay here—inside—when you greet them. *Please?*"

"I'm sure they'll understand. Not easy for me either. I've never met John. We've talked on the phone a few times. That'll be fine. Sam always said he's a great guy."

The incoming call warned Geo and Kate of the small entourage's imminent arrival. Geo provided final directions.

Their arrival was anti-climactic. He supposed that was by design, but still surprised him. A dusty white Ford Edge with a Hertz sticker on the rear bumper parked on the gravel road in front of their distinctive rig.

Before anyone got out, thirty seconds later, an identical red version of the white mid-size SUV rounded the curve at the end of their row. It stopped a vehicle length behind the white one. Both four-wheel-drive cross-overs looked at home out here.

Geo recognized President Stevens after a few moments of reflection. First, he was the oldest of the four. Second, his casual demeanor could not hide his regal carriage. And last, he looked like a model from LL Bean's Autumn catalog. Like trying to dumb down a rock star traveling incognito through Mayberry, USA. Geez. But then he was looking for a president.

Per Cheevers' phoned instructions, Geo waited for *them* to approach *him*. What was *that* all about? He could guess. The team looked wired. John led the way toward the front of site sixty-nine, their site.

Million-dollar smile, arms spread wide and above his shoulders as gravel crunched underfoot.

"Lee! How's my favorite nephew?"

"Uncle John! Char and I are so glad you all could make it."

Geo didn't think anyone was watching or listening, but per Cheevers' instructions from which he dared not deviate, they took no chances. They would be a family for at least the next week.

As they shook hands with stiff formality, Geo's eyes widened to porcelain dinner plates as President John W. Stevens drew him into a warm embrace.

Uncle John's *sons*, Mick, and Derek, along with Derek's *fiancée*, Darla, all tensed. Derek even flirted with an offensive step forward before John glared at him now off to his left. John's hard look screamed, *Freeze!*

He whispered into Geo's right ear. "George, I feel I already know you through your stories and for what you did, what you gave up for our grateful nation. I'm glad we're here, son. I mean, nephew. That serious light-haired gentleman to our left is Derek."

As they drew apart, Geo recovered from his momentary shock— the prolonged hug helped disguise it. He smiled with a genuine glow and made the rounds of introductions meant to look like a family reunion. The two alpha males in this trio were not huggers, and that was okay. Some families didn't hug.

"Char wanted to greet you too, but she's recovering from a nasty headache. Cousin Derek! How long has it been? Welcome to the desert."

He grabbed the Captain's hand with both of his. Cheevers, not much of an actor, offered a stiff but untrusting smile—more a smirk of unpleasant amusement—attempting what he knew to be a necessary facade. He offered a good-natured slap on the side of Geo's right shoulder while he gripped Geo's right hand, shaking it with an artificial vigor.

"Good to see you again, Lee."

Had anyone been watching, they might think these two harbored a dispute over Uncle John's inheritance.

Geo stumbled, regained his balance after the Captain's friendly shoulder slap that threatened to knock him off his feet. Would have if Cheevers hadn't still clamped his hand in that vice he called his right fist.

"Geez, Derek, you been working out? Good grip, man!"

Retreating from Derek's test of manhood, he swiveled his now-tearing eyes toward Dar, the only female, and Mick, the only other man in John's little entourage. The president was taking a huge risk with such a small detail. This trio must be extraordinary.

Then he realized he must stop massaging his right hand, still drained of all blood and feeling after its encounter with Derek's destructive grip.

Is he marking territory?

"Mick! Darla! You guys look great!" A civil but abrupt handshake from Mountain Man and a merciless hug from Intensity Girl. Her beautiful smile failed to find its way to her eyes.

He never met such an edgy and serious threesome. It appeared John was in good hands. Then why should that surprise him? John was a freaking *president!*

∽

C̲HEEVERS BRISTLED.

A camper walked his dog thirty yards from them and then headed away from them.

In a softer voice, Geo said to the group, "Okay, guys, Char and I are thrilled you are here. After the weirdness washes away, we can talk more if you wish. I want to help. For now, you already know this is our motorhome and trailer. Those two units across the way are yours. Here are your keys."

This Geo Janis impressed John. He was handling extraordinary circumstances well. Smart to keep his wife under wraps if she couldn't perform.

Geo handed one key to John with a *Black Rock RV Campground* fob connected to it on a split ring. The other key he tossed to Mountain Man Mick. He just feared Captain Cheevers.

Feeling like an informal Welcome Wagon, Geo offered his best synopsis of their accommodations.

"You can park one car under each port. It's traditional in an RV park to greet new neighbors and then to disappear so they can get set up. John, Derek, you both have my number, or just wander over and knock. If your cell carrier is AT&T your phones should work, but the Wi-Fi ranges from crappy to non-existent."

"Thanks, Lee. We carry our own comms."

"Oh. Yeah." Another embarrassed grin.

"Sir, we should not remain in the open so long." Cheevers admonished his president.

"You're right. Enough with the theater. That was fun. Lee, thanks again for the welcome. Later, then?"

"Yes, um, Uncle John. Later."

Geo stared for a too-long awkward moment as if John Lennon just hugged him and called him by name.

Cheevers repeated, "Well, later then?"

"Huh? Oh, yes. Sorry. Bye."

Geo scurried off to report to Kate who must be dying with anticipation by now. He thought he spotted her peeking around the edge of the windshield shade as he walked toward the bus.

~

"JOHN, LET'S GET INSIDE. PLEASE? NOW?"

John nodded to Derek, then looked at the key. Someone handwrote the '7' with a ballpoint pen on a scrap of white adhesive tape on the black plastic fob. The thing looked like an elongated triangle with rounded and chipped corners.

He grinned.

*Not the Plaza. And **way** off the grid. Perfect.*

Distinct from any security concern, this trip was already a salve to his beleaguered soul. He might just understand what attracted George and Kate to this lifestyle after all the other curve balls associated with a lifetime of responsibility and service.

THE SETUP

W ASHINGTON, DC

He was elsewhere in the White House and connected him with the president.

Stan cited an urgent security briefing regarding a request from President Stevens. The president wished to prepare for a call with the former president and required the VP's input.

"Norman, thank you for taking my call. I can't shake my serious trust issues, as you know. At least we can trust each other."

The VP presumed awareness of the agenda for the call with Stevens.

"Of course, Stewart. If President Stevens can help incarcerate what remains of this treasonous scourge, I'm glad to help in any way possible."

"Thank you, Norman. I've asked my security chief, Mr. Farley, to sit in. He is on the line with us.

"Mr. Vice President…"

The president continued, "Norman, in the carriage of your duties, have you learned *anything* of this Patriot Brotherhood that might be of use in this call with John?"

"I have not, Stewart. That is so far outside my purview, but I can't imagine much of that organization still exists. President Stevens still campaigns against various activities he attributes to that group. He isn't tilting at windmills, is he, Stewart?"

"Norman, I'm just not sure. But he requested this call with us from some place called Black Rock outside Brenda, Arizona. I believe we owe him the courtesy of accepting it. We'll try to keep it short."

"Agree. President Stevens served this country with passion his entire life. He is a true patriot. I'm glad to listen in and help if I am able."

"Some state business demands my time for the next thirty minutes, Norman. I'll finish early if I can. Please join me in the Oval by four p.m. We'll call John then. Agreed?"

"Of course, Mr. President."

WE HAVE STEVENS!

With no time to return to his secure communication cocoon in his den at One Observatory Circle and still meet with the president at four, Vice President Sealey risked a call to Martino with his white-hot news.

From his office in the West Wing behind closed doors, he dialed.

Sealey whispered, "Michael, Stevens is in a place called Black Rock outside the town of Brenda, Arizona!"

"Sealey, you fool! You're calling me on an un-encrypted cell?

Click.

THE STING

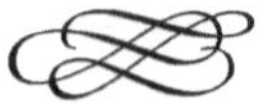

P OTOMAC, MARYLAND

MR. M SAID, "WE'VE LOCATED OLD SOLDIER.

"Stevens is at a place called Black Rock outside Brenda, Arizona. Let's finish this thing, Van."

Thirty minutes after Michael Martino's secure call to Van Stockton who was still with Malc Frieburg in Maryland, the two killers boarded Martino's private jet. It awaited them fueled and warm at Leesburg Executive Airport.

Their mandatory flight plan listed Phoenix Sky Harbor as their destination.

If they would have flown commercial, the two-thousand mile trip would have taken five hours plus intolerable airport wait time. But Michael's Gulfstream G550 would get them over Sky Harbor in less than three hours, tarmac to approach.

The FAA flight plan system raised no red flags when en route they diverted to Desert Skies Executive Air at the Lake Havasu City general aviation terminal. A simple distraction from their true destination.

From there, a short and discreet two-hour drive would deliver them south to Brenda, Arizona in two rented GMC Acadias that awaited their aircraft's arrival at Desert Skies.

WASHINGTON, DC

REED BENNING WAS LIVING HIS DREAM.

He protected his old commanding officer, now Job One.

This presidential protection detail was even better than MARSOC —Marine Special Operations Command—where he served with Stan Farley under Stewart Atherton, until they all aged out, that is.

Reed briefed Stan, his boss, after talking with the analyst assigned by the president's friend at NSA, Admiral Mahoney. A small circle under tight control. This recording was white-hot nuclear and treated as 'eyes only' by a handful of folks who knew how to keep a secret.

Geez, the VP? We are so screwed unless we resolve this.

"Stan, based on names mentioned on Director Stavers' recording, we found a Malcolm Frieburg. He's registered as the sole proprietor of an LLC that owns a large house in Potomac, Maryland. Address is 10666 Falls Road.

"Plus, get this, one Michael Martino, the other name, used to be the freaking CEO of Greater Global Solutions before he resigned and disappeared in 2008. Been a ghost ever since. Now *that* guy knows how to evaporate. But this Frieburg dork? Not so much. We only have old PR photos of Martino, but we found Frieburg's face on a Christian dating website."

STANHOPE FARLEY'S DEVOTION TO HIS BOSS?

Well, he had dedicated the last eight years of his life shielding his president, and twelve years before that, his favorite senator.

He considered Stewart Atherton a brother. They shared mud and blood in the Marines prior to politics, and a few other adventures.

Stan's lifelong purpose was to repay the honorable man who saved his life in Viet Nam.

"Nice work on these IDs and getting us an address, Reed."

"Thanks, Stan."

"I'll liaise with the locals. You and your team get out to Frieburg's house, contain the scene and mine that property for intel. By the time you get there, I'll make sure Potomac PD, DC Metro SWAT, and a search warrant await your arrival. Don't be shy about using your credentials. Clear?"

"Yes, Sir! What about Job One?"

Stan said, "I'll stay with One. Stay alert, soldier!" Reed enjoyed being called that. He missed the Marines too.

"Roger, Boss."

THE PRESIDENT IS EATING OUT OF MY HAND!

With that happy thought, Vice President Sealey arrived at the Oval Office from his own in the West Wing at four o'clock on the dot. President Atherton's assistant ushered him in straightaway.

The sight of three Secret Service agents including that weasel Stavers shocked him. President Atherton long distrusted the Secret Service, and no individual agent more than Adler Stavers. For him to be here?

The president stood behind his desk gazing out the window, his back to the room.

"Have a seat, Norman. By the desk, if you please."

This was an ill omen. The VP always sat on one of the two sofas.

After Vice President Sealey seated himself, with the president still at the window, his voice carried over his shoulder.

"Adler, if you would be so kind."

At volume, the recording played with the press of Stavers' finger…

∾

"Yes, Mr. Vice President.

How may I serve?"

"You can do your damn job, Martino!"

"Sir, no names, please. I know Old Soldier is a burr under our saddle, and he could sink us…"

"Stop already with your sophomoric mixed metaphors. John Stevens is not only a threat to our brotherhood, he's jeopardizing our chances for success in the upcoming election. Now you've not only failed to rid me of Atherton, you can't even handle an old ex-president…"

AND AFTER A BRIEF SILENCE…

"Michael, Stevens is in a place called Black Rock outside the town of Brenda, Arizona!"

"Sealey, you fool! You're calling me on an un-encrypted cell?

∾

"TURN IT OFF."

Sealey's face and neck, already pasty, transitioned through several shades of apoplexy. As if someone was both inflating and deflating him. They had set him up. He said nothing.

Unlike the movies, he knew not to incriminate himself further, even though that recording sealed his destiny.

He avoided eye contact. With anyone. Not embarrassed—defiant, and pissed off at getting caught. He no doubt still maintained his residual self-image as a patriot.

President Atherton turned around in a slow arc to face his vice president and to gaze perplexed into his misty eyes, now bloodshot and puffy. Astronomical blood pressure, perhaps?

In a soft voice, he said, "You held my trust, you treasonous bastard. I do not wish to hear *one more word* uttered from your seditious lips. Get him out of here."

To the room the president quietly said, "Let me be very clear, ladies and gentlemen, *nobody* hears about this."

After two of Stavers' most trustworthy agents ushered the vice president from the Oval Office, the president addressed Stavers.

"Adler, I owe you a debt of gratitude. Thank you."

PLANNED AND UNPLANNED

BLACK ROCK, ARIZONA

Off the grid, and then some...

The four of them congregated around a small circular table in the tiny eat-in kitchen of Number 7, a compact park model mobile home.

Derek thought, *A funky RV park outside a nearly non-existent town with the unlikely name of Brenda? Good grief.*

He summarized their situation. "Sir, from a tactical point of view, this place is brittle Swiss cheese."

He addressed his next remark to his two veteran Delta Force teammates, Darla Evans and Mick Sandstrom.

"Guys, we'll stand watches but we dare not do so outside. Can't draw attention. We're full black here."

John, former President Stevens, said, "How could anyone find us way out here?" But even before Derek's you-gotta-be-kidding expression faded, he added, "What am I saying? They always find us, don't they?"

Derek continued, respectfully passing over John's comment.

"We'll wait til after midnight to move the armory in from the vehicles. John, tomorrow we meet with your fan-boy to get a better tactical briefing on the surrounding area. We need to understand all contingencies.

"Sir, if you agree, one of us will rotate watches in here with you at all times. When you need privacy, the sentry will loiter out on the covered porch. I assume that would appear normal. I suggest we use Number 6 next door as our command post and bunkhouse.

"We maintain radio contact on tactical channels with the sentry through earbuds whenever we lose visual contact. And we'll rotate and sync channels each four-hour shift. Questions?"

John said, "Derek, what is your recommendation for blending in here? Won't it appear odd—maybe even attract awkward questions—if we rotate each of you between the two trailers every four hours?"

Derek pondered this for a moment before conceding.

"Good point, Uncle John." Snickers.

"Okay, new plan. I'll establish the schedule, but we'll stand watches from *within* our respective units. Somebody's always awake and alert for their shift.

"Mick, you bunk in here with John. Dar and I will be next door. Otherwise, same plan. Meet here at 0600. Okay?"

After receiving a round of serious nods and a thumbs-up from their boss, Derek said, "Good. Mick, first watch. Then you, Darla."

More nods acknowledged their team leader's orders.

As everyone arose to retrieve their go-bags from the cars to settle in, John tugged on Mick's sleeve. "Mick, could you take your time? I need to make a call."

"Of course, Sir."

~

"Lee, this is your Uncle, John.

"Thanks again for making us feel welcome. Derek is serious about his job. No offense."

"Oh, you saw me nursing my hand?" Geo sniggered, embarrassed that was so obvious.

"He'll warm up. But if he doesn't, he'll have his reasons. Do you understand, Lee?"

"Sir, he's doing his job, a tough job. I respect that. And even though we've never met, I've seen those eyes before. Those are Sam's eyes. I can only imagine."

"You're observant, Lee."

"I'm a writer. Writers observe. But thanks for your concern, Sir."

"Okay, then. We'd like to ask you to visit us in Number 7 at 0600 for a briefing on the area. Will that be possible?"

"I look forward to it, Sir."

"Good night to you and, ah, Charlotte."

~

JOE STRETCHED HIS LANKY FRAME.

His eighteen-foot travel trailer required certain adjustments. While the short bed stretched sidewall-to-sidewall, he could only fit at an angle.

Daylight faded outside, so he pushed the button to operate a small twelve-volt sconce light above his head.

Boxers and a sleeveless tee were de rigueur for bedtime. He looked goofy with his white cotton socks normally hidden by his boots. But his feet did not appreciate cool temps at night, especially if he pressed them against his poorly insulated trailer's wall.

He rejected using covers and hated burning propane to feed his furnace. He called his trailer his aluminum teepee. It fit his needs. About the time he decided to close his eyes for a few minutes before throwing on his jeans for his next walk-around, his cell rang to the tune of *America, the Beautiful.* The boss. Again.

"...Cassie, I'll tell them when the time is right."

"Okay, Joe, but expect fallout from keeping this a secret from them."

"Hey, Geo and I have much in common and that made it easy to get in and stay close. Besides, he likes us redskins."

"Joe, that self-deprecating humor might play well with your protectee, but I am not amused, Deputy Marshall Blackfeather."

"Sorry, Doctor Marshall Nobles. I'll handle this. Thanks for the consult. And maybe you need to follow your own advice."

Joe hung up on his boss. He could just imagine Cassie thinking her guy has *gone native.* Fine. He'd handle it. His priority was protecting the Janis clan who were also his friends. Besides, she hadn't told Geo that in addition to being his therapist at the VA, she was also his supervisory guardian angel.

Darkness fell early in this desert.

Their boss was racked out and Mick stood watch next door.

Derek sensed a smoldering volcano threatened to erupt after lying dormant for decades.

Still in her khaki shorts, hiking boots, and a tight white sleeveless t-shirt only eight feet away on the queen bed in full view, Dar Evans stretched and purred like a cat on a warm windowsill. Seemed deliberate.

He hunched over his laptop on the coffee table as he perched on the edge of the ugly red velvet loveseat in the open living space. Smelled new.

He risked a quick glance toward her lithe form in the bedroom of the small trailer, as if he was seeing her for the first time, but afraid to stare.

Starlight twinkled through the skylight as the evening air drafted in from an open kitchen window. Tickled the hairs on his bare chest and legs. He trembled, but not from its chill.

His forehead glistened from perspiration as he pulled his attention toward the micro eat-in kitchen at the street end of the park model mobile home.

Too many windows.

ALONE WITH DEREK. COULD SHE? MAYBE?

As she looked at her former commanding officer and now her civilian team leader in Unit Number 6, Darla moved with one swift cat-like motion. From the bedroom she joined Derek in the main living space. Sat down beside him.

"How come you've never made a pass at me, Derek?"

They had often slept side-by-side in tents pitched in different hostile deserts and jungles and on mountains on different continents, not knowing if they'd survive.

After all these years of working together on countless missions, how many times had they saved each other's lives? Or shared body heat in order to endure?

"To make a pass at a teammate is not professional. A distraction."

His eyes remained resolutely locked onto the computer's small screen.

"I get professionalism. But a distraction? Does that mean you find me attractive, even though I could kick your butt at will?"

He closed the laptop and turned to her. His smile was gentle. He could not believe he was allowing this conversation to happen. After so long.

He said, "Look, we've been through a lot. We know each other. Better than we know anyone else. You're one of the best operators I've seen, and I admire you. We trust each other, no matter what. I don't want to screw this up.

"Besides, after that South Carolina thing, I figured you'd hate all men, including me. And you'd have every right."

They had held Dar captive, drugged her, interrogated her, tortured and raped her, for two days.

"When I found you…" His voice faded. He didn't need to finish.

She frowned. "Derek, that was combat. We've come home now. We leave that shit on the field of battle. I refuse to be a casualty. Just another mission, with consequences. We manage consequences and emotions—done and done. Okay?"

Derek hung his head, then looked over at her with dewy eyes.

"Dar, seeing you naked and bloody tore my heart into little throw-away pieces. Something happened when I held you in my arms—the way you looked up at me—delirious. You're telling me that affected me more than you?"

"Not at all. But we move on. I want to move on. I love being on your team. I love what we do, and we're damn good at it. But we're people too, not just operators."

～

SHE SAT AT AN ANGLE.

Their knees touched. Nobody pulled away. She placed her small calloused right hand on his left knee and let it rest there for a time before she spoke again.

"Derek, I want more than to be an operator, don't you?"

Oh shit, he thought. *What the Hell are we doing here?* But this woman was a force of nature.

He laid his hand on hers, still resting on his knee.

"Dar..."

"Shut up, Captain."

She snaked her limber body onto his lap, straddling him. So quick. Leaning into him, she kissed him hard, drove his head against the back of the couch.

Geez, she's strong!

Even as her fingernails dragged across his chest, she slithered down between his legs and onto the floor in front of him. The feather light touch of her small hands drifted over his olive-drab boxers. She had melted his lifetime of steel-reinforced discipline in an instant, and seared him with years of her restrained desire.

His once impenetrable defenses crumbled as her pouty lips enveloped him. He was rock hard from years of loneliness and desperate need.

It felt good. She felt good.

She purred, "We can still be operators, my love, even as real humans, with real needs. I've trusted you with my life, now I trust you with my heart."

He threw her onto the couch and covered her.

Now nothing can happen to her.

Ever again.

0545 CAME FAST.

A short night with little sleep found Derek alert, but a beat off. He admonished himself. Was this what guilt felt like? Another frickin' first. But no, that was wrong. She was right. They could be operators *and* human.

Still, the knock on the door of Number 7 at 0600 sent a bolt of electricity to his every nerve ending. John directed him to remain in his chair. His voice carried as if he were about to deliver the State of the Union. "Please come in, Lee."

Once again anchored in the present moment, Derek avoided eye contact with Dar. With anyone but Lee. Not because he regretted last night, but because of uncertainty, of how he might react to those damn doe eyes should they gaze back at him. He wondered how their working relationship *must* change. Shit!

"Good morning, all! Sleep well?"

Geo chirped with enthusiasm. Derek rolled his eyes and considered vomiting. Mick offered a perfunctory nod, Dar a sweet smile. The whole team knew *Lee* was an alias, but that had nothing to do with protecting John. Besides, John liked his little secrets, and he trusted Lee, or whatever his name was.

"Fine, Lee. Thank you. Derek, would you kick off our discussion?"

Derek guessed now was when John expected his rehearsed speech.

"Yes, Sir. Lee, no hard feelings from yesterday. This is not a scenario with which I am at ease, but I am adapting. We good?"

After a pause, Geo said, "Derek, I get it. You're good at your job. I'm clueless here. Just wanna help. Fair enough?"

Derek cocked his head sideways as he took in this tall and somewhat overweight older guy who John seemed to respect. Maybe he's okay, even if he *is* a soft geeky fan-boy.

"Fair enough, Lee. So let's get to work. We need info on our local environs here. First, the land. Second, the people. And third, we'll share with you our perspective on security. Tell us about this place."

Geo launched into the briefing.

"Cool. First, the area. As you know, we're about seventeen miles from the nearest town called Quartzsite, almost due west of here. Not much there. I think they have a Sheriff's station. Not sure about the nearest State Police Post.

"The fence behind your units separates this private park from public land managed by the Bureau of Land Management. Locals call it government land or BLM land. Millions of acres, including the low mountains to our east and south.

"You'll hear all-terrain vehicles called side-by-sides roaring past during the day, but never at night. Only trails out there with deep gullies called arroyos. No roads. All the way to Yuma, and Mexico beyond that. The low mountains called the Harquahalas are honey-combed with box canyons and shallow caves. Wild country.

"If you're not used to the desert, touch nothing you don't under-stand, always take water with you, wear boots, not sandals or shoes. This time of year, as things warm up during the day, rattlers and scor-pions might lash out. Gets mighty cold at night. Low forties."

Derek looked at Mick and Dar as Geo continued. They all smiled and cocked their heads. Geo picked up on that and said, "Right. You guys have been around. Sorry."

Derek said, "What about civilians? The locals, that is?"

"Most folks stay here long term—seasonal residents. Snowbirds. Some year-rounders too—lower income because this place is cheap this far out. People here get bored. Bored folks get nosy. They mean well, but you need to know they're just looking for something to do or someone with whom they can visit. It's just that simple. Normally.

"Not much to do, although they have a nice hot tub here, even Alcoholics Anonymous meetings most Tuesdays that Ka... Char and I attend."

Derek said, "We heard about your friends in Tucson. Sorry. You're here incognito because of that. What's your view of what we might expect?"

At the mention of his murdered friends, Chet and Jessie, who someone mistook for him and Kate, he fell silent and grew reflective for a moment.

"Thanks, Derek. They were good people. Here, I don't know. The civvies are curious, but that's about all. We know some folks, but most, not so much.

"Sam—Doctor Braxton—warned us to be vigilant and to move. As you said, that's why we're here. These Brotherhood assholes? I really have no idea. You guys'd know better. John told me about your beach house adventure."

Derek looked at John with surprise as if to say, *You told him about that?* John's head projected a subtle sideways shutter.

Geo continued. "As far as other people, I'd like you to meet a close friend at some point. He's a local I met in Tucson. Moved down here last week. He's a tech guy who works from his trailer. Knows the area since these are his stomping grounds. Name is Ernesto Blackfeather, but everyone calls him Indian Joe. A good guy with lots of insights. He knows a lot of the Natives and locals around here, including quite a few of the seasonal transients. Got a level head. Okay?

"Yeah, why not?"

Derek saw the surprise in Lee's face as if he were expecting resistance.

Derek continued. "We *should* familiarize ourselves with any local assets you feel might be useful. In fact, why don't you call this Indian Joe right now?"

"What? Oh, yeah, sure. Why not?"

Ten minutes later, Joe knocked on the plastic front door of Number 7. He still wore twin bandanas, one around his neck, the other high on his forehead. Faded Levis, the ever-present frayed jean jacket, and his turquoise choker over a tee completed his ensemble. Geo expected a few raised eyebrows when they saw him. He started to introduce his friend.

"Everyone, this is Joe."

Curt as ever, Derek interrupted with, "Good morning, Deputy Blackfeather. Nice to meet at long last. We've heard good things."

Geo wasn't sure what Derek had said. *Deputy?*

"What?!"

Joe said, "Sorry, brother. US Deputy Marshal Indian Joe, at your service."

Everyone let that marinate for a good thirty seconds.

"Son of a bitch!"

"Geo, I…"

"You *lied* to me? Has our friendship been a lie too, *Deputy?*"

"No! Geo, to know you is to love you, man. I didn't lie, I left out a few salient details."

"So all this Native shit was for me, another gringo *tourista?*"

"C'mon, dude. Throttle back or I *will* kick your ass. Now listen, started out I was on assignment. Protecting you and your bride. The lady I work for thinks I've gone native on her because I put our friendship above my job. It's you and me, man."

Geo fell silent and sullen. Joe tugged at his choker, looked embarrassed, realized he and Geo weren't the only two people in the room. Their little spat took place in front of a freaking US president. *Holy Hell.*

Joe spoke. "Very nice to meet you, Mr. President. Y'all. How can I help?"

Geo still stewed in his own juices. He wasn't yet ready to move on, even though he knew he must. Before anyone could say anything else, he took a quick step toward Joe, threw his arms around him, whispered in his right ear, "Asshole! Thank you."

Derek said, "Well, drama aside, ladies, we will need help, Deputy Blackfeather."

"Just Joe."

"Okay, Just Joe. We were told you might offer up some assets."

They spent the next hour reviewing the topographical maps Joe whipped out of the large inside pocket of his jean jacket.

They agreed Lee Randle's four visiting *family members* would want to take advantage of their proximity to the extensive trail system next to the park. Trail-riding was a popular avocation around the area. They needed desert-worthy transportation.

One of the many ATV—all-terrain vehicle—rental agencies in Quartzsite delivered three high-end rigs that afternoon. Joe offered to guide them on a tour of the trails later the next day. They had trails to explore, venues to choose, and people to meet.

GYPSY CAMP

B LACK ROCK, ARIZONA

ATVs—side-by-sides—scurried.

Everywhere.

Most Black Rock residents either owned or rented them. The magnificent trails were extensive.

Joe had rented a side-by-side upon his arrival from Yuma the previous week. Said he scored a favorable seasonal rate in Quartzsite. Rates were negotiable, at least for locals and hard-asses.

"C'mon, Lee. Even though most of the folks we're gonna visit today would consider you and your huge diesel-burning rig a poster child for conspicuous consumption, you're still a kindred spirit.

"They'll appreciate a fellow itinerant vagabond, an orphan of the road. But only you. Remember the flute circle Randy and I invited you to? Not far from their camp. They don't advertise."

Geo wouldn't find out until later why they weren't taking Captain

264

Cheevers and the others straightaway. Joe said this was a recon mission before punishing his local friends with the others.

A twenty-minute high-velocity romp across the arid terrain carried them over gentle-rolling dunes littered with a rich ecosystem. With the monsoons still months away, the most dominant colors remained earth tones and pale greens.

Even a sparse rain would cause this crunchy landscape to burst into bloom. The aftermath of a monsoon rain would inundate this broad valley with colors, smells, and scurrying critters coaxed from their cool underground lairs. He knew this was contrary to most folks' stereotype of the Arizona desert.

An almost total absence of flying bugs amazed Geo. His native Minnesota joked the mosquito was their state bird.

As they ascended from a twisted three-meter-deep arroyo, they rounded the base of a hill they called a mountain in these parts. Joe stopped their ATV on a rise with a grand view of a broad valley below and killed the engine. They could see the Fringers' dry camp in the distance. Those folks prided themselves on their self-sufficiency.

The sight below warmed Geo's heart: a splash of saturated hues leaped out at him among a sea of scratchy browns and dull blue-greens. A lopsided series of circles composed of camping vehicles clustered in several neighborhoods appeared contrived in their asymmetry.

Geo wondered if these circles of trailers and vans painted in bright psychedelic colors—even the tires on some rigs—represented reviled cliques he loathed in high school. He asked Joe as he stared through his mil-spec binoculars.

"Not at all. Those circles represent shared interests. These free thinkers are creatives. Most get along with almost everybody, but best with like-minders. That larger circle to the north, for example, are where writers congregate: poets, novelists, anyone who paints with words. Some freelance for a living, but most just pursue joy and freedom, or are trying to leave a legacy.

"To the south sprawls that smaller circle of visual artists. They spend a lot of time sketching, drawing, and painting. Even a few sculptors. They like to spread out more. Farther to the east is a sizable but tight group of fluties. See Randy's Airstream? That's his winter 'hood."

Some rigs like Randy's appeared opulent, but most ranged from modest to ramshackle. The latter were the most aggressively customized to match their owner's eclectic tastes. Some with a spray can or a brush, and lots of decals.

Geo said, "I'm surprised at his age Randy still dry-camps way out here. But he seems content. And the way he plays his flutes? Inspiring."

There was a comfort already knowing some folks in that camp from the circle.

"You kidding? Try to keep Randy away. Wild horses! Remember number ten in his flyer?"

Geo recalled:

10. CHOOSE THE TIME, PLACE, AND CIRCUMSTANCES OF OUR OWN PHYSICAL DEATH EVENT.

"So you're saying Randy came out here to die?"

"Look, Geo, er, Lee, we humans think we're so damn smart. We assume everything we think and do is so important. Most of our lives we even ignore the fact that we all are on a slow death march that starts the moment we're born. We're so wrapped up in our self-importance that despite the inevitability of our own demise, we act as if we'll live forever. A lot of stuff like that."

"Wow, Deputy Marshal Blackfeather. You've thought a lot about this."

"Geo, that is the precise point. Most folks don't. While we're all dying a little more each day, we ignore or rationalize the consequences of our decisions, of our actions. We ignore the impact each of us makes on our temporary home, Planet Earth. It's like we're driving it like we stole it.

"Do we not feel we have the *right* to over-populate with as many kids as we desire as if it were an entitlement? And most of us don't recycle, or worse, we litter, because it's not that big a deal.

"Then only because of our wants we consume more resources than Mother Nature can provide, and we're running out. Yet we do little or nothing except to consume at unsustainable rates and to pursue our own self-centered agendas.

"For many, nothing is *ever* enough during the time they rent space on this tiny rock.

"There is no limit to the arrogance and greed of our species. And some, like the Fringers, take that deep into their hearts, to resist their natural greed. For them and others like them, it is personal at a profound level.

"Quite a few Fringers follow the tenets of a forward-thinking self-proclaimed conservationist—Henry David Thoreau. Others, like myself, pay attention to the ways of the Old Ones, my ancestors. Many intersections.

"See that large lopsided circle of trailers in the center of the camp? That's where the hardcore conservationists hang out. Most of all, they fear we as a species will consume our way into extinction. So yeah, like these crazy lunatics, I've put a lot of thought into this, Geo. I mean, Lee."

"Okay, Joe. I get it, I think. Makes me feel guilty for burning so much diesel. A slippery slope."

"Aw, forget the diesel, man. You burn something else much more important and potent, dude, you burn calories to feed your open mind. You've already made quite a few friends from the flute circle. Let's get on down there."

With that, Joe once again fired up the ATV's noisy engine. He said he'd take shit from the hard-cores for burning fuel in such a *toy*, but he could take the heat.

It's all relative.

Joe explained they were to meet someone named Bob Fell.

"Many look to Bob for leadership. He denies that, suggesting sometimes he mentions his plans, and some folks choose to follow. But nobody denies Bob's influence in the group."

Joe explained the guy's humility is legendary. The mere mention of his influence embarrasses him. But give Bob a mission? He becomes a steamroller with a small army behind it.

"And he's no shrinking violet. Bob's a retired probation officer from Brooklyn. You'd never know that to look at him though. You'll see."

As they weaved their late-morning way at a lumpy idle through the sprawling camp, they stopped near the southern edge of the spacious center circle.

Dozens of threadbare and dilapidated lawn chairs surrounded a smallish fire pit with a pile of cold ashes in the center. A short stack of what Geo guessed might be mesquite lay in a haphazard heap alongside the pit. Reminded him of another circle reported to be close by.

Joe powered down the rather noisy *toy* as soon as it stopped rolling, but not before attracting lots of attention in this otherwise ear-ringing setting of silence. Most hid from the mid-day heat in the shade of their rigs or make-shift awnings.

A few heads poked out of trailer and van doors as Geo's eyes danced over the decorated trailers that surrounded them with primary colors and bold designs. They reminded him of a cross between a hippy commune from the sixties and the small camp he once spotted on a road trip through North-central Spain. That camp also nestled in a valley as he skirted the Pyrenees—a mountain range separating the Iberian Peninsula from the rest of Europe.

Geo always remembered that sight as a *gypsy* camp, though only he would use that word. Like the Basques beneath the Pyrenees, these folks chose their own way of thinking and of viewing their place in the world with pride and purpose—living way out here in an isolated valley between mountains.

Like the Basques, he perceived they existed as strangers in a strange land where each spoke their own language.

Oh, he knew at least some of these gentle folk spoke various dialects of American English, maybe some Spanglish or something more ancient. But based on Joe's introduction, their beliefs, their lifestyle, and their culture set them apart, like that group of Basques in Spain.

Geo admired that.

By his rough count of eighty trailers, smaller motorhomes and vans, Joe told him every single rig displayed their extended-stay BLM sticker. They were proud of their law-abiding status however unlikely a Bureau of Land Management ranger might ask for such proof way out here.

While almost two hundred dollars per season was a fortune for some, none of them would put a price on their pride.

Almost none of the rigs in this circle seemed a prestige purchase. Instead, they seemed to shout, *We've reduced life to its essentials.*

Indian Joe said, "Most of these free spirits believe simplicity clears the mind of clutter that stands in the way of contentment and contemplation of wisdom so invisible to so many.

"They believe that by removing obstacles littering their path to a more enlightened life, purpose shines without the otherwise inevitable shadows of doubt and deceit, or the blinding glare of shiny conceit. The worst clutter enables deceiving one's own soul, defiling the earth beneath one's feet, polluting the air all around us and the energy within us."

～

JOE AND GEO SAT IN SILENCE.

The engine behind them in the now-near-silent ATV ticked and pinged as its hot aluminum engine block contracted. They waited for someone to approach them. Joe suggested this was only because he wondered who was most inquisitive and attentive in the camp today.

He told Geo, "I bet old Baldy is the first one out."

"Who?"

The voice came from Joe's side and behind.

"Indian Joe? Son-of-a-bitch, man! Why you not come around so much like before? Too proud?"

Joe's voice carried with some force.

"Naw, Baldy. Just busy white-man business. Keepin' the wolves outta camp, ya know, amigo? This here's my brother from another mother, my friend Lee. Lee, say hi to this sidewinder everybody calls Baldy."

As they crawled out of the ATV still ticking away with embarrassing loudness, Baldy made his way around the front of the rig to Geo's side. He maintained continuous eye contact with this new curiosity.

"Lee! A friend of Joe's… *Lee*, ya say. Huh." Sounded like disbelief.

"Very nice to meet you, Baldy."

"Huh?" Baldy presented Lee with his right ear. Hearing-impaired, Geo guessed.

Louder, Geo said, "Nice to meet you! Baldy? That's a joke, right? Man, you have the thickest hair *ever*! Shouldn't they call you *Wolf?*"

Then Baldy broke eye contact with Geo without swiveling his head away from Geo, glanced sideways at Joe still crawling out of the ATV's far side.

"Ha! Kid speaks his mind. Like that!" Every word out of Baldy's mouth seemed maximum volume. And Geo thought, *Kid? I must have fifteen years on this hairy buck!*

Joe explained. "In ninety-one, Baldy's air defense artillery battery in Desert Shield pummeled Saddam's ground troops in Kuwait. He was a loader. Ended up with his ears bleeding because the ignorant old desert rat refused to wear ear protection throughout a forty-eight-hour bombardment. You always were an ignorant old cuss, Baldy."

"Wha'?"

"I SAID, LOST YOUR HEARING IN COMBAT!"

"Yeah, hated those goddamn ear muffs. Made for pussies."

Joe spoke to Geo, but loudly for Baldy's benefit. "BALDY CAN'T HEAR FOR SHIT, BUT HAS THE EYES OF AN EAGLE. THAT'S WHY FOLKS CALL HIM *BALDY.*"

To Geo, Baldy said, "Damn right. Saw you come up over Sand Flea Rise three miles up yonder. Been waiting for ya. You here to see Bob." Not a question.

Joe just air-checked with his right index finger. Baldy nodded over his left shoulder as if to say, *He's in his trailer. Head on over.* Joe nodded in return. Tossed Baldy a peace sign, two fingers, right hand, spread wide, followed by a fist to his heart, same hand. Dipped his head toward ole Eagle Eye.

Joe responded to Geo's amused grin and unasked question. He said, "Easier 'n trying to get him to understand by shouting at him. Means I understood his go-ahead, as in *Two*, and then *Respect*. Baldy's a good shit."

Geo also recalled radio protocol during his time in the teams. *Two* also meant, *roger*, or *got it.* And a fist over the heart spoke for itself.

They wandered the forty feet to a seventeen- or eighteen-foot vintage bumper-pull trailer that looked to be at least a half-century old. Even sported ornamental wings high on either side of its trailing edge. Backed up to within a few inches of its tongue crouched an even older Datsun pickup and matching bed topper with the worst case of cancer imaginable.

Must be a truck from up north with all that rust. But the few areas of non-perforated metal or plastic are spotless.

He forgot how tiny they used to make these trucks.

"Knock knock."

"You know what a door is for. Use it, friend."

They entered the small but airy space—open windows on four sides along with the entry door latched open against the outside wall. No screens anywhere. Geo couldn't help but stare at a man he guessed was fifty-something, snugged in amongst several huge pillows in the trailer's tiny booth reading a ragged paperback the size of a hardcover.

Walden Pond, maybe?

That book did not release his gaze. His chin-on-chest posture pushed out his bushy beard—more salt than pepper, with some red— like a wreath of dirty snow exploding in all directions.

The chest of his coveralls allowed the bottom portion of a peace symbol to peek from underneath his whiskers. Looked like it had been *spray-painted* on the bib of his black-and-white-striped coveralls.

He wore the coveralls' legs rolled up at least twice into broad cuffs to mid-calf length.

No shirt, hairy legs and arms, but shaved armpits?

His bare feet and calves rested on the padded bench. Bob showed lots of whitish more than reddish hair the consistency of straw straying out back and down as it hung over the settee's back cushion. And his pink balding forehead peeked out above his yellow bandana worn low like a sweatband.

Not what Geo expected. Didn't know what he expected. And this wiry spit of man smelled of lavender. Wave after wafting wave. Like clean after a shower.

"Bob! Good to see you, brother."

"Good to be seen, redskin. Take a load off."

Bob pulled his bony feet in to allow them to pass to the far side of the tiny booth. Joe waved a hand at Geo to slide in first opposite Bob in his semi-reclined position. Joe slid in next to Geo who thought, *Tight quarters. Bob's a tall man. Like an aged Abe Lincoln gone native?*

"You communing with ole Baldy over in the next county? Refuses to go to the VA for hearing aids. Wouldn't cost him a solitary centavo. Claims those devices will eat his brain. Won't own a microwave for the same reason. Besides, his rig's batteries run on fumes trying to push a haywire inverter. Stubborn, that sod. And ignorant, but *nobody* sneaks up on us."

He addressed his remarks to both Geo and Joe.

Geo found it unusual that Bob expressed no curiosity who the stranger was that Joe had brought into his home and whom he was looking in the eye. It seemed what he *saw* or *sensed* he found more insightful than any spoken word.

"Enough banter, already, my friend. Joe, your eyes possess the purpose."

While Bob's demeanor broadcast nothing but laid back, his speech reminded Geo of a small caliber machine pistol. No wasted words.

"Yeah, I'm not *only* here to enjoy your ebullient personality. Oh, this is Lee."

"Hey, Lee. Sorry you got tangled up with this injun. Your life has already changed forever, has it not?" A rhetorical question, but…

"Um…"

"Joe, he's a nice looking kid. You already know that. Not too quick on the draw, though, huh? Don't worry, Lee, hazing rights. Welcome."

"Yeah, we spent some time with Randy. Lee's been to a couple of flute circles. Randy likes Lee too. Glad to see the old boy made it down here."

"Ha! He keeps circling number ten, bless his heart. Well, Lee, if you're good enough for Randy. You hear voices too, huh?"

Not sure why Geo felt comfortable enough to talk about this, here and now, with a total stranger, but he did."

"Yeah, Bob, I've had a few conversations with a deceased friend who just passed."

"Well, don't talk about it like you're embarrassed, man. What's his name? What's his gig?"

"Sam. His name was, is, Sam. He was a doctor, and a spy. Shot at ninety-six. He was, is, protecting me and my wife Char from some bad people."

"Well, I bet was-is-Sam has shared a few pearls of wisdom with you already even though he's in transition, eh? Be patient. No doubt he's still confused too."

Geo blurted, "*He's* confused? Okay, guys, this is some weird mojo. I just met you Bob, and I'm telling you stuff I don't even share with my wife of over fifty years! What is going on, here? You aren't punkin' me, are you?"

Bob said, "'Punkin'? Isn't even Halloween yet, kid."

Joe smiled. "Well, now you've met Bob," as if that was all he needed to say.

Good grief!

Bob grinned like a cat with a snack 'a nip. Joe pressed on with a sense of urgency.

"Bob, we have a common foe. And they're coming here."

Geo found this choice of words strange. Not an *enemy*, but a *foe*.

"Some folks who ooze with negative energy aim to bring chaos, violence. We affiliate them with other assholes who propose unspeakable harm not only to people but to our Mother. To speak in plain language, fuckers are aiming to spread some evil. Are you ready?"

Without the slightest hesitation, Bob answered. "Whatever is just and necessary, brother. No more, no less."

"After we talk some, I'd like to bring someone else out to meet. He's a vet too. Bet y'all could share stories. But he's real serious and has serious skills. You two need to talk about what's coming. His name is Derek."

"Strong name. Kindred spirits with common goals but different hues can still blend."

This enigmatic exchange preceded a half-hour of scenario analysis and tactical planning. Geo had envisioned these people as bland pacifists whose only interest lay in their isolation from society and for intellectual masturbation. He could not have been more mistaken.

Joe radioed Derek their coordinates. He showed up thirty minutes later with Dar beside him. So for another half-hour after that, Bob served herbal sweet tea and ginger snaps during their pow-wow. And he flirted with Dar, but was perceptive enough to avoid offending her. Or Derek.

This tribe of gypsies prepared for the battle that would be brought to them.

EXPLOSIVE EVIDENCE

P OTOMAC, MARYLAND

A half-dozen police cars plus the SWAT command vehicle transformed the already-busy ten-thousand block of Falls Road into an impossible gauntlet. Long mysterious shadows announced the day's weariness.

But the day demanded still more.

The entrance to the small estate bore the number 10666 as an inlaid mosaic of black on a rather crude square stone column encased in blue and white Spanish tile. Out of place in Potomac. This column and its identical mate across the drive served as hinge posts supporting ornate wrought-iron gates.

Those gates, however, now lay half-buried in the pea-gravel driveway after SWAT's forceful entry blew them off their hinges.

A quick search of the house and grounds revealed no other occupants or staff.

Reed Benning headed straight to the rotund bald guy mopping his brow with his sleeve. He displayed the most gold on the hat currently in his hand, shoulders and collars. As Reed approached him standing near the SWAT van in the middle of Falls Road, he flashed his White House credentials while reading the officer's name tag: *Silas Hampstead, Chief of Police, PPD.*

"Chief, I'm Reed Benning. My boss briefed you?"

"Yes, Mr. Benning. Mr. Farley asked us to wait for your arrival before breeching. But we started taking automatic gunfire from the gatehouse as we began establishing a perimeter down the block. Somebody in there panicked. I became concerned for public safety, so we proceeded.

"Since we're a small force, we appreciate the help from DC SWAT arranged by your boss. The scene is secure."

"I understand. Now I need your team to vacate the scene, just for a while. Will that be an issue?"

"Ah, no, I suppose not. May I ask why? I was about to send in our local forensics team."

"Chief, we seek evidence of a national security breech. That comes from the president, but… your jurisdiction."

"Ah, geez. Well, you do what you need to do, Mr. Benning. So far, all the action's been outside, anyway. One of the three gunmen survived and is on the way to UMC in the District. Will you want to question him if he survives?"

"Yes, Chief. Now, the house? With your permission? The president believes time is of the essence."

"Ah, yes, yes. Truth is we're way out of our ballpark here if we're talking national security. I get it. So you guys do whatever you need to do."

"Thank you, Chief. We'll let you know when we're done. For now, please make sure nobody disturbs us, alright Sir?"

"Yes. I will. Glad you and your team are here to help sort this out."

Benning, his four teammates, and three members of the DC Metro Crime Scene Investigation unit formed a caravan. Their three vehicles snaked up the long curved pea-gravel driveway to Malcolm Frieburg's house.

WASHINGTON, DC

It took eight years, but he'd arrived.

Adler Stavers basked in the good graces of his president. At last. Just before the end of his second term. He was proud of his team's performance; the president was alive because of them, even if he hadn't known that. *And* because of Stan Farley and his team too, he must admit.

Director Stavers smiled. He and Stan Farley sealed their common goals with an optimistic handshake and a brief shoulder-slapping bro-fest yesterday.

And today they found time for a brief discussion after Farley's top five investigators left for Maryland, including Farley's favorite second, Reed Benning.

Adler only felt a little guilty; he toyed with stealing Benning away from Farley. He was that good. Maybe he'd go after that entire team now that President Atherton was leaving office. The Service could always use fresh blood. Now more than ever.

The monumental exposure and arrest of the VP would precipitate a major political scandal. But that was no longer his primary concern, nor the president's. They agreed this discovery in Maryland held the potential to change the landscape of their multiple-decade hit-and-run relationship with the Patriot Brotherhood, *and* its impact on the national political stage.

The mention of this Frieburg guy by the VP in that recording meant he was a high-level PB operative, or even senior management. He must know much of their treasonous operations.

The other name caught in the VP's recording, Martino, proved far more elusive which only piqued the service's interest in him even more.

The VP's arrest shook President Stewart Atherton to his patriotic core. While he was ecstatic at being able to trust his Secret Service team again—at least the agents Director Stavers had already re-vetted —they nevertheless kept their circle tight. For now. One never knew…

From the Oval Office, the president gathered them close, including himself, Stan Farley, and Admiral Jake Mahoney, Director of the NSA.

Stavers knew the president would take heat for excluding the rest of his National Security Council as this colossal betrayal unfolded, but he said he'd manage that later. Events were developing too fast with trust remaining in short supply.

With a nod from Stan who hovered over the speakerphone, "Mr. Benning, this is Director Stavers. I'm here with Mr. Farley. You're on speaker in the Oval Office. Speak freely. Please update the president and Admiral Mahoney."

Adler couldn't help but smile. Benning's voice sounded stiff and formal. The poor guy had had little opportunity to personally brief the president.

On a hunch, Adler recorded this conversation on his own iPhone's voice recorder app as he manned the White House landline connection to Benning's cell, breaking a few rules for the sake of expediency.

"Yes, Sir. Formalities aside, Potomac PD and DC SWAT subdued three gunmen before our arrival, two succumbed, a third is critical. The scene is secure.

"The DC crime scene team and we are searching the house. No sign of either primary suspect on the premises. We found Frieburg's computer. I'm looking at the bottom of its router as we speak. I just texted a photo of the IP and MAC addresses along with his landline number to your phone, Director."

The admiral and the president allowed the staccato briefing to continue without asking about this tech-speak. The president could only guess it was important, but the admiral understood.

Stavers checked for the text. "Got it. Can you access the computer's contents, Mr. Benning?"

"No, Sir. Password protected. DC CSI will take custody for analysis. They assure me it's just a matter of time.

"Doodles on the desk blotter here reference *Hat Trick 2.0*, although none of us has any idea what that means. There's also a safe deposit receipt in the trash for the Wells Fargo branch here in Potomac. And we see some alphanumerics jotted on the desk blotter here: N63ZCZ, that's November, Six, Thuh-ree, Zebra, Charlie, Zebra.

We're also gathering…"

Abrupt static. Then silence. For two seconds, five seconds.

"Mr. Benning? Reed? Reed!"

Stan's gut churned as Adler checked the status of the phone connection. He croaked, "He's gone."

Adler tried to reconnect to Benning's cell. Nothing. He referred to the text from Benning and dialed the house's landline from his iPhone.

Seconds later, he said, "Sorry, Stan. Sirs. No joy. It's as if that line just disappeared."

Stan grabbed the speakerphone from in front of Adler. With his right index finger, Stan punched out a number, a death grip choked the handset of the presidential speakerphone in his left fist. "I'm with the president and the admiral. Find out what happened. I need on-scene intel *right now, goddammit.*"

The phone on the table between the two sofas in the Oval Office didn't break when he slammed it down, but he'd order full diagnostics anyway. Tomorrow.

The admiral and the president shared a look and a memory. Both feared the worst. They'd both lost men in battle.

President Atherton placed a paternal hand on Stan's shoulder. Reed Benning was like a son to Stan.

POTOMAC, MARYLAND

THE CHIEF WAS DOING HIS JOB.

Outside the Malcolm Frieburg estate on Falls Road, Chief Silas Hampstead updated the mayor on his cell.

"Ma'am, three men opened fire on us with automatic weapons as we arrived to set up a perimeter. With DC Metro SWAT, we returned fire. Two killed, one wounded. No officers were hit. The scene is secure and the Feds just arrived. Yes, ma'am. I understand."

Chief Hampstead returned the cell phone to its clip-on holder attached to his equipment belt. He reflected how important that damn thing had become as a tool of his trade. He wished for a larger screen, easier to read.

His granddaughter told him he could make the text larger, but he needed some down-time to figure that out with her help. That fetched a smile.

He reached for the radio mic through the open door of the nearest squad, stretching its cord so he could speak to his dispatcher while standing outside and staring at the gatehouse across the street.

The Chief wondered what happened during the next few moments as a wall of super-heated air tossed him into the driver's side of the squad behind him. Next, he found it difficult to breathe—as if some unseen force prevented him from inhaling.

From the ground, his disorientation prevented lifting his face off the asphalt.

Silence.

Moments later, radio static, car alarms, and shouts of confusion gradually returned, but equilibrium remained elusive. The Chief realized he was regaining consciousness after the brutal affront of a concussive blast. He still drifted within a shroud of blurred vision—like peering through a veil of loosely draped lace.

He imagined he saw a perforated shell where the large house up on the hill stood moments earlier. Flames escaped through windows and doors and where its walls once stood and where a roof once rested.

He could see little else, but was sure he spotted a profusion of debris littering the grounds. All the way out to the now-flattened gatehouse ten yards from him. He *was* lucid, wasn't he?

The certainty his team would find eight corpses in the wreckage once the chaos subsided delivered more pain than his bleeding fore-head. Chief Hampstead's head had struck the corner of the open car door behind him. His ears were wet. So were his trousers.

Curious.

Disbelief overwhelmed him. Mr. Benning and his team: gone. The CSI team from DC: gone.

Through the clearing fog of his sideways cheek-to-asphalt view of the estate's remains, he spotted one of the team's three vehicles. Misshapen, on its crushed roof, it had come to rest in the middle of the vast lawn.

Now on his hands and knees next to the squad car, its rooftop light bar no longer broadcast a message of confidence, of authority. The entire assembly had shattered, but he saw no debris from it anywhere nearby. The radio's microphone dangled from its spiraled cord near his left shoulder, swinging in a pathetic arc, almost kissing the blacktop.

Onto the street between his hands he hurled the giant apple fritter and twenty-ounce black Breakfast Blend devoured quick-time two hours ago from Dunkin' over on Tuckerman Lane.

As he passed out again, face down in his own vomit this time, he thought, *A concussion? Or a TBI? Or worse? Son-of-a-bitch.*

He recriminated himself for not scrubbing the scene for explosive devices. *Hindsight. Let it go, Silas. Somebody else's problem now.*

Warm black velvet embraced Chief Silas Hampstead of the Potomac PD as his enlarged heart ceased to negotiate with inevitability.

FOXES EN ROUTE

LAKE HAVASU CITY, ARIZONA

NOW WHAT?

Moments earlier, on final approach, Malc's phone buzzed from the inside breast pocket of his tweed blazer. It could wait until they landed and taxied. Gulfstreams were not quiet when reverse thrust slowed these swift birds once on the ground.

Three minutes later, they taxied to the service ramp. Next to the Havasu FBO—Fixed Base Operator—the simple sign above the low-slung building announced their arrival at Desert Skies Executive Air.

A soft chirp from the landing gear as the brakes' discs stopped rotating announced their arrival. The plane rolled to a stop near an entrance to the private customer lounge. That chirp precluded a brief curtsy by the nose gear before the front of the plane bobbed back to level.

Still strapped into his seat, Malc retrieved his phone. An alert from his security system at the house? Strange. He speed-dialed his security chief from his recent calls list. No answer. Dialed his backup from his contact list. The same. Now he worried.

Crappy cell service out here.

He opened the *SafeHouse* security app on his phone to query the property's systems. With only one bar, the connection took three tries before the app retrieved the breech code.

Breech code?

He tried to access the CCTV cameras in the house. Not enough signal strength to sustain video. Shit!

"Van, something's going on back at the house, man. I need a better signal to learn more."

"Did you secure all materials before we rushed off to the airport, Malc?"

He didn't want to incur Van's wrath—again—so he lied. Just a little.

"Yes. All returned to the bank's safe deposit box until we go back to complete our analysis. All the computer stuff is password-protected and encrypted even if they get in. Plus I only use a secure TOR browser. No history. We're good."

"We can afford to take no chances. Let's get inside where they're sure to have a cell boost. Now."

Malc continued to ping his app to get video from his house as they hustled from the plane to the lounge. Equipped with eight exterior cameras and eight inside the house in Maryland, he then snagged a strong enough signal to stream video.

Horrified, he saw his house overrun by various law enforcement types as he scrolled through the camera feeds. He showed Van who did not hesitate.

"Blow it."

Malc was about to succumb to his court of last resorts. But his lovely home. All his stuff.

Van sensed his reticence. Pulled his huge forty-five caliber Glock 41. Leveled it against Malc's right temple. Van's action would have been the same even with other passengers or flight crew in the small but luxurious lounge. There were none other than their own team.

The barrel pressed against Malc's head hard enough to bobble it, warm to the touch from its recent proximity to Van's torso.

"Do we have a problem, Malc?"

Eyes opened so wide they hurt, Malc didn't move his head, but tried to look to his extreme right to see Van's eyes. Or that gun. Thought better of it. Instead he peered down at his phone.

He pressed the custom app's big red button in the center of the screen while holding down the phone's home button. A message layered on top of the camera feeds asked, "Are you sure?" Malc ignored *No*, pressed *Yes*. A moment later, all cameras went black on his Android's screen. On a field of black he read the message, *Command Executed*.

"No, Sir. No problem. Done."

With no further words, Van returned the over-sized pistol to his well-worn but still handsome blonde leather shoulder holster. The weapon disappeared beneath his ragged sport coat in a single smooth motion as if he were returning his wallet to an unseen inside pocket.

Their four mercs milled nearby to avoid eye contact with either of their bosses and to avoid reacting to the developing drama.

As if nothing happened, with an eery calm Van said, "Our cars are waiting. Let's attend to loose ends, okay Malc?"

"Sure, Boss. It's just, well, all my stuff, my fuckin' house!"

"As long as we've swept our trail, you will buy more stuff, Malc. Now I expect you to get past this. Doable?"

"Yeah, sure. No problem. No problem at all, Bossman. Just getting used to the idea."

WASHINGTON, DC

THEY CIRCLED THEIR WAGONS.

Admiral Jake Mahoney, Director of the National Security Agency, remained Stewart Atherton's longtime friend.

Still fearing compromised communications after the vice president's arrest, they kept their comms tight at the top. Other than the president's trusted protection detail, only Jake and his lead analyst were in the loop per President Atherton's explicit command.

Admiral Mahoney briefed the president on this matter of national security via one of the most secure landline connections in the world.

"Mr. President, per your instructions, we are holding our cards close to our vests. Armed with the intel from your field team in Maryland, my top analyst consulted with Director Gerald Banfield of Homeland's Domestic Terrorism Division—eyes only.

Director Banfield recognized these six alphanumeric characters as an aircraft tail number. After a cursory search of the FAA aircraft registry and their flight plan system, he surmised three important pieces of information for us.

"First, the number your agents found is a valid aircraft N-number, or tail identification number.

"Second, we verified that a Gulfstream G550 registered to an LLC in Maryland with that N-number filed a flight plan from Leesburg, Virginia to Phoenix, Arizona an hour ago. Leesburg is a short thirty-six miles from where your guys discovered this number.

"And third, the FAA flight plan system shows eight souls aboard, including two crew and six unspecified passengers. Confidence is high these are your bogies, Sir."

"Thank you, Jake. You came through with all of this in less than thirty minutes? Impressive, my friend. It gratifies me that our team did not perish for nothing. Please bury this analysis."

"Yes, Sir. Now my analyst, and I must go develop amnesia. My deepest condolences on the tragic loss of your... *our* team, Sir."

~

My team, thought Stew Atherton.

The worst part of this job is losing loyal patriots to the actions of traitors on US soil.

It was as if Adler Stavers, his exonerated Secret Service director, read his mind.

"Sir, these are solid leads. You are not the reason our team is gone. Those treasonous PB dogs are. And we've performed our duties to the best of our abilities, including you, Sir."

"Thank you, Adler. Now what do we need next to best help our friend, my predecessor, who is running for his life in a place called Brenda, Arizona, for God's sake?"

"Sir, not within my purview, *but* in the spirit of containing this at the highest levels, I suggest Stan and I get back with Director Banfield at Homeland. We should ask him to use his resources at FAA and law enforcement to track this aircraft. To an unspecified destination in Arizona or California since Brenda is so close to California's eastern border. I googled it.

"The flight plan to Phoenix may be a ruse—they could land anywhere—but we know where they're headed after they land.

"Once we discover their destination airport, I will personally alert Captain Cheevers on President Stevens' protection detail with an ETA of the in-bound bogies to their location. He and his team will deal with the situation in the field. His plan is sound."

"Excellent, Adler. I'm thanking you with great frequency these days. Perhaps a subliminal effort to make up for the last eight years of you protecting my unworthy ass while I thought you were a Brotherhood mole?"

Stewart thought, *Did my Secret Service director just blush? He is a good man, by God.*

∼

"ADLER, YOUR CREW JUST LANDED.

But in Havasu, not Phoenix."

"Thank you, Director Banfield. *What* crew?"

"I too have *no idea* what we're talking about, Adler. Now I suggest you get back to work, son."

Adler smiled at the old NSA war dog's gruff demeanor.

∼

"CAPTAIN, CONFIRMED.

"Six foxes en route to the hen house. ETA two to three hours by ground transportation. Incoming from Havasu."

"Copy. We'll keep the egg warm."

"And Captain, per Job One, no rules of engagement."

"Affirmative. Out."

Adler Stavers smiled. He loved working with these hardcore field guys. Cheevers' reputation preceded his grizzled ass. *HOO-yah.*

Former President Stevens was in good hands. He hoped. He harbored doubts over this bold plan, but if it worked, everyone would breathe easier.

BLACK ROCK, ARIZONA

"MS. JOHNSON?"

"Call me Sandy, hon. Are you here to protect and serve?"

She disguised her consternation at seeing this handsome but stern young man and his partner by drawing on her extensive repertoire of pithy humor.

She batted her blue-lidded eyes with just a touch of sparkle this morning. These two young men, children, were in law enforcement, armed 'n all. And they looked oh-so-yummy in head-to-toe black!

"Very well, Sandy. We're federal agents, and we need to evacuate your residents as soon as possible, quickly and quietly."

Shaken, her demeanor changed from flirtatious to fabian. "Oh, my. Well, what's this about? I'm not sure. I must notify the owners of the park."

"It's for the safety of you and your residents. Now our team will knock on doors. We'll offer vouchers for them to stay overnight at the Best Western Hotel in Quartzsite. Are you alone?"

If Sandy weren't so unnerved she might have exercised her lascivious wit yet again.

She said, "Yes."

"Here is your voucher, ma'am. Leave the office unlocked and unattended. We'll assume responsibility from here. Thank you for cooperating, Ms. Johnson. Please leave now."

The Homeland agent stared at her, waiting. Startled, she said, "You mean *right* now?"

"Yes, ma'am. Grab a few necessities, but you need to be on the road in less than thirty minutes. Enjoy your stay at the hotel. I understand it is very nice. Even a free breakfast. Now go. Hurry."

If *flustered* were a color, Sandy would be saturated, but she complied.

FOXES IN THE COOP

B LACK ROCK, ARIZONA

Their GPS led them: Havasu to Brenda.

It retrieved no info in its database for the Black Rock Campground, however.

But the town was so small they found it near the town's only street which was also two-lane Highway 60.

Trailers clustered behind the sole retail business in town—Buckaroo's Country Store & Diner. An entrance road wound around Buckaroo's to a small building marked *Office,* a hand-painted sign. They bypassed it to reconnoiter.

Van suggested one of them hike around the tiny campground looking for any sign of their quarry while the others stayed in the SUVs.

Dega might do, but he couldn't trust these other neckless steroid skid marks to be discrete despite their contrived disguises of jeans and over-sized t-shirts.

Might be time for an upgrade.

He took the walk himself and returned in fifteen minutes. His cursory search revealed nothing. So he sent Dega and Malc back to the office to rent a trailer as their base of operations until they were ready to strike.

With several units available according to a young guy in a black t-shirt, and per Van's orders, they chose one toward the west end of the park. They left one car by the office, and the other by their park model.

Once they all crowded into the small mobile home and settled in, Van sent Lita Dega out for an evening stroll. Her sensei in Cali told Malc he taught her more than martial arts. He always said, "A beautiful woman's appearance is her passport."

Van suggested she use her passport.

So she donned her workout clothes to jog the roads of the small park.

She wore a blinding white tank top tight over a sports bra. Her skin-hugging Lycra workout pants started just above her twenty-four-inch waist and ended just below her knees. And stylish running shoes with near-invisible white sock liners completed her cover.

SHE SMILED. JUST ENOUGH SKIN.

Lita's exposed neck and well-muscled calves, along with a ribbon of hard abs, flashed a generous hint of her bronze allure. She splurged on all this finery once she received her first ridiculous paycheck from Malc. Columbia was still her home, but she loved Los Estados Unidos.

Her run afforded her time to ponder. Armed with only one such change of clothes for this quick trip, she worried about laundry. Brutal daily workouts made her petite hard-body not only a lethal weapon but an irresistible anti-weapon. Of that she was proud.

Lita's thick black hair started high on her dominant forehead, tied into a taut ponytail far above her long slender neck. That hair still extended to the middle of her back. It danced as she ran.

Malc said she reminded him of a teen-age version of Jennifer Lopez, whoever that was. But she liked the sound of *teen-age*.

She estimated there were less than a hundred trailers within which their quarry could hide. Maybe a mile of streets broken into a half-dozen parallel gravel roads with pretentious street names: Saguaro Boulevard, Apache Way, Sunset Strip. Lita planned to run them all several times.

If she spotted something of interest, she would run in place to check her pulse and to look around before continuing. The least conspicuous recon. Women would get it, and men would stare. That overworked sports bra could only contain her exuberance so much on a cool evening.

Her first circuit through the park revealed nothing. Few folks were here this time of the year. And even fewer spent time exposed to the evening desert chill that descended with the swiftness of lowering a stage's curtain.

On her second circuit, however, she noticed a couple relaxing on the elevated porch of a small mobile home next to the rear fence of the park.

Nothing but the sprawling desert behind them, and good emergency egress with the right vehicle. An excellent tactical location.

After a moment of jogging in place to check her pulse, Lita recognized the woman. She remembered spotting her carted on a big man's back while firing her sidearm toward the hill on which Lita lay prone.

Yes, the last time she saw this fierce little warrior was in the reticle of Brick's sniper scope on the Maryland coast. And she'd had the man sitting next to her on the porch in her sights too. He was on the boat protecting...

She had located their quarry. She glanced up at two-thirds of President Stevens' protection detail. The survivors.

Malc's briefing said the woman's name was Darla Evans. She recognized the Veteran's Affairs file photo. The muscular sandy-haired man next to her must be Derek Cheevers. No sign of the president and the third surviving member of their team, however. Not surprising. She saw a large Number 6 on the front of their tiny mobile home.

~

DAR NODDED AND WAVED.

This Hispanic girl's appearance seemed too spectacular for the middle of nowhere.

"Hola! Nice evening."

Lita said, "Sí." She puffed as if out of breath. She wasn't. Still, she jogged in place.

"Where are you from?"

Mr. Janis said this was a popular ice-breaker in an RV park.

"Oh, I'm up from Mexico City, visiting mi tío—my uncle. You?"

"Out east. Here with mi tío también!" Her nervous chuckle signaled uneasiness at the unlikely coincidence. The non-verbals grew too obvious to miss. They saw something in each other's eyes, as only one woman's intuition reads another's.

What was it? Not the uncomfortable smile that felt artificial. They both might dismiss those stiff grins as superficial politeness between strangers, but they didn't. Nor was it their eyes that darted, each searching for sincerity.

Something else passed between them. Was it a modicum of mutual respect? Mutual distrust? A deeper understanding of what they might enjoy given the right shared circumstance? Then the moment passed.

Lita said, "That is nice. Family is important. Enjoy the rest of this beautiful but chilly evening, chiquita."

Dar nodded and offered a small wave from down by her hip as she might offer to a congenial colleague without the hard man sitting next to her seeing it.

And Lita jogged on her way. Derek pretended to be reading.

~

"WELL, DEGA, WHAT DID YOU DISCOVER?"

"This, uh, compound? This, park? It is small, but we already knew that. A hundred trailers, and mobile homes near a perimeter fence with another three dozen bus-style or trailerable recreational vehicles within that perimeter. Beyond that, nothing but open desert nearby and low mountains in the middle distance."

"Any sign of Stevens or his team?"

"No, Señor. But I saw only a few people. Too chilly this near sunset."

"Very well. Thanks for the effort, Dega. Good tactical analysis."

"De nada, Señor. If there is nothing else, I will shower at what they call the clubhouse."

She didn't add that as the only woman in this tiny mobile home with all these men, she craved privacy. The four men at the round eat-in kitchen table ignored everything except their five-card-stud hands. Except for Malc. He raised an eyebrow, swiveled his head to watch Dega.

Van offered a dismissive wave giving Lita his tacit permission. She gathered her change of clothes, a towel she found in the bathroom, and her shower kit before slipping through the exterior door in the living room.

Dar lay on the bed next to Derek.

She researched the surrounding mountains, valleys, and canyons on her iPad using Google Earth.

She heard it first—a quiet thump from the front porch. Reaching for her compact Glock 19 wedged just beneath the edge her pillow, she nudged Derek who was reading a brief.

Both alert within a heartbeat, she stayed low as she approached the side of a small window in the door, using the flimsy door frame as partial cover. Peeked through the cheap curtains, saw no one. Derek waited, tense, with his sidearm drawn.

"Nothing. Lots of wildlife out here, they say. I'll check it out."

Dar opened the door a crack and stayed in her low squat. She poked her head out. All appeared normal, except for one anomaly.

"Derek, back me up here. A rock on the porch. Something under it."

"Go."

Right behind her with his larger weapon held tight to his right thigh, he waited and watched. Dar stepped onto the porch with bare feet, wearing nothing but her boxers and a sleeveless t-shirt a size too small. Near the porch's top step, she retrieved the small scrap of paper, but left the nondescript rock that had kept a chilly breeze from blowing it away. When she returned to the kitchen and closed the door, she caught Derek staring at her.

"What?"

"Sorry. I covered you. Doesn't mean I can't enjoy the view."

She slapped the front of his considerable chest with the back of her left hand before turning her attention to the curious piece of paper. A single three-by-five-inch page, ripped from a small notebook spiral-bound at the top and folded in half, contained three lines of text and a signature.

It read:

> 6 of us from "out east"
> 4 guns, 2 management: Van Stockton, Malc Frieburg
> They don't know where you are yet, but will soon
>
> *- The Jogger*

As they read the note together, heads side by side, more like lovers than colleagues, Dar said, "Son-of-a-bitch! We have an ally behind enemy lines!"

"Or it's another ruse, like the flight plan to Phoenix."

"Fact or fiction, it's intel. She used Malc Frieburg's name, same one Homeland warned us about. Supposed to be a PB big-shot. The other name? Not sure. She also said, 'out east.' I mentioned earlier that's where we were from—exact words.

"It's her. And she's under deep cover, whoever she is. Let's get this to Director Banfield."

From memory, Dar dialed the Homeland chief on their secure sat phone, a number provided by President Atherton's people.

Derek said he trusted her instincts, sensed she was right. Dar handed her team leader the phone, already ringing.

As soon as he hung up he said, "We need to brief the others. Right fuckin' now."

CAMP PLAN

WASHINGTON, DC

"REPORT, CAPTAIN."

On the secure satellite phone Homeland Director Banfield spoke in clipped tones with Derek Cheevers, Captain, US Army, retired, somewhere on the backside of Southwest Arizona.

"Sir, we're ready to activate our plan. Just confirmed the opposition is on site. Odds are good our precise location is not yet compromised. We don't expect engagement until first light, but we're falling back now as a precaution."

President Stevens remained under the low-profile protection of three veteran Delta operators—that team was legendary. Director Banfield was savvy enough to have his own local Homeland team stand by as a backup.

Falling back meant they were evacuating Stevens into the desert near their location to prearranged coordinates within a sizable camp of friendlies. The local US Deputy Marshal vouched for them and his supervisor suggested in the strongest terms they trust his instincts.

Since they didn't yet know if the Brotherhood had placed other assets in the area prior to the arrival of their crew from Lake Havasu City, they hadn't evacuated Stevens earlier either. They considered evacuation by road too risky.

Besides, that was not the plan.

The deputy's trusted local recruits and the Deltas would whisk away President Stevens in the night aboard all-terrain vehicles.

Banfield couldn't help wonder, *Who really is hunting who out there?*

Captain Cheevers continued. "And Sir, we believe we've received confirmation—at least two very high level operatives from the Brotherhood are likely among the opposition."

Banfield heard of the remarkable reputation of this team. They're not only protecting their charge, but looking to score valuable intel. Impressive.

"Copy that, Captain. Use your discretion."

"Yes, Sir."

Click.

DESERT OUTSIDE
BLACK ROCK, ARIZONA

THE DARKNESS CONSUMED THEM.

Distant from any light source other than that cast by their vehicles, the desert out here felt both expansive and claustrophobic at the same time.

An enormous half-moon hung within a lacy diagonal veil carelessly flung across the heavens. A solitary glance skyward at that celestial brush stroke, of translucent white-silver above an ink-black horizon was all it took to realize one's singular insignificance within the scope of the Milky Way Galaxy.

John W. Stevens, former President of the United States, sat in the passenger seat of a side-by-side all-terrain vehicle, the second of three hurtling across the lumpy valley in single file. Kate Janis drove.

Deputy Marshal Blackfeather—Indian Joe—led the way with Geo Janis in his passenger seat. Derek Cheevers and Darla Evans brought up the rear. They were all armed except Kate and Geo.

Mick Sandstrom stood an invisible vigil back at Black Rock.

The headlights from Derek's rig blasted the two units in front of him sporadically with the brilliant LED light bar atop his ATV. John found that erratic strobe effect from behind unsettling, but took comfort knowing he was in good hands, and in a good place. This far from the oval office and from his ivy league pedigree, he felt whole.

And real.

They were driving at a swift but deliberate pace enabled by Joe's intimate knowledge of the area.

They made the long drive more tolerable with light conversation. But the engine noise in the open cockpit forced them to speak louder than normal.

"I'M DRY-CAMPING WITH A PRESIDENT."

Kate was embarrassed to say it out loud. But she might as well speak her mind if they were going into exile.

She smiled at the notion. That was something Geo might say. *Exile.* He always found the drama in every situation. More so of late. But that's no doubt what honed his skills as a great author of fiction. Or so people said.

While she admired his skill, she didn't care for his books, but as Geo would say, "Not every book is for every reader. Each book chooses its own."

"*Dry-camping,* Kate? We won't have access to water? In the desert?"

"Not exactly, Sir."

"Oh, for Heaven's sake, Kate. Call me John. If one more person calls me Sir, I'll scream."

"Sorry, John. Okay, time for RVing 101 since you're now one of us, at least for the next day or two. Most sticks and bricks dwellers—folks who live in houses—perceive our lifestyle as full-time RVers similar to camping. That's far from reality, at least for some of us.

"We live in nice houses too, but they have wheels. And bus-style RVs like ours have engines too. Oh, but they *are* much smaller than most houses. At three hundred square feet, ours is considered large by RV standards.

"Most often Geo and I move our home to parks like Black Rock that offer full hook-ups—electricity, water, and sewer. When we're roughing it without full hook-ups, we call that *dry-camping* or *boon-docking*."

"So we won't be able to use lights, drink water, or have access to, ah, facilities?"

A look of consternation and slight embarrassment passed over John's face visible in the red lights reflected from the ATV's dash. But he was prepared to endure any hardship in return for this lovely woman's safety, *and* for his own.

Kate chuckled. "Oh, John, you are adorable. Next lesson. RVers, boondockers in particular, waste little time dancing around life's essentials.

"When you've been out here for a while, you see people for who they are, not for what they want you to see or think. Peel away all the empty trappings of society, the bondage of shallow social climbing, and what's left is a more altruistic concern for our fellow human beings.

"Compared to most, I'd suggest most RVers show a deeper appreciation for our natural resources, including the most precious natural resource of all—each other. I might also suggest boondocking—dry-camping—might be a useful boot camp for every president-elect."

This bold assertion earned her the famous heart-stopping John W. Stevens campaign grin. Even in the dim reddish glow, that smile devastated Kate. Just a little. She shook her head and blinked a few times before returning her eyes front.

"Many boondockers, for example, like Joe's and Geo's friends who we are visiting, live the way they do to minimize their footprint on the planet. So no hook-ups, but they get electricity for their minimal needs from solar energy and store it in batteries for later use. Like lights at night. Though most sleep when it gets dark to conserve. Like nature intended, maybe?

"They get their fresh water from onboard tanks filled before venturing out. And because of supply constraints, they excel at conserving—by using water at least twice. For example, most use dishwater to flush toilets later. They even make a game of it, an art form, even. I bet you've never heard *mellow yellow, brown goes down,* have you, John?"

He regaled his ability to fit into any situation or any crowd with aplomb, but had enjoyed advantages in life. Grew up in an affluent family, attended private schools, and completed his education at prestigious institutions. But he also appreciated self-sufficiency. The last eight years taught him valuable lessons. Now this extreme? Yes, a new challenge, and a chance to meet folks with an old-fashioned pioneer spirit? He liked that.

"Well, I can guess, but I'd rather you tell me, Kate." He knew his body language broadcast he wasn't sure he wanted to know, but the odd thing? He did.

"John, we do not waste time dancing around fundamentals. *Mellow yellow* means when you pee in the toilet, you don't waste precious water flushing every time, not until it's good and *mellow yellow.* With number two, however, you do. So *brown goes down.* Even that, however, is subject to negotiation.

"Plus men take every advantage to pee behind a tree in the mountains and woods. Or over a dune, or behind a big rock in the desert.

"Excess dishwater might get tossed in a nearby gully so as not to fill onboard waste containment tanks too fast. When close to full, tanks get emptied at a dump station in town later. Or variations on that them. You get the idea, John."

"Tell me more, Kate. This is all *so* foreign to me, but fascinating." Now his morbid curiosity at this focus on earthy fundamentals drew him in. He could not explain why.

"When there's trouble, we offer help or we ask for help. If we have left-over food, we share. For other people's dogs, we carry dog biscuits—puppy cookies. We're open and friendly with everyone... until we're not. Then we smile and walk. Most of the time, anyway. At least we try.

"The universal ice breaker? *Where ya from?* Yeah, bad grammar. Nobody cares. These people are genuine, open, honest, and they—we —look out for each other. Oh, we meet the occasional asshol... uh, less agreeable person, but they are rare around the RV parks, even more so in dry camps, at least in our experience."

"Fascinating. Frontier America!" He beamed at distilling his observations to a slogan.

Ever the politician, Kate thought.

She paused in her response, hesitant to dampen his enthusiasm. She cautioned him, speaking loudly over he engine noise.

"Careful, John. Most view themselves a little different from that. Take my Geo. He's an erstwhile sophisticated member of twenty-first-century society who decided on a more austere and adventurous life-style—his words. A refined but world-weary urbanite who has tran-scended life's trivialities—*so* not my words. He still hauls a fragile ego around with him.

"If you call Geo a member of Frontier America, it might not be a compliment, although it should be. He does envision himself a pioneer of sorts, though. But Frontier America sounds somewhat, well, elitist, coming from you, anyway. No offense.

"I don't know. I just feel I can say anything to you, John, and want you to enjoy your own *frontier experience* without alienating anyone.

"Among boondockers—dry campers—you will also find folks entrenched in hard times. They live in a trailer in the desert. Not by choice, but by necessity. And not surprising. Almost half the folks in this country live at or below poverty level. That does not mean they don't share the same ideals.

"You may find a few resentments smoldering, but they too are free spirits and grateful for what they have. It's refreshing, John, and one reason we love this lifestyle and the people we meet."

She realized her words flowed like a waterfall brimming with bubbling energy. That was fine. She was chauffeuring a president *and educating him!*

"I understand, Kate. This is all so new to me, I'll listen more and speak less when we arrive. Your candor is a delight. My goodness!"

FRINGER FRIENDS

D ESERT
NEAR BLACK ROCK,
ARIZONA

John sat in a tattered lawn chair.

After introductions and a brief awkwardness, he surreptitiously glanced across the small fire at some of the Fringers. Those present numbered almost three dozen. He was not the alpha here.

After several campers floated a few political opinions, including one topic popular with this group—EMP, or ElectroMagnetic Pollution, or *Poisoning*, depending on who was speaking—the former president listened to the dialogue between a half-dozen vocal locals with great interest.

One old gentleman named Randy, designated his host for the night, was vocal but soft-spoken. Everyone craned to hear him. This man's quiet voice carried weight.

When such conversations took place in most other venues, John was accustomed to being the center of attention, answering the questions. Not in this setting so foreign to him.

They didn't ignore him. Neither did they expect him to field questions. This erstwhile President of the United States became just another occupant of another recycled lawn chair around a campfire.

Thanks to Kate's earthy wisdom, he offered no opinions as he was here to listen, to learn, and to stay alive. He suspected when he and Randy were alone in his trailer, he'd want to pick his brain.

Randy seemed a profound and learned man. Kate drifted off to chat with a few of the ladies along with a few men. *She* was learning from *them.*

Before long, someone blew life into a soft flute. Others joined in or took turns. A drum appeared in front of one lady who began a soft and regular rhythm, brushing its vertical sides with a large hand-crafted mallet.

And there was Joe, Deputy Blackfeather, of the Yavapai-Apache Nation, Geo had said. Seated in a low beach chair called a sand chair out here, Joe joined the flutes and drum with a soft chant that grew louder as he found his balance. Sounded atonal and tenuous to John's classically trained ear.

But that quivering melody, with its pitch and volume extremes, seemed perfect for this occasion. Reminded him that one of their protectors belonged to a proud nation within his nation, or his within theirs. So easy to forget until special times like these.

This group honored John by allowing him to be here. He felt privileged.

Less than an hour later, Randy led him to his trailer to show him where he'd sleep.

"Randy, you have only one bed."

"Oh, no worries. I won't be sleeping in the trailer. I'm growing accustomed to my *new* home."

John grew reticent. Randy appeared to have one foot in the grave. But with miles of empty desert in every direction, Randy compelled him to ask.

"*New* home?"

With candor and so casual as if explaining where to find the bathroom, Randy said, "Oh, yes, I've found the perfect spot to complete my transition. I've dug a nice deep hole in a holy place. Get it? Since the time is near, I'm camping in a tent at its edge.

"John, I didn't vote for you back in the day, but if you ran again, I would do so now. You have a beautiful spirit."

John reeled from Randy's bizarre revelation and abrupt change of topics. He recovered, at least on the surface.

"Sorry. Two terms is all any president gets. Besides, I continue to serve outside that cocoon with new freedom. If anyone understands that, I'm sure you do."

"Yes, I do. *This* is *my* bit." He waved his arms around his small trailer, and by extension, the desert all around them.

"John, would you do me one small favor? Since no one in our group is a notary, would you witness my last will and testament? I suppose the signature of an ex-president will do, even without an official stamp."

Randy offered John a weary grin as they both sat at his small table.

"I wish to leave my meager larder to a fellow Fringer, one Ernesto Joseph Blackfeather. Including my trailer, my truck, and an old family trust fund I had forgotten about, but thought might be useful some day. It seems I am to be denied one last trip to town."

Randy produced a document and slid it across the table toward John with his deformed hands along with a cheap pen emblazoned with a logo: *Fifth Third Bank.*

John thought, *What a strange group of people! No, that's not right. They're just different. And old Randy here is saving himself for what might be his last hike.*

He felt honored to be a part of his *transition*, but he was also feeling shaken.

"Randy, a bonus: I am a former president *and* an attorney." Both smirked at each other.

"It's normal for you to wonder, John. Yes, we are different, and I'm more different from most. One more thing. You'll note in this will I've asked Indian Joe for one last favor—to shovel sand over me and to place my chosen rock when the time comes. Not that I need to document that.

"Please stick this flyer in your pocket and read it at your leisure. We've been discussing number ten. John, I am honored to have you here, and to share in the joy of my transition. Thank you, Sir."

John thought, *How could I say no to this wonderful man?*

Randy said, "Oh, you can say no, and you think I'm wonderful?"

"What? How?"

"Don't worry, John. Just another of life's little mysteries. Sign, please?"

"Ah, um, oh, yes, okay. Randy, you amaze me, and I'm not amazed much any more. Here."

John slid the signed document and the pen back across the small table to Randy with his mouth still gaping. Now he was spooked *and* amazed.

They both stood. John shook one of those crooked hands that seemed to tingle his own.

Good grief! This little trip to the desert is changing my life.

The cadaverous Randy patted John on the shoulder, came in close for a brief man-hug, still shaking hands. He whispered into John's ear, "Change is often a good thing. It makes new paths possible."

Without another word, he pulled away, left him with one more shoulder pat, turned, opened the screen door, and disappeared into the night at a slow and visibly painful gait.

Ridiculous purple robe and all.

John wandered back outside.

Too rattled to sleep, he sat in the empty chair next to Indian Joe. The large circle of compatriots around the fire had fallen into a comfortable silence.

His security team was invisible, guarding the camp's perimeter.

He whispered to Joe, "It saddened me to hear of Sam Braxton's death. He was a great patriot and a true friend. I understand you met him."

Joe said, "Yes. A true friend to Geo and Kate too. Geo spoke of him all the time. His death devastated both of them."

He could say nothing more. Nor could John. They sat in silent respect for this fallen soldier and compadre.

"Mind if we talk business, John? Here's the plan for tomorrow."

Instead of waiting until morning, for the next five minutes, Joe quietly briefed him on an overview of the plan he formulated with Derek. Then he sensed John was troubled.

"Joe, I just had a most unusual conversation with Randy. He…"

"Told you he is completing his transition?"

"Yes."

"These last few days that subject has consumed him. He came here to die. Knows it's close."

"He dug his own grave?"

"Randy doesn't want to burden anyone. The only favor he's asked of me is to cover him up and place his stone."

"He camps by the grave he dug for himself." Not a question.

"Like I said, he doesn't want to burden anyone. He'll no doubt roll himself into his hole. But he's scared to roll in too soon, wake up in its bottom and not be able to get himself back out until it's time. It's a whole thing with Randy. He fears a premature roll.

"He reads my mind!"

"John, it's okay. I'm guessing his spirit guide is playing with you."

"Oh."

Aghast, John then raised his voice a half-octave and twice the volume. So unlike him.

"*Goddammit!* These are good people, but nobody prepared me for all of this!"

A few nearby glanced his way. Most just smiled.

"Yes, they are good people. And nobody ever *is* prepared, my important friend. So we're content with trying. It's just another thing. John. Breathe, brother."

After patting him on the shoulder, Joe kept his left hand resting there to comfort him, squeezed a few times to settle him. Shook his shoulder with a gentle cajoling motion to prevent him from hyper-ventilating.

"Shit!"

"Welcome to the real world, Mr. President. Now, with respect, get your ass to bed. You'll have a full morning of worrying here in camp when we go fetch your bad guys for you tomorrow."

ATTACK!

B LACK ROCK, ARIZONA

"We'll finish this at first light."

Without a precise location for their opposition, and their own force so small, Van felt searching further in darkness made no sense. In the morning, however, he *would* complete his mission, and damn any collateral damage.

A half-hour before sunrise, he and his team sat in their vehicles, scanning for signs of life. Van sat in the back seat on the passenger side with Malc behind the wheel of their lead SUV, a red GMC Acadia. Their white SUV waited behind them.

Van figured it foolish to assume no one had detected their presence, so he assumed they'd evacuate Stevens. But he was told nobody travels the desert at night.

With a man on watch non-stop since Dega returned from her jog the evening before, this watch-stander reported nobody had departed the park's entrance road. Come to think of it, nobody had entered either.

"Malc, where in Hell is Dega?"

"No idea, Bossman. Pisses me off. Maybe some female thing. I'll deal with her when we find her."

"Please do. We have work."

With their radios tested and active, the neckless guy in the passenger's seat in front of him—Van couldn't remember his name—croaked, "There!"

He pointed toward several sets of headlights darting about behind the row of mobile homes a hundred yards north of their position. Through the windshield they saw the lights skittering between the motorhomes and trailers in front of them.

Sunrise approached, offering a golden view. Still dim with long suggestive shadows, daylight proper peeked over the low mountains in the distance, hinting at a brilliant day.

They crept forward, sans headlights, until they approached to within twenty yards of the back of the property to the east. The row of small mobile homes near the chain-link perimeter fence dead-ended their street.

On the fence's far side they spotted a trio of ATVs gathered and pointed away from them, toward the desert. Five men and one woman were boarding the machines, casting surreptitious glances in their direction.

Headlights or not, their two large SUVs in this small campground stood out.

They were blown.

❧

THEIR PACE QUICKENED. VAN TENSED.

When they spotted Van's SUVs, they averted their faces.

This has to be them.

All but one carried themselves like military. And that tall one disguised himself under a floppy hood, a ball cap, a kerchief, and sunglasses. Sunglasses at this hour? Could that be Stevens? Must be.

Van keyed and spoke into his radio to inform the other truck.

"Found them. Five combatants protecting one package. Three four-wheeled all-terrain vehicles. Two in each, six total. Let's go."

Malc had to turn left or right. No gate and not enough room between the trailers straight ahead. He turned left.

"Boss, I don't see a gate through that fence. Are we headed out into the desert?"

Van stared at Malc's unsuccessful attempt to hide his trepidation at heading off-road even though their vehicles featured all-wheel drive.

"We don't need a gate. Space between those two trailers. Go!"

THEY LOST SIGHT OF THE PRIZE.

But only for thirty seconds as they looked for a place to break through the park's perimeter.

As they plowed through the four-foot wire fence between two park models, they spotted a vague dust plume rising now south and west of them in the pre-dawn twilight.

Van stiffened and pointed through his side window. "There!"

Malc veered to the right to follow the dust. The second SUV, the white Acadia, clung to his tail.

Van said, "The ground is flat and firm. Faster."

He could sense Malc's continued uneasiness about their pursuit over unknown ground even though it seemed solid enough. So far, anyway.

"Faster."

They flew toward the low mountains at over sixty miles per hour. The terrain roughened. The ride became tailbone-jarring. But every time Malc eased up on the accelerator, Van threatened him. They sped up. Seventy miles per hour.

"Faster, Malc!"

The three ATVs commanded less than a half-mile lead. They weren't visible, only their dust trail. Were they running for Mexico? Wouldn't matter. Jurisdictions held no meaning.

PEQUEÑA HARQUAHALA
BOX CANYON, ARIZONA

THE MORNING BRIGHTENED, THE DUST FADED.

Drifted toward them and to their right on a stiffening northerly breeze.

That's when Van paid attention to the rugged mountainous terrain that arose on both sides *and in front of them.* The fools were running toward a dead-end—into a narrowing box canyon.

As the dust continued to drift, he saw they had abandoned their ATVs a hundred yards ahead and to their left. They were trapped. And they now sought cover on foot.

He expected them to be armed, but so were they. His crew, however, drove heavy American steel behind which they could hide. Those little ATVs were Swiss cheese. Must be inexperienced to make such foolish tactical mistakes. That surprised him.

As their SUVs approached the now-empty trio of Polaris RZR side-by-sides, Van shouted, "Stop."

This could be an ambush. The opposition numbered five combatants, they numbered six. He assumed they were at least as well-armed. He'd leverage their heavier vehicle advantage. He must assume they held the home-ground edge, but that wasn't a given unless they recruited locals.

Tactical ambiguity now a given, they'd proceed with caution until they regained visual contact and better situational awareness.

"Bossman, looks like caves over there."

Malc pointed to the rocks rising to their front and left.

Van said, "Might be caves, or deep shadows. Whichever, that's where they took cover. We'll form a barricade with our vehicles close enough to contain them; we remain distant enough for a broad field of fire since we don't yet know their precise location."

On the radio he ordered the two thugs in the other truck to follow bumper-to-bumper. They crept forward at five miles per hour.

"Stop here," Van said in an unnecessary whisper. Malc stopped with a light touch on the brake pedal, but the buffoon following them bumped into them.

Nobody saw Van roll his eyes.

Ping! P-p-ping! P-p-ping!

Van said, "Ah. Small arms, a single range-finding pop, followed by a pair of triple-taps."

All the rounds hit their windows but they only starred their lead vehicle's windshield. None penetrated.

Van said, "So they carry small-caliber automatic weapons, but are conserving ammo. Smart. At least one accurate shooter. Stay low. Slide out of the passenger-side doors. Prepare for an assault."

They took cover behind the axles to avoid under-vehicle shots.

Bap-bap-bap-bap-bap!

Two of Malc's guys were spraying the rocks with their larger-caliber weapons. Good odds they'd score from ricochets. Malc raised his head just high enough over the hood to pop off two rounds from the little Glock G17L long slide he carried everywhere. But he let his mercs do the heavy lifting, ducking as more incoming fire peppered their truck.

P-p-ping!

"Got 'em spotted, Bossman. To the left of that reddish pointed rock."

As Malc spoke, a steel shaft penetrating his shoulder threw him forward, against their SUV. Went down like wet cement from the shock of the heavy hit.

No time to check the idiot's pulse.

But too late, Van realized they had been flanked. How was that possible? He had made a green boot's mistake. As he lifted his gaze, defeat sculpted his face. Looked behind him at over two dozen deter-mined faces, each armed with either handguns, rifles or cross-bows. *Cross-bows?*

STEEL RESOLVE

T HEY WERE PROS.

But Malc's two surviving soldiers were not suicidal, not with the boss down along with two of their own.

And not with a significant force of hostiles surrounding their exposed position.

THOSE GUTLESS APES ARE SURRENDERING?

While they were placing their weapons on the ground, Van still contemplated finding Stevens and finishing the business at hand with his backup weapon.

He laid his beloved Heckler and Koch HK MP7 machine pistol in the sandy dirt at his feet.

From the shadows, across the vehicles from Van's position, he heard, "Hands on your heads, right fuckin' now, or you are dead."

The voice didn't shout. A matter-of-fact statement issued with barely sufficient volume as if the shooter looked for an excuse to fire. An easy shot from ten yards. But six thousand pounds of American steel still stood between him and these skilled shooters.

The aluminum engine block ticked away as it cooled, like a bomb on a timer.

The local rabble behind me? Not too worrisome. I bet not a decent shot among them, except for one crossbow, and they're still fifteen yards away.

As Van rose, he plucked the subcompact Glock 26 with its ten-round mag from his coat pocket. But he kept it hidden in his sizable palm as he eased his hands behind his head—as instructed. He had practiced this.

The skilled shooters were far enough in front of him they wouldn't see that little spot of gray-brown. And the yokels behind him were farther away still.

When two of the surviving attackers appeared submissive, three down, and the last surrendering, the five combatants and their protectee approached from the shallow caves where they were hiding. As Mr. Ball-cap-under-hoody appeared and approached amidst his protectors, Van saw the kerchief over his lower face.

Stevens must be paranoid. He should be. Or is he allergic to desert dust?

Van waited. *Not yet, not yet...* There would be a sweet spot between close enough for the tiny Glock to find its mark, and too close when they'd spot the weapon. Van accepted he would not leave this place alive. His priority remained the mission.

Not yet.

He waited for three of Stevens' detail to reach for their supply of restraints...

Now.

He spoke to provide a distraction. "President Stevens. An honor, Sir."

With his hands behind his head as instructed, he had raised them in a slow deliberate motion high overhead, palms pressed together as if in a praying gesture. He concealed the tiny semi-automatic pistol between his palms, his right index finger tucked into the trigger guard.

In a slow deliberate non-threatening motion, Van lowered his pressed palms down toward his chest to complete the faux praying pose of complete submission and deference. All that remained was to extend his arms in a smooth arc, aim, and fire. He couldn't miss at this range.

His arms accelerated as they extended. Aimed at Stevens' chest now only twenty feet away over the hood of the Acadia, he increased the pressure on his trigger.

Just then, another steel crossbow shaft pierced the back of his right calf.

Van had heard nothing but a faint *snick*, but collapsed to his right even before Stevens' lead guy had even processed his movements. The silent impact of the two-foot chunk of solid steel devastated him. With his leg failing, on instinct, Van shot his hands forward and to his right to break his fall. The little pistol skittered in the dirt into the long shadow of the vehicle in front of him.

He fell, eyes wide with surprise and awe. Gritted his teeth and grimaced from the shock, but made no sound. As he crawled forward to reclaim the gun just a few feet away, the pointed end of the shaft protruding from the front of his leg dug a tiny furrow in the dull red dirt.

The insane pain heightened his awareness. If they were to lose this battle, they must not lose the war. First, he would shoot Malc, then himself.

The Brotherhood must survive.

Joe muttered to himself, "Gotcha!"

Their lead guy down, he still crawled for the shelter of his SUV. One shaft remained in his triple-threat crossbow, so he used the integrated lever arm to re-cock.

As he and his most capable Fringer brothers and sisters advanced on these assholes, armed with sub-standard weapons, they nevertheless sampled the sweet taste of victory. Meanwhile, Derek and his crew closed from the far side of the two trucks.

Baldy, the Fringer five yards to Joe's right, wasn't a very good shot but with his superior eyesight and with a better angle, he hollered, "Joe! Tall one's goin' for a gun under the car!"

Joe thought, *What the Hell? He's thinking he's gonna shoot one of his own guys, and then himself? Don't think so.*

And with a click-swish-snap, his remaining shaft leaped from the bow, ran true, found its mark less than a second later.

HE AIMED HIS GLOCK AT MALC'S FOREHEAD.

Van lay on his side, with his right arm about to reach full extension, Malc curled on the ground six feet away.

Can't miss.

Now conscious again, Malc watched, frozen in horror.

Another shaft pierced the back side of Van's right forearm just below the elbow at the precise moment he fired. His bullet left its barrel and stabbed a neat little hole low in the front right quarter panel of the red Acadia four feet away—instead of in Malc's pink forehead.

This time Van screamed, more in frustration than in pain. And that's when he figured blood loss caused him to feint. He remembered thinking, *I hope I'm dying.*

THE SHORT ONE WASN'T GIVING UP.

With his still-functioning left arm, and with the tall one now laying unconscious, the little guy reached for the machine pistol that flew just out of his reach.

Derek, Dar, and Mick swept around both ends of the two-vehicle caravan like triple dervishes. The two FBI agents in their company— on loan from the Tucson field office—provided cover.

From the front, Dar kicked the weapon out of the short guy's reach. At the rear, Derek covered the remaining two uninjured mercs who had already thrown their hands over their heads.

They made short work of binding the survivors with zip-cuffs, still holding their weapons at the ready as a precaution while they double-checked the two whose blood puddled and soaked into the desert dirt. Both were down hard.

Deputy Marshal Blackfeather and his local recruits approached from the far side of the narrow box canyon. Derek smiled at the wild-looking cop wearing one bandana around his forehead, another under his throat, and his neck-to-boot denim uniform.

Indian-looking hick *and* a nasty crossbow sharpshooter?

Derek could not believe such a sentence even made sense. Joe now carried the unloaded bow over his shoulder. A valuable antique, no doubt. And lethal. Three shots, three precise hits.

Now they stood six feet apart. With grim amusement, Derek watched Joe stoop to grab the barbed head of the shaft protruding from the tall one's calf with a gloved hand. A muddied mixture of blood and dirt obscured the razor point and its edges.

Joe planted his heavy boot against the guy's leg. Drew the shaft clean through in one *slow* motion and transferred it to his left hand. Then he did the same with the second shaft sticking out of the guy's right arm. The same boot held that arm as he pulled the second shaft through. Mister hard-case no longer remained silent.

"Aaaaahh!"

Joe stooped down, looked the guy in the eye, and said, "Hi, there. You ain't from 'round these parts, are yuh, pardner? Welcome to Arizona."

Then he wandered over to the shorter bandito to collect his third and final shaft from the little guy's shoulder. Same routine, same scream.

Derek and his team chuckled. Didn't even feel guilty about that.

Joe said, "What? These babies are expensive! 324 stainless!"

Baldy and a few of the twelve other Fringers behind him added their nervous post-action laughter to the mix. Three were combat veterans, the other ten had never held a weapon intending to kill before, but they were patriots.

Derek admired their grit. Bob Fell had merely suggested one possible course of action, and here they stood.

With venom in his voice, as he lay there bleeding, the tall one looked up into Joe's eyes, said, "You son-of-a-bitch!"

As if Joe had violated some Geneva Convention prisoner shit or something.

~

INDIAN JOE RETURNED THE TALL ONE'S STARE.

He peered at the guy at his feet with curiosity. He probed into those treasonous eyes, as if deciphering a cryptic epitaph. He idly rolled the three bloody crossbow shafts together between his thumb and fingers. They tinkled with their own micro-melody in his half-closed palm.

Joe whispered, "Kimosabe, my mother was no bitch. She was a saint. And shame on you for not honoring yours. You are a dishonorable man. Thanks for returning my shafts, and for failing to kill my friends, or your little buddy there. I suspect somebody somewhere will have more'n a few questions for all y'all, amigo. I will pass on your thoughts about how incompetent you think Michael Martino is, *Van*. Or should I say *Palmer*? Yeah, definitely time for an upgrade."

"*What* did you say? How? You couldn't…"

With that, US Deputy Marshal Ernesto Indian Joe Blackfeather merely offered an enigmatic smile and walked back with pride to join his group of desert rats who call themselves the Lunatic Fringe. His kindred spirits, that delightful tribe, helped defeat the forces of evil this day.

They'd be talking about this "legendary battle" around the campfires for years.

They deserved it.

~

VAN STILL HOPED TO MEET HIS QUARRY.

He assumed ex-President Stevens would come forward to gloat after their captors bound their prisoners, and he was not disappointed. Yet.

As the capped and hooded figure approached, Van sat bound and bleeding in the red dirt. Looking up into the sun, Stevens was more a silhouette than anything. The tall figure eased back his hood, dropped his kerchief, and removed his ball cap.

But something was wrong.

"Hello, Palmer. I will need at least twenty percent from you. Wait. Let's make that one hundred percent—of the rest of your sad little life."

Van knew that voice, a voice from the distant past, but it wasn't the president's. If only he wasn't looking into that dazzling morning sun.

For the second time in two minutes, he once again said, "What? *What* did you say?"

His composure crumbled, and it wasn't from the pain of his leg and arm wounds. Despair threatened to choke the voice that had sounded so calm and controlled and arrogant minutes earlier.

"A hundred percent is impossible you say? Well, you need to gain some distance. You know, perspective."

Geo relished repeating the cold words verbatim that Palmer Xavier used on him so many years ago as his boss, the chief operations officer at Greater Global Solutions. *So* many years ago. He had been raping Geo's budget—twenty percent at a time—to divert funds to the Brotherhood, Geo later discovered.

"Janis. I should have known. But you're dead."

"Well, you can see that is just not true. Not altogether, anyway. And no thanks to you. Your merc turds killed two innocent friends of mine in Tucson by mistake. Their names were Chet and Jessica Braverman. And now you have failed *yet again*, Palmer. Do you not grow weary of incessant *failures?* You know what? I will pray for your blackened soul, you evil asshole."

"You always had a small mind, Janis."

"And yet, *you* are the one sitting in the dirt, bleeding, with your wrists and ankles zip-cuffed, and in custody. For attempted murder in full view of witnesses. Only takes a small mind to know you fucked *yourself* this time, Palmer. Must feel just awful. Embarrassing too?"

As Malc listened to this exchange, he said, "Van, *you* were Mr. X?"

"Shut up, Malc."

Geo experienced profound guilt at enjoying this so much, but scoffed anyway as he strolled over to Joe and the Fringers. Time to move on. He was eager to re-join Kate who took shelter in their camp with President Stevens last night.

He swiveled his head to toss a few words over his shoulder.

"Derek, I'm done with this guy. Thank you."

"But where is Stevens?" Van's neck now swiveled in a jerky arc of dismal expectation.

Derek's flat voice said casually, "Oh, him. Yeah, well, he's already en route to Washington to join President Atherton and the NSA Director. They're having a party to review the details of *Hat Trick two-point-oh-so-sweet*." The president had taken Derek into his confidence on this after he swore him to secrecy.

"But we blew up the house and the computer!"

"Can't blow up a cloud, Xavier, or whatever alias you're cowering behind these days."

Palmer—Van—looked over at Frieburg and spit in his direction. He muttered, "Malcolm, you idiot."

NEW FRIENDS, OLD ENEMIES

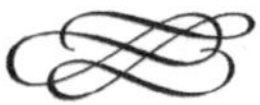

B LACK ROCK, ARIZONA

The time came to take out the trash.

Derek and Darla transported their bound prisoners and the two bodies in the bad guys' own bullet-ridden vehicles from the box canyon where the skirmish took place. Geo and the two FBI agents delivered the ATVs back to the campground.

Back at Black Rock, Derek formally transferred the survivors to the team of Homeland agents who had blockaded the entrance to the RV park per Director Banfield's instructions.

The coroner from Quartzsite, who was also the town's general practitioner, retrieved the pair of corpses. He received instructions to retain them for eventual transfer to the FBI forensic team from Tucson.

Homeland then moved Van Stockton and Malc Frieburg to an undisclosed location for interrogation by unidentified government agencies.

Mission managed.

PHOENIX, ARIZONA

Happiest of hours... Martini time.

Former President John W. Stevens awaited his team's arrival in comfort aboard Air Force Two on a secure service ramp at Sky Harbor Airport.

A dozen FBI agents stood guard around the perimeter of the aircraft and the ramp, while three of Adler Stavers' senior Secret Service agents kept John company inside. The rest of the crew went about their business.

They weren't taking any chances after this entire team escorted the president from Black Rock earlier in a caravan of four Suburbans borrowed from the Phoenix FBI field office.

Mr. ex-POTUS admitted to himself it felt damn good to witness the apprehension of these treasonous dogs after almost a decade of skirmishing with them as a civilian. More work to do, but today was a banner day.

How ironic I'm sitting here in comfort in the VP's plane with an exquisite Bombay Sapphire birdbath martini in hand. Meanwhile, the vice president of the United States is under house arrest for high treason. What a remarkable turn of events!

"Another martini, Mr. President?"

"Oh, dear me, ah, why not?"

He still bathed in the afterglow of the previous night's campfire and extraordinary companionship with those wonderful patriots who call themselves the Lunatic Fringe. How very unlikely!

He looked forward to a celebratory meeting with his friend Stewart Atherton at Camp David. Stew was still recovering from the most recent attempt on his life, but he was doing as well as anyone could expect. A complete recovery from slow arsenic poisoning might not be possible, but Stew was a rock.

John's lids grew heavy.

Well, after the next drink, maybe I'll just grab a short nap—in Norman Sealey's bed.

A horizontal victory lap!

BLACK ROCK, ARIZONA

Mick hiked to the front office.

He paid their bill, including Stockton's, and thanked the management for allowing the quiet evacuation of the RV park's few residents as a precaution to the previous evening's and this morning's festivities.

He looked forward to a pleasant flight to Andrews with his president and his team on Air Force Two.

About time they publicly recognized John for his contributions as a civilian and a great American!

Time to leave.

As Dar threw her heavy duffel into the back of their rented Ford Edge, a familiar face bounced up. Her eyes widened as she reached for her sidearm but stopped short of drawing it. Rested the heel of her palm on the hip holster now that concealment no longer mattered.

"You're the jogger from yesterday!"

"Guilty as charged, Señorita Evans. But don't shoot. Lita Dega, CIA, and before that, Brazilian Fuerzas Militares de Colombia, Contrainsurgencia—my country's national counterinsurgency unit. I am so pleased to meet you at last, as myself. And that your tío is now safely away. How is your leg?"

Dar's jaw dropped. After staring at this surprising woman jogging in place for a full ten seconds who waited for her response with unnerving patience, Dar found her voice."

"My leg?"

"Sí. From the beach below el casa grande overlooking the ocean in Maryland."

With her suspicious nature once again aroused, she unsnapped the smooth leather retainer on her holster, as she said, "And how do you know about that, Ms. Dega? *Officer* Dega?"

"Just Lita to mis amigos, and I'd like very much to think of you as my friend, Darla. The big hombre carried you with little effort. And you were, como se dice en ingles, muy valiente? Very courageous. Firing your weapon up at me from the big hombre's back? I saw the courage on your face, in such white eyes, magnified in the rifle's scope. Estuviste feroz—ferocious."

Dar's head spun in a diagonal double-take with a wrinkled brow. So many surprises coming from this surprising little woman so fast grew exhausting.

There they were, just two gals standing in front of park model Number 6, one packing up her car. The other bouncing in place in her skin-tight workout pants and thick insulated vest over a long-sleeve tight white tee with white ear buds bouncing at her neck. The Latina danced to keep her heart rate up, as if that were her priority.

"Wait. *In your rifle's scope?* Did *you* kill my friends and colleagues at the beach house? *Lita?*"

Dar's voice rose an octave as she spoke, her final word dripping with accusation and disgust. Dar's eyebrows took on complex shapes below a forehead with furrows so deep they looked sculpted in emotional clay. Her knuckles whitened on the grip of her sidearm, now half-drawn.

"No, I did not, Darla. I commandeered a weapon from the sniper who shot you. A moment too late—lo siento. Your gentleman, the one just inside up there, killed him. He is an excellent marksman. After I took the weapon, I saw you in its scope, and then I saw your gentleman, and your *tío*, in the boat. Señor Brick would have shot you all. He was also a very good marksman.

"In case any of my comrades happened upon me at the ridge while you were making your escape to the sea, I continued aiming the rifle. I did not find it necessary to fire the weapon in your direction. It was a fine weapon."

Lita offered a small closed-lip crooked smile in response to Dar's expression of disbelief and shock. Her right cheek dimpled.

Then Dar softened, now with a less-wrinkled forehead, as her shooting hand lowered to her side after allowing gravity to drop her weapon back into its holster. Dar acknowledged she not only believed Lita, but felt obligated to thank her for saving the team's lives, and that of her president.

"Lita, we owe you. Gracias."

"You are welcome. I have been under the deep cover since before I left Columbia. I will share anything I have learned, which is not much. These men I work with? They are evil, and only seek to destroy. We will be friends, yes?"

Her hardscrabble but perfect smile lit up the brilliant desert morning. Dar would still check her story, but this little Latina appeared legitimate. And she was an ally.

Dar said, "We will be friends, yes."

"Bien. Your tío, he is away." Not a question.

"He is."

"Very good." And with those words, Lita Dega swiftly extracted the small caliber weapon strapped to her middle back under her insulated vest, extended her arm, and fired. Dar dropped.

DEREK WAS ABOUT TO EXIT NUMBER 6.

He dropped his duffel when he heard the shot, took cover behind the door frame at the top of the porch. He drew his weapon in a single swift motion and swung it down toward the young woman—*the jogger!*

She had already laid her weapon in the dirt in front of her, held her arms high in the air, and shrugged with an apologetic smile.

Derek screamed when he saw Dar on the ground.

"What the Hell? Dar!"

Then Dar, who had covered her head with her hands, uncovered and opened her eyes. She took in the tactical situation within the next two seconds. Saw Lita's gun on the ground two feet from her face, snatched it, pointed it up at Lita, her arms still raised. Heard Derek behind her. She hollered to him.

"I'm okay, Derek. *Lita?*"

The petite Latina said nothing, but pointed with her still-raised right hand toward the rear corner of Number 7 next to the fence between the park and the desert. A corpse lay crumpled, sprawled over a large Agave. A weapon hung from his left hand, finger still inside its trigger guard.

"Señor Stockton would call that insurance, Darla. I am sorry. There was no time to warn you. He was preparing to fire, but I am uncertain whether at you or at me, or both. I did not show up for la fiesta in the desert this morning."

As Dar picked herself up, she brushed a copious amount of reddish dirt crumbles and dust from her dark hair and from her traveling clothes. She chuckled with gratitude all the while although her ears would jangle for a few hours.

"Again. Thank you, amiga. Captain, c'mon down and meet our new friend—the jogger—*Officer* Lita Dega. CIA."

As he descended the porch steps while securing his weapon, he said, "Seems I can't leave you alone for two minutes without trouble finding you, Dar. I thought…"

"I know, Babe."

A look of comprehension flushed over Lita's face before she displayed the broadest smile between the pinkest pouty lips.

"Ah! Amor! Bellísimo!"

Derek shook her dainty hand, cocking his head with a crooked smirk, he said, "Oh, she's good. And her hands are calloused like yours, Dar. Huh."

UNDISCLOSED LOCATION

· · ·

Both Van and Malc survived.

After addressing their wounds from the conflagration with Cheevers' team, Indian Joe, and his local recruits, the Fringers, Homeland transferred Palmer Xavier—aka Van Stockton—Malcolm Frieburg, and their two surviving crew to the CIA's Counter Terrorism Unit.

By Presidential Order, they held them as domestic terrorists for enhanced interrogation under the USA Patriot Act of 2001.

Interrogators used a recent highly classified development euphemistically referred to as *the cocktail* which extracts the truth as they know it from anyone. Its unfortunate side effect is damage to the frontal lobe of the brain, causing memory loss and disorientation.

Frieburg revealed Martino's location. And they extracted the identity of the Eastern European Patriot Brotherhood leader—along with dozens of that cabal's members—from Stockton.

WASHINGTON, DC

Congress began its work in earnest.

The testimony of a whistleblower from within World Horizons led to a bi-partisan inquiry. This motivated the Justice Department to pursue a full-scale investigation into the potential public health hazard from the deployment of World Horizon's latest telecommunication strategy, another nefarious enterprise sponsored by the Brotherhood.

This inquiry lent widespread public visibility and outcry with respect to the hazards of device *and atmospheric* electromagnetic poisoning.

As a result, World Horizons retreated from their original strategy under threat of federal prosecution, and of greater significance, the probability of negative customer perception.

They vowed to invest in a sweeping program of research and development to discover a "more efficient technology that will provide even greater benefit to our valued customers worldwide." Other carriers had no choice but to follow suit.

THE BROTHERHOOD'S DEFEAT? COMPLETE?

The FBI and the Justice Department exposed Jefferson Davis Redding as a PB lackey. He found it necessary to withdraw from the upcoming presidential race because he was on his way to prison for conspiracy and treason.

They also learned that Frieburg was not a US citizen. He had been living in the US as an illegal alien for twenty-two years. He was an Austrian National in possession of a superb counterfeit identity—the best money could buy.

No matter.

Not now.

OLD FRIEND, NEW LOVE

BLACK ROCK, ARIZONA

Geo sat alone in his lawn chair.

His favorite spot beside his trailer shaded him. Kate slept inside, exhausted from an excess of intrigue and high adventure and worry. He was grateful she was on the mend.

Another beautiful desert sunset rewarded him, the first he enjoyed as Geo Janis, *retired* tech exec. He and Kate had also retired their cover identities, now useless artifacts of an eight-year side trip down America's byways, backroads and alleyways.

He heard Sam's voice, plain as the end of this day.

We did it, old son. They're finished, you and Kate are safe, and it would seem so is Democracy, at least for now.

And how thoughtful of our old friend John to share with you that Malcolm Frieburg was the one who ordered your friends killed, thinking they were you and Kate. Turns out only he had a vendetta against you and me. John and President Atherton were the only Brotherhood-sanctioned targets.

Lots of folks are on their way to prison, or worse. Those sons-a-bitches—pardon my French—will hurt no one ever again.

Geo thought, *I assumed I was a threat to the PB because of my podcasts. Leave it to an author to create a sense of inflated self-importance!*

Sam's disembodied voice echoed through his mind, *It **was** 'Redemption Alley' that got Frieburg to suspect you were his target under two layers of assumed identities—Lee Randle and Jack Rhodes. Frieburg's bitterness toward you and me for getting his friend and mentor incarcerated is what led to his reckless behavior, and to his demise. But now it's done, old son. You and your lovely bride are free. It has been a long crooked road, and once again, you have served your country.*

Geo thought, *So have you, my friend. And you gave your life protecting Kate and me. I'll be forever grateful. But is it done, or do we continue hurtling ourselves toward some dark alley of future history?*

George, we do what we can, and we live our lives. I lived mine with no regrets. I suggest you find some peace on that path as well.

Sam, since you passed, I know you're merely an artifact of either my TBI or PTS, or both. Or you're my spirit guide, as Joe would say. I don't care. I just know that our conversations mean so very much to me, but must remain contained in my thoughts and within pleasant memories revisited. Instead of me screaming at the interior walls of my trailer.

A sound strategy. The civvies might not understand. But your new friends of the Fringe get it.

Can a guiding spirit smile? Because he envisioned a crooked little grin from the crooked little man that meant everything to him—even if he *were* dead.

Geo vowed to only mention the *memory* of Sam to Kate and others. Even his therapist at the VA did not understand. A delicious crooked little secret between him and his memory.

~

"Happy Anniversary, Kate!"

"What's this?"

"I'm a writer. I've written you a note. A poem. A verse!"

"Ooh. Can I open it now?"

"Yes, silly! Open it now!" She opened the elaborate linen envelope with care. She would save that like she saved old Christmas wrappings as mementos of treasured moments. Its scarlet lining cradled a single folded piece of rich linen stationary.

"Geo! Calligraphy written in burgundy ink? So elegant, and my favorite color. This must have taken you *forever*. It's beautiful. Let's see."

The more she read aloud, the shakier her voice grew:

A half-century gone, we still enrapture one another,
Now older, no wiser, we push forward together,
Blood and water mingle, sweeter than red wine,
My heart, your mind, our souls intertwine,
With dulcimer wings, on a bough sprung from Heaven,
In our bus, our chariot, our redemption, our haven.
No alley, no side street will again ever do,
Our journey down main street, just us two, our coup.

"Oh, Geo, that's lovely. But, does this mean what I think it means?"

"It means I'm calling it quits on *The Alley* so we can spend more time traveling down the Main Street of our own lives—together.

"Kate, even after all that's happened, and more than a decade of retirement, of living in fear, I'm still struggling to discover who I am. That's not fair to you. I'll continue writing because I believe that's good—for both of us—but this other stuff, well, we'll get somebody else to do that. Okay by you, partner?"

She hesitated, choking back a lump. "Okay, partner."

Tears tumbled down her cheeks, now reddened from wiping them while reading Geo's verse. Marriage involved concessions, and she felt touched he made this one.

She knew he remained troubled, but then, who wasn't? They had weathered a tempest. Yet again. Now she could hope for calmer seas, or smoother dunes, or whatever remained ahead.

"I love you, Babe."

"I love you, Geo. Shall we say goodbye to Lee and Char Randle forever?"

"Why not? They'll remain old friends well-remembered. Lee, Char, may you rest in peace."

He had brought a large manila envelope from inside the bus and laid it on the small table between them. The time had come to open that envelope to withdraw its contents. With that, they tossed their false identities into the campfire: driver's licenses, social security cards, credit cards, passports, library cards... the works.

They agreed that silly act felt damn good.

Geo and Kate said their goodbyes.

Indian Joe had just told them he had resigned—no longer a deputy.

He *was* to hang up his spurs—his words—*last* year. But stayed in the saddle long enough to complete one last assignment: to protect a sweet couple who had done their nation a great service and were facing a longstanding and renewed threat.

He said he had made two dear friends in the process and helped destroy an evil cabal in the bargain. A pretty good deal.

But their tearful goodbyes were just *hasta la vista*—until they'd see each other again. Joe assured them they would. Both Geo and his soulmate vowed to spend more time with that lovely group of desert dwellers who helped them reclaim their lives. They would see each other again.

Joe said the noise had grown too strong at the USMS. His spirit guide told him in no uncertain terms the time had come for him to seek refuge. Joe would alternative between his Fringe brothers and sisters in the deep Southern Arizona desert and kindred spirits within his tribe farther north near Camp Verde, sliding between the two as his spirit and his truck moved him.

Geo understood.

The Fringers had moved since *the battle,* as they called it. Joe left

Kate and Geo GPS coordinates, but warned they'd need something more stout than their little red Toyota Yaris to get *there*.

Joe delivered one last parting shot.

"Geo, don't take this the wrong way, but I know you've been seeing a therapist at the VA named Doctor Cassie Nobles. She is a wonderful multi-talented lady. She was also my boss, *Marshal* Cassie Nobles."

Joe did not expect what he saw and heard next.

Geo smiled and said, "I know, Joe." As Kate collected empty iced tea glasses on the nearby picnic table, Geo whispered, "Sam told me. The US Marshal's Service is truly multi-faceted."

Joe smiled too, "Huh. Well, Hell, tell Sam howdy from me. Pardner."

THEY SAT WITHOUT WORDS FOR A WHILE.

Derek Cheevers, Captain, US Army (retired) occupied the lawn chair Joe often used while in the shade of Geo's trailer.

Geo looked at him with appraising eyes, revisiting in his mind their encounter in the desert with the forces of evil. The author in him dramatized, well, everything.

"That went pretty well, didn't it, Derek?"

"It did. You're a decent operator for a civvie, Geo, along with that wild injun friend of yours. And hey, I never had a right to be so hard on you."

"No problem. Any friend of John's."

"That's Mr. President to you, civvie."

Both laughed like neither had for a while.

COLORADO ROCKIES

THE WEEKS DRIFTED BY.

Derek looked forward to double-dipping. He wouldn't experience the slightest guilt from collecting two pensions—one from the US Army, and one from the United States Secret Service. He had Adler Stavers to thank for that. Ditto for his teammates.

And John's generous separation bonuses for him and the team now that Stavers' agents protected him? Who knew John held the reins to obscene personal wealth? The president would be okay.

He and Dar would be okay too. More than okay. They had served their country and their president with honor. Now it was time for him to serve breakfast to that pocket rocket he had *always* loved.

"You awake, soldier?"

"Mmmm… Just… Come back to bed, you bad-ass hunk of beef."

He set the tray of peeled hard-boiled eggs, fruit, granola, coffee and juice for two on the dresser across the small room that comprised an eat-in kitchen, living room, and bedroom.

Dar couldn't see his mischievous grin as he padded barefoot across the knotty pine floor to the too-small bed. She hid her head and her cold nose.

Derek lifted the covers that battled the cool air of the poorly insulated mountain cabin they'd just purchased. Witness the tiny pile of snow at each of the *inside* corners of their north window's sill.

He snuggled against her plush flannel PJs and purred like the mountain lion they spotted on their ten-mile hike the day before.

He echoed, "Back to bed? Hunk of beef? Affirmative!"

AND SO IT BEGAN IN EARNEST.

With the cloud copy of *Hat Trick 2.0* in the hands of trusted authorities, and mounting interrogation results, the thorough dismantling of the already fragmented Patriot Brotherhood proceeded with all haste.

Meanwhile, the nation mourned the tragic death of Vice President Norman Sealey who took ill and passed away in his sleep during the final days of his second term as vice president.

The American people would remember him as a decent governor

of the State of Maryland, and only a side-note vice president to the effective first black American president who was awarded the Nobel Peace Prize.

Some wondered about two VPs passing away during Stewart Atherton's two terms, but only for a news cycle or two. Every president has critics.

President Atherton transitioned leadership to an honest woman who America voted his successor and the country's first female president. The election was a landslide as she essentially ran unopposed after Jeff Redding withdrew at the eleventh hour.

During her first term, her administration would engage in an endless battle with an opposition Congress. At least the democratic process gained another chance.

Three months after they swore in President Grace Levinson, Jefferson Davis Redding also tragically passed away from injuries sustained in a skiing mishap.

Former President Stewart Atherton never recovered from the last of one-hundred twenty-three assassination attempts. The nation and hundreds of friends on both sides of the aisle mourned the death of a great president.

Mr. M's organization was in tatters.

Federal law enforcement threatened to batter down the beautiful door to his manse at any moment. Michael Martino sat in the chair his predecessor occupied before his demise.

Never wavering from tradition, he ensured a fire roared in the library's fireplace. One last artifact remained from the Brotherhood's founding patriarch—Mr. Z—and of their eight-decade fraternity: the old Makarov pistol waiting patiently in his lap.

Michael Martino, Mr. M, harbored no regrets. His life had been full. He had performed his patriotic duty as he saw it. No one would miss him. He would die alone on *his* terms—*before* they broke down that beautiful door.

The brief echo of the single gunshot faded, and so faded the glory of the nefarious and once far-flung organization known only to a few as the Patriot Brotherhood.

The fire died to a pile of cold and insignificant ash.

It is done.

CAST OF MAJOR CHARACTERS

IN ALPHABETICAL ORDER

- **Stewart David Atherton**: Current US president, and John W. Stevens' successor.
- **Gerald Banfield:** Director, Homeland Security
- **Bearfoot:** Ed Insner, Indian Joe's spirit guide and deceased partner from the US Marshal Service Felony Apprehension Team.
- **Reed Benning:** Member of President Stewart Atherton's private security detail under Stan Farley
- **Chet & Jessica Braverman:** Geo's and Kate's RV neighbors in Tucson and old agency friends of Sam Braxton.
- **Doctor F Samuel Braxton:** Retired US Army Colonel; retired Chief Medical Director, NSA; friend of Geo and Kate Janis.
- **Carmelita Dega:** Assassin recruited by the Patriot Brotherhood from Cali, Columbia.
- **Captain Derek Cheevers:** Team leader of former President Stevens' private security detail and retired US Army.

- **Cyril Dunstone:** World Horizons project manager and whistle blower.
- **Darla Evans:** Member of Derek Cheevers' presidential protection team. US Army retired.
- **Stan Farley:** Leader of President Stewart Atherton's private security detail.
- **Bob Fell:** Eccentric and very unofficial mayor of the group calling themselves the Lunatic Fringe.
- **Malcolm (Malc) Frieburg:** Leader of the Patriot Brotherhood's organization of thugs and dirty tricksters; Enoch Slattery's successor.
- **George (Geo) Janis (aka Lee Randle, aka Jack Rhodes):** Retired technology executive, now a popular author and podcaster.
- **Kate Janis (aka Charlotte Randle):** long-suffering wife of Geo Janis.
- **Indian Joe (aka Ernesto Joseph Blackfeather):** Friend and compatriot of Lee Randle (aka Geo). Also a Deputy Marshal charged with protecting the Janis's.
- **Admiral Jake Mahoney:** Director, NSA and friend of President Stewart Atherton.
- **Michael Martino:** Mr. M, leader of the enigmatic Patriot Brotherhood.
- **Cassandra (Cassie) Nobles:** US Marshal protecting Geo and Kate as part of WitSec (Witness Security), the government witness protection program. Also Geo's Veteran's Affairs therapist.
- **Randy:** An aged Lunatic Fringer who is only known by his first name and is a dear friend to Indian Joe.
- **Doctor Elijah Rudstone:** Consulting White House physician and friend of Sam Braxton. From Johns Hopkins Medical Center.
- **Doctor Joshua Sampson:** White House MD, from Walter Reed National Military Medical Center.

- **Mick Sandstrom:** Member of Derek Cheevers' presidential protection team. US Army, retired.
- **Norman Sealey:** Two-term US Vice President under Stewart Atherton.
- **Adler Stavers:** Director, Secret Service.
- **John W. Stevens**: Former two-term US president until 2008.
- **Palmer Xavier (aka Van Stockton):** Former GGS Chief Operations Officer & Geo's boss; later, briefly known as Mr. X, head of the Patriot Brotherhood.

~

Are you curious to learn more of Geo's *Redemption Alley* podcasts? Well, wonder no more.

Turn the page to explore *"BENEATH the Mayhem,"* Book One of the *Dateline* series for the all-too-plausible near-future adventures of rogue journalist and podcaster Isaiah (Zaya) French. His raucous story unfolds within and around the podcasts published by Geo Janis (aka Lee Randle, aka Jack Rhodes) in *"Fractured Dreams."*

~

Turn the page for a peek...

BENEATH
THE
MAYHEM
DATELINE UNDERGROUND:
2048
GK JURRENS

BENEATH THE MAYHEM

DATELINE UNDERGROUND: 2048

Available Summer 2020

2050 Fiction Podcaster of the Year?

Unbelievable. Considering…

Now Isaiah (Zaya) French aims his sites toward investigative journalism via what he calls "informed fiction." He tackles his most challenging case and publishes the wildest story of his checkered career. There is treachery afoot on a frightening scale.

Zaya lives in a home that flies as he squeaks out a meager income by leveraging the curiosity that so often gets him into trouble.

His current caper sounds like a bad joke: *an ex-Jesuit priest, a nun, a Chicago detective, a goggled and hooded telepathic girl who hides in a tunnel all partner with a storyteller who lives in a flying bus to solve a string of murders meant to look like accidents or suicides.*

This is no joke. Why are these people dying?

Zaya and his new friends reveal a conspiracy of planetary proportions as they unravel this mystery. They will not be silenced. But will they survive? Will *anyone*?

Keep reading for an excerpt of "BENEATH the Mayhem."

~

TUNNEL VISION

EXPRESS SKYWAY
OUTSIDE NEW WASHINGTON,
MARYGINIA
JUNE 2050

Zaya French *was* ready to die tonight.

Or much worse—*if* his plan failed and they caught him.

Surely bad for him, but much worse for everyone else. But they'd need to catch Zaya before *he* could interrogate *them*. And that would be the trick. Yet he *had* to know.

He could grow just as passionate about a spirited street scrap as much as drawing bad people out of the shadows and digging out their secrets. His passion was *his* secret weapon. But now they knew it too.

Every one of his scars told its own story, and Zaya had earned so many. Even though he avoided fights, they did not avoid him. He suspected someone embedded a trouble-locator chip under his skin and wired it to his brain—Zaya never backed away. Constitutionally, he was incapable of accepting defeat. He could not explain it. Nor would he try.

His house—his home—screamed down the skyway at a hundred knots as it sliced through a late Spring drizzle, commanding just a single meter of altitude above the big plasticrete slab. Reflections from his road beams revealed a hint of its pitted surface ahead.

The ride roughened with every additional knot. Zaya's loose white pony tail shimmered with the excessive vibration until it disappeared, wedged between the middle of his back and the once-creamy, now-cracked contraband leather seat.

As he tweaked the old transport's controls for the sixth time in as many seconds, Zaya mumbled to himself in risqué flamboyance, *In the eight years this beast has owned me, I've never pushed her past seventy-five knots, nor above ten meters. Oh well. She'll always give me a little more. She had better.*

But then he softened his internal monologue just in case the old girl was...

Good grief! What the Hell am I thinking?

He had already coerced the eighteen-year-old forty-ton bus twenty knots past her theoretical maximum hull speed as they rocketed through the hazy darkness.

A sweeping network of intermittent spider-lace lightning flashed across the oxygen-deprived sky just ahead. Not enough air for thunder. Now and then, that crisp blue skyfire dimly illuminated the all but deserted thoroughfare.

All eight thrusters, one nestled just inboard of each tire shield, canted their business ends fifty degrees aft demanding beyond-reckless levels of horizontal thrust. That meant less vertical thrust.

If he pitched them any farther aft, the entire rig would drop like a lead ingot. But what choice did he have mere seconds ahead of a horrible death? He needed to control their precise point of confrontation, otherwise...

Sparse commercial traffic dominated the New Washington-Philly skyway this late at night, all ponderous by comparison. Truck drivers never slept, it seemed, although most rigs required no drivers. But those that did never drove this low or this fast.

The periodic red lane lights atop sensors embedded in the magnetically-repelled roadway offered subtle night-vision guidance for those stupid enough to drive in manual mode. Zaya's bus ripped over the red sensors so fast and so close they appeared as near-invisible solid lines.

But this low, and at this speed, the bus would have been quick to respond to those sensors' emitters, had he allowed that.

He grumbled to himself, *Not this fool. Not in this bus. Not this night.*

◦⁓◦

A HASTY GLANCE CONFIRMED HIS FEARS.

All the mirrors and cams confirmed they had closed the gap.

His pursuers had identified him as a dangerous thief. Of secrets. A whistleblower.

But worse than his own demise, if he didn't outlive these hired thugs, a story of heinous malevolence on a monumental scale would go untold and unchecked. He had *so* many questions!

The legislation sure to follow his demise, his story untold, would legitimize government-sponsored mass murder by time-elapsed assassination.

ZAYA FELT INVINCIBLE. MOSTLY.

But even with his potent physique, no matter how buff, *nobody* outran pulsers. He slammed the heel of his left hand on the dash and grimaced at the pain.

God, I hate those things. Like outrunning death by toaster.

Zaya's moments of reflection usually arrived unbidden and always at the worst times. He had learned he must always keep his emotional armor lubricated, in good working order. That took movement. Always movement.

He had shed his armor only three times in his life, allowing exposure to the deep affection of only three women. He outlived them all.

Just outrun the toaster. Tonight.

THE BUS WAS OLD BUT CAPABLE.

His ancient transport pre-dated pulse weapon technology by at least a decade.

While the bombardment excited the molecules of his bus's shiny fuselage, trying to fry its ancient systems, the barrage did nothing to disable his flight controls or drive-train.

He swiped at the sweat running in rivulets down his temples and checked the gauges.

*It **is** getting warm in here. Gotta do something before I'm roasted.*

Zaya smirked at his foolhardiness.

Manual control at this speed and just a meter above certain death? Ha!

But he needed everything the old AppleSoft transport could deliver, and he knew her better than his old auto-fly *Cruise* system ever would. Besides, the little extra lift from the ground's proximity gave him a boost, albeit a small one.

Despite the risk, he put even more forward pressure on the stick. As he gripped it with white knuckles, he resisted the forces applied by turbulent side winds generated by a sudden drop in barometric pressure. That seemed to happen a lot these days. They tried to whip his twenty-five meter articulated rig from the skyway.

Yet one more reason manual control is a stupid idea!

With little choice, he kicked in a touch of linear stabilizer to negate the transverse forces, though that would cost him a knot or two. That fancy crap seldom worked anymore, but the old bus surprised him again. Tonight it worked.

THE GAGGLE OF GOONS GOT CLOSER.

Zaya cursed that flat-black Samsung Trans-Sport as it further narrowed the gap.

Geez, that thing is fast! This is not going according to plan!

As he edged the stick forward, he pushed it a millimeter too far. Typical. The transport's alumasteel nose bounced off the roadway with bone-shattering finality.

His forward momentum overwhelmed the skyway's far weaker mag-lev field below. Magnetic levitation was never designed to overcome so much horizontal thrust and so little vertical.

That's when he heard the voice coming from within.

"The ditch is your salvation, Zaya. Use it! Now!"

When he lost vertical thrust trying for more forward speed, the nose of his forty-ton transport kissed the edge of the plasticrete roadway a second time. He obeyed the voice, slammed the stick to his right.

That command granted him a few meters of grace. The forward skid plates under his fuselage dug into soft earth of the broad emergency ditch as wide as a barren field. Far better than augering into the unforgiving slab.

Another chance to live a while longer.

Time for a new tactic, he thought.

Zaya eased back on the violently vibrating stick and returned it to amidships. The fuselage regained an uneasy course a few meters up, at least less ground turbulence, but now hurtled him toward a galaxy of lights twinkling in the hazy atmosphere.

If he maintained course and altitude, hundreds would die. But stopping in time wasn't possible. If he climbed in the bus's current state, any failure would plummet him to certain death.

Well, an easy choice. Let's do it, old gal.

He jerked back on the stick and jammed both feet to the floorboard, dumping raw pressurized hydrogen into all eight thrusters now swiveled to near *Full Vertical.*

The ponderous bus shot up faster than its design should have allowed, and just nimble enough to clear the sixty-floor housing complex on the far side of the dusty field. His pursuers kept pace.

"Head for the flood tunnels that run parallel to the skyway, just on the far side of these apartment buildings. Turn left. **Now.**"

He trusted the voice that already saved his life once tonight. No, he trusted *her*, although he acknowledged fear of capture, torture, or death more easily than the widening gap in his emotional armor.

She makes my stomach flutter.

He smiled.

Aw, what the Hell. No way I'll outlive her anyway.

Zaya jammed the stick forward.

At the same time, he stomped more pressure onto the pedal under his right foot, less on the left, stick to the left. The bus obediently dived hard and skewed left with this cross-control maneuver.

A tunnel entrance appeared as if by magic in front of him. Black on black. No lights. Illuminated only by occasional skyfire. The oval maw looked to be about twice as wide and high as his transport, but he understood why she suggested the tunnel. Precision driving—his specialty.

*Let's see if those assholes can do **this**...*

Zaya brought the stick to its center detente and eased up just a little on both thruster pedals. At the same instant he nudged the stick forward, using his starboard thrusters and his trim's fine-tuning controls on the dash to tweak his course without banking. His stomach churned. He ignored the clammy goo in his throat.

Hang onto your clenched glutes, you idiot.

Was this tunnel long and straight? No telling. Neither would it gave him any visual frame of reference once it consumed him and his bus, but he gambled he had flyway.

He throttled back, but only to sixty knots, punched in *Cruise. Can't steer if I can't see. Thank God Cruise doesn't need satellites. Hope this proximity shit still works!*

As he wished functional karma on the old bus's control and propulsion systems, he touched another button on the cockpit's dash screen to lower the garage's ramp door.

The aft fifteen feet of the transport—his garage—housed his chocked-and-strapped 'forty-two Road Commander, blacked-out from its handlebars to its thrusters.

He boarded the bike in place and fired her up. When he jerked the thruster control to full *Aft Horizontal*, their position was confirmed on the dash screen above the bars. But he kept the throttle at a low idle and waited. Wind whipping in through the open tail created a maelstrom in the garage.

I sure wish I'd thrown on a hat and tied up my damn hair!

The garage's interior was as black as the bike's paint and the invisible tunnel walls meters away in all directions. Brilliant road beams of the pursuing transport rendered the dim blue glow of his bike's idling thrusters insignificant.

Zaya's WristPad enabled him to raise or lower the garage's ramp door and to tweak the transport's cruise speed, but not its altitude. He assumed all that little-used finery still worked.

Astride his Harley-Victory Road Commander, he waited until his pursuers closed the gap to four lengths. Watched them via the bike's rear cam monitor on the dash screen. They must be on *Cruise* too— nothing else seemed possible.

Not willing to entrust his next moves to voice commands, he touched the transport's *Slow Ten Knots* button on his WristPad. Within two seconds, the bus responded with unquestioning obedience.

Zaya cranked the right handlebar grip that shot one hundred percent power to his bike's twin thrusters over the top of the horizontal ramp, blistering its paint.

The pursuing transport flew into the hottest portion of twenty-foot white-hot hydrogen flames and stayed there long enough to melt its windscreen. Anyone or anything in the cockpit? Charbroiled in seconds.

*Oops. Overkill. No answers tonight. Dead goons tell no tales. I **do** feel bad. Oh well...*

The gap widened an instant later. A sea of sparks showered the tunnel's interior from the now-grounded and roasted pursuers as they faded into a distant tumbling twinkle.

Zaya killed the bike. The fifty-knot draft around the ramp sucked out the fumes in seconds. He touched the *Secure Ramp* button on his WristPad while rushing forward through his living and office areas, up the steps, and back into the cockpit once more. Just in time.

Sensors thought the tunnel ended up ahead. Or was it just a curve? The bus couldn't tell the difference. So it was screaming a warning.

God, I hate tunnels!

Throttling down too fast, his nose dipped before re-leveling. Zaya shifted *Thruster Attitude* to *All Vertical* again with a downward swipe on the dash and waved at *Hover* a second later. Power dropped to five percent in response to the *LLH—Low-Level Hover—*command. *Cruise* might have handled this swift command sequence if he trusted it more. He didn't.

A ground check seemed prudent before he'd allow his dear old house and home to settle into the unknown.

Besides, he needed time to think, to research this tunnel system. Even if the burning wreck of his pursuers didn't now block the way back, without room to turn around, the only practical egress lay ahead. Yes, he needed to pull up the relevant charts. If they existed.

An old journalist's adage crept into his mind: *Trust is sometimes necessary, but direct confirmation is essential.* So he cautiously cracked an inspection port in the floor toward the rear of the cockpit at the centerline. At least the steamy smell that accosted him from below, as foul as it was, didn't seem toxic, and no flowing liquid. Yet.

Time seemed suspended. He rubbed the back of his sweaty neck with both hands after closing and locking the port. Energized by a few deep breaths, he leaped down the three steps from the cockpit. Three paces later he stood staring at his desk reviewing the events so far.

Zaya's hands trembled.

Not from fear—from an adrenaline hangover. An annoying disequilibrium forced him to gravity-drop into the chair on a floor-mounted pedestal at his starboard-side workstation.

Damn, I'm still alive!

His obedient screens awaited. Because of his basic distrust of voice control, his fingers flew over a keyboard under each hand.

Well, that's interesting...

Analysis proved the ground solid with only nine percent instability beneath all projected jack sites. Acceptable. Instead of returning to the cockpit, he lowered just four support jacks from his WristPad. He'd not be staying here long, but saw no reason to plant his tires into this sewer muck and whatever else lived down there. Nor did he need all eight jacks. Plus these days he only operated essential equipment.

Besides, sinking the tires and his beautiful bronze-tone rims into... whatever... might also expose his still red-hot thrusters to something too nasty to be healthy. They needed time and space to cool.

And since the altimeter said he'd descended a hundred meters over the last kilometer, no telling when the stormy skies outside might open up and flash-flood these tunnels.

Zaya expelled a sigh of relief.

The old girl performed with aplomb, even though she ate some dirt. Now another fricking repair bill I can't afford...

"Who are you calling 'an old girl?'"

A surprising laugh escaped.

Sorry, PodGirl. Not you... it's this needy old bus. Thanks for the heading. Now how the Hell do I get out of here?

No response. On his own.

Have I pissed you off with my driving? Or...? God, if you only knew how much... What am I saying? You know.

Zaya slumped in the reflected teal glow of the cockpit's instrumentation that lit his left shoulder. And the softer orange glow from the array of indicator lights in the panel overhead along with those in front of him.

He had wanted to question those goons, but failed. Allowed his emotion to run away. They held a key to unlocking the mystery he had chased for over a year, but since they all died by thruster roast, he'd dig out another angle. He always did.

A year-long investigation into several murders revealed a vague connection between them. Now, Zaya's podcasts had generated sufficient buzz to move his name in some villain's ledger from the annoyance column to the problem-elimination column.

He had captured unwanted attention from Congresswoman Libby Blade's goon squad. If he could just survive this day...

While Zaya planned his egress from this tunnel, he pulled up chart after chart, but that revealed nothing helpful. So he stared at vague blueprints on the two-meter screen that arose from the back edge of his ebony desk, reflecting in the blue-green glow how all this started.

His antennae had begun to tingle before his first podcast two years earlier when he had leaped into this preposterous plot…

DOOMSDAY? LATER!

Redemption Alley Podcast Episode 6:13

UNDISCLOSED LOCATION
MAY 2048

[Somber orchestral music climbs to a crescendo,
then fades to a soft background drone of strings before its segue to
the ponderous ticking of a grandfather clock. One chime of the huge
clock precedes several moments of silence before the narrative
begins]

HEY. MY NAME IS ISAIAH FRENCH.

Some call me *Mister If.* Because I'm always asking, "what if," I guess. Plus I.F. are my initials. Funny how names stick. *Please,* just call me Zaya.

I am a freelance writer, a self-professed investigative journalist, storyteller, historian, and podcaster. And I am but a dream that begins as a nightmare, as many dreams do.

It does *not* have to end that way, however.

Insatiable curiosity transformed me into the profession that now defines me. And that gets me into every flavor of trouble. You might think you are listening to a fictional account of events as I discover and report them, and you are not altogether wrong.

In case something happens to me, though, you need to understand the vagaries of my current project. My danger is in its telling.

So while I cannot share with you my location for safety reasons, I come to you from my home studio. It's pleasant here. Lots of sound-absorbing surfaces and cozy surroundings. But don't let the warm glow you hear delude you into thinking I am detached from the world. Quite the opposite.

Two-dozen real-time and recorded national and global newsfeeds on the big screen always front and center keep this storyteller apprised of relevant events. Why should you care? Because I want each of you, dear listeners, to feel confident this podcast is *well-informed fiction*. Allow me to illustrate with heat from the steaming meat.

I've already discovered evidence of large-scale intrigue and corruption which conspire to make my current efforts high risk. But you, dear listeners, need to know. Remain confident that I vow to continue sharing this story with you wherever I can remain long enough to 'cast in relative safety. *And* whenever I am able to bring more info to you, God willing, I pray you will understand.

But I am grateful you stumbled into my quest. Because the guts of this report, brought to you in weekly segments as my investigation of informed fiction progresses, will touch each of your lives.

If you listen with an open mind, you might just survive. You have a right to hear of epic events unfolding from ignoble roots in front of your very eyes.

I call this podcast *Redemption Alley.* Don't ask. You'll see. Just walk *The Alley* with me each Thursday. If possible. Stay close as it may get dark from time to time. Do you have a courageous heart?

Enough rambling preamble. So let's get moving with a story, *our* story, before… well, you know.

~

THE TICKING COMES NOT FROM A CLOCK.

It comes from a doomsday device called greed. The end of life approaches, unless…

I report to you not of some imagined movie apocalypse, but to tell you that soon all we know and love will no longer be sustainable.

My job? To impede this conspired but unintentional march to the end of days by informing you—or even inspiring you to take action—before it is too late. For all of us.

Look, I imagine and plan for the worst, but I hope worrying about the worst will remain trapped in my imagination.

Some will claim my methods are dubious. But the evidence must speak for itself, no matter how I uncover it or what that evidence may reveal. Let there be no doubt, however, a conspiracy is afoot. And it is big.

Be patient, dear listeners. I will explain through this series of informative yet entertaining podcasts that I am not just another conspiracy nut making baseless claims. I confirm each nugget for its veracity before reporting it to you—as informed fiction, of course.

Despite learning of widespread corruption driven by greed, I maintain a sense of brightest hope for our future. Or at least not worse as we adopt new normals. Redemption is at hand for all of us if we defenders fight for what is important.

The redemption of truth, and love, and a bright clear voice anchors us to this more brilliant hope for our future.

But that is not enough. More of us must act. I must act.

So what can *I* do?

I can dig.

And I can write.

And I can publish.

So I am. You will see. And hear.

Oh, my... Gotta scoot! Listen to next week's episode as a sweet young girl places herself in the cross-hairs of unknown assassins. Why? Only for discovering and threatening to reveal the truth—her version of informed fiction.

So until, and wherever, mask on, Zaya out.

FIRST AIDE

Redemption Alley, Podcast Episode 6:14

NEW WASHINGTON, MARYGINIA
MAY 2048

(Silent backdrop other than long fingernails
tapping on a hard surface sequentially and repeatedly. The sound
stops.)

∾

HI. ZAYA HERE. I'M BACK.

The following was assembled for you from reliable sources.

∾

SHE SLOUCHED. ALONE.

In the small reading room, she admitted the Georgetown Library was her sanctuary. Again. How many thousands of hours had she spent here over the last few years?

She loved the smell of old paper-bound books and the yellowish lighting reminiscent of long-obsolete and now-outlawed incandescent lamps.

This earthy place of long tables and endless walls of books included actual books printed on real paper. Felt like it should be dusty and musty, but it was spotless. Still...

The quiet and cozy room shut out at least some mental clutter causing her sleepless nights ever since she intercepted one voxmail that changed everything.

Sometimes, she'd just drop her head to the table on a book or a keyboard and slept when her eyes disobeyed her will. Now, when not dozing, her every motion remained focused, hurried, and urgent.

Even though every cell deep within her primal lizard brain compelled her to run and hide, she did not.

Lucy Candelson, aide-de-camp to Speaker of the House, Congresswoman Elizabeth Blade of the United Americas 145th Congress, seemed unstoppable. At twenty-four, Lucy's star shone brightly.

She had achieved her Masters in Political Science from George-town in less than a year. That had been two years ago—an eternity. Now with the priceless experience and prestige of working for the influential speaker?

Her matchless work ethic and ambitious demeanor, coupled with an eidetic memory and unforgettable pixie features, represented the complete package of an up-and-coming political fast-tracker.

Lucy loved her country and worked to make it better. That's why she sought a career in politics.

As a closet environmental activist, however, she led a double life. She wanted to change the system from within, but the system was swallowing her.

It started with her incidental access to that after-hours voxmail from a cabinet member—the Secretary of Defense, Madeleine Haley—to her boss. In her message, Secretary Haley apologized for egre-giously breeching security protocol by leaving such a bombshell in a vox message. She said she had her reasons.

Lucy told no one what she had heard, not even her boss, until she could learn more, but dared not delete the message either.

So on her own, Lucy dedicated herself to discovering the heights to which this obvious conspiracy ascended. What she learned left her stunned.

Speaker Blade's ambition scaled a ruthless dimension she could not comprehend, it seemed.

Lucy thought, *I admire Libby as a strong female role model, but this! I need to know more.*

She spent most of her scarce free time on the familiar Georgetown University campus far from the Capitol's prying eyes. Close to her home, her infinitely patient stay-at-home husband awaited. But Lars' limits were not boundless. If only she could tell him of her suspicions, but that would only put him in danger too.

She sifted through endless data related to telecommunications, climatology, and the science of electromagnetic waves.

Lucy could only describe her discovery as a preposterous abuse of political power. The most appalling dimension? Somebody created the opportunity for a government-sponsored public health hazard on a global scale—a technology-driven pandemic, or worse.

Despite her own ambition, it appalled Lucy to learn of a horrifying conspiracy comprising a strategy developed by the Grandy Group, a non-government organization, or NGO. A disenfranchised policy guy within Grandy was the key. Then he turned up dead!

Suicide? No way.

Lucy's doubt consumed her. Was her boss a party to some or all of this dreadful plot? She could not deny her strong suspicions, though she tried.

Speaker Blade takes part in too many off-calendar meetings and secret voxcons. And that snake Mayfield Bailey from Gray and Foster Telecom Consulting? Whenever I enter the speaker's office, why do the two of them fall silent and share furtive glances? But not with me. What in Hell?

Once, she met Anderson Dean from Capitol Security Services whom she disliked for no good reason. Her instincts? He was little more than an ivy league thug in a five-thousand-dollar suit. Oh, he's slick, alright, but something about him caused the hairs on the back of her neck to bristle when he was in the room.

And why so many calls between Madame Speaker and this guy, but never face-to-face? They both work in the Capitol!

Lucy continued torturing herself with endless self-interrogation.

So why does Speaker Blade feel it necessary to surround herself with such unsavory characters if she is innocent? ***Just how far does political expediency carry one's ethics into darkness?***

Knowing she could trust no one, Lucy took unilateral action to research Secretary Haley's fears. She imagined the secretary was in for a rough ride too.

Counter to the secretary's beliefs, Speaker Blade's position on the

HR 8897 bill before the House was no secret, but the scaffolding it apparently provided for high treason, was.

Lucy harbored no doubt she needed to bring her frightening suppositions into the hazy light of day. That remained her only option, no matter the risk. Someone was playing a very serious game with the highest stakes.

The warm and welcoming ambience of the Georgetown Library Reading Room had grown bone-chilling.

Her decision made, Lucy realized she must confide in someone. But who to trust? Certainly no one in politics. She scanned the twenty-four-hour-access room. Only a few others shared the smallish space with her this late in the wee hours.

Lucy committed to pass her private journal to her new friend, Lamatte Foliére. She knew she was in mortal danger and needed a backstop.

And he is still here, she thought.

"Lamatte, may I have a word in private?"

WHAT'S NEXT?

If you like what you've seen of *"Beneath the Mayhem,"* please go to
GKJurrens.com
or purchase a copy from your favorite online retailer when it becomes
available Summer 2020. Shortly thereafter it will be available
worldwide in eBook, paperback, and later, audiobook.

BEFORE YOU GO

Please *subscribe at* <u>*GKJurrens.com.*</u>

And don't forget to leave a brief review where you bought this book.

- If you're eligible to post a review on **Amazon** (if you've spent at least $50 on Amazon in the past year), these have the highest impact and broadest coverage. Click, type or paste this link into your browser: *https://bit.ly/ FracturedDreams* and scroll down to "Write a Review."
- And/or post a review on **Goodreads** (an avid reader site), they have the next highest impact. Click or paste this link into your browser: https://www.goodreads.com/ and then search 'all' for "GK Jurrens Fractured Dreams" to rate & write your review.
- *And/or **email** your review with any other comments to me at* <u>***author1@gkjurrens.com***</u>*. I'd* love *to hear from you.*
- **One final offer I made to near the front of this book:** Once you subscribe to my email list, you'll be invited to optionally join my ARC team. I'll then send you my next book two weeks before it is published (an Advance Review

Copy), absolutely free. You keep the book, and if you are moved to write a short review and post it, you *stay* on the team for the book after that! Not bad, eh?

Remember, other readers and I really need to know what you think. **I gratefully read every review.** *Thank you! - GK*

Note: *While planet-wide ElectroMagnetic Poisoning (EMP) sounds like a bizarre fictional concept, serious studies have already forced many scientists and leaders around the world to consider this a potential health hazard for all life on Earth. They claim some species have already fallen prey to this invisible threat. They are taking a stand. See* **www.5gSpaceAppeal.org** *for more information.*

ABOUT THE AUTHOR

GK Jurrens writes with undiluted passion.

He also teaches writing and publishing on the road. GK and his wife live and travel in a motorhome. They find wandering their beloved North America a source of endless inspiration.

After four years of government service, GK earned several college degrees while mounting a successful three-decade career in high technology.

Now he practices Yoga and Transcendental Meditation, writes, paints, and plays Native American-style flutes, some of which he handcrafted while living in the Arizona desert. GK's favorite quote: *"The difference between ordeal and adventure is attitude!"*

Subscribe at GKJurrens.com to be notified of new releases and giveaways.

Also follow GK on:

amazon.com/author/gkjurrens
goodreads.com/gkjurrens
twitter.com/gjurrens1
facebook.com/genejurrens